ACCLAIM FOR
WHERE DARKNESS DWELLS

Darkness and shadows. The glowing bones of the dead and paths lit by bioluminescent fungi. The eternal struggle of good versus evil plays out in a way that is both fantastical and yet so very real in *Where Darkness Dwells*, Renae's powerful debut novel. With unforgettable characters and lyrical prose, we are reminded that no matter how dark things may be, the light can always be found.

—AMBER KIRKPATRICK, *Until the Rising* & *Unleashed*

In a time of morally gray heroes and romance driven narratives, this refreshing tale brings to light the importance of foundational gospel truths. With focused themes of forgiveness, redemption, and faithfulness, *Where Darkness Dwells* stands in stark contrast to most fiction being produced today.

—AMANDA AULER, *Daughter of the Sun* & *Children of the Earth*

Powerful and gripping, *Where Darkness Dwells* is a debut novel that keeps readers wondering what happens next. At every page, thought-provoking prose catches the attention and engages them in the battle between Light and Dark. For fans of gritty yet wholesome novels, this is a story you won't want to miss!

—V. ROMAS BURTON, *The Heartmaker Trilogy* & *Fortified*

Within these pages, Andrea masterfully crafts allegory and characters that embrace flaws as well as strengths. Revealing the beauty of community that makes us stronger and what happens when pride gets a foothold, *Where Darkness Dwells* captures the eternal battle of light versus darkness, hope versus despair, joy versus grief, and how good will always prevail.

—ANNA AUGUSTINE, *the Taletha Series*

Andrea Renae has created the kind of story that takes root in your heart and never lets go. Set in a town that literally dwells in darkness, this book will keep you turning pages as you follow the characters' emotional journeys to find light. Themes of hope and love are intricately woven through the heartbreaking seasons of loss, fear, and secrecy they experience. With strong spiritual allegory and beautiful prose, *Where Darkness Dwells* is a book that shines brightly.

—CRYSTAL GRANT, *Shadowcast*

Renae's world will grip you the moment you sink into its inky depths and immerse you in a richly textured setting that is as heart-achingly beautiful as it is complex. As her characters each grapple with what it means to live in a world of darkness, their journey to find hope amidst seemingly insurmountable odds will keep you thinking about this story long after you turn the last page.

—KATEE STEIN, *Glass Helix*

Where Darkness Dwells holds timeless themes penned in refreshingly unique ways. The atmospheric world combined with Renae's lyrical prose is like warm honey. Hope sings from every character as they seek truth and light. This fictional tale resonates deeply with reality, and I highly recommend it to anyone who wants courage to face life's challenges.

—EMILY BARNETT, *Thread of Dreams*

where
darkness
dwells

A NOVEL

ANDREA RENAE

where *darkness* dwells

First Edition printed July 2023

Edited by EditElle — Writing & Editing Services
editelle.com

Cover Design, Interior Formatting,
Graphic Design, Map, and Sheet Music by Andrea Renae
Chapter Heading Graphic by Emily Barnett

ISBN paperback: 978-1-7388647-3-7
ISBN hardcover: 978-1-7388647-1-3
ISBN ebook: 978-1-7388647-2-0

Website — authorarenae.com

For those who long for the light.

.

PART ONE

awake

You have slept long.
While you slumbered
the shadows have grown.
But the seed I planted
cannot be marred by the dark.
It sends down roots, drawing strength
from the fertile ground of your heart.
Soon, a tender shoot will emerge,
but only when it has struggled
through the decay.
Awake, sleeper.
Rise up from the dead,
and light will shine on you.
Awake!

I

AMYRAH

I HAVE KNOWN DARKNESS ALL MY LIFE.

The valefolk say it isn't sinister, it should not be feared. It is for our good. For seventeen years, I've pretended to accept it. But when my eyes are closed, I imagine I can see everything that lies around me for miles and miles. When sleep takes me, I dream of lights that burn unimaginably bright and banish every hint of shadow.

The tightness in my chest eases, and I know I was never meant to dwell in the night.

When I open my eyes, the brilliance fades, exchanged for the melancholic glow of bioluminescent bolétis. The stubby mushrooms huddle together in a woven branch cage, bathing our cottage in frigid blue light. Nothing can banish the unceasing blackness that defines our lives, but these humble bolétis push against the night in their small way.

I lie here a while, listening to the passerine birds chirping a racket in the treetops. They never bother with the ténesomni—the darkness. It doesn't seem to inconvenience them. I brush a lock of wavy hair away from my face and rub my forehead, blinking up at the cottage's roof as I admire their fearless refrains. It's easy to imagine they sing to Elyōn, the Highest.

My father's snores from across the room provide a rumbling bass to their high melodies.

Careful to keep the woolen coverlet around my shoulders, I sit up and feel for the clothes I left draped over the end of my bed. A frosty chill still permeates the air even though the season of ice has passed. Shuddering as the blanket falls, I pull my linen frock over my undergarments. I don't know why I put so much effort into dying it with bloodroot and onion skins. The color, an earthy red-orange, is only recognizable directly under the lights of the city. Even then, it is only a hint of a shade.

I swing on my cloak, then contemplate bringing some sort of order to my impossible hair. In the end, I give up and rub some oil into the ends with my fingertips, leaving it to hang, thick and loose, down my back. It always finds a way to escape. And who will even care?

Creeping across the room and holding my hands up, palms out, I feel for heat at the hearth. The ignati went out in the night, but a subtle warmth remains. Perhaps a few hot embers are ready to catch with a bit of encouragement. I stagger a few wedges of wood in the fireplace and use a thin branch to poke at the dregs of fire. A ruddy glow blooms as the coals spring to action. Not wanting to underestimate the reach of the flames in the gloom, I keep my distance.

When the logs have caught, I snatch up the lantern and crack open the door of the cottage. Even though I know every rock and root of our homestead, Father does not permit me to go anywhere without light. He insists any number of creatures could lurk in the shadows, but his need for caution feels arbitrary after seventeen years.

The air is heavy with the night's frost, invading my lungs with its icy presence, awakening me fully. I like the stillness of the morning. Everything is watchful, expectant. Hopeful, even. Calmness pervades the atmosphere, and even the ténesomni that shifts all around me seems languid and less threatening. I like the thought of it sleeping too.

Beneath the fabric of my skirt, my bare legs tingle with cold. I pause to take in the sounds. Other than the brilliant avian symphony, all is still.

My feet find the smooth path that leads to the animal sheds. The trail is so familiar, as if seared into my mind by routine and memory, that even if there was no light in the world, I would know exactly where I was.

Calm but alert, the goats bleat their greetings. I scratch behind their ears, and they repay me with affectionate nudges. After breaking the ice that has formed over their drinking trough, I turn my attention to the neighboring coop where the chickens cluck at me ominously. I smile at their woeful tales as I free them to roam the edges of the trees. The abundant eggs suggest the girls can't be as hard-pressed as they'd have me believe.

During the early hours of the morning, I tend to the rest of my chores. I milk the nanny goats and brush down their stiff coats, then shake out the frost from the rags left on the line the previous day. Soon, the shadowy skies will warm, and I won't need to worry about battling the cold any longer. I can almost taste the enatuberries ripened by Zomré's heat.

By the time I am finished, the swirling blackness all around me has lessened ever so slightly. During the day, you can almost identify the shapes around you, or at least be aware of where things are. Even though the valefolk are accustomed to it, I have never been able to make myself believe it is natural. For me, the feeling of being adrift never really goes away.

A mournful sound shatters the morning stillness. Its tone starts out low but climbs to a steady, high blast. I turn toward the noise but can't make out anything in the dense blackness. The sound rings out again and again, louder and more fervent. It feels very near, but the cold air likes to play tricks that way.

At the same moment, a strange sensation crawls over my skin, starting at my core and radiating outwards. A heat that doesn't scorch yet burns all the same. Is it my imagination, or did the ténesomni shudder around me? I almost drop the basket of eggs in my scramble to reach for the lantern. I've never seen the shadows do that.

Holding the light close, I feel a bit calmer. It won't do a thing to protect me, but I want it anyway. I need it.

Another sound rings out, causing me to spill half the goat milk all over my cloak. But it is only the bell that signifies that the day has begun. My cheeks warm at my childishness, but I manage to make it back to the cabin.

My father is awake, roused by the disturbance. I want him to explain away the eerie horn and chide me for my girlish fright, but he does neither. Instead, he blunders around the cabin, grabbing blindly, frantically, for his cloak, shoes, and weapons.

I freeze where I stand. The unknown sound unnerved me, but my father's complete lack of composure terrifies me.

"What is it?" I say, once my tongue has unglued itself.

Father doesn't even glance my way. "The call of Sola Vinari."

My brow crinkles at the odd phrase. Pada doesn't speak in the Atsunic tongue often anymore, although some words still trickle into conversation. Vinari means 'hunt,' but hunting is a necessity of survival in the Vale. I can't recall a single instance where it has been heralded by such a strange instrument.

"Why have I never heard it before?" I ask, still clutching my bolétis lantern, eggs, and milk.

"You have, thirteen years ago." His voice drops to a strained whisper. "Although I always hoped you would not remember it."

He moves to the back of the room where the dry goods are stored on high shelves to keep them from spoiling. His fumbling hands send a whole basket of tree nuts crashing to the hard planks. It snaps me to my senses. I set down my haul and drop to my knees to help him gather the wayward nuts.

"Sorry," Father says as he tosses the last shell into the basket. He sinks back on his haunches. Even in the weak light, the lines in his face appear deeper than usual. "I need to take control of myself."

"Just explain it to me," I say, barely able to whisper. My cold fingers find his forearm, pleading with him to look at me. When he does, something strange flickers across his countenance. His brows descend, and I cannot still the tremor in my touch.

What does he see?

After a moment, though, he softens. "I will. I promise I will. But there is not enough time right now. They will not wait for me."

"Who?"

"The men of the city. One of the solas has been sighted."

The hairs on the back of my neck stand to attention. "A Light Creature? In the Vale?"

My father nods and pushes himself to stand. "And we need to hunt it down before anything worse comes."

I have only ever read stories about the solas. Most valefolk children believe they are nothing more than fables, creatures of myth. Their bones light the market of Utsanek, the City of the Vale, but they've been there forever. I stopped wondering about them a long time ago. Now I'm having a conversation that assumes their existence—a conversation that centers around the need to snuff them out.

Father, composure regained, assembles himself a hasty breakfast of ripened goat cheese and the crusty end piece of yesterday's bread. He fills a waterskin from an earthenware pitcher, secures its closure, and sets to work lacing his boots and cloak. Satisfied, he takes a spear and dagger in hand, safely tucking the latter into a sheath at his waist.

"I need you to stay here today. Please."

I shake my head. It's market day. "Pada, I don't underst—"

"*Amyrah.*"

My name, like a slap to the face, silences me. Wide-eyed, I gape at him as he takes a moment to calm himself and lean his spear against the door frame. My pulse hammers in my throat. He turns to me and pushes my heavy hair behind my shoulders, resting the heels of his palms on my collar bones and turning my chin up with his thumbs.

The light of the bolétis limns his face. Like roads on a well-worn map, the creases point me to the home of his eyes. Bottomless pools, heavily shadowed under prominent brows. His wayward hair is the same soft shade as mine, although his has begun to shine with silver threads in the last few years. The corners of his mouth angle down in concern, but it is hard to see in that thick, silver-streaked beard.

I have never seen him look at me with such intensity.

"When will you be back?" I whisper, trying to diffuse the pressure of his gaze and failing to hold back tears.

He closes his eyes and takes his time exhaling. His lips curve into a somber expression that is almost a smile. It's lighter, at least. My shoulders relax under his weighty palms.

"I should return before the shadows deepen."

My courage wanes. The prospect of facing an entire day of isolation and uncertainty makes me protest, but he holds up a palm to still me.

"Do not venture beyond the clearing. I need you to promise me that."

Irritation blooms like an itch that can't be scratched. Why must he always forget I am seventeen years old? I don't need his protection, or for him to always keep me tucked away.

Disheartened though I am by what feels like a lack of trust, I summon up the resolve to push the hurt aside and nod.

He catches me up in one of his all-consuming hugs that makes me feel small and childlike, but whole at the same time. I sigh and decide I don't mind being his little girl, for a short while longer, anyway.

A scent of fresh air, leather, and wood smoke hangs about him, and I am comforted. Everything I can't make myself say aloud, I squeeze into that embrace.

I feel his reply.

I love you too.

Too soon, he takes up his spear and waterskin and plants a whiskery kiss on my forehead. Then, my father steps over the threshold of the cabin and into the darkening day.

2

TÉRON

FURY FUELS ME. It races through my veins when my daughter looks up at me with those pale eyes. Eyes that seem to hold a light of their own. She is too innocent for this. Too vulnerable.

I don't know what the solas, or the valefolk, would do if they knew of the strange phenomenon I witnessed in her only moments ago. If they knew who she is. All I care about is keeping Amyrah safe.

But the horn of Sola Vinari has sounded, and I fear this carefully crafted life is beginning to crumble.

My grip tightens on the wooden shaft of the spear in my hand.

Today, I will make it right.

With the tinkling noise of the stream to my right, I set off in the direction of the horn blast. I take no lantern. Hatred gives me sight, and I could walk this path in my sleep.

In little time, the faint silhouette of the city looms before me. I navigate its web of streets and emerge into the central square where an excited crowd has accumulated underneath the strings of bones hung across the area in swooping arcs. These sola brossa illuminate Utsanek's heart with a sickly luminescence, substantially brighter than the negligible bolétis my daughter loves to gather. Unlike the mushrooms, the glow of the bones can last decades, although I can see these are coming to the end of their usefulness. They have been here for at least thirteen years.

It is time for the lights to be renewed.

A group of men brandishing weapons splits off from the rabble. They regroup in front of the steps to the ancient shrine, the fanum, where the few devoted valefolk that remain heap their offerings to the kaligorven—the guardians of the darkness.

I am not too late. Hastening to reach them, I keep the tip of my spear high and out of reach of the civilians. Soon, I am within earshot.

". . . sighted it northeast of here, about halfway through the forest, near the base of the mountains."

"And you think we will be able to track it?"

"Yes, if we hurry."

"We will only take the most capable among us. You, Bruel, Trafton, Akir, and myself."

I plant myself in their midst and raise a palm into the air. "I am here to volunteer for Sola Vinari."

The group silences and regards me with skeptical looks. My knuckles gleam white against the spear shaft, and I am breathless.

Wrapped in a heavy bearskin vest, a towering man stands at the head of the company. A pale, curved horn and a double-edged sword are strapped to his side. He carries a longbow and quiver on his back. Black tattoos ring one of his bare arms, signifying the elevated rank of his family. He is Dravek Kovah, the Foremost of the Vale. No one has challenged his position in years—since before the last sola dared to step foot in the valley.

Dravek's low timbre carries well. "Téron. I thought you might come." He shakes his head, and his eyes narrow. "But I am not sure we want you to join us."

Some of the men grunt in agreement, but I am determined. I strike the butt of my spear on the stone-laid square, ensuring every eye is on me.

"I have as much of a right to hunt that thing, and you know it. Or have you forgotten it was a sola that took my wife from me thirteen years ago?"

The Foremost chuckles dryly. "No, Téron. How could we forget? We all paid the price for weeks afterward. The kaligorven unleashed their punishment on all of us for that blunder, if you recall."

The men's faces are grim, vengeful. I ignore them.

He continues, "You have always insisted a sola killed her, but I seem to remember your wife did not always approve of the Hunt. You say sola, but I say she made herself a target of the Shrouded." He uses the common term for kaligorven. His glinting eyes narrow on me as a murmur ripples through the group.

Striding forward a pace, I beat my chest with a fist. "Let me rectify it."

Whatever reaction Dravek expected, his weather-worn face reveals nothing. He stands with arms folded across his broad chest, staring at me, willing me to back down. But I will not relent. I have been both dreading and hoping for this moment for thirteen years.

"For too long, my daughter and I have been pariahs in the Vale. Ten years ago, when I could no longer bear the reproach, I removed us from your midst and sought to be as little of a burden as possible to this city. I have kept my daughter from the awful truth as much as I could. Why punish her for my crimes? For my wife's death? Have I not already paid the price?"

My words crack in my throat, and I pause to drag in a steadying breath. When I begin again, I must fight to hold back the emotion.

"You may still think ill of me, but I will not let another second of that girl's life be spent as if she has committed some crime against the Vale. No young woman should grow up accepting she will always be an outsider in her home. It is time I, and I alone, bear the weight of my wife's actions. Let me remove our debt to the kaligorven."

Silence falls, my speech cloying the air like a mist. In the weak light, it is impossible to tell what the men are thinking. One by one, they look to Dravek, awaiting his response.

We hold each other's stares. He is imposing and fierce; I am broken but unyielding.

With an almost imperceptible nod from the Foremost, the tension eases, and I am accepted into the hunting party without another word.

Sola Vinari has begun.

After brief preparations, our hunting band moves off. Several massive, stretched-leather game bags are dispersed among us, along with four reinforced sacks with narrow openings, resembling very large wineskins. Each of us receives a coil of rope. Thus equipped, we exit Utsanek through the northernmost gate and cut through the dense trees like the teeth of a comb. We possess no ignati to guide our way, only the innate understanding of direction and keen senses developed through a lifetime of existence in this darkness-laden land.

Krandel, the one who brought the initial report of the sola, takes point for the first leg of the pursuit—a grueling slog through thick underbrush. We do not stop to drink or speak or even relieve ourselves.

Gradually, the landscape transforms as we approach the foothills of the Askonnet Mountains. After hours of punishment, Krandel holds up a hand and nods to the Foremost. Dravek motions to spread out in an even line and follow his lead. We are getting close.

My heart thumps a wild beat in my chest. For thirteen years, I have dreamed of taking revenge on the creatures that stole my Ellehra from me. Worth more to me than my own life, she left a gaping wound in my soul when she was torn away.

For thirteen years, I have looked into identical, glassy eyes in my daughter's face and wondered if things would have been different if I had prevented my wife from leaving the house that day. But knowing her, it would not have made a difference.

Ellehra had always been headstrong. She was determined to prove the solas meant no harm, that they were a thing needing protection rather than elimination. But might will always determine right, and the power of the kaligorven has always been the only thing worth considering in the Vale. Still, she persisted in her trust of the Light Creature's goodness. And how had those burning beasts responded to such unwavering faith? By leaving her mangled body to feed the carrion in the middle of the forest. The memory of finding her lying there still haunts my dreams.

Whatever Dravek might say, I know a sola slayed her. I saw the fatal wounds, exuding an unnatural light that drove the tendrils of ténesomni away, shining like a Light Creature. Only a sola could cause something to glow in such a supernatural manner.

But the fact that the solas had carried out their own sentence had not mattered to the kaligorven.

For centuries, the valefolk have existed in an uneasy alliance with the cryptic beings that thrive in the darkness. They are rarely seen, except when a sola appears. Then, payment is required: the blood of a Light Creature poured out at the Reckoning Grounds and witnessed by all the people. When Ellehra meddled with custom and threw off the Hunt—at the expense of her own life—the kaligorven took out their fury on the citizens of the Vale. The darkness deepened tenfold for a fortnight, and every living thing that could not find shelter was slain.

The snapping of a twig brings me back to the present. We halt our approach at the raised hand of the Foremost and strain to discern anything between the phantom-like pillars of the trees. As far as I can tell, nothing is out of the ordinary, save the peculiar bolétis that dot the forest floor.

We wait.

Without warning, the unnatural spectacle of a scla unfurls from the roots of the mountain above us. Only sixty, maybe fifty, yards ahead, a daunting rock face separates the predators from the prey. Fortunately, we are downwind of it, but that is our only advantage. We cannot all make the climb that would put us in striking distance.

It appears we don't need to. For whatever reason, the sola makes a careful descent, right into the heart of our trap, with the craggy incline fencing it in from behind. It will not easily escape.

As the glowing thing draws near, I will myself to look at it, curious despite my hatred. What form does it take? I have heard tales of monstrous bruins and fearsome horned rams. The solas never seem to take the same shape twice. I struggle to identify it, unable to bear looking at it for long. Blinding brightness floats and ripples around it like featherlight ribbons caught in a lazy breeze. But sooner than should be possible, my eyes adjust, and I behold the most glorious living thing I will ever see.

It is like a lion, or at least a lion is the nearest comparison I can draw. Four enormous paws grip the earth with silent precision as it approaches. Its huge body is sleek and muscular. It has a long, thick tail that ends in a blazing flame of strange ignati. The fur around its strong neck grows thicker than on the rest of its body, parting into a thousand shining locks —or are they feathers? Its muzzle is smooth and whiskered, with a velvety nose and long, pointed fangs.

The awful beauty of the sola cannot be fully comprehended, nor can its piercing brilliance. It burns with a myriad of licking tongues of flame. Great beads of liquid light splash into a thousand twinkling droplets at the slightest shiver of movement. The lion-sola sends the grasping tentacles of ténesomni retreating away, like oil meeting water. The creature eclipses everything I have ever imagined.

I am transfixed. My spirit swells with an unexpected awe. I clamp my eyes shut.

No. Remember Ellebra. I must remember what they did to her.

But it is not possible to hold this beast in contempt. How can something so magnificent have been the cause of her demise? The effort of resisting its otherworldly magnetism causes my body to tremble.

When I open my eyes, my fellow hunters are moving ahead without me. I hasten to follow, berating myself for faltering when revenge is so close. Though I try, I cannot push aside the nagging thought that I have been mistaken.

We only advance ten yards before Dravek issues more wordless commands. As the resplendent creature crouches by a mountain stream, slaking its thirst, the Foremost raises his bow. The other hunters follow suit, some brandishing spears. We will attack as one, ensuring there will be no escape for the sola. It is oblivious to our presence. How does it not sense us? I lift my spear but find it unnaturally heavy. I cannot hold it steady, and as our leader gives permission to let fly, its tip sags to the ground.

A ghastly shriek shreds the atmosphere, followed by a surge of terrible heat that casts every man to the ground. I scramble to my feet as soon as my body permits and find myself at the side of the immense, fallen creature. The others are close behind.

What I behold breaks me.

The sola lies in a tangled heap of fur and feathers. All its light has been extinguished, except for where the five arrows and spears pierce its hide. Flowing from those mortal wounds, glittering blood gathers into glowing pools. My legs give out, and I collapse to my knees, soaking my trousers with the strange substance. The beast's face is noble, even in death. I rest a hand on its huge shoulder. Already cold to the touch. Its warmth was released the moment it perished.

The similarity to how my wife looked in death strikes me like a physical blow. Her wounds, too, had shone impossibly bright. I assumed there had been some strange effect from contact with a sola, but a new and incomprehensible thought invades my mind. Perhaps, somehow, the light came from within her. Like she was a Light Creature herself.

It is too overwhelming and illogical to consider. My insides quake. I scramble aside in time for my stomach to project its contents into a bush.

Dravek's cynical laughter barely registers over the ringing in my ears.

"Too much for your delicate sensibilities, Téron?"

The other men chuckle. I wipe my mouth with the back of a quavering hand. Calm begins to return to me. Making no reply, I get up to retrieve my spear from where the sola's shockwave threw it to the ground.

When I return, Dravek's eyes lock on my unused weapon. The Foremost's demeanor darkens.

"Did you not even join the attack, coward?"

He throws his longbow aside and eliminates the space between us. His tone is dangerous, and I refuse to meet his eyes. At this lack of acknowledgment, he plants both hands on my chest and shoves me hard. I am thrust back, falling to one knee.

"You spoke of making things right. Was this your plan? To come along and threaten Sola Vinari, just as your wife did last time?"

I remain reticent. I can hardly hold myself together. How can I possibly form the words to refute this allegation?

"Answer me, *fool*. Did you intentionally put our entire city at risk by losing us this kill?" Dravek shouts. "Because if that was the case, your debt to our people would be considerable. We would not tolerate a second betrayal from your pathetic family."

At the mention of my loved ones, I rise to full height and look my accuser in the face.

"I would never put my family in the line of fire or willingly place any of the valefolk in danger," I say with quiet intensity.

Dravek snorts in disgust.

"Then explain yourself," says Krandal. He seethes with anger, as do the others. The murder of the sola only exhilarated them.

My pulse intensifies. The dread almost chokes me, but the confession cannot be contained. "I-I think we may be wrong."

Dravek cocks his stubbled chin to one side and raises an eyebrow. "Excuse me?"

"I think we may be wrong to hunt the solas."

The Foremost and the rest of the hunting party stare at me, uncomprehending, but the silence does not last. Dravek's face hardens, and he steps forward, pulls back a fist the size of a small boulder, and unleashes his rage on my jaw.

I know nothing more.

3

BELWYN

*S*HOULDN'T THE FIRSTBORN *of the Foremost deserve more than this?*

Balancing yet another large stump on its end, I sigh deeply and take up my ax. Settling into the proper stance and filling my lungs, I raise the implement high and arc it to its target. The log springs apart in two neat halves. I repeat the motion again and again, dividing it into precise quadrants.

Completely filled. My father gave clear instructions before he left for the Hunt this morning. He expects the ceremonial firepit to be completely filled with firewood by the time he returns. I hadn't understood just how big a task lay before me. But when I got to the ancient Reckoning Grounds on the edge of the city and saw the expansive, stone-laid pit, my spirits sank. It is at least ten paces across, dug five feet into the earth. So many years have passed since it was last in use, I forgot the immense scale of it.

As I bring the ax down for what must be the thousandth time, my palms explode with pain. My freshly acquired blisters have burst. Chucking the tool away in a fit of rage, I throw myself down on a nearby boulder.

The worst of it is knowing my friends are partying in the heart of Utsanek, along with the rest of the Vale. I can hear the festivities in the distance. And I am stuck here, chopping wood.

It has been so long since a sola has come anywhere near the Vale, I had started to think I would never see one in my lifetime. When I was younger, their absence meant only temporary disappointment. As I have approached adulthood, each year that passed meant a greater possibility that I would get to be among those hunting it. Each year, the frustration has grown.

I am the oldest. I have earned it.

All these hopes were dashed this morning, when my father dismissed my request and sent me to play the part of lumberjack while he took on the role of victorious hunter.

And I don't even get to enjoy myself while they're out there.

I rake my agitated hands through my hair, forgetting the open sores and cursing when even that small action invites a fiery pain.

A familiar chuckle sounds. "Bad day?"

Rhun, the eldest of my three younger brothers, steps out of the shadows and smirks at me with crossed arms. He has a knack for finding me when I'm on the verge of implosion.

"What do you care?" I grumble, tenderly dabbing the burst blisters with the hem of my shirt. "I bet Mother let you off without lifting a finger to help."

Rhun angles his head and lifts an eyebrow. "I have my ways of getting out of things if I want to."

"That's because you're her favorite."

"Ah, but you're the one she depends on." He saunters over and slaps me hard on the back. "Come on. You've done plenty. Let's go have some fun. It's not every day we get to celebrate because something will die."

I roll my eyes. He makes it sound so macabre.

By the crook to his smile, I can tell Rhun already knows he's won me over. I stand and stretch my shoulders. Rhun's right. I can hardly grip the ax handle, my back aches, and I am in a foul temper. I glance at the pile. The wood already chopped will have to suffice. Maybe my father will be pleased, but the odds are low. Nothing is ever good enough for that man.

Rhun's grin broadens as he watches me retrieve the ax and sink it into an unobtrusive stump. I snatch up my metal lantern and follow him into the city with only the slightest twinge of remorse.

The festival is even livelier than I had hoped. Valefolk delirious with anticipation burst from every seam of Utsanek. Is the thought of more light so intoxicating, or is it simply the break in the monotony that thrills them? A smile spreads across my face when I catch sight of my group of friends, who have concocted a crazy game involving knocking each other off a precarious balance with one hand held behind the back. In the middle of the crowded square, they've cleared a circle wide enough for two combatants.

"Aren't you going to join in?" asks Rhun as we get closer, and he sees me scanning the market booths.

"Maybe later. I'm going to have a look around."

He nods and dives into the game with an enthusiasm appropriate for his fifteen years of age.

I laugh under my breath and turn my attention to the extraordinary gathering.

There is much to see. It looks like every person from the farthest reaches of the city has turned up for the occasion. Troubadours battle for the attention and arlum of the masses, spouting poems and songs that collide in cringe-worthy discordance. Various tricksters perform mysterious illusions by sleight of hand that have the young ones gaping and tugging at their mothers' skirts. Everything around me drips with merriment and indulgence. The square vibrates with the energy of it all.

The merchants are giddy at the uptick in sales. I pass numerous booths so crowded with patrons that I doubt there will be anything left. Though it has been over a dozen years since the last Hunt, it is evident the valefolk have not forgotten the extravagant feasting that will follow. I won't be surprised if I come across my mother and two youngest brothers caught up in the festive preparations. They have probably been peeling onions and potatoes since before the bell sounded. Grudgingly, I admit chopping firewood might not have been the worst fate for one of the Family Foremost.

Ignoring the hunger pangs that gnaw my insides, I decide to let the excitement brought on by Sola Vinari carry me as far from my troubles as it can.

4

AMYRAH

HOW CAN I STAY HERE while a creature of legend meets its end, maybe even at my father's hands?

The rough planks of the cottage walls eye me with condemnation as my hands struggle to complete tasks which I mastered years ago. Agitation festers within until my stomach churns. I cannot keep my mind from what is happening in the woods, if they have yet found the sola, or if my father is safe. Pain pulses through my temples, and the muscles of my back coil tight. For the hundredth time, I retrace my steps to remind myself what I was doing. But there really is little to be done at the homestead. Yesterday, I made sure to work doubly hard so I could attend the city market today. Washing out my cloak before the goat milk sours is the only job left.

The jarring angles of the washboard rattle my whole body as I throw my weight into scrubbing the fibers. I am drained by the endless waiting, waiting. . . for what? For Father to come home and explain everything to me? He had seventeen years to educate me on the strange custom of Sola Vinari, yet he has never mentioned it. Was my mother's death, all those years ago, connected? It must have been. The last time a sola appeared was also the last time my mother was seen alive.

No wonder its coming has unhinged my father.

I wring out the cloak with extra vigor. The gray water splashes into the bucket abrasively.

My mother died when I was four years old. The recollections I have of her are more glimpses and impressions than solid memories. A skipping laugh. Swaying, warm hugs and soft hair tickling my cheeks. The scent of sage. Odd melodies hummed while she worked, while she walked, while she tucked me into heavy blankets. A hollow sadness winds around my heart and constricts its function. I'm not sure what I miss more: my mother or all the days I never had with her.

As the hours crawl by, agitation seeps into my bones, compounded by my father's desire to keep me tucked so conveniently away from the world. I want to know what is happening outside of this claustrophobic homestead, and I no longer trust him to tell me. It has always been difficult living so far out from the city, but today, I find it especially suffocating being in this cabin. Alone.

Marching out of the house with an armload of wet clothes and a basket heavy with eggs, I make up my mind. I fling the garments on the line to dry, then stalk down the trail that will take me to Utsanek.

I reach the outskirts of the city before I realize I left my lantern at home. The stinging cold of guilt threatens to deflate the purpose that drove me here. I have now both disobeyed my father and spurned his efforts to shelter me. But as my eyes dart around wildly, probing the shadows, the blackness does not swallow me. My heart stills. A warmth of satisfaction soon pushes out the ice of regret, and I stand a little straighter. Maybe Father is just overprotective, and I am not as fragile as he imagines. Maybe the ténesomni isn't what he thinks. Maybe it really does mean me no harm.

But my instinct tells me it's something else.

The city center swarms with activity. I am accustomed to a busy marketplace, but this is something entirely different. Valefolk pack every inch of the square, spilling into the side streets. A thousand words and shouts and guffaws hum in my bones. I've always shied away from crowds, but this one draws me in. Haltingly, I sidle through the shifting throng, resorting to using my elbows and shoulders to make passage. It is exhausting but exhilarating all the same. A new sensation. By the time I make it to the market booths, my cheeks are hot from exertion. I feel alive.

Dozens of movable structures line the edges of the square, each with its own peculiar flavor. There are tanners' booths piled high with hundreds of animal skins; millers' tables sagging under the weight of heavy sacks of flour; weavers' displays draped in luscious linens and wools; produce stands overflowing with the bounty of last Elberu's harvest. I could spend hours looking at all the Vale has to offer. There has never been such a delicious variety.

The savory aroma of venison stew drifts toward me, making my stomach squeeze with hunger. I wonder if I have brought enough arlum to spend on such a luxury until the smell mingles with the pungent scent of new leather from a cordwainer's stall. My nose wrinkles at the strange combination.

Through a gap between the bodies, a table glittering with gently glowing jewelry catches my eye. I manage to shove myself through to it. Slipping the handle of my basket so it sits in the crook of an elbow, I free a hand to touch the cool gemstones. What I thought were sola bones are intricately carved shards of a peculiar soapstone. They are all so beautiful, shining in hues of gold, blue, scarlet, and indigo. Some are as big as an egg, others like a drop of rain.

A girl of about my age with rich brown skin sits behind the stall. The corner of her cheek bunches in a shy half-smile when our eyes meet, but it disappears as soon as I return it. One of her hands traces the grain of the counter, and the other pulls absentmindedly at a coil of her dark hair.

"Did you make these?" I ask.

Her quick nod makes the stones dangling from her ears wiggle. She bites her bottom lip and watches my hand.

"They are such pretty colors," I say, my fingertips exploring the smooth shapes of leaves, animals, and ancient Atsunic script. The language is dying, valefolk preferring the simpler common tongue over such slippery words. I wonder if there are still people who can read it.

"You can't find them in the Vale." Her voice is low.

Not in the Vale? I meet her gaze.

Her eyes widen like she has surprised herself, but she shakes the reaction off with a skittering laugh. "I mean, you can't find them *here*. There are many more varieties of bolétis in the forest if you know where to look."

I raise an eyebrow, not quite sure if that was what she meant. And I don't understand how the bioluminescent properties of bolétis can be imbued into stone. But since she looks like she wishes her market stall would swallow her, I decide not to pursue it further. A weight of tension releases from her shoulders.

My eyes come to rest on a delicate pendant the size of my thumbnail. It has a peculiar shape, with eight sharp rays radiating from a single point, alternating in thickness and length. This one isn't made of stone, but an odd metal. It glows with a silvery-white light. Pure.

"What's this?" I pick up the necklace by its leather cords, the shiny jewel swaying gently in front of my face.

"Oh, that?" she asks, like I've startled her by finding it.

I peel my gaze from it, tilting my head and trying to make her out. She has a slight frame, and her clothes, which are threadbare and mended in places, hang loosely off her shoulders. They aren't homemade like mine. They could have been expensive at one time. Dozens of bracelets ring her arms, glowing like the articles on the table. All except one, which is nothing more than a few pale, braided strings with their ends knotted together. Her eyes enlarge at the sight of the jewel dangling from my hand, following its subtle movement. She slips her index finger under the simple bracelet and twists it around her wrist.

"That's . . . that's called a star, or istilatum ideralis. It's a shape from . . ." She frowns and scratches the nape of her neck. "From . . . history."

My silence must betray my skepticism because she clears her throat and changes the subject. "That one is actually made from argentilum. There are big veins of it in the Askonnet Mountains. It can absorb the light around it and store its energy . . ." A look of deep thought claims her brow.

Everything she says leaves me with more questions. But I don't have room for them right now.

"Well, thank you for sharing your art with me," I say, laying the necklace down. It outshines the rest of the jewelry. "It's beautiful."

I don't even want to ask how much it would cost. She raises a hand to chin-level, pointer finger extended. Her lips part like she wants to say something more, but I pretend I don't see and bob my head in gratitude. More people crowd in, so I step aside to make room. Before I am out of sight, however, I glance back. Disappointment crosses the girl's face.

As I continue through the market, I study the strings of sola brossa more closely than I have in a while. Their brilliance has faded, the light struggling to reach the ground. That must be the reason for the dozen newly erected street lanterns around the square. Their muddy glow isn't worth the effort. Has Utsanek ever gone so long without replacing the Light Creature bones?

I don't have a moment to consider any of it further as a shrill and distinctly aggravated voice emerges from the cacophony of the crowd.

"Oy, come back and face me, yeh insolent brats!"

A commotion erupts farther down the merchant line. People spring to the side with disgruntled cries as two filthy boys barrel through the throng. Grinning maliciously from ear to ear, they hurl themselves along, each clutching large loaves of bread.

Close on their heels, a storm cloud of billowing skirts and wind-whipped, silver hair descends. Those who avoided the first wave are knocked off-balance by the second, and the ambient cursing increases. The face of my old friend, Orlagh Bekyr, comes into view, contorted with anger. The flappable woman nearly plows right into me, but I reach out and catch her just in time, pulling her into my side.

The erratic pursuit ends as quickly as it flared up, but not before Orlagh has a final say. She leans over my shoulder and bellows with all the air in her lungs, "I better not see yer sorry, dirt-smeared faces skulkin' around my stand ever again."

I wince at the painful volume of her final threat while laughing inwardly at its vehemence. I would never want to be on Orlagh's bad side. As I pull her close and hold tight, the woman's body relaxes.

"Did you need to be so hard on those poor little dears?" I tease, releasing her and letting a smile dance in my eyes.

"Eh? Who're you callin' a dear? Those rascals couldn't be 'dear' to their own dear mothers."

Fighting spirit revived, Orlagh unleashes her fury on the onlookers. "And a fat lot of good yeh all were, watchin' and doin' *absolutely nothin'* about it."

I laugh, but no one else does. The irritable marketgoers shake their heads, mutter insults, and return to their business as if nothing happened.

She seethes in disbelieving silence while I attempt to tame her frazzled mane of hair. The action has a calming effect on the aged woman. She closes her eyes as my fingers deftly plait and wind the strands into a simple, silver rosette at the nape of her neck.

"Child, yeh are too gentle on this bitter ol' soul." She sighs, all her bluster spent.

I secure the knot with a ribbon of fabric from around my wrist. "There. I can recognize you again."

Catching my hand in hers, she squeezes firmly. She picks up the basket of eggs, loops an arm through the crook of my elbow, and leads me back to her market stall.

The enticing scent of fresh bread pulls me in. Orlagh's baked goods are legendary in Utsanek. Along with several dozen golden-crusted loaves, her stall is laden with spiced fruit-filled rolls, herbaceous flatbreads, and buttery biscuits. How the woman manages to accomplish all this every day with no one to help her, I'll never quite fathom. She is a true artisan. My father constructed an impressive stone oven for her several years ago, to her very exacting specifications. At least three times the size of most people's ovens, it takes up nearly half of her tiny apartment.

Fanning herself with a cutting board, Orlagh deposits the basket on the counter and heaves herself onto a wooden stool behind her booth.

"*Mercy*, what a ruckus. I shouldn'a let myself get so hot and bothered. I'm too old for such nonsense." She squints at the many-hued eggs and nods approvingly. "Oh, Amyrah—what a lovely bunch of eggs yeh brought me today."

"The hens are just happy the season of sowing is here," I say with a shrug.

Orlagh clucks her tongue. "Plenty of chickens wouldn't give half so beautiful eggs. It's yer tender care that really makes 'em thrive." She pats my cheek, and I don't mind.

She is the closest thing to a mother that I have. Despite her long hours baking bread for her patrons, Orlagh has never missed an opportunity to help me out. She taught me to mend my own garments when I was only five years old. She ensured I knew the basics of making a satisfying stew, no matter the ingredients, by the time I was ten. And, I blush to recall, she helped me transition into womanhood when the time came upon me. No matter what new challenge life demanded of me, she has always been my confidant.

"But child," Orlagh says, growing serious and leaning in so only I can hear, "yeh shouldn'a come to the city. Not today. Not with the first Sola Vinari in thirteen years."

I study her dim, stone-gray eyes, surprised to see an uncharacteristic fear lurking within them. Again, the guilt-chill washes over me for having rebelled against my father's instruction. Maybe there is something to his behavior, after all.

But it isn't right for him to keep me in the dark, I argue with myself, failing to ease the sickening remorse gathering in the pit of my stomach.

"Orlagh, please." I clutch the knitted wrap draped around the woman's bony shoulders. "Please, tell me why. What's so dangerous about this Hunt? And why has my father never spoken of it?"

She watches me silently for a moment, an internal battle playing itself out over her countenance. Finally, she sighs. "It's not the Hunt itself yeh need to be wary of. It's the repercussions of the last one."

A shiver runs down my arms, circling my wrists and making my fingertips tingle. "Did it have something to do with my mother?" My voice is hardly audible amid the surging clamor of the valefolk.

The old woman nods slowly. A vacant look claims her eyes, as if a vision of the past plays out before them. "Aye. Poor Ellehra. She was a light snuffed out too soon."

I swallow hard, my throat tight.

"And—and was it them, the hunters, who . . . *took* her?" I ask, fearing the answer.

Orlagh shakes her head and scowls. "No, not the hunters. They had nothin' to do with it. But your father was the one that found her."

I squeeze my eyes shut and tears slip off my lashes, cool against my hot cheeks.

"Yer mother was the most strong-minded lass in all the Vale, and she let everyone know what she thought about Sola Vinari. She was the only person I've known with the courage to challenge it, though heaven knows I've had a mind to do the same over the years."

"What were her reasons?" My brows hitch together as I wipe away the wet trails of tears with the back of a hand.

"She insisted the solas were no' the problem in the Vale. Caused quite a stir in the city, she did. Yeh see, for ages past, we've been accustomed to huntin' those ethereal creatures, tellin' ourselves it'll keep us safe from the kaligorven and bring light to our city in exchange, and that one sola's life was worth the peace and protection we received from the Shrouded in return. It made folks uncomfortable, thinkin' all this time we've been in the wrong. But her words had a ring o' truth to 'em, and a few good souls were swayed to see it her way."

The leaden feeling plummets deeper within me. "What happened?"

A customer prevents her from responding—a tall man with dark hair and broad shoulders. Irritated, I pretend to be too deeply engrossed by the bread rolls to notice him, hurriedly wiping my face clear of tears.

"And do yeh intend to pay for that, or squeeze the life out of it?" Orlagh asks.

I glance at the intruder, bread in his hands. A guilty smile cracks his lips as he secures his lantern to a strap at his waist and fishes the silver coins out of his pocket. He barely manages to pay for a loaf when someone barrels into him, laughing and spewing nonsense.

"Watch it, Flip." The man chuckles. "You're going to take someone out."

"Bel, you're missin' all the fun," the assailant slurs, sloshing a cask filled with an unidentified liquid in the air. "The games are just gettin' started."

"Whatever you're drinking, I think you should dump it." The man—Bel, was it?—attempts to turn him toward the heart of the crowd with one hand while protecting the bread clutched in the other. But the belligerent Flip interprets the help as an insult. Lurching away from his friend's reach, he loses his footing and knocks me over, whooping hysterically. I grimace, grit stinging my palms as they take the impact of my weight against the cobbled ground.

When I fling my disheveled hair out of my face, a hand extends to me. I look up and see it belongs to Bel. He's younger than I thought. His face, which had shown amusement, is now full of concern. He bends lower, searching my eyes with dark irises that glow golden in the warm ignati light. His jaw is angular, and a ring of polished metal threads through his left nostril. A clump of auburn hair flops over his forehead while he waits. He does not appear the least bit inebriated.

My cheeks flush under his gaze, and amusement toys with the corners of his mouth. I don't want his help, but I also don't want to be rude. When my fingers find his hand, his warm grasp swallows them. He pulls me to my feet with one easy motion. I withdraw my hand sharply, his scratchy calluses grating against my palm. A quick smile of thanks is all I can muster. My squirming insides confirm how handsome he is.

His lips part like he wants to say something, but a second onslaught from his intoxicated friend spares me that mortification. Ushering the drunkard away requires all his attention, but right before they disappear into the crowd, he throws me a suggestive wink. Certain I am as red as enatuberries, I busy myself with brushing off my clothes.

Orlagh purses her lips. "The Hunt brings out the worst in everyone, I'm afraid."

I nod faintly, waiting a few moments for my heart to slow and the heat to dissipate from my face. Never mind them. Turning back to her, I ask, "What happened to my mother?" as if there hasn't been any interruption. I have no time for delicacy. I need to know. *Now.*

My wise friend considers me curiously, taking a long moment to think. She squeezes her wrinkled eyelids shut as if the memory pains her.

A flare of regret plagues me for putting her through this, but it can't be helped.

"Oh, child." Orlagh's eyes mist over after she opens them, and I cover her soft hand with both of mine. "There was something special about yer mother that most couldn't put a finger on. Some thought it was just her manner, but I knew it was somethin' more."

"Like what?"

She opens her mouth to speak a couple times but struggles with words. As she cocks her head to one side, the furrows in her brow plunge to new depths. "I don' rightly know myself. It was like . . . like the ténesomni had no effect on her. Like it . . . left her alone. Gave her space."

Recognition flickers in my mind. Did I experience the same thing on the way to the city? Back at the homestead? It's hard to say. Father has always made me carry light wherever I go, but it isn't all that strange. Very few people ever venture anywhere without it. But after arriving in Utsanek easily, without a shred of illumination, I know better. The shadows had not been nearly as debilitating as they were supposed to be. They let me be.

"I've often wondered if that was what did it." Orlagh is oblivious to my tangled thoughts. "The Shrouded are not exactly known for their patience. And if word of a darkness-repelling maiden reached them . . ." She shudders. "Well, it wasn't long before they sighted a sola to the north of the Vale, much like today. Yer mother couldn't let another one of those dazzling creatures be taken because of superstition. She set out to head off the hunting party before they could reach it."

Tiny bumps prickle down my arms. The scene plays before my mind's eye, as if I am witnessing it firsthand. My breath lodges in my throat until my lungs burn for air. I need Orlagh to finish, but the woman is awash in tears. Inhaling sharply, I slip to the merchant side of the booth and put my arms around her. It's a while before the baker composes herself.

"Dear, sweet Ellehra," she chokes out. "Yer father found her broken body, thrown to the ground, not a sola in sight. No matter how they searched, they caught no glimpse of the beast that did it."

A knife-like pain pierces somewhere around the center of my being, and my face goes numb. The voices of the multitude mesh into a single, deafening roar in my ears. When I lick my lips, a briny taste fills my mouth.

"And yer father. Yer poor father." Orlagh sobs. "He took it badly. He swore the solas had been the ones that took her from him."

The absurdity of his conclusion pushes through my fog. "But . . . that can't be. Why would they kill her?" The evil word scars my throat.

Orlagh holds a handkerchief to her face and shakes her head too fast. "No, child. It doesn't make sense, does it? Nay, what I have always believed is that the kaligorven murdered your mother because they were threatened by what she had. What I believe ye possess as well."

"What's that?" I breathe, although I already feel the answer rising within me, clawing to be let loose.

She frees herself from my grip and pulls my face close, so that we share air.

"*Light.*"

An unnatural silence descends upon the crowd, as if a single word from an old baker holds the power to freeze time. I spin around, eyes wide.

Can they sense the threat? Do they know what I am?

But Orlagh's whispers aren't what stole the people's attention. The long and grievous tone of a single hunting horn holds them in its grip.

Orlagh gasps and tugs her shawl around her with a shiver. We stand together, shoulders pressed, transfixed along with the rest of Utsanek. Waiting.

The horn blasts again. This time, it is met with cries of relief. The square bursts into celebration, but my heart fills with a sadness I can't explain. The hunters are returning, victorious.

5

BELWYN

I DEPOSIT FLIP IN THE RELATIVE SAFETY of a deserted alleyway that branches off from the square. He's too sloshed to perceive much of what is going on, and I decide it's best to leave him somewhere out of the way while he has a chance to sober up.

Anyway, there are other things on my mind.

Like the girl I just met. Even in her indignation, she was striking. She hadn't spent hours plaiting her hair into intricate designs or painting around her eyes with reflective ink. There is something about them I can't quite figure out. They were pale and . . . piercing. How her cheeks flushed when I helped her up and how she yanked her hand from mine showed both her innocence and her spirit.

I tear into the loaf of cheesy bread and plunge once more into the heart of the throbbing mob to join in my friends' games. And with any luck, I'll find the girl again too.

I've only just spotted the group when the first horn sounds. A sigh wheezes out of me. Nothing about this day is going as I imagined.

The throng surges at the second bugle blast, catching me up in the jubilant deluge that flows to the outskirts of the city. It is not so frenzied out here. The darkness deepens away from the torches and gleaming sola brossa of the streets, and many people carry lanterns that glow with the reddish tints of fire. The excitement of the valefolk crackles in the air, infecting me despite my grumblings, and I quickly become as jovial as the rest of them. We are, after all, about to see a sola.

The horn blasts again, and a hush falls. Nothing but the shifting ténesomni with the pinpricks of bioluminescence lies before us until a ray of light slices between the towering torsos of the trees. A greedy roar rises from the people.

Out of the gloom, the mighty men of Sola Vinari materialize, highlighted by the tremendous skull of a strange sola creature strapped to my father's back. Each man stoops, shouldering loads of flesh and bone and sloshing waterskins filled to bursting with iridescent blood. It looks as though not one cut of the animal has been left behind.

The hunters' return parts the crowd like the prow of a ship with my father at the helm. Valefolk slap the backs of the hunters and congratulate each other as if they have vanquished a thousand deadly foes instead of a single creature. As I look at the remains of the sola, the bubble of anticipation in my chest deflates. In the end, it's just an animal like any other. The most I can say about this one is that its skull is big. And bright.

The infectious conduct of my companions swallows my disappointment. Flip was right. The fun is just getting started, and I might as well give myself to it. I'm not surprised to find Rhun in the mix.

Always the comedian of the group, he climbs onto someone's shoulders and shouts bombastic challenges at any bystander that dares glance his way. Some people are affronted, but most choose to excuse his youthful mischief, barely withholding their own chortles. I can't help but laugh. He has a likable way about him, even if he's being a buffoon.

My other friends, I realize with a nagging sensation, are getting a little carried away, especially when it comes to the girls that tend to follow us around like starved canines.

My own shadow has materialized at my side, like she always does. Ketra leans into me, laughing in a way that tells me she's not quite there. Her blond locks are professionally arranged tonight, and her dainty features are outlined with skillful strokes.

Rhun points at us and whistles suggestively, and the group around us hoots with delight. It's nothing out of the ordinary, but tonight it chafes me coming from my brother. He's only fifteen.

Ketra waggles her eyebrows and pecks me on the cheek. I am not a stranger to her charms, and I know most of the guys here would jump at the chance to be in her company. But at this moment, I think with mild surprise, I don't find her the least bit attractive.

Oblivious to my thoughts, she leans in closer and thrusts a sticky flask into my hands.

"Where have you been, Bel? You look like you could use a drink," she purrs. "Have some of mine."

I take one appraising sniff but hand it back. It isn't appealing, and I'm not eager to give her leverage over me at the moment.

Ketra pouts dramatically, frowning up at me with playful annoyance. "What's the matter? Don't you want to enjoy yourself? It *is* a party, after all." She traces my arm with a finger, a coy smile tugging at the corner of her mouth.

Disgust builds like bile in the back of my throat as I shake my head. "I'm not interested."

"Oh, come on. Have a little fun."

I brush her hand aside and direct my attention, instead, to the progression of the hunting party. She pushes her body into my side, shamelessly attempting to force me to acknowledge her. Heat crawls up my core.

"Not now, Ketra," I say through a clenched jaw.

Her demeanor flips instantly. She pulls back like I've burned her. "Fine. If that's how you'll treat me, I'll gladly find someone who isn't a complete prude."

When she vanishes into the crowd, all I feel is relief.

With difficulty, I make it closer to the cleared path in front of the hunters. I stop short when I perceive a lone, feminine figure standing before them. The glare of the sola skull throws her into silhouette.

"What have you done with him?" the shadow cries, her voice like a twanging of her heart.

The pull of familiarity hitches my brow. I move through the crowd, apologizing as I go, until I can see her. I recognize that homely wardrobe, that unbound hair.

I glance at my father. The austere man does not look at her as one would expect, with pity or forbearance because of her size or sex. His face is devoid of emotion, almost predatory. If he wasn't my own father, I would feel compelled to place myself between him and the girl. But he's my flesh and blood, a man I fear more than any other. I am well acquainted with the subtle clench of his jaw, the flexing of his hands at his sides.

But this time, his cruelty comes in the snap of his words. "We bound him and left him at the site of the kill."

A mortally wounded animal could not make such a feral sound of pure anguish. The girl wheels round and darts between the bodies, but not before I glimpse her fair face and those clear eyes.

I bolt after her.

It isn't hard to follow her trail through the mass of affronted people, but that changes when I reach the forest. Dirt sprays as I skid to a halt, the lantern at my side almost extinguished from the whiplash. My breaths are labored, whether from exertion or rage at my father, I do not know. I shake my head, willing myself to shelve the panic his cruelty has stirred up within me.

The girl. Which way has she gone? My eyes scan the darkness, but there's no sign of her. A shiver runs through me. Does the ténesomni feel thicker than normal? I untie the lantern and hold it out, but it doesn't help. It can't cut through the sable mists. I curse and thump a fist on a tree trunk, the bark scraping my knuckles.

"Consider your actions carefully, Belwyn."

The low voice makes me jump. I spin around to find the tall frame of one of my father's most-trusted men barely illuminated in the glow of my lantern. My shock gives way to anger.

"What are you doing here, Krandel?" I huff, fighting to remain in control of my emotions. "Did my father send you to fetch me, like a trained hound?"

Krandel smiles wryly, letting the insult bounce off him. "He simply wishes you not to make a fool of yourself."

Or of him, I think bitterly. But I say nothing.

"You know the significance of Sola Vinari. You understand the risk in angering the Shrouded."

The lantern bangs against my thigh as I step toward him. "No, I don't. You forget I was five at the last one. And maybe that's a good thing, because I seem to be the only person who recognizes that there was something really wrong with the scene back there."

Nonplussed, Krandel's lithe form advances to match me, his tone hardening. "The girl is not your concern. You should be focusing on your responsibility as son of the Foremost, not on the impulsive gallantry that led you here."

I part my lips in protest, but Krandel holds up a palm.

"Look around, Belwyn. Can you not see how deep the shadows have become? The kaligorven are very near now. They expect complete subjugation at the Reckoning, and if they find something amiss, they will unleash their fury on us, as they did thirteen years ago."

I feel my resolve slipping. What do I know of the solas and the kaligorven, or the way things need to be? Nothing. I scan the forest behind me with misgiving, but thoughts of the girl being out there alone give me courage. Shaking my head sharply, I turn my back on Krandel.

"And what about the girl? She won't be there. I can't leave her to fend —"

An iron grip clamps around my forearm. Warning exudes from the man's touch. "Amyrah Cantar does not matter. She is nothing. You are the eldest son of the Foremost. Your duty is to your father, and the Shrouded will know if his house is not in line."

We stand locked together, as still as stone, for a tense moment. I seethe and consider yanking myself free, but I know I cannot overpower or outrun Krandel. It is useless.

The hunter perceives the change in my eyes and releases me. "Good man."

I rub my arm and scowl.

"And now, before anything else unfortunate happens, let's get you to that ceremony."

Pride bruised by my swift defeat, I follow Krandel in fitful silence. I hate my cowardice as much as I hate my father. And yet, as the ceremonial grounds come in sight, I have something I didn't before.

A name.

6

AMYRAH

RAINDROPS PRICK MY FACE like icy needles from the sky. My eyes flutter open. Springy moss and leaves form a damp cushion under my head. The scent of wet dirt fills me, and I dig my stiff fingers into the cool earth.

What happened?

I recall hearing a scream issue from the region of my chest, but it didn't sound human. It had to be from something else, not me. My body aches everywhere, as though I've flung myself through a hundred fists and elbows. Or were they flung at me?

And I remember running. A wild, frantic chase. No, not a chase. An all-consuming need to find someone.

Not someone. *My father.*

A strangled sob escapes me. What happened to him?

I swallow and try to make my mind focus, but my thoughts are a muddled blur. What knocked me out? There was a sudden blindness and then . . . silence. Groaning, I press a palm to my forehead. It feels like I collided with a wall.

With painful effort, I push myself up and look around. Nothing but stoic trees, quivering ferns, and oblivious fungi encircle me. It seems I am alone, although I cannot shake the feeling of being watched.

A breeze picks up, and the treetops, obscured by obsidian darkness, converse among each other with whispers and creaks. Water slips off their leaves and slaps the soggy ground. The droplets on my skin become icy cold. I wrap my arms around my knees to ward off the chill, but my body shakes uncontrollably. I think of my cloak, which I left to dry on the line back home. The drizzle persists, becoming steadily heavier until my clothes are drenched, and my hair snakes in ribbons across my forehead. Water dashes in rivulets down my face, mingling with my tears.

I have to get up. I have to get moving.

But to what purpose? I have no idea where to begin the search for my pada. Continuing in the pitch-black night could be suicidal. And there is the unthinkable possibility he isn't even alive. My gut twists so sharply, I feel I will be sick. The sensation soon abates, but only because something much more sinister has taken its place.

Maybe I should stay here, let myself sink into the earth, let the darkness claim me.

The thought seduces me.

But there must still be a spark within me, something buried deep and eager to spring to life, like the coals in my fireplace. It roars into existence at the mere thought of extinction, catching and growing and giving strength to my limbs.

It is not in me to give up.

Pushing aside the feeling of unease, I stand, wincing at the stiffness. The pouring rain has leached all the warmth from my body. I won't last out here long, but all I need to do is put one foot in front of the other.

I hesitate, unsure of which direction I should go: back to home and hatred, or forward on a doomed endeavor?

The clamor of a mighty wind rolls through the forest again, stronger this time. The rain stops. Several great cracking noises cackle nearby, and my breaths come in sharp gasps. Something large must be pushing through the trees. I turn my back on Utsanek. Whatever comes, I will meet it head on.

Tremors course through my limbs as I wend between the pale tree trunks. The tumult of the approaching calamity makes it difficult to think, but that spark within me has been lit, and it drives me forward with burning insistence.

Dimly, I notice that my circle of vision remains constant, like a protective orb around me. Like I carry a lantern. My eyes test the limits of my sight, and I am alarmed to find I can see where the snaking tendrils of darkness, like wisps of ebony-colored smoke, end. They reach out toward me, desperate to claim me. But they are unable to reach their target.

How?

The uproar is on top of me, and the thick trees sway. An explosive sound rends the air, and I throw myself forward just in time to avoid the crushing impact of the gigantic, cage-like crown of a tree. Adrenaline flooding my veins, I flip to face the obscured sky and scramble backward until I come into contact with something cold, hard. Immovable. A rock face, or a very large boulder, at least. I feel along it with soggy hands, not daring to take my eyes from the danger above, until I come across a slight depression in its side, big enough to curve around me. Really, a poor excuse for a shelter, but it reaches ever so slightly overhead in such a way it might provide protection if another tree should be snapped in two above me.

My fingernails bite into my shins. I stare out wildly into the ghostly hurricane, waiting to see . . . what?

The Shrouded?

Childhood frightfables are not supposed to come true.

As suddenly as the wind and the creaking and cracking began, it ceases. It becomes impossible to hear anything beyond my own heartbeat. My eyes strain. The little bubble of light remains intact around me, but the darkness beyond it thickens like tar.

No sooner has the pounding retreated from my ears than a heavy thumping emanates from the night. Slow and rhythmic, it advances nearer. Footfalls.

My exhausted brain struggles to grasp at a logical conclusion. It has passed the point of fear and entered a realm of disbelief. The solas and the kaligorven aren't even supposed to be real. None of this is supposed to happen.

As I shiver and hug myself in the cleft of the rock, surrounded by a strange halo of darkness-repelling light, my head screams in denial. I am watching this happen to someone else, not me. Some other poor soul huddles at the threshold of death.

The footfalls halt, and intense silence descends. Something must have happened to my hearing. I force myself to scan the concave wall of shifting darkness. My eyes dart to the left, a subtle movement calling for my attention. A shape pushes through the blackened barrier. A deformed, clawed shape enrobed in inky tatters of shadow, conjured out of the darkness itself.

Panic returns in full measure. I open my mouth to scream, but there is no sound.

A leg, bent at the joint. A shoulder. And the looming outline of a hulking, crouched creature.

The nightmare is interrupted by a thing absurd and foreign and wonderful. A timid, lilting melody pierces the air. Sweet and sad but permeating the roots of my terror. The veiled being freezes in place. The song persists, growing stronger and clearer. It is a warm, bright sound, and I can feel it pouring into me like warm honey, drop by drop, note by note.

Somehow, I know the song. I can sense which notes come next, like they spring from my own soul. And I know if I sing it the kaligorva will flee.

If only I could recall the words, I could join in too.

But I *do*.

They well up within and find my tongue. My lungs, which had refused to utter a sound, now fill themselves and give power to the haunting, hopeful refrain that feels as though it has always been inside me.

> *My eyes have seen a glim'ring beam*
> *Piercing through doomed bracken's core,*
> *And although it has made my heart to hope,*
> *I fear I shall see it no more.*

The ténesomni shudders as my voice, timorous at first, rises to join the melody of the first singer. With each word, courage blooms, and my tone becomes steady and pure.

> *Thus grows the ever dark'ning gloom*
> *From the glen to the ne'er ending moor.*

And although Light has filled me with wealth unknown,
I fear it has left ye poor.

A change slips into the forest. The tongues of shadow retreat on themselves, like water pouring in reverse. The kaligorva screeches and withdraws before it can be revealed.

All around me, the gloom starts to lessen. Still, I sing, the words coming to me out of some deep well of memory.

Long past, on that ill-fated night,
When the hearts of men grew weak,
There came by the woods a Shrouded beast,
Of which we now do not speak.

And on that day no spear was raised;
The strong did not shelter the meek.
Then all the brilliant goodness fled,
And of that light we now do not speak.

I pause to listen, forgetting the terror that had crippled me moments ago. This is something greater than my fear, a force so mighty it drives the malicious darkness away. The forest settles into its usual grayish hues.

Above me, my unseen ally continues the melody, and I spin around, looking for the brave soloist. Such a peculiar noise. No human or instrument could issue so lusty, so unearthly a sound. It streams like a river from above.

The rocky ledge behind me, dripping from the rainstorm, is jagged enough for me to climb without much danger of slipping. At least thirty feet high, it's taller than I thought. The handholds are abundant, however, and I ascend without great difficulty. Even so, by the time I reach the top, my lungs burn, and my strength is spent. I don't have time to consider my exhaustion, though, for what waits at the crest drives all other thoughts far from my mind.

It is as if all the light I have ever seen in my life—ignati and bolétis and sola brossa—has gathered into one single point in space and time. High up in a spreading chestnut tree, the fantastic scintillation reaches with hundreds of arms, curling around and embracing everything within a fifty-foot radius. Upon stepping within its reach, I feel all traces of wet and cold vanish.

From the heart of that glorious, blinding orb, the song continues, undiminished. I join in once more.

> *Lo, there will be a coming day*
> *When bird, beast, man shall see,*
> *For all the darkness will fade away*
> *And all of the Vale will be free.*

> *Thus grows the ever bright'ning day,*
> *From the fields to the ne'er ending sea,*
> *And the Light of Life will shine on all,*
> *For rich and whole we shall be.*

The creature repeats the melody of the last line, and everything stills.

My chest rises and falls with exhilaration as I soak in the strange light. I steel myself to look at the brilliance head on. Strangely, it doesn't hurt my eyes—it's just more than they can handle at once. The longer I look at it, though, the more a form begins to take shape in the heart of its crystalline flames. And I see it.

It is nothing more than a tiny wren! Surely, this must be smallest sola there has ever been.

A warmth of joy bubbles up inside me, escaping my lips in a breathy gasp. Can such an innocuous thing as a songbird really have the power to banish ténesomni?

I hold out my hand.

The brave bird cocks its head to one side and hops a couple times on the branch. Even the tiniest movement sends out a wave of shimmering light daggers. It propels itself down, gives a few soft flutters of its perfectly mirrored wings, and lands lightly in my open palm. My eyes well up with tears, and I catch my bottom lip between my teeth.

The beauty of this diminutive songbird is indescribable. Its eyes are burning coals encased in glass. The delicate, white beak glints and gleams. Its feathers are softer than silk. Up close, I can make out intricate patterns ringing its neck and continuing down its fluffed breast. The long tail feathers brush my fingertips. Warmth from its gentle, clawed feet spreads up my arm and makes the hairs on the back of my neck stand on end. I laugh again and wipe my eyes with the sleeve of my frock.

"Thank you, sweet one, for saving me."

The sola twitters a cheerful reply and hops on the spot, regarding me curiously with one gem-like eye. It spins to face the other direction, and with a look over its wing as if to make sure I am paying attention, it takes flight.

"*Hey*," I shout, scrambling to follow.

The wren alights on a branch at a fair distance. When I make it there, it flaps its wings and leaves me behind again. I am too enraptured by the miniature sola to be greatly annoyed, so I trail it to the next tree, and the next, the bird waiting for me each time. It chatters at me encouragingly.

We go on in this fashion for a long time, but I do not grow tired. Simply being close to the sola renews my stamina, and I trust the golden creature is leading me to something important.

The slope of the forest floor changes, bending upward. When I reach the tiny creature this time, it does not fly away. Catching my breath, I lean against a tree trunk.

"Would you mind telling me what that was for?"

The enigmatic wren merely fluffs out its feathers and begins to preen itself. I scrunch my brow and open my mouth to protest, but a faint noise stills me.

"*Amyrah.*"

Whipping around, I look from bush to tree to lichen-covered rock.

"Pada?" I whisper, hardly believing what I heard.

"*Amyrah,*" the voice repeats, choked with emotion.

I scramble toward the steep rock face at the end of my range of vision, nearly tripping over my father's outstretched legs. I collapse next to him, burying my face in the warmth of his neck and dousing it with my tears.

"Amyrah . . . my girl . . . *my girl,*" he murmurs into my hair. All the sorrow and fear I have been harboring all day pours out. When my tears are spent, I tuck my hair behind my ears and gently lay my hands on either side of my father's face to inspect it. He winces when my hand grazes his jaw. I pull back quickly, sickened from causing him pain.

"Oh, Pada," I breathe.

His beard is matted with sticky, dark blood. I sit back and look him over before I hurt him again. "What else did they do to you?"

He sighs and shakes his head. "Nothing." A groan follows, even the smallest word bringing him incredible anguish.

My tears threaten to return, so I shuffle to the back of the tree to which he is bound and begin working at the knots. They are pulled so tight, no doubt from his struggling, my efforts are wasted. I grunt in frustration.

"Amyrah," Father says, exhaustion plain in his voice.

"It's ok, Pada. I'm going to free you. I just need to work at it harder. Maybe I can find a piece of . . . of . . . shale, or something, to pry the knots loose." I mop my eyes furiously and clamber to the rocky incline.

"Amyrah . . ."

"I'm sure if I can get a thin enough shard, I'll be able to, I don't know, wear the rope down or something."

"I have a dagger."

I turn on my heel, cheeks warming. "*Oh*."

Of course. I knew that. I saw him slip it into his sheath this morning. He nods toward his right hip. Carefully, I pull it free and saw the rope, well away from my father's wrists. I do not trust my shaking hands.

The bonds snap. He slumps forward with a moan, rubbing his wrists and shoulders in turn. I kneel beside him, my mind reeling.

"What happened to your jaw?"

Father's shoulders lurch in a mirthless laugh. "I told Dravek we shouldn't be hunting the solas, and he took it out on my face."

My eyes widen. He was certain as of this morning that killing the sola was the only way forward. What's changed?

He gestures for me to help him up. "What I want to know is how you managed to find me." Leaning against the tree, he coaxes the blood to return to his extremities.

I pale. There is no hiding my disobedience now. Haltingly, I relay how the day unfolded, from my conversation with Orlagh amid the ruckus of the square, to the Foremost's pompous return. I tell of Dravek's hardness of heart toward me, and my wild rush into the forest to find my pada.

Father gives his head a shake and scowls. "That was foolish. Completely foolish."

Ice water forces into my veins. "I know, Pada," I cry, desperate for him to forgive me, to understand. "I know you said not to leave the homestead, but I—"

My father holds up a hand. "No. It was foolish of me to hide all this from you. I was an idiot to think ignorance was your best defense. I'm the one who put you in danger's path." He draws in a ragged breath. "And I was a fool to desire to kill a sola."

Something has happened to him, out here in the woods. The closed-off man has been cracked open, and all his insecurities are exposed. He's punishing himself for the events of the day, taking blame that ought not belong to him. The wounds he sustained go deeper than flesh, and my heart breaks for him.

There are no words to make this right, but one thing may bring him a small measure of relief.

I take his hand in mine. "I want to show you something."

7

BELWYN

T HE FIRE BLAZES WITH UNIMAGINABLE HEAT, crackling
and consuming the enormous pile of wood within. This colossal
stone-lined pit is one of only a few locations where an open flame is
permitted in the Vale. The clearing in front of it is big enough to fit the
entire valley's population—some ten thousand individuals—and it is
packed. Even with ignati reaching twenty feet high, only the first couple
rows of people are illuminated. The darkness beyond is suffocating.

On the western edge of the blaze, I fidget with my raiment. Having
last attended a Reckoning when I was five, I have very little, if any,
memory of the rituals the ceremony requires. I didn't recall that, as a
member of the Foremost family, I'd be forced to put on this heavy cloak
adorned with thousands of beads carved from sola brossa. I squint down
at it with disgust. Ancient and gaudy, the thing's bones have long since

lost most of their illuminating qualities. The scent of the cedar chest from which the robe was unearthed is not enough to conceal its overpowering musk. My only comfort is that each of my brothers is similarly bedecked, the awkwardness spread out evenly among us all.

I crane my neck to see my mother standing next to Rhun. Her endless smile and pearly teeth glint in the firelight. The sight of her makes me forget my own mortification. She's alive with jubilation, and I can't fault her for her good humor. Being the wife of the Foremost is, supposedly, a position of honor, but there has been precious little opportunity for her to be in the spotlight. I suppose her moment has come.

Her hair is beautifully arranged, inlaid with glittering gemstones and luscious plumes. The elaborate creation of featherweight fabrics in rich shades becomes her. Delicate designs in thin, golden strokes bloom from the corners of her eyes and across her temples. They catch the flickering light and enhance her striking features. She is a piece of art. I wonder if she has been planning this outfit for thirteen years.

On her other side, my father is more imposing than ever with a heavy mantle of fur draped over his shoulders. It hangs in glossy black folds to the ground, where it pools luxuriously at his feet. A skillfully crafted breastplate laced with Light Creature teeth and claws hangs across his chest. The embellishments still glow with considerable fortitude, despite their age. Illuminated from below, his features are thrown into an eerie relief that makes him appear skeletal.

He holds a twenty-foot-long, spear-like shaft in hand. Instead of coming to a sharpened point, its tip is a half-circle bar of metal that forks to the sky. Its prongs curve downward at the very tips, like the talons of a raptor. Krandel stands opposite him, on the other side of the bonfire, grasping a nearly identical implement. It has small rings atop the crescent instead of hooks, perfectly spaced so the two tools can be latched together. They will form a perfect circle.

The real spectacle, however, is the oversized urn that stands in front of the fire. It issues the most astonishing tendrils of light. The vessel itself is made of clay, unadorned and utilitarian in form, but large enough to hold all the blood of the slain sola. And it is dazzling with a pure, white heat that easily eclipses the inferno raging behind it. The light tumbles from the urn and shifts around its base, fighting to gain ground against the ténesomni. But the shadows are more tenacious than I have ever seen, and for once they hold the advantage.

Father moves forward and raises a hand to silence the valefolk. Their murmurs fall away until the only voice is the breeze whispering through the trees.

"People of the Vale," he booms, "we have long awaited this day."

A deafening cheer arises. My father allows it to build and crest before motioning again for stillness. The people obey.

"Year after year, we waited and watched, yet no sola entered our land. We sent out scores of hunters well beyond our borders. Still, the burning creatures hid themselves away. What used to be a ritual of celebration deeply ingrained within our very identities as valefolk has become nothing more than a story our children have begun to pass off as legend."

A shiver runs up my spine. Even I doubted the old stories, son of the Foremost though I am.

"But tonight we can agree the time of disbelief is at an end."

The valefolk cannot hold back any longer. They roar and laugh and pump their fists high into the gloom.

"Let us observe the rights of Kuvror Erovantus once more."

Blood Reckoning. The ancient Atsunic words for the ceremony are like a noxious vapor in the air. I am jostled as the energy of the throng surges. My father does not wait for it to calm this time but rides the swell, his deep voice projecting with unusual volume above the tumult.

"Tonight, we offer the blood of a sola as a tribute to the mighty kaligorven that jealously guard this land." He raises the ceremonious spear and shouts, "Habith ténesomni eth noér lurum."

No one below the age of sixteen knows what the phrase means, but that's one thing I can recall. *Dwelling in darkness is our good.* The words feel heavy on my tongue as I echo them with the voice of thousands.

As if it awaited a proper introduction, a wind picks up and moans through the forest beyond, bending and snapping trees like twigs as it draws near. A collective gasp echoes around the clearing. All become mute, save the frightened children who mewl into the night.

I strain to see beyond the blinding sola blood and the towering flames, my abdomen tensing. I can't make out anything, but I sense a malignant force. It is very close. It presses in on me from all sides, harder and harder as the approaching gale grows to a deafening volume. Pulsing like a wound, the blackness constricts forcefully. I might pass out. Either the dark really is so thick even the sola blood is being blotted from sight, or my vision is failing.

My chest heaves as I breathe through the terror, willing it not to crush me. Sweat soaks the ceremonial garment, and I think of my youngest brothers at my side. Are they as affected as me? I shoot out a hand to locate Shemai, the baby of the family, feel his scratchy cloak, and attempt to tug him closer.

"Lay off, Belwyn," the nine-year-old says irritably, following it with a forceful shove. I can't see him, but from the sound of his voice, Shemai is anything but afraid. I press against the bridge of my nose with my knuckles and try to focus on breathing. I am supposed to be the brave older brother. It is for me to be annoyed by my sibling's babyishness, not the other way around.

What is wrong with me?

The wind-racket ceases as a new sound emerges. It is low, guttural, almost animal in tone. Yet also rhythmic, like great footfalls or drums. Thrumming, it keeps beat with my pulse, one beat for every three of mine. I feel it pull, drawing my mind with irresistible force, like the barbed hook that reels a fish to its captor's net.

Boom, pulse, pulse. Boom, pulse, pulse.

Even if we wanted, not a soul could utter a sound. Everyone freezes under the spell.

Boom, pulse, pulse. Boom.

Every eye fixes on the unknown point past the roaring fire, past the column of sola light. However eager the valefolk are to see the awesome thing that lies beyond, the wicked darkness prevents them. It still manages to grow thicker by the second. Rolling in like a heavy curtain, it advances nearer as the volume of the otherworldly sound increases.

I do not like being so close to the trees from which the Shrouded will emerge, but being shamed by my little brother pricks my pride. Resisting the urge to cower, I hold my ground, but my heart continues to thud. I conceal my shaking hands in the deep folds of my robe, suck in cold air through gritted teeth, and turn to face the blooming wall of black.

With each beat, doom draws closer. It envelops the entire tree line now. Am I mistaken, or are there ghostly shapes in those swells?

The change in atmosphere acts as the cue for Father and Krandel to assume their positions. I don't want to look away from the spectacle, but I force myself to observe them. The men take their spear-like instruments and hook them together, crescent to crescent, around the wide mouth of the clay pot. In this way, pushing with equal force and aided by two additional men on either side, they raise the giant urn a few feet from the ground. It takes an incredible amount of exertion. The weight of sola blood and earthenware must be considerable; the muscles of the men's thick arms bulge, glistening with sweat. Together, they march their load toward the bonfire, careful to keep it level, not willing to waste one drop of gleaming blood. When the flames are near enough to lick around the base of the urn, periodically obscuring it from view, they halt.

At the same moment, the rhythmic pounding ceases. I turn toward the forest, and my blood freezes.

An enormous figure emerges from the center of the cloud. It can't be seen naturally, using light to reveal the hidden. Instead, it's like an image turned inside out, with undulating ribbons of thinner darkness outlining the edges of its limbs, shoulders, and head. I only get brief glimpses of its form, but they accumulate in my mind like the burning trails of light that cling to retinas. I am left with a fading impression of something inexplicable and grotesque.

I feel the kaligorva's towering height—at least nine feet. It is roughly human in form, but the powerful hind legs on which it balances are not like a man's. These are haunches, bending backward first, then forward above frightening, clawed feet. Sheets of darkness wave behind it like flags in a spiteful breeze, resembling a cloak. Or perhaps they are wings.

What cannot be obscured are the molten pits of its eyes. Filthy and fierce, the thin crust of darkness that surrounds them barely contains them. A shudder passes through my frame when I lock on to those burning chasms. They go on inside the beast forever, down, deep down, into the very heart of its sludge of a soul. My mind screams to look away, away, anywhere but at their smoldering ruin, but my body cannot act.

"Eternal Beings of the ténesomni."

My father's voice makes me jump. It demands the attention of the entire Vale. I am vaguely impressed to see, when I force myself to face the fire once more, the men have been suspending the urn above the blaze the whole time.

Father's voice does not betray his physical strain. "We are honored by your presence."

This time, no one dares cheer. The mood is now one of apprehension rather than triumph.

"We beseech you to accept the blood of the sola as an offering of peace, a sign of the covenant we have held with you, our protectors, for generations."

His elocution is perfectly timed. He barely finishes the words when the vessel shatters from the heat of the blaze, sending sola blood gushing like an angry, glowing river over the remnants of firewood. The moment the blood contacts the ignati, the fire extinguishes with one last blinding explosion of light. Hot air tinged with a musky, spiced scent blasts my sweat-drenched hair off my brow. The valefolk gasp, staggering to keep their footing in its wake. A whoosh of frigid wind sweeps in from the opposite direction. Darkness rushes to fill the void left by the sola blood's light, like a pack of jackals diving in for the kill.

At this plunge into blindness, cries emanate around the clearing. This is a darkness so complete even people bred and raised to live in a black-stained land are alarmed by it. I am too young to remember the Reckonings of the past, but I wonder at all those older than me. Do they not know what to expect? Maybe the ceremony is something to which one can never really become accustomed.

But this is not my father's first Reckoning. Quickly, the Foremost steps in to take control before the ceremony deteriorates into chaos. "*Be still*," he shouts with unquestionable authority, and all thoughts of deserting are banished. "Do not be so weak. We are in the presence of the kaligorven."

My limbs quiver as a rumbling growl emanates from the thickest core of shadow. Persisting, it climbs in volume until the ground trembles, the pebbles skittering across the hard-packed earth in rhythm with the vibrations. The sound crescendos and changes from a bestial moan to something almost human. For a moment, I imagine I hear words.

I *can*.

You have not obeyed . . . All of you will pay. This ténesomni must remain . . . Unbroken . . . Until we return.

The beast's words linger in the air, growing weightier by the second. The people are too terrified to speak. Even my father remains uncharacteristically silent, his large hands wrapped tightly around the spear-like implement. The tension bears down on me, drawing my shoulders slowly upward. What does it mean, the dark must remain?

But no explanation is offered, and time passes by in uneasy silence until a sudden and violent gale picks up around the clearing. It courses like a cyclone, faster and faster, whipping shawls and beaded necklaces painfully at unprotected faces and eyes. The women cry out and draw their children into the safety of their bosoms, bewildered and afraid. I wrestle with my own bead-adorned wardrobe, which the tempest has made deadly. I try to pin it to my body, but the heavy thing lashes wickedly, threatening to strangle me with the strength of a hurricane. The wind is impossibly fast, flinging debris and knocking people down as it tears around the stone firepit. The men join in, shouting their disbelief, endeavoring to protect their loved ones. I look around desperately, seeing nothing but shadows penetrated by darting trails of light cast by flying bits of sola bone.

The ténesomni must remain . . .

I clutch at my chest, feeling the cool, luminescent beads under my fingers.

... Unbroken ...

Their strength is feeble, but still, they shine.

"*The sola brossa,*" I yell through the tumult. No one hears.

Throwing myself into the vortex, I lurch toward my father. The formidable man clings to his spear like the mast of a ship. When I am near enough to cut through the screaming winds, I try again. "The bones, Father—we must hide them."

Father gapes at me in confusion, but when I rip off my robe and begin to ball it up, inside out so the offending sola brossa are concealed, he clues in. Frantically, he follows suit, tearing the breastplate from his chest and throwing the fur cloak over top. The gale's force lessens almost imperceptibly. He grabs my shoulders, his eyes wide.

"Spread the word," he says, then shoves me as he turns and dashes into the crowd.

I waste no time, narrowly escaping a flying tree branch as I dive back into the midst of the people. The instruction is difficult to communicate at first, but as more people catch on and more sola bones are obscured from sight, the fury of the Shrouded begins to be assuaged.

The message spreads rapidly, and in short order the ten thousand valefolk stand in an oddly quiet, oppressively black night with heavy breaths and heaving shoulders.

A few flames still flicker in the last lanterns that lie unbroken on the ground, but the ténesomni has rendered them almost as useless as the bolétis. The kaligorven don't seem to care about ignati.

My legs tremble beneath me as I struggle to catch my breath. There isn't so much as a breeze, but I shiver. A few nervous laughs crackle the silence.

But the relief will soon snap when the valefolk realize that we have been condemned under an order of complete darkness—and we have no idea how long it will last.

I fumble along with my useless lantern held out before me, carving a path through the blackness for my family, when the aroma of home cooking hits me like a warm swell.

Right. The feast.

We are expected to celebrate after Kuvror Erovantus. I doubt anyone will participate in the festivities now. I know I can't stomach it.

The moment she steps through the door, Mother drapes herself across the fur-upholstered couch. An arm anchored with jewels presses dramatically across her forehead.

"I've never been so embarrassed in all my life," she says into her sleeve while I begin to chase down the sola brossa strewn on every surface in our house. I turn away to hide my rolling eyes. What happened back there had nothing to do with her.

Just leave it, I think, knowing it won't lead anywhere good. I focus instead on removing all the bones from the sconces secured to the rocky walls. I don't want to take any chances with the kaligorven, or my father.

He enters the house and chucks his cloak at me, knocking a glowing talisman out of my hands. I bite my lip to keep from reacting and stoop to retrieve the carved bone and the fur garment.

"Quiet, Ketur. Your shame is nothing to mine," he says.

The younger siblings, Shemai and Korvin, burst through the door, arguing about which one of them is hungrier.

"*Boys* . . ." Mother says, a groan dragging out the word. She pinches the bridge of her nose between two manicured fingertips and scowls. The golden embellishments on her face crinkle.

They ignore her and continue shouting. I manage to catch Korvin's eye and give him a subtle shake of the head as I lay down Father's folded cloak and resume my pursuit of the sola brossa. He may be a little aloof most of the time, but Korvin can read when I'm serious. Clamping his jaw shut, he grabs Shemai by the collar and drags him into the kitchen despite his flailing limbs and deafening protestations. I have no doubt their appetites and the mountain of food on the dining table will have a quieting effect.

Mother sighs heavily when their banter recedes. She motions for me to bring her a cushion. I have to set down all the sola brossa to fulfill her request.

"The first Sola Vinari in over a decade, and it was an absolute joke." Mother rests her head on the fluffed pillow and begins the long process of loosening the haggard braids from around her crown.

Father paces the length of the front room, his anger practically a visible cloud around him. He spins on his heels.

"What are you doing with that light?" he bellows.

My heart lodges itself somewhere in my throat. I shut my eyes and wait for my vocal cords to loosen before responding. "I thought you wouldn't want to risk another encounter with the Shrouded."

After a long pause, during which I don't dare to look at him, his reply comes as an ugly snort. I take it to mean I should continue.

Mother refuses to let the matter drop so easily. "Dravek, it was a disaster. A complete humiliation. Look at the state of me." Her voice has a high, pinched sound to it. She might even be crying actual tears. I'm impressed.

"After all that planning, the hairdressing, and the expensive jewels . . . And what was the point?" She sniffs loudly, a bitter laugh bubbling from her throat. "And my dress . . ."

Father snatches a bone from my grasp and hurls it into the fireplace. It explodes into a myriad of sparks. "I have more important things to worry about than your dress, woman."

My eyes dash to my mother's face, which has taken on a darker tinge. She sits up, eyes flashing. Half of her light hair is still secured to her head, and the rest cascades in tight waves over her shoulders. "Well, with that failure of a ceremony, I'm sure our family is the joke of Utsanek."

This time she strikes a nerve.

"This has nothing to do with us."

"Of course not, my dear," she says sweetly, mollified as her words hit their target. She settles back into the couch and resumes untangling her hair. "But I had hoped you would do everything in your power to redeem yourself after the last Reckoning."

She provokes him on purpose. The hairs on the back of my neck raise in warning. Father won't ever raise a hand against her, but I know that doesn't mean I will be safe. I dump my blinding load of sola bones into the kindling basket near the hearth and hope I will be able to light the fastest fire of my life. Because even though this room is the last place I want to be, I know there isn't another person in this house that will lift a finger to help. If the command of darkness will last any length of time, we will need all the firelight we can get.

In response to her barbed words, my father grabs another sola brossa from the basket to hurl past my head. This one merely lodges itself in the pile of ash, sending up a cloud of dust. It takes all my resolve not to shrink under his overhanging form. My hands grapple with flint and kindling, desperate for it to catch so I can get out of this situation. As my breathing quickens and my gut twists itself into a painful spiral, a single spark jumps away from the steel to ignite the pile of feather sticks. I thank whatever power that gave me success and blow it into flame. In no time, the ignati licks at crackling logs. I move to make my escape.

"Where do you think you are going?"

I cringe. Something venomous bubbles under the surface in my father's tone. I'm used to his words pouring out in angry torrents, not this barely controlled undercurrent. Frozen with my back to him, I hold the basket of kindling and sola bones to my chest. My eyes squeeze shut, my shoulders tense in anticipation of his forceful hands. The moment drips by like an eternity.

"Oh, let him go, Dravek," my mother drawls, breaking the silence with her apathetic tone. She waves dismissively.

For once, she came to my rescue.

I look back at Father, but he has already left the room. Not willing to risk one more altercation, I head for the stairs, my supper forgotten.

"Belwyn, where is Rhun?" my mother calls after me.

Pausing at the banister, I inhale through gritted teeth. I almost escaped. "Wasn't he with you?" My voice is terse, and I don't like it. Too much like my father.

"I lost track of him in that . . . well, whatever it was. Why don't you take a look for him?" She sighs, and when I look over my shoulder, I see her settling back into the sofa with eyes closed, her long hair flowing across the cushions.

"I'm sure he'll show up eventually," I mutter, tired of always being the one to hold this family together.

Before she can guilt me into doing what she asked, I bound up the steps.

The light leaves with me.

It is pitch black when the creak of the door startles me awake.

"Welcome home," I mumble into my pillow as Rhun stumbles into our shared bedroom. He swears and closes the door much too loudly for the middle of the night.

I raise myself onto one elbow and peer uselessly into the darkness.

"I'm surprised you were able to find your way home."

He snickers like a maniac. I hear the muffled sound of his cloak dropping to the floor. At the same moment, our small room fills with blinding light. I throw up a hand to shield my eyes.

"We snagged a couple of these after that awful ceremony." He barely controls the fit of laughter that wants to run away with him. When my eyes adjust, I make out two sola brossa in his palm, no bigger than a carving knife.

"*Shades*, Rhun!" I say as loud as I dare, now fully awake. I lunge at his hands to douse their light. "What are you doing with these?" The bones clatter to the floor, and I throw my pillow over them. Pain bites at my kneecaps. I pin the bones to the planks with the pillow as if to keep them from skittering away.

"What's the matter, Belwyn?" he asks after catching his breath. His boots thud dully as they hit the far wall. "They're just bones. It's not like the kaligorven even know we have them."

I peel the pillow back a fraction. The light hits me in the face. My hands grow slick with sweat. I should hide them again, but I can't stop staring. They are more luminous than any sola brossa I have seen. One shard could illuminate the entire market in Utsanek. "These are new, Rhun."

He shrugs. "Yeah, so?"

"Where did you get them?"

He flops down heavily on his bed. "From the shack where the hunters left the sola meat to hang for the night." Glancing at me, he lets a smirk creep across his face. "Ketra took me there."

I sip in a quick breath and try to control my surprise.

Ketra's always been my . . . what? Girlfriend? That word doesn't seem right. Whatever she is, I've always taken for granted that she wanted me. I realize I'm an idiot, and it makes me want to spit hurtful things at Rhun, like *When has she ever shown interest in you?* Or, *You know she only did that to make me jealous.* But it isn't his fault. I'm the one who completely ignored her at the ceremony. I just didn't think she'd run off with my brother. Grimacing, I push it aside.

"And you, what? Thought it would be funny to hack off a bone or two?" My exhale comes out as a laugh, sharp and mirthless.

He rests his arms back on the mattress and slips his fingers into his mop of dull-blond hair. At fifteen, he already has my father's muscular frame, but his features are those of Mother. "Don't worry," he says, "we took them from inconspicuous places."

Is he honestly this obtuse? I stare at him, bathed luxuriously in the fresh sola bone light. "There's no way the Shrouded, or Father, will let you get away with this."

Rhun's eyebrows raise. "Ooo, look at the brand-new convert they made out of you."

An exasperated sigh escapes me as I try to knead the tightness out of the space between my eyebrows. Sometimes, I find it hard to believe he is only three years younger than me. "What are you talking about, you morvus?"

He folds his hands on top of his chest. "You can't pretend you actually believed in all this kaligorven garbage before today."

His smug expression makes me want to punch him. Instead, I sit back on my heels and rest my hands on my knees.

Of course, I didn't. But what does that change?

Pain throbs dully in my left temple. I grit my teeth. Somehow, he always manages to get in my head.

This isn't about me. It's about my stupid brother.

"So, you're saying you didn't notice the entire Vale threatening to implode on us?" I say, my voice barely controlled. "You didn't feel the wind try to rip trees out of the ground? You didn't hear that . . . that *thing* speak?" I shudder thinking about it.

Shrugging, Rhun rolls his eyes and stares back at the ceiling. "It was a good show. That's all." He closes his eyes as if to sleep.

"Rhun, this is serious. Your actions could have severe consequences—not only for you. For all of us."

"I'll believe it when I see it."

My fingers clench into tight fists. Will nothing get through to him?

"And what happens if Ketra gets the blame?"

Rhun examines his fingers, scraping the dirt from the crevices with a thumbnail. "You honestly think she means anything to me, other than a good time?" His eyes assault me with a look of superiority. "If you care so much about her, why were you such a prick at the festival?"

Heat rises to the collar of my tunic—whether it's because I can't stand his egotistical face, or because there's some truth in what he says, I don't know.

Standing up, I snatch the bones from the floor and loom over him. I'm done with words.

"Get up."

He cocks his head, challenging me. "What?"

"I said, get up. You're going to get rid of those things. Now."

He yawns apathetically and tries to roll over. I catch him by the arm, yanking him to his feet.

"*Hey*," he protests, but I've already thrown open the door and dragged him halfway down the hall.

He's only an inch shorter than I am, and he's built like a stone wall. I have him off-balance, however, and he's at my mercy. He stops fighting me when he nearly falls down the stairs.

"What do you want me to do?" The new tone of seriousness in his voice satisfies me slightly, but I'm still on fire. The sola brossa burn in my eyes, and my anger burns in my heart.

"You're going to bury them."

We reach the back entrance. I open it, thrust the bones into his naked arms, and push him through. I point to the shovel leaning against the house.

"And I don't care if the kaligorven see you doing it."

His head jerks up from the bones, and right before I slam the door shut, I see the whites of his eyes.

The ténesomni must remain . . .

I am half awake. The oath of the Shrouded reverberates around my brain, but the voice is all wrong.

. . . Unbroken . . .

It twists and mutates into a screeching wail, snapping through my semi-conscious state.

"My boy, my darling boy . . ."

I lurch upright, flinging the bedclothes to the floor. Dread gnaws at my intestines.

"Oh, Rhun, my *baby* . . ."

Mother's voice, transformed by the unearthly tones of grief. My hands and knees collide with the scraped wood floor for the second time tonight as I throw myself from the bed, but I have lost the ability to feel.

Out in the hallway, the other boys' door cracks open. Korvin's murky eyes peer from the shadows. All I can do is shake my head desperately at him as I pull the door closed.

"Why, oh *why* . . . my baby . . . *Rhun* . . ."

I reach the kitchen. My father's broad silhouette dominates the doorway. A lantern hangs limply at his side. His shoulders are slumped, his head low. An aching cold spreads down my arms as nausea rushes up my core.

"Not my boy . . . Not my son . . ."

Father's fist tightens around the lantern's handle. He turns around when he hears me approaching.

"What—what happened?" I say through a throat that has tried to seal itself shut.

The ignati barely manages to reveal his hardened face, taut and murderous.

"The kaligorven took your brother, Belwyn." His detached tone does not match the muscles twisted so tight they might snap.

I try to look past my father to see, but I can only picture Rhun's wide eyes as I shoved him out the door, the sola brossa gleaming against his white arms. Father shifts to block me.

"No, Belwyn. He is gone. That is no longer your brother." He lifts the lantern so he can see my eyes, so I can see his.

"But why . . ." I gulp down the words. I know why. He's dead because his self-righteous brother exposed him to the night.

Father drops the lantern. It smashes on the flagstones, and the fire goes out. In the darkness, he grabs me by the shoulders and shakes me violently. "It does not matter why. Do you understand?" He jolts me again. Pain fires through my neck. "He was a sacrifice the kaligorven demanded."

A cold sweat breaks out all over me. Whatever he may say, I know it's my fault. It was me.

I am glad he can no longer see my face.

His grip loosens, and he bends to retrieve the lantern. My mother's ugly wails rend the early morning air. "We will go to every single house in the Vale and rip every last sola bone from the greedy fingers of the valefolk."

I bob my chin in agreement, though it's just a habit. I am not really here. This is not really happening.

"Not one more person will violate the command of darkness," he growls dangerously, "until the kaligorven lift it."

8

AMYRAH

IF WE DIDN'T HAVE THE SOLA'S LIGHT shining like a beacon in the distance, I don't know how we'd find our way. Even with my gift surrounding us, there isn't much to give us direction except the feeling of the ground slanting away beneath our feet. I try not to worry. Clutching my father's arm tightly, the tension drains from my back and escapes through my fingertips. We are together. The inexhaustible bird flutters ahead of us from branch to branch, so I must believe the world will be right again.

But my father refuses to look at the sola.

It is the early hours of the morning when we emerge from the trees and into the clearing on Utsanek's north side—at least that's what my instincts tell me. But there's no real way of knowing. My brows pinch together. Something feels wrong. I slow down to listen. Father sighs deeply, and I feel his agitation as a swell of guilt. He wasn't ready to see another sola. I should have known.

I do my best to push the feeling aside, though it is hard. I hate how this thing that brought me hope has caused him even greater torment. The creatures he set out to kill, that he thought he was justified in hunting . . . he owes them his life.

We cross the hard-packed earth to the stone pit. The wren darts to the treetops, as if it knows this is no place for a Light Creature. Even somewhat removed, it still casts enough illumination to reveal the clearing.

It is in disarray. Broken branches and other debris congest the ground. I slip my arm out of my father's elbow and approach a bundle of clothes lying in the dirt. Crouching, I lift a corner with my forefinger and thumb. From within its folds emanates a sickly light. Sola brossa. I let it drop back to the earth, perplexed. Straightening and dusting off my hands, I return to my father.

He is a statue, immobilized at the edge of the spent fire, staring down into its charred depths. I lay my hand on his forearm, cautious not to startle him.

"What is it?"

"Kuvror Erovantus," he mutters, like the words will catch and spread. When I open my mouth in question, he clears his throat and nods his chin toward the ashes. "They burned the sola blood. Look."

I peer into the pit. Shattered pieces of pottery and blackened remains of wood litter the ashy earth in a ring around its circumference, swept clean to the edges as if a forceful blast has pushed it aside.

"It is what happens when sola kuvror, Light Creature blood, meets fire. It does not mix. The reaction is . . . unpredictable."

From the forest's edge, the sola chirps out five sweet notes. I look at it, wincing for the thousandth time at its brightness. How can you explain such great power dwelling in something so small?

But the bird's refrain does not comfort my father. He keeps his chin down and wraps an arm around my shoulders to turn me away from the wreckage, toward Utsanek. If it wouldn't take an extra hour, I know he would rather take me around the city. Not through it. But we are on the wrong edge, and I'm sure he is as desperate for home as I am.

As we approached the veiled streets, the shadows converge upon us. Glancing behind, I see only ténesomni. The light has gone. I don't blame the sola for abandoning us, but I can't help feeling sad. The little bird felt like a friend.

When I turn back to the cobbled path, I find even though the lanterns are lit, they barely cast any illumination. I've never known ignati to be so concealed by ténesomni. If it wasn't for the strange orb that surrounds me wherever I go, we would not be able to see anything. I glance up at my father. He has made no comment about my peculiar gift. I dare not draw attention to it at such a fragile moment. If he wasn't aware of it before, it would surprise him now.

The burning embers of anger threaten to catch in my chest again. He must have known about it for a while, perhaps my whole life. Why has he kept the truth from me, as he kept the existence of the solas secret? Has everything in my life been a farce?

I let the tide of fury drain away from my muscles, the cool wind of reason taking their place. Now is not the time.

Down the winding streets and past towering structures that lean threateningly overhead, the air grows thicker. Suffocating. No misplaced sola bone gives the darkness chase, even from within the dwellings.

Drawn curtains and latched doors stare at us morosely. We are the anomaly, the only things possessed with life.

"Why aren't people up yet?" I give my swirling anxieties a voice. The merchants always battle with each other to make it to the square as soon as the morning bell tolls, with the hopes of gaining an advantage over the competition. I've spent my own share of early hours running Orlagh's booth.

Father shrugs, lost in his own restless thoughts. His shoulders curve forward, and the downward turn of his face conceals his expression in shadow.

We emerge from the maze of the residential sector and into the market square. An inhale rushes past my lips.

It's unrecognizable. Even here, there are no sola brossa left to illuminate Utsanek's center of trade. The smudges of red ignati behind the lanterns' glass can hardly be seen.

We keep to the edge of the square, coming across overturned merchant booths and refuse littering the cobblestones. A tingling sweeps down my arms and pools in my fingertips. What could cause the valefolk to rip down the glowing strings of bones they depend on and lock themselves indoors? A new day approaches, but the Vale dares not to greet it.

A sharp clatter startles me, and I swallow as my pulse lurches. Father's tendons stiffen beneath my fingers as we approach the sound together. Down the line of booths, a small shape materializes out of the gloom. It scrounges carelessly around a familiar stall, knocking over a stool.

"*Hey,*" I shout, fierce loyalty displacing the cold from my veins. That booth is Orlagh's.

The figure bolts upright and regards us, a defiant desperation shining in his black eyes. His thin chest rises and falls rapidly as he conceals a soiled loaf of bread behind his back. I stare at him, speechless.

"Leave him be," my father murmurs, breaking the silence. His fingers dig into my shoulder, scraping the linen of my dress across it like coarse sand.

I glance from him to the scavenger, and all at once the inconsiderate thief transforms into a terrified, helpless child. My brows unhitch themselves.

"It's ok," I say. "You just startled me." I gesture at the disorder around us. "Can you tell me what happened here?"

The thick layer of grime on his face does nothing to disguise the hollowness of his cheeks. Flashes of white shine from huge eyes that dart side to side, taking in the strange, bright sphere that surrounds all three of us. His arms go limp, the pilfered treasure falling to his side. His jaw slackens in wonder.

"What's wrong with the shadows?" he asks with a voice too soft to belong to one condemned to the cruel streets of Utsanek.

I wish I could offer him some explanation that would make sense. I shrug. "Nothing, really."

Father tugs me close.

The child cocks his head, unsatisfied. "They don't get near you."

"We need to go," Father says.

I tune him out and address my small interrogator. "It's just like I have a little light, that's all."

The gaunt face scrunches as he tries to work it out. "But we're not allowed to have light anymore," he concludes, as if it settles the argument.

I wish I could make sense of this strange comment, but my father's grip distracts me. A weak smile wobbles across my lips.

"Well, I'm sure we're allowed to use it to find you a bit more to eat than bread." I want to pull away, but the hand holds me tighter. The boy retreats, his eyes widening and his head shaking too fast.

My father's voice grows stern. "No, Amyrah. We need to go."

How can he willfully ignore this starving child?

"I'm sure if we both look together—"

"*Now.*"

His fingers root themselves into my very bones, and I gasp. I fix my eyes on the boy. Some of the light of innocence leaves his eyes, his face aged in an instant. Now an icy mirror, it reflects my father's indifference as if he has seen it a thousand times before. That heartbreaking reality saps the last of my strength.

"I'm sorry," I say weakly, yielding to the pressure, powerless to help without defying my father again.

The child's face contorts as he spits on the stony ground and slips into the darkness.

Heaviness pools into my limbs. This city was alive with hope and energy yesterday. Now it is a place of hunger and mistrust, and I'm nothing more than a feeble ignati within it. I stare down at my feet as they carry me forward without my consent.

The street rolls along under me, dusty and dim. I cannot tell where my body ends and the ground begins, nor do I perceive what objects make me stumble.

A glimmer catches my eye from the cobbles. It wakes me from my stupor, draws me in. I yank my arm away and veer out of Father's reach to see it closer.

An argentilum necklace, fallen to the rocky earth.

It's worth more than I could earn in a year, but that's not what draws me. I wrap my stiff fingers around its angular shape. Warm to the touch.

I stand, slipping the minuscule treasure into the pocket of my dress, and rejoin my father. The tiny circle of heat from the pendant spreads through my palm and up my arm, dispelling the cold that had begun to turn me to stone.

Maybe a weak flame is still better than no flame at all.

9
WEHNA

YOU NEED TO BE STRONG, WEHNA.

I'd take strength from these words—the last my mother spoke to me—if I hadn't driven her to say them every day of my life. If I'd been braver.

"Wehna . . ."

A tug on my tunic follows the plaintive voice.

"Wehna, I'm hungry."

I stare at the wrinkly tubers in my hands. Four lanuum. That's all we have. Just thinking about what we'll do after we've eaten them makes me sweat. I inhale slowly, masking my worry with a smile.

"Well, that's good, because I was about to make some lanuum cakes for you."

I drop the tubers into the little boiling pot above the fire and turn to give Arvo's hair a playful tousle. His green eyes search mine, and my lips quiver. Have I convinced him? Does he believe everything is fine, or can he see through me?

I turn my back before my smile can falter completely and pull out a board crisscrossed with knife marks. "The question is, do you want them to be flavored with onions or dill?"

Arvo sighs, and I hear his tiny body collapse into the chair by the hearth.

"I don't like onions. When's Mada and Pada coming home?"

My shoulders tighten at the whine in his voice.

I don't know, my mind answers while the words "soon, I hope," find my tongue. It shouldn't be this easy to lie.

His toes scrape at the stone floor. "I wish they let me come with them."

The fresh herbs crush underneath my fingertips, and their fragrance intensifies. My knife hand trembles. I grip tighter. It is not a good time to be chopping things.

"Hey, Vo, can you do me a favor?" I don't wait for him to reply. "See if you can stab a fork into the lanuum."

I hear Arvo muttering as he attempts to conquer the bubbling water and spear a slippery tuber. With his attention off me, I let my shoulders sag, close my eyes, and raise my face to the ceiling. After three years, I feel like we only just arrived in this horrible city, and I'm suddenly being forced to navigate it alone. The tears sting when they come.

"Keep your toes away from the fire this time," I say, my voice strangely breathy and high. My little brother is too preoccupied to notice.

You need to be strong, Wehna.

"Got it," he shouts, like he's landed a fish and not a hot potato.

My tears disappear into the sleeve I drag across my face. "Good job."

Arvo spends the next few moments trying to rescue the others—long enough for me to prepare the other ingredients and compose myself. His grin is infectious as he saunters up and dumps them into the clay mixing bowl. I hand him a slotted spoon, and he sticks his tongue out the side of his mouth while he squashes the lanuum into a white paste. When he tries to drop in the dill, the damp herbs stick to his fingers. A wrinkle forms at the bridge of his nose. I crack in an egg and tip in a small scoop of flour.

With his hands plunged into the savory dough, I turn to the fire and unhook the heavy iron pot and replace it with a flat, rectangular plate that sits above the ignati on knobs that protrude from the sides of the fireplace. When the oil I drip on it begins to shimmer, I beckon my brother over. He's formed six lumpy cakes out of the dough, varying greatly in thickness and size. I reserve comment and transfer them to the hotplate, one by one. The sizzle fills my mind, and the aroma overtakes my senses. An antidote, for a moment, to my anxious thoughts. I sink to my knees on the hearth, and Arvo nestles into my side. Stomachs grumbling, we watch the cakes cook.

Little fingers play with the bracelets around my wrists. "How come you wear so many pretty things, Wehna?"

I look at the strands with blurred eyes. The colors bleed into one another, consuming my vision. "They help me to forget the darkness, little one."

Arvo's brow furrows, and he sticks out his lips like a duck's bill. "That's silly."

A weak chuckle I did not anticipate puffs from my lungs. "And why is that?"

"Because you can't forget something that's always around you."

I squeeze him tighter. His curls tickle my cheek. "Well, I can pretend it's not there, can't I?" As if it's that easy. "Although, I don't think I'm very good at it. Wanna help me?"

Arvo continues to pull on a bracelet in silence. It's unique, with angular beads in the shape of flying birds in hues of indigo, turquoise, and blue. I envy the birds of the Vale, with their ability to fly above it all. I have to make myself imagine it, because it's easy to believe this night goes on forever.

"Here," I say, tugging at the knot underneath until it springs free. "Why don't you keep this for a while?"

The beads glint off Arvo's widening eyes, their fresh green joining in perfectly with the mosaic of colors. "Really?" he asks, breathless.

I nod and fasten it around his thin wrist, gritting my teeth in concentration. "You made one for me, remember? I owe you."

Arvo holds his arm to stare at it. "That one doesn't have any fancy beads on it, though."

I tousle his hair. "That doesn't matter. Yours is still my favorite."

He brings the bracelet close and fingers the beads, studying them intently. His lips and brows shift and pucker. I have always loved watching thoughts play out on his sweet face. He moves so he can be sure I am paying full attention to him. "Wehna, how can the birds see where they are flying if it's so dark all the time?"

My chest tightens as his innocent eyes clap on to mine, wide in anticipation of my response. Sometimes I forget the ténesomni is all he can remember. I try to ignore the way my throat has tightened and force my mind to formulate a response.

"What do you see when you look into the sky?"

Arvo squeezes his eyes shut and ponders intently. It looks almost painful. I can't help but smile. He scrunches his nose and nods with finality before looking at me again. "Blackness."

I bob my head. "That may be true for us, but the birds don't see it like we do. Neither do the animals"

"How come?"

"Because this shadow is not meant for them."

Arvo shifts onto hands and knees. He leans forward and peers at me as if he's trying to assess my sanity.

"Wehna, you don't make any sense."

I roll my eyes and reach over to tickle his exposed armpits. He collapses in a fit of giggles. When we both get a chance to catch our breath, I hold his arm up and finger each of the flying bird beads. "Remember, fledgling, there's a place where this darkness ends. One day, we'll find it together." I let his arm drop, and he grins when it smacks softly onto his face. "Then you'll get to see the stars."

The lanuum cakes don't take long on the grill. I stack them into a little tower that wobbles precariously, purely for Arvo's benefit. He snickers as I struggle to balance them. I kick two cushions from the huge pile reserved for the caeruméni gatherings my parents host.

Hosted.

I bite my lip.

I need to be strong.

"Do you want to pray tonight, or should I?"

Arvo makes a show of thinking it through, his lips pressed into a tight little line. He points at me.

I nod. Setting down the dish between us, I reach for my brother's hands. Squishy and warm. The way his fingers cling to mine sends a little shot of comfort to my heart.

"Elyōn, we thank you for all you have provided. We have nothing that you did not give us. We trust you to use this meal in us to shine in the ténesomni like stars." A twinge of guilt tugs at the words, a tether restricting the bird-like flight of my prayers. I don't want to shine. I just want to survive.

"And keep my mada and pada safe."

The sincerity in Arvo's pure voice shames me. I squeeze his hands and echo his plea in my heart.

"Elyōn érit agértu," I whisper. The Highest will act.

Our supper is simple but satisfactory. Arvo inhales two whole cakes, and I force myself to stop at one. We can still get another meal out of them if I am disciplined.

With a full belly and the warmth of the fire curling around him like a cloud, Arvo soon dozes off. I stoop to pick him up, slipping my arms under his knees and shoulders. He is light, like a hollow-boned bird. I press my cheek to his forehead, letting his warmth chase away the chill that tries to grip my every waking moment. The bed we've shared since he could walk dwarfs him in size. I pull the heavy wool quilt over him, trapping the beautiful bracelet between it and his heart.

"Sleep, sweet boy," I say, brushing my knuckles across his smooth, light-brown skin before slipping out the door and down the rickety stairs with a lantern in hand.

At the first landing, I pause and knock on the door, trying to ignore the chill of darkness that presses against my spine. A grisly faced woman opens it a crack, scowling at me from under fleshy brows.

"I need to go out, Gotrel," I say, my voice more confident than I feel. "Will you keep an ear out for Arvo? Help him if he needs anything?"

The woman's thin mouth opens in a sneer. "Out, you say? Leavin' that poor boy alone again, are ya?" She shakes her head. "What would your ma and pa say, I wonder?"

My throat squeezes at the mention of my parents, and air whistles in through my teeth. "*Please*. Please just say you'll be there for him if he goes looking for me."

Gotrel's eyes are like faded violets. They narrow, and I squirm inwardly under their gaze. She nods.

I touch the hand that holds the doorknob in its wrinkled grip. "Thank you."

Descending the last flight of stairs, I am swallowed by the night.

10
TÉRON

YOU WERE THE MOST BEAUTIFUL THING I have ever seen. When you and I met in the market that day, the ténesomni seemed lighter. You made it lighter. I know that now.

I never dreamed you would see me too. But you did. You must have unearthed something deep inside, something even I did not know I had. You never told me what it was, but it made your eyes sparkle and the dimples that punctuated your lovely mouth deepen.

The day you said yes, my heart swelled to absorb every single drop of light that shook from your laughter. It took on a new shape. A you-shape.

Did I really get to wake up with you every morning, molded to my side, entwined in the blankets you stole during the night? Or was it a dream? It feels like a dream. But I remember the way your nose wrinkled in the bolétis light when I bestowed you with bristly morning kisses. I can see your freckles scrunching together. I know it happened. The tiny details make it real.

When you brought our daughter into the world, your strength humbled me. Pain carved crevices between your eyebrows. Joy sculpted rays at the corners of your eyes. I laid her tiny form on your chest, skin to skin, and wrapped my naked arms around you both. My world.

Nothing bad would ever happen to you. I would not let it.

You were the mother our daughter needed. I know you second-guessed every word you said, every touch you gave, but you were so good. I could not bear seeing the blackness of doubt taint your brightness for even a moment. Always, when the shadow passed, you shone clearer. And you gave that light to her.

I never counted the days with you. I never thought I needed to. They rolled over endlessly, gently carrying us along in spiral after glimmering spiral. I should not have let you slip from my hands. But I did not hold on. Why didn't I hold on?

All I am left with are these memories, clinging to my thoughts like spiderwebs. One careless breath, and a strand snaps. Tiny threads, nothing to them, yet enough to hold the weight of my world.

What lies led me here, to this moment, when I am questioning all that has kept me going since your warmth embraced me for the last time? My thoughts are an endless cavern, too deep for light to reach.

My Ellehra, why did you have to leave me?

A new heat consumed me after you were taken. It was not life-giving, like yours. Caustic and powerful, I began to crave its flame's acidic intensity. It sustained me for thirteen years. It owned me.

The crystal waters of our daughter's eyes—*your* eyes—threatened to extinguish the blaze. I should have let them, but I was a coward. I believed I needed it, and without it, I would drown.

In the end, it was you. You were the one who overwhelmed that cancerous inferno. It may have been a beast lying amid the trees, but I saw you, in all your fading sola radiance.

So many questions assail my every waking moment. I want to find the answers, but the thought of searching makes me weak. I feel the exhaustion in my soul.

What now becomes of me?

I have held on to this anger so long, I fear my heart will only ever be anger-shaped.

II

BELWYN

MY SHOVEL IS A CLEAVER, severing plant roots and marring the smooth ground, taking more life out of this world.

You can't pretend you actually believed in all this kaligorven garbage before today.

Rhun's words throw themselves around my brain like an untamed beast. I want them out. I fling a mound of dirt over my shoulder and thrust the implement down into the soft earth again.

Maybe I didn't believe. Maybe I hoped it was all a lie.

I glance at the heap of old sola bones awaiting their burial. We scoured all Utsanek. This meager pile represents all the bones my father's men could find, every scrap of sola light the people possessed. Some of the pieces are so old they emit almost no light. They have belonged to the people for generations. All are a putrid, waxy yellow. It's fitting that they resemble the death which befell their hosts all those years ago.

If I had truly believed in the kaligorven, if I had understood what it meant to incur their wrath, would I have abandoned my brother to their domain?

A bead of sweat slips off the tip of my nose, splashes the back of my hand. This didn't need to be my job, but I asked for it. Father doesn't know why. He probably believes I'm being the dutiful son again, trying to make him proud. The thought of telling him—of telling anyone—that I am at fault for Rhun's death makes the air in my lungs solidify to brick.

I keep digging. The hole is up to my waist, but it still isn't deep enough. It will never be deep enough. I breathe in the sharp scent of decay that surrounds me, a bitter perfume rising from the wound I've inflicted on the forest floor.

He *stole the bones*. He *taunted the kaligorven. I was protecting our household. I did everything right.*

But the Shrouded do not show mercy. I believe in them now.

I throw myself into the task until my spine feels like it will snap in two. I need this pain. I need it to distract me from my guilt—a physical ache to displace the emotional anguish. But my mind will not be stilled.

I hate myself, my obsession with doing everything right.

What a morvus you are.

In the moment he needed me the most, duty became more important than my own brother. How could I have been so fixated on making sure our house didn't break the command of darkness that I didn't care what happened outside of it? A miserable sound—not quite a laugh, not quite a groan—escapes my throat. The early morning mists press against the noise, making it sound like I'm sealed in a tomb.

If they took me in the same way, right now, I would welcome them.

But that is a selfish thought. I deserve to live with these consequences. And maybe my father does, too, for how he failed me and failed Rhun. But my mother does not. One more loss will shatter her.

I lob the shovel out of the grave and climb out after it. The dirt mingles with my sweat when I try to brush it off my hands and arms, smearing my skin with dark streaks. I stare at them, barely illuminated in the dying sola light. I imagine the cords of darkness have been burned into my skin. The darkness *is* me. I sink to the ground, clutching my left wrist in my right hand and resting my forearms on my knees. My head stoops below my shoulders.

I don't care anymore. Let them have me.

The woods watch, but they are hidden from sight. A hundred feet above my head, trees sway and creak. Whatever wind shakes them does not touch me. I am nothing but a tiny pebble in the midst of this wild immensity. I know nothing of it. This is the farthest I have ever ventured into them alone, and it isn't far.

Coward.

My entire life has been spent within the confines of Utsanek. This moment makes me feel pathetic in a way I have never known before. Logically, I can justify it. Immense trees with trunks as thick as small houses hem in the valley on three edges. They gradually disperse into the Askonnet Mountains, leaving the stony precipices to guard us. To the southwest, the vast Loch Skythe forms an impassable barrier between us and the Southlands. Beyond that, who knows? In this never-ending darkness, people want to stay where it's open and where light, no matter how feeble, can be found.

The pile of bones to my left represents nearly all of it—the glowing trinkets we ripped from the fingers of the frailest grandmothers.

I can still see the fragments Rhun brought home a week ago when I close my eyes. I never dreamed sola brossa could be so bright. A hundred piles of these old bones could not equal them. No wonder Sola Vinari is such a sacred rite.

Time drifts by, but I don't care. My kneecaps press themselves into my arms, like I press myself into the darkness. Like it presses into me. I wish it would swallow me. My eyes strain for any variation in the shadows, but there's nothing. Always nothing. The ténesomni has reduced the bolétis to greasy smears that streak off into the distance. It reaches in determinedly at the sola brossa, still powerless to snuff them out, weak though they are. The black fingers claim me, painting me with their bold strokes. I am powerless to resist it.

A crack of thunder propels me to the present, making my heart lurch to catch up. I go from stone cold to flushed and sweaty with the sudden injection of adrenaline. My head snaps back and forth, but no shadowy monster has found me. I close my eyes and wait for my pulse to relax. When I am able to stand, I am conscious of how vulnerable my aching back and numb appendages render me.

Good.

I glance around one last time, daring—hoping for?—the kaligorven to face me. But nothing does. I kick the bones and they scatter, hitting the earth with soft thuds. How have I sat beside a hundred sola bones for at least an hour, yet I go unnoticed? Rhun was out there—what, five minutes? They wasted no time hunting him down.

My anger burns itself out within moments, and a kind of bewildered desperation fills the gap. It's been so long since the Vale has been visited by the Shrouded. Why now? I was content with the shadows. I thought I knew them. But now I know I don't know anything. Like why I get to live while my brother dies.

I do not understand this present darkness at all.

The yawning mouth in the earth waits patiently to receive the bones, but not me.

Fingers tightening around the handle of the shovel, I finish the job.

"*Belwyn.*"

I pinch my eyelids shut and stifle a sigh. How in Elyōn's name did Ketra find me? I can't even register my surroundings. Except for the small circle of cobblestones my lantern manages to illuminate, I wouldn't know I was in Utsanek at all. I navigate the city from memory, not sight. Ketra's footfalls echo dully behind me. If I wasn't so bone-weary, I'd make sure she couldn't catch up.

"Belwyn, wait."

Ketra's hand finds my forearm and tugs me to a halt. I sigh and turn around reluctantly, holding my lantern up to keep space between us. She's the last person I want to see right now. When I am facing her, she slides both hands up my arms until her palms rest on my collar bones. Her touch is like a thing not living. Dim though it is, I can see the hunger in her eyes when she leans in. I can smell the alcohol on her breath.

"Why haven't you come to find me?" she asks, her cool fingertips pulling at the neck of my shirt. Her chin tilts up, but there is no longer that characteristic playfulness in her expression. I break her gaze and focus past the top of her head. I can't do this.

"I haven't been able to leave my room in days," she says, her hands tightening into fists.

When I refuse to look at her, she sobs and rests her forehead on my chest. The lantern does not yield between us.

"Say something."

I inhale slowly. My free hand traces one of her white arms and clamps down on her fingers, prying them off. Ketra pulls back. She lets go with the other hand, and her arms drop listlessly by her sides.

"What's wrong with you?" she asks, her voice tinged with hurt and anger.

If she really wants to do this, so be it.

"Are you really this stupid?" I ask, noting how my voice has a knife-like quality about it. "I know how Rhun got the bones that night."

Ketra opens her mouth, then shuts it. I look at her hard, noticing how her hair is dull and unkempt, and how her eyes swim in dark circles. She may be a wreck, but I won't let her get into my head. I cross my arms and hope my expression communicates anger rather than guilt and a childlike desire for comfort. "If you hadn't run away like a spoiled brat, if you hadn't been so intent on getting back at me—"

"How unsurprising that you're making this all about you." She laughs dryly, shaking her head.

I am the bewildered one, now.

"What are you talking about?"

"Rhun is" —she chokes on the word, like something bitter— "*dead*, Belwyn." Long fingers twist at the front of her dress. I should be comforting her, but I'm stuck on how we still say *is* when a person no longer exists. Her face contorts. "And you're acting like daring to have fun with someone else for once is the worse crime."

"I know he's dead," I say quietly, focus returning, eyes narrowing. My voice is so low it almost doesn't make a sound. "I know that." I can feel my shoulders drawing upward. The buildup of tension surrounding my lungs gives increasing power to my words. "He was my brother. Mine. Not yours. Not some amusing pastime."

I step forward, and Ketra retreats, her eyes huge. "I'm the one who saw him last, and I'm the one that has been spending a week trying to clean up the mess you made." I'm yelling now, and the corrosive words rip at my throat. "Were you there when he died? Do you even realize *you* handed him the very thing that destroyed him?" I press a shaking hand to my forehead, trying to gain control. I can feel my heartbeat pulsing through every part of me, like something fighting to escape.

Ketra cowers in the ignati glow, and I think how small she seems.

With enormous effort, I reel in my fire. My next words slip through gritted teeth. "Don't you dare tell me I cared more about your pathetic tryst than I did for my own brother."

Her lip trembles. Tears shine on her cheeks. "I needed you, Belwyn." She steps toward me, her plaintive voice weak. "I needed you the night of the Hunt. I needed you when Rhun died." She sniffs. "And I need you now."

I want to scream away her meaningless words, but she pushes the lantern aside and erases the distance between us before I can. Her lips find mine in nothing more than a passionate last effort at self-defense. For a moment, I consider giving in, but I feel nothing. Nothing except this depression seeping into my bones. She is using me like she used Rhun. I don't kiss her back.

When she pulls away and looks at me with shadowed eyes, I turn my face away from her and stare into the black. Maybe I would have accepted this—whatever this is—a week ago, but not now. I can't.

"What's happened to you?" All the softness has left Ketra's voice.

I shake my head.

I don't know. I don't know.

12

AMYRAH

BOLETIS WASH ME IN MULTICOLORED HUES. Instead of quiet blue, I am illuminated by vivid green, purple, and orange tones. Nothing compared to my dreams but still more than I knew existed in this world. Several days of searching the darker corners of the forest proved worth the effort. I've made six trips home with baskets full of these treasures. Every day yields more tiny beauties. I have ventured farther into the trees than I would ever have dared before meeting the sola. Before discovering the darkness can't reach me.

Father wouldn't like it, but he has barely acknowledged my existence since the Hunt.

Expecting him to be confined indoors, like he has been for more than a fortnight, I bound into our yard, to the lean-to along the far wall of the cottage. As I reach for the latch, the slatted door swings open, exposing his hunched form. His beard sticks out at odd angles below his sallow face. The buttons of his shirt are mostly undone. He stares, blank-faced, at the rows of bolétis, neatly arranged along rough shelves in old, clouded glass jars. The necklace dangles from his hand. It glints in the bolétis light.

"Amyrah," he says, as though I hadn't been gone for hours. His voice cracks from days of silence. "What is this?"

I bite my lip. What can I say?

The brilliant gem quivers as his fist clenches. He raises it to the level of his eyes and scowls before twisting his shoulders toward me.

Strange. It does not glow when he holds it.

"I asked you a question."

Swallowing, I lift my chin and straighten my back. He doesn't get to judge, not after shutting me out for nearly a month. Not after refusing to work. Not after making me keep our little farm running on my own.

"I found them."

"You *found* them," he repeats, and his eyes fix on my face, checking it for any hint of untruth.

I blink but remain silent.

Father's lower jaw tenses and shifts forward. Teeth gritted, he lowers the necklace and scans the shelves again. The tension snaps between us like static electricity.

"Do you have any idea how dangerous this is, all this light in one place?"

I shift my weight to one leg and lower the basket to my side. "Dangerous for whom?"

His face snaps back to me, and something not quite stable taints his expression.

"For *you*," he says. "For the whole city. For your—"

My head tilts to one side. "For my what?" I step closer, daring him to tell me the truth.

He glares at me for a moment, but then his eyes focus somewhere far away. I wait, breath held, wondering what he's seeing. Coming at me, my father yanks the basket from my hand and tosses it into the furthest corner of the lean-to. The little bolétis tumble out all over the floor. I shrink back, shocked to see him so changeable.

"Your mother thought she was beyond their reach too," he spits out like a wild animal in pain. His voice makes me shudder. "It brought her nothing but death."

Tears gather in the corners of my eyes. I chew on the inside of my cheek.

"They're just mushrooms," I whisper.

He closes his eyes and shakes his head, laughing bitterly as he grinds his free palm into his temple. "They are so much more than that."

"Then *tell me*. Explain this whole broken world to me. Please."

Father walks past me into the open air. I follow.

"I can handle more than you think," I say, close to yelling now.

He wheels around, his shoulders heaving like he has run here from Utsanek. Even this short exertion has the power to exhaust him. I should be ashamed of myself for vexing him like this.

But I'm just angry.

"What do you know of life?" he returns, fixing me with a withering look.

My back goes rigid. It's not like him to cut me down like this. "I know enough to keep things running while my useless father wallows in the past." The acidic words spew from me, and I can't get them back.

The argentilum necklace in my father's hand slips through his fingers, plummets to the earth.

If I wielded an actual weapon, I would have hurt him less.

"Do you really think," he begins, stops, wets his lips with his tongue. "Do you think I want to be this way?"

I wrap my arms around myself and make no reply. There isn't a right way to answer, except to apologize, and I'm too upset to do that.

He approaches me hesitantly, no doubt afraid I will lash out again. I turn my face away and squeeze my eyes shut. His touch makes me start. The warmth of his hands brushes my arms, then my back, as he pulls me in and holds me tight.

"When your mother died, I lost everything. Everything I was." His breaths shake the both of us. "I thought—I—I could shelter you from it all."

"But you can't," I say into his shoulder. "Not anymore."

Father's chest rises and falls four times. "I can try."

I untangle my arms from between us and gently push him far enough away to see his face. The fingers of ténesomni strain in but do not touch us.

"And what about this?" I ask, motioning at the darkness and where it ends. "Why do you pretend you don't see it?"

His mouth tenses, but his eyes don't leave mine. His answer comes out in a tight, pointed burst. "You think this makes you special, but it means nothing."

I pull away and shake my head, eyes narrowing. "You still won't tell me, will you?"

"Tell you what?"

"About her."

Father's hands drop to his sides. "What are you talking about?"

I study his face, noting the angle and pinch of his eyebrows. He's afraid.

"Your wife. My *mother*."

Hardness chases away his apprehension. "She has nothing to do with any of this."

"Except with *me*." I beat my chest. "Her daughter. And the peculiar gift she and I both possess. Or didn't you notice?"

My father grabs my shoulders and thrusts his face within inches of mine. His eyes are wild, desperate. "Your love of light will get you killed. Is that what you want?"

Shivers run up my spine. "Like her?"

Great tremors assail his arms. A wrenching sob shatters him, and his head sags between us.

Shame drenches me from head to toe. I know he is not strong enough for this right now. A confrontation is the last thing he needs. Why can't I hold my tongue, go on with life, and ignore the troubles that threaten to close in?

I sigh and lay a cool hand on his flushed cheek. "No one will care about my collection of bolétis, Pada."

For a moment, we stand like that, and I begin to hope something has been mended between us. But he brushes my hand away from his face and stands to his full height. If I hadn't just witnessed his grief, I would not know it could have ever existed. His eyes are cold, his jaw set. "If you are intent on ruining yourself, I want no part of it."

Pushing past me so I struggle for balance, he storms toward the cabin and barricades himself inside.

I stand there a moment; I stand there forever. The rhythm of my heart slows, my breaths calm, but the turmoil within my soul refuses to be stilled. A soft wind cuts through the clearing and lifts the hair off my damp brow, bids me to awaken.

Scooping up the necklace and brushing it off, I rise and tie the straps so it rests in the little hollow between my collar bones. It shines clearer than ever.

If he refuses to help me, I will have to help myself.

This time I remember to carry the brightest lantern possible. I hope it will keep the valefolk from noticing the impenetrable sphere around me. With how thick the darkness is and how useless ignati has proved against it over the last two weeks, entering the city is a risk. But it's one I feel compelled to take.

I don't know what I will find in Utsanek. More than I can expect at home, I hope.

What I didn't anticipate was an entire square filled with angry people.

Distinguishing any words amid the passionate shouts and cries polluting the air is difficult, but from the far end of the gathering, a stronger voice carries above the rest. Every time it pauses, the valefolk yell even louder, more enraged with each passing moment. I am not close enough to catch any of what the speaker says. The crowd presses in so tightly that I cannot penetrate the heart of the square to see what's going on.

Frustrated, I make my way around the edge of the throng, sometimes having to scrape my back against the stone-clad buildings and hold the lantern above my head so it won't be smashed. I am surprised anyone can keep theirs alight with the way people jostle about. They must carry them out of habit, not necessity. The flames really don't do anything anymore.

I almost make it to the northeast corner when an explosion of pain and light knocks me against a wall. A warm, sticky liquid dribbles over my lips and chin. I sputter and gasp for breath. By some miracle, my lantern is intact, but I fear my nose may not be. I slump down and curve myself around the ignati while attempting to stymie the flow of blood.

"Are you alright?"

A concerned voice edges through the cacophony. Startled, I peer up to find its source.

Heat rushes into my cheeks. The young man from the marketplace, the one with the thoughtful eyes and the nose ring, stands over me again. This time, he looks surprised to see me. Or relieved, which is a bewildering thought. How is it possible that, out of all the people in the Vale, I have come upon this same young man in a multitude—twice?

He crouches to one knee and digs in a pocket of his trousers, offering me the cloth he unearths. I hesitate before accepting. Inspecting his face, I find only a disarming kindness.

"Thank you." I hold the square of fabric to my throbbing nose.

He stays on my level, watching as I mop the blood off my chin before it dries. I am painfully aware of his gaze, of how disgusting I must look, of the awkward silence that drowns out the riot around us.

"You're the bread-stand girl." There is a softness in his voice. "Amyrah."

Mercifully, the bleeding stops, and I am spared having to answer through a bloody rag.

"I—" I crinkle my nose, which smarts, and avoid his eyes. How does he know my name? "I'm not sure what to think of that title."

He laughs, and it's a strange sound under the circumstances. Wrapping a hand around my elbow, he pulls me up with him. We shuffle over and take shelter in a small alcove between buildings. "Well, you don't have to call me 'market boy.'" Turning to me, he releases my arm and smiles, but it doesn't quite reach his eyes. "I'm Belwyn Kovah. And I'm relieved to see you're alright."

The way he says it makes me think he means more than just from getting elbowed in the face. Maybe he witnessed me make a spectacle of myself in front of the Foremost. I sweep my hair out of my eyes and tuck it behind my ear. It springs free immediately. He keeps looking at me, and warmth creeps down my neck.

"What's going on here?" I ask, partly to break his attention, partly to distract myself from how close he is.

The lightheartedness vanishes from his face. "Things are getting worse," he says. I follow his gaze to the north end of the square.

"Worse?" I repeat, confused and annoyed that I've stayed away from Utsanek so long. All I can see is a moving mass of gray and black, with orange smudges flickering in and out of sight.

"Yeah," Belwyn replies. His tone lowers, laced with emotion I can't identify. "There's been another attack."

"Another?" *What have I missed?*

He nods but doesn't elaborate.

I grab his forearm, and he turns to me in surprise.

"Tell me."

Ignati light dances feebly across his features. His eyes slip to the necklace at my throat. I drop his arm and quickly cover the jewel with my hand.

Curiosity drags one of his eyebrows down, the other up. Before he can pursue my strangeness, I persist. "Tell me about the attacks. I don't know anything."

His mouth gapes. "How—"

I shake my head. "I don't come to the city often."

A thunderous shout from the horde interrupts us. The energy is escalating quickly, and the whole rabble pulses together, shifting closer to the person speaking, then pushing back out like a wave. Even in our tiny square of privacy, we could be crushed.

"We should go."

Belwyn makes to grab me again, but I recoil from his reach and glare at him.

"Why would I do that?"

He regards me a moment, takes a hasty look at the mob, then leans in close and speaks so only I can hear. "Look, you want to know about the attacks, right? And I get the impression you have something to hide."

I clamp my mouth shut. This boy is too perceptive.

A brawl breaks out nearby, and Belwyn makes the decision for me. He grabs my hand and drags me behind him. I scramble to keep my feet, unable to see anything but the heels of his boots kicking up in front of me. We duck out of reach of the flailing appendages and slip down a narrow alleyway. He doesn't stop there but leads me down several twisting streets until the sound from the square reduces to background noise. Without my lantern in front of him, I don't know how he can see where he's going. I almost run into him when he stops. He glances around, opens a creaky door, and pulls me inside after him.

I yank my hand out of his. "Where are we?" I demand. It's a low-ceilinged kitchen with a massive hearth glowing at the far end. An expansive sitting room filled with squashy chairs is visible through a cased opening.

"A friend's." He takes the lantern from me and sets it on a roughly hewn dining table. The scent of fresh herbs, which hang above it to dry, fills my senses.

I raise my eyebrows.

"Don't worry," he says in a dry tone, "she won't mind." He gestures to a stool at the table.

Not sure what else to do, I sit. He pulls out another stool from underneath and does likewise. Clasping his hands and leaning onto his forearms, he studies me.

I fidget with my shirt sleeves in the sudden quiet.

"So."

Behind me, the fire crackles. I feel my cheeks heating up again. What am I even doing here? In some stranger's house, uninvited? With a boy I don't know? My neck could splinter with the tension. I sweep my windblown hair over one shoulder. My hands disappear into the mass of waves and instinctively start working the knots loose. The sensation of the strands slipping between my fingers is enough to convince my heart to slow.

I'm thankful not to be trapped in the middle of a riot.

"Tell me what you want to know," Belwyn says.

The strain in my neck eases a little now that he initiated the conversation. I chew on my bottom lip. My hands fall to the table. "Start with the attacks."

He nods subtly and takes a few slow breaths.

"The first one—" he swallows, pain flitting across his face. "The first death was three weeks ago. The night of Kuvror Erovantus." He inspects his thumbnails absently, running one under the other. "My brother."

My lips part. I should say something, but there are no words for a thing like that. Is that what drove Utsanek into the state of panic that night? I focus on the lines where the boards of the table meet and allow him to continue when he feels ready. His chest expands and contracts with measured breaths.

"The second happened about a week later, after I—well, the men—searched the entire city for all the remaining bones."

My eyes abandon the table and seek his.

"Who?"

Belwyn shrugs. "A man and a woman foolish enough to keep sola brossa with them. They were never identified. The bones were in their pockets when they were found."

I'm about to remark on how callous he sounds, but nothing would feel significant after losing your own brother. At least, I can imagine.

"Since then, there has been a death every day."

His words advance where the ténesomni dares not, tightening around my chest until it is hard to breathe.

"Every day?" I gasp.

He nods but doesn't look up.

"Did they conceal bones as well?"

"That's the thing. No one knows why they were targeted. They had nothing on them." He clenches his jaw. "And it hasn't only been people that should know better. Today, they killed a . . . a child."

The weight sinks down and pools in my stomach. Belwyn must feel it too, because his eyes pinch shut, and his head appears too heavy for his shoulders.

"That's why everyone's so angry. They have given up all their light, and now they are afraid they will be forced to give up their children."

It is difficult to speak when there's no air in your lungs. "And is it certain—do we know—was it the kaligorven?"

Belwyn raises his head. His eyes mirror the firelight. He doesn't need to say anything to confirm it.

How could this be? I have been exploring the forest so carelessly since the Hunt—bringing home bolétis, of all things. I could have met a kaligorva at any moment.

I don't know how I'm still alive.

My fingernails scrape the wood. I wince when a sliver embeds itself, but I make no move to dig it out.

"What else did you want to know?" Belwyn asks. He sounds tired.

I shift on the stool and trap my hands between my knees. I want to know about any rumors of people with the ability to repel darkness. I want to know I'm not alone. The questions expand inside me until I feel I will burst, but my father's words play over in my mind.

Do you have any idea how dangerous this is . . . for the whole city . . .

I didn't want to believe him. I reasoned that my actions could only bring harm to me, which was a risk worth taking. Nausea climbs up my insides and grasps me with clammy hands when I realize I could be the reason people have died.

No, I will not be telling this stranger anything about my gift.

I shake my head, look him in the eye, and smile wanly. "Nothing."

He lifts his clasped hands and rests his chin on them. "You really didn't know about any of this?"

I shake my head. I wasn't forbidden from coming to Utsanek, but I felt bound to my father. The black mood that possesses him is deeper than any I have seen him endure before. I can't allow myself to imagine what would happen if he didn't have anyone there for him. And I went and called him names, accused him of wallowing. How could that possibly help him? The regret tastes bitter on my tongue.

But these are not things I can tell someone I've just met.

Belwyn says nothing for a while, his thoughtful eyes staying on me as though he can read my mind. The idea is ridiculous, but still, I can't bear looking at him for more than a few seconds. I find the grooves of the tabletop much more agreeable.

"I wanted to go after you, you know."

"What?" My eyes dart up.

"When my father came back from the Hunt, and you confronted him. I saw the whole thing."

A chill quickly chases away the heat that races up my arms. He wanted to follow me? I try to swallow and find my mouth has gone dry. Instead of asking him why he would do such a thing, all that comes out is, "Your. . . father?"

He nods, a grimace gripping his features. "Yeah, I'm the son of the Foremost. Or at least one of them."

It's like I have been hit by a mighty wave, tossing me between the unexpected admission that he cares for me—at least in some unexplored way—and that he is the son of the man I hate most in the world. I was right to be cautious around him.

The stool screeches against the stone floor as I get to my feet. "I should go."

Belwyn's eyes narrow. "Look, I know he can be harsh, but—"

"This has nothing to do with him," I say, fumbling to slide the stool back under the table.

"Are you sure?" he asks, brows descending as he gets to his feet. "Because that's not what it looks like."

I give my head a feverish shake. "No, it's—I'm not sure I should even be here right now. And . . . with the riot and everything—"

He crosses the room and places himself between me and the door, suddenly severe. Unpredictable. "I am not my father, you know," he says, his voice affected, his dark eyes flashing.

I bite my lip and meet his gaze, struggling to breathe when he's so near. "You are close enough." *Too close. Dangerous.*

He stares at me intently, and for an instant, I am afraid. Some unstable emotion rages behind his eyes—because of me or because of his own familial ties, I cannot tell. When his hands tense, I flinch. His eyes graze my jaw, my throat, landing on the pendant. His voice flattens. "You should get rid of that thing, you know. It could get someone killed."

My fingers find the precious metal. I know each angle by heart. The tiny shape is warm, shining with a light untouched by the ténesomni. Perhaps it is dangerous, but there are far worse evils. I press it to my skin and raise my chin.

"And you might want to question why we think killing the light will free us from darkness."

Without giving him a chance to respond, I step around him, unlatch the door, and escape down the street.

13
BELWYN

A COMMOTION SOUNDS IN THE ALLEY. Something's happening. But my feet fuse to the spot.

She was afraid of me. I saw it in her face.

My fingers curl inwards, inch by inch, until the blood flow in my fists stops, and the palms of my hands scream out in pain. I forget to breathe.

All these years, I've done everything my father asked, everything I could to be the son he wanted. I told myself I could meet all his demands and still be myself. That I wasn't him. That I would never be him.

But now I wonder if I'm closer than I realized.

Who is this girl who makes me question everything I thought I knew? Who is she to treat my family status as something to be ashamed of? She knows nothing. She *is* nothing.

My lungs are on fire, but I refuse to let instinct take over. I consider how the pain laces out from my core like plant roots, forcing my entire body to convulse for air. When black begins to grip my vision, the reflex grows too much to fight. I drag in lungful after lungful of ash-scented oxygen.

I am no more capable of changing myself than I am to keep my body from breathing. Maybe there's a part of me that will always thrill to be cruel.

More shouts echo from outside, followed by the tromping of feet. The door flings open. Ketra tumbles in, catching herself on the doorframe. Out of breath, hair disheveled. People race down the street behind her. It takes a moment for the adrenaline to clear her eyes and confusion to take its place.

"What are you doing here?"

My fists unfurl as I cast around for an answer. "I needed a place to have a conversation."

She makes a face, still holding the doorpost like it's the only solid thing in the room. "And you thought my home would be the appropriate place for this?"

When I say nothing, she clicks her tongue. Her eyebrows raise, and she closes her eyes, touching a hand to her forehead.

"By all means, do what you want." She sighs, dropping her hand as she closes the door and gestures at the room. "Take what you want. I'm at your disposal." The disdain is slick in her voice.

The tone grates on me, makes me want to respond in kind. "I'm doing as you do, Ketra. You always manage to get your way, no matter what it costs."

For a moment, her face blanches, but color quickly returns. She comes right under my nose and scrutinizes my face with her arms folded.

"Was it a nice conversation, then?" She tilts her head. An eyebrow arcs in derision. "Catching up with your invisible friend?"

"I don't know. You'll have to ask her," I say, unruffled.

Ketra's eyelids flutter. Her nostrils flare slightly with a sharp intake of air. I've succeeded at inflicting pain, but it doesn't sit right. Why is it so easy to lash out at her now, when we only ever shared amity before? I'm so tired of it.

I exhale and pace toward the entrance, running my fingers through my hair. "I'll get out of your way now."

"Don't do that."

My hand on the doorknob, I peer at her over my shoulder, waiting for an explanation.

In the homey kitchen, Ketra is an odd sight. Nothing about her dress and demeanor could ever recommend her to domestic life. The herbs hanging over the scene are almost certainly the work of the aging aunt who is, no doubt, tucked neatly into her bed on the upper level of the apartment, completely unaware of all that happens below. The aunt that indulges every simpering word with an adoring smile and a pouch full of arlum.

Ketra pulls her cashmere shawl close around her, mouth working at the bottom lip. I'm sure she'd rather do anything than help me out at this moment. A breath heaves her shoulders, and she gives in.

"Your father has called a gathering at the Reckoning Grounds."

That makes me stand to attention. I let go of the handle. "What for?"

A reluctant grin dimples her cheeks.

"Another Hunt."

The desperation in the air is palpable. It takes a great deal of effort to navigate the city streets when no one seems to have a care for anyone around them. I don't know if I've ever seen such a frenzy before.

When I make it out, I find a weak circle of light at the north side of the ceremonial grounds. The Foremost perches on the back of a wagon wheeled to the tree line for the purpose. A select few men closest to him —his thugs—carry lanterns to illuminate him as much as possible. I approach the scene hesitantly, unwilling to be associated with them. Father nods approvingly at my presence and returns his attention to the scene unfolding before him.

People arrive from all directions, trickling out of the streets of Utsanek as if it is a dam on the verge of collapse. My father towers over it all, arms crossed. The tattoos ringing his bicep twitch when they flex. He is not a patient man, but he waits with remarkable calm. As the crowd thickens before him, his men step closer. They form an impassable wall of muscle, holding back a city at its boiling point.

A wiry man with a tunic in tatters approaches the Foremost, a manic expression dancing in his face. "Where is the beast? Let us have it."

"You can't keep it for yourself," another chimes in, joining his comrade. All within earshot shout in agreement. I look at my father. He needs to get this under control quickly.

"Save our children from the kaligorven!" a mother shrieks, a squalling babe wrapped in strips of fabric tight to her chest.

Father nods to his men, and they bellow at the mob to settle down. It only serves to further enrage them. Seizing the moment, the Foremost raises both hands and addresses them, projecting his deep voice above the ruckus.

"I know you are all hungry for retribution for the loved ones you've lost," he begins, the passionate outcries diminishing only slightly. "And I do not blame you. Even my home has not been left untouched by the kaligorven."

I avert my eyes. I don't want to know his thoughts.

"You have every right to demand a part in this Hunt. But it is only one sola. If we all go after it, we do not stand a chance at tracking it down."

At this sensible conclusion, the valefolk begin to calm. Father lowers his hands and hops off the wagon. His men make way as he walks among the people.

"The kaligorven have every right to be angry with us—have we not proven ourselves unfaithful? Keeping light for ourselves, growing to resent our protectors?" A myriad of eyes drops away from him. He continues to pass through the crowd, placing his large palm on a few shoulders as he goes. "They have only repaid us with what we deserved. But they may yet have mercy reserved for us if we do not act rashly."

"What would you have us do?" the wiry man retorts, his fists shaking at his sides. Father faces him.

"Every family who has suffered a loss will choose one representative to join the hunting party. In this way, you will satisfy your need for revenge, and we will make restitution with the Shrouded."

A murmur washes through the valefolk like a wave.

"I will give you time to decide who that will be. Go to your homes and prepare. When you are ready, we will be waiting here. But be warned: we will not wait long."

With that, the rabble disperses. Assuming I have no part in this, I turn and follow the exodus.

My father's stern voice calls to me. "Belwyn."

I halt, letting him catch up. He plants his feet in front of mine and waits for me to look him in the eye. When I do, his expression chills me.

"You are responsible for the reckoning of your brother's life."

I shake my head. Nothing in me wants to go out there, where I will be forced to confront the shadow and the light and everything in between.

Father claps his hands around my arms.

"Think carefully, son. Would you defy me in this? Would you give in to the coward I fear you are?"

My shoulders tense, and I look away. He grabs my chin roughly, forces me to regard him. I am sure his fingertips will leave bruises.

"You're the eldest son of the Foremost. It's time you act like it."

I stare into his eyes, level with mine. They frighten me, both warm and cold. But they are my father's. Whatever pain he has caused me, whatever embarrassment I've bestowed upon him, he is my kin. Maybe if I say 'yes' this time, maybe if I do one more thing for him, those eyes will see me.

My throat squeezes tight, and I nod.

"I will."

Thunder rumbles in the distance. I shiver and slip my arms into the sleeves of my soft leather jacket—a present from my mother for my eighteenth birthday. She spared no expense, choosing the highest grain and having it tailor-made so it fits my shoulders and torso, with the right amount of slack for ease of movement. Comfortable. I prefer it to a cumbersome cloak.

Taking up my bow and quiver, I turn to say goodbye to her, but she stares out the window. She's wrapped her arms around herself, fingers digging into her sides. I decide to leave her be and make my way to the Reckoning Grounds.

It is not a surprise when the wiry man strolls up to the wagon brandishing a rusty spear and dagger. Nine others follow him, including two fierce-looking women. The group isn't as intimidating as my father's lackeys, but I still wouldn't want to mess with them. Grim purpose tends to make a person deadly.

No one shows up to represent the couple who hid the sola bones.

My father nods at each person in turn, assessing the gear they managed to scrounge up. I look down the line doubtfully. Who's to say any of these people know how to hunt? I'm decent with my bow, at least when it comes to stationary targets. Father has always made sure of that. But there are so many other factors to consider. One being that I have never actually shot an arrow outside of Utsanek.

Flanked by Krandel and another man, the Foremost motions for the troop to follow him. He moves off casually into the trees. I'm perplexed. He does not appear like one taking caution. And the three of them carry lanterns.

Our band settles into a rhythm behind them for some time, the thunder booming steadily closer. I bring up the rear, and I'm glad, because every little thing makes me jump. I can't risk shaming my father with a show of cowardice. The man in front of me darts his head from side to side, all the muscles in his back tense. But my father continues before us, steady and unwavering.

I notice a glow ahead that can't be attributed to three little lanterns. We stop. Father calls for the hunters to come near, and we spread out on either side of him. Gasps break the stillness.

A massive pit lies below us, filled with a blinding form that paces the bottom. The other hunters circle around the opening, holding up hands to shield their eyes. Though the light enters my pupils like daggers, I am too awestruck to do anything but stare.

I think it's a stag, or something resembling one, but it's twice the size of any deer I've seen. A swell of delicious warmth exudes from it, creating an updraft that sweeps my hair from my brow. A kingly rack of antlers like a twisted tree spans nearly the entire width of the pit. Confined within the dirt walls, its ribbons of light have the appearance of a roiling sea. I wonder how the creature does not drown in them. Illumination tumbles over itself, teased by the snaking ténesomni grasping at it from above. In the midst of its sleepless intensity, the animal's mournful face inclines to regard us. And looks right at me.

It is the most exquisite thing I have ever seen.

"Here is your sola," says my father, drinking in the astonished faces surrounding him. As the air around us starts to swirl and flashes of light fill the sky, fingers clench tighter around weapons. A greedy glint passes around the circle.

"Take aim."

Some alien force animates my body, makes my feet stumble backward. A wild thumping fills my chest—is it the thunder or something else?—as a burning question possesses my mind.

Will killing the light truly free us from the darkness?

My head shakes, no. No, no, no. It won't, it can't, it won't.

I should do something to stop this. This is wrong.

But I keep stepping back with a reckless desire to get as far away as possible. Yet I am unwilling to turn my back on the scene.

"Ready."

I am going to intervene, if only my legs would obey. I am.

As my father opens his mouth to say 'fire,' a geyser of light shoots upward. Confused, I think it's a bolt of lightning until all the hunters around the pit react, throwing their spears and shooting their weapons blindly. A scream erupts as an arrow flies and embeds itself in a man's shoulder. Lightning strikes nearby, so close I can feel its heat. I blink several times, trying to focus my mind on what is happening. But there is no time to think, because the gigantic sola stag leaps toward me through the gap I left in the circle.

"Kill it, *kill it!*" my father bellows.

A primitive instinct bursts inside me. I see Rhun's white eyes. I feel my father's crushing hand clasped around my jaw. I hear my mother's death wail. My bow is raised, the arrow straight. As I pull the bowstring to my cheek, my arm shakes from the strain. With a scream that tears my throat to shreds, I let the arrow fly.

It finds its mark, disappearing where the creature's gilded neck and chest meet. An impossible shot. The beast continues far enough to collapse at my feet. The moment it hits the ground, all its light escapes from it forever, blasting the bow from my hands and eviscerating every last good thing inside of me.

Lightning flares, nothing more than a flicker in comparison.

I no longer blame Amyrah for being afraid of me.

I am afraid of myself.

14
AMYRAH

STEAM CURLS IN SEDUCTIVE RIBBONS from the tea in my mug. I slide it close to my chin and breathe in the spiced aroma.

"You didn't have to do this, Orlagh. You're so busy."

Her eyes flit to mine between pounding and folding the large lump of dough on the table. Capillary waves spread out across the surface of my tea with each thrust of her flour-coated hands.

"Never too busy for yeh."

A grateful smile spreads across my lips. I know.

The hot liquid flows over my tongue, teasing it with warmth and spice and sweetness. The perfect brew.

"But what about yer father? Why haven't I seen him lately?"

I set down the cup and slip my fingers around its circumference. "He's . . . not well right now."

Orlagh straightens and wipes her hands on her apron. Her expression says she understands. I am relieved I don't need to explain it further, because I wouldn't know what to say.

A dozen rattan bowls congest the table on either side of me. I run a finger across the textured glaze of the mug and watch Orlagh divide the dough into six equal portions. With a deft twist of the hands, she transforms the craggy heaps into smooth mounds and deposits them into the proofing bowls. Flour puffs up and drifts through the air.

The stately wood fire oven, glowing on the other side of the room, stands ready to transform the work of her hands. It provides all the light in the space. But it is still abnormally bright in the warm room, because of me.

My shoulders draw in. "What do you think it means?"

A heavy bowl thumps onto the work surface. Orlagh rests her hands on either side of it and peers at me.

"Child, yeh have to be a bit more specific than that," she says, her breaths escaping in short bursts.

I sigh and stand up, leading her out the door and into the humid night.

"This."

Arms raised at shoulder-height, I rotate slowly. The clawed fingers of the ténesomni grow desperate in their attempt to push through my invisible barrier. My hands stretch out as far as they can go, and still, there is space between where they end and the shadows begin.

Only when the darkness pulls back can you truly see how thick it was.

Chin raised to the sky, I breathe in. "I don't understand how this gift is mine."

I face Orlagh and let my arms fall. She pulls her shawl taut around her shoulders, but no hint of surprise shows in her features. I search them, pleading silently. *Make this make sense.*

Her brows and jaw work for a while, tensing and relaxing as she formulates an answer. "There's a callin' on your soul, Amyrah. It's always been there, since yeh were a wee babe."

A sharp inhale inflates my chest. My pulse picks up pace. *Don't stop.*

"Yer father didn't see it for years, not in the presence of yer sweet ma. How could he? She never let you stray more'n five feet from her reach. But on the rare occasion when she left yeh with me, I saw what he could not. No matter how deep the dark, somethin' always kept it from reaching your heart. It was so small tha' no one woulda ever noticed who wasn't lookin' for it."

My hands move of their own accord to cover the place where I can feel my heart lurching in my chest. "Where did it come from?"

Orlagh shakes her head. "Tha' I can't know for cer'ain. But if I had to guess, I'd say Elyōn put it there himself."

I frown. *The Highest?*

An airy laugh shudders from my lungs. "That's ridiculous. Why would he be concerned with my life? I thought he finished his work a long time ago." A guilty grimace puckers my face. "I have never so much as uttered his name other than in a passing reference."

Her smile is a little sad. "Neither had I, until recen'ly. But I am more and more convinced tha' he's more'n just a story mothers whisper to their bairns as they fall asleep. He's keepin' all things together, an' he's workin' it all according to his purpose."

Something inside me has always drawn my thoughts toward Elyōn, although I hardly know who he is. Even still, everything that is beautiful in this black-stained world, no matter how small, has always screamed his name.

My eyebrows come together. "But that doesn't explain why I am more deserving than everyone else."

If anything, I deserve it less. I know my heart.

"I'm not sure it has much to do with deservin' anythin'. Yer of a different race."

A chill runs down my spine.

Orlagh continues, "I can't say where yer from or what yeh are, except that yeh don't belong in the Vale. That much has always been cer'ain. Somethin' is bent on setting you apart. And I fear for yeh, that the fate of yer mother will find yeh if yeh don't find a way to escape the land of the kaligorven."

I've always felt like I didn't belong in the Vale, but that had nothing to do with me. I thought my father made me that way.

My father.

My stomach twists at the thought of him shut in our musty cottage.

"What can I do for Pada?"

Orlagh steps out of the darkness. I clutch her hand and draw her in so she can use me for support. We walk down the street at her easy pace. "Yeh must be gentle on him. I don't think he knew all Ellehra's closeness did for him, as it did for all who got near enough to feel it. But his entire bein' must have depended on it. And when the bond between them snapped, he lost more than the love of his life."

"That's why the darkness has such a pull on his mind," I say, a crack of thunder accentuating my words. "She became his light."

The old, strong hands squeeze my forearm tight as Orlagh comes to a halt. I turn my head. She lifts a palm to my cheek, and I am comforted by its easy warmth.

"However yeh are tempted, yeh must not become that for him. He needs to find a light of his own."

I look into her misty eyes, wondering, not for the first time, at their depths of wisdom. My chin bobs, and her wrinkled cheeks bunch under her eyes.

Another peal of thunder sounds, closer this time. The wind begins to pick up. Orlagh turns to go back, but one last question keeps me from moving.

"Why do you think my gift has grown like this—now?"

Holding out a hand to me, she gives me a moment to catch up. "Tha's not something I can answer, my dear girl. But I suspect it has somethin' to do with the solas comin' back to the Vale. Don't yeh think?"

I walk in uneasy silence, the ominous weather looming overhead. Each step I take solidifies my conclusion further, like a hammer driving a nail deep, deep into the inner reaches of ancient timber.

Yes, I think they have everything to do with it.

PART TWO

emerge

It has begun:
hope is kindled
within your heart.
Though now all that can be seen
is this veil of shadows,
your soul strains toward the light.
But be on your guard.
The moment you started
this journey upward,
adversity set its eyes on you.
Do not fear.
O, child, do not fear.
You are not alone.

15
MYRZETH

RAIN FALLS IN DROVES FROM THE SKY.

The man moves through the forest, ribbons of ténesomni whooshing out of the way when his feet touch the ground. The darkness parts for him as a sea of grass. He holds out a hand, a smile teasing the corners of his mouth. Raindrops splash against his palm like tears, but the shadows don't dare brush his skin. They gather above it like a submissive black cloud until he releases them, and they absorb back into the gloom.

Journeying alone, he slips between the trees without a living creature noticing his presence. The loose black tunic helps him blend in, even pressed to his flesh as it is by the rain. A well-worn satchel crosses his torso, bulging with a rectangular shape. He pushes it behind him and comes to a stop on the edge of a cliff.

"Praecéro," he commands, and the ténesomni opens. Without the dark mists preventing him, he sees all the way to the valley below. To the city, glowing dimly in the distance. It almost looks welcoming.

For him, it is. He was invited.

If someone in Utsanek had stood in a precise place at that moment and lifted her eyes, she would have been able to see up the strange tunnel in the shadows. She could have spotted the man's solitary outline, perched on the tip of the rock, but she would not have been able to identify the wolfish look in his pale eyes.

He breathes in the scent of pine needles and dirt. A second order, "caelaveth," rolls off his tongue, and the gap in the ténesomni disappears.

The smile doesn't merely play with his lips—it possesses them. White teeth glint against skin. Thin lines stretch around his mouth to his sharp jaw. Loose, white-blond hair frames his pale face.

"It's good to be home."

16

WEHNA

COLD SWEAT AND RAIN trickle down my scalp as I try to find the next caeruméni meeting. Before my father left, he had made me repeat the directions over and over again. His patience and the calm pressure of his palm on my cheek had given me the confidence I lacked.

Now that I need to recall the directions perfectly, and I am all that Arvo has left, doubt's grasping fingertips sneak in and steal what I thought I knew.

I need to be strong.

With a slow inhale, I press on, but I'm lost after several turns. I raise the lantern, spinning in a slow circle as I try to get my bearings. The buildings all look the same—or at least, similarly dilapidated. They tower around me like old trees, wrapped in peeling panels. Terraces reach out, branching toward each other. Lines draped with forgotten laundry lace them together, creating a dripping canopy overhead. Unlike the real thing, this forest is deafeningly silent. It presses uncomfortably on my eardrums, and my pulse fights back with a frantic pressure of its own.

I strain to see something beyond this gallery of decay and the streaks of rain, but there is only the spreading cloak of night heaping in on itself.

For a moment, the plumes of black part. In the span of a heartbeat, I catch a glimpse upward, as if I am looking through a tunnel that comes out at the knees of the mountains.

And feel as though death holds me in its sights.

My limbs go numb, my legs shake beneath me. An attack of nausea distorts my vision. I fight it all as long as I can, but I am weak, so weak. I crumple under the force of the ténesomni.

"Elyōn, help," I gasp, my forehead scraping on the wet gravel.

I can't do this on my own.

Something heavy and warm rests on my shoulder. A hand. My body quakes, but the hand stays firm and secure. It is real. It exists. My mind latches on to it long enough for my fears to stop whispering their lies in my ear.

"Wehna?"

I raise my head a fraction. Warm light spills out of a doorway in front of me.

"What are yeh doing out here, poor child?"

When I don't answer, my rescuer comes down to my level with no small amount of difficulty.

My hands find the ground, and I manage to push myself up.

I need to be strong.

"Is this where we are meeting tonight?" I pant, brushing the wet dirt from my palms.

A wizened face comes into view and nods reassuringly. Silvery hair frames it. I cast around in my memory for a name. She recently joined my parents' meetings, after the Kuvror Erovantus. She has kindness in her eyes. The smell of bread wafts out the open door. I sigh. "Orlagh."

The old woman nods and slips her arm underneath mine. I don't allow her to help me up, however, but find new strength to be the one to offer her support.

She leads me out of the streets and into the most marvelous light. I pinch my eyes closed and feel the invisible cords that constricted my chest snap. I can breathe again. Touching a hand to my forehead, I wheeze out a breathy laugh.

Murmurs of welcome ripple around the room. I open my eyes and glance around. A dozen concerned faces encircle me bearing the expression of friends.

Orlagh directs me to an empty cushion, right in front of a truly gargantuan oven. I sink into the softness. The luxurious heat dries my rain-soaked garments within moments. Someone hands me a basket filled with golden biscuits studded with little gems of dried fruit. I listen to the hum of polite conversation around me and sink my teeth into the buttery baking. My shoulders relax.

After a few minutes the conversation ceases, and I find myself at the center of attention again. A man I recognize as an acquaintance of my father's perches on the edge of a chair. Bryn, with his ebony hair and deep-set eyes overshadowed by a furrowed brow.

"Wehna, what happened to your parents?"

My breaths quicken, and I set the unfinished biscuit down in my lap. I close my eyes and exhale slowly.

I need to be strong.

17

TÉRON

H ER HAND SPREADS WARMTH TO MINE. I pull her along through the trees, our footsteps silent in the springy moss.

Where are we going? she asks between sprinklings of breathless laughter.

You will see. My eyes fix on the glow in the distance. We are almost there.

Like birds, we flit between trunks and over bushes. The miles race past, sped along by the curious melody trickling past my beloved's lips. The song falters, then stops. I peer back to see if she is alright, but her face turns down, and silvery blond hair floats in the breeze to obscure it. She holds up the skirt of her goldenrod dress in the other hand, uncovering bare feet that move cautiously through the bracken.

The air grows warmer and brighter as we go, calling us in. But the closer we get, the colder her flesh feels.

Almost there, I promise, urging her to keep up. Doubt pinches my brow when I feel her struggle, but I keep my grip tight. I won't let her fingers slip.

The forest thins. We break into open air and a shimmering cloud. I cannot keep my face from beaming when we stop. But her hand stiffens. When the wind shifts her waves of reflective hair, I can see her face. Colorless.

What is this? she asks, her voice flat. A chill passes from her body into mine. Icy accusations pierce me from pale eyes.

I want to smooth her fears away. I reach to touch her cheek but find my fingers wrapped tightly around a dagger. My knuckles shine white, and though I try, they will not let go.

Something about the light demands my focus. An inexplicable desire fills me. *Is* me.

We must take it. We must take all of it, I say in a voice not my own. I should look away, but the dancing flames are bewitching. *It is the only way.*

When I advance toward the inferno, my shoulder snaps back. Ellehra will not move. Her grip is iron, her feet planted in the earth like pillars of granite. I plead with her. I try to pull her toward it, but her porcelain face moves slowly from side to side. Tears gather in her eyes.

Would you really ask this of me?

Of her? I do not understand.

Why do you let her hold you back, Téron? asks a derisive voice. A man wrapped in strips of dark cloth appears at my side. He is barely there, shifting in and out of reality like a yawning chasm. His strange garb tangles around him, mingling with the darkness. *She doesn't understand what's at stake. But you do. Don't you?*

My chin bobs. *Yes.*

Then do what she cannot.

Ellehra's hand slips from mine. Her lips part, but I cannot let her speak, cannot let her change my mind. Lunging away from her, I dive into the heart of the brilliance and strike with all the force I possess.

A cry rends the air. I wheel around. The dagger, no longer in my hand, protrudes from her chest. The light which I sought to extinguish pours from her heart like water. She sinks to her knees, but when I try to catch her, a muscular arm holds me back.

The ghost-man, who mirrors so closely Ellehra's features, sputters in wicked laughter as he keeps me from my love. Excruciating spasms shudder down my core with each cachinnation.

You deceived me, I exhale, my sole reason for living escaping with the sound.

His laughter multiplies. I shake in his unyielding arms. An eerie wail rips me apart, but the incandescent flow gags me. It pierces my flesh, blinds my eyes, and forces itself down my throat until my lungs burn.

I jolt awake, gasping. The air in the cottage does not satisfy me; it has become putrid, stale. I press an arm across my forehead and squeeze my eyes shut. My head pounds against the weight. I drag in a breath, but it is like I am sucking through a mouth stuffed with cotton. Tears dampen the hair at my temples and sweat soaks through my garments.

It was a dream. It was a dream. But the tremors continue.

Swinging my legs over the edge of the bed, I stifle a groan. My eyes are open, but I cannot see. I cower in the dark, my pulse surging in my ears. Fingers dig into my kneecaps, and I struggle to make myself believe I am awake. That I exist.

Where is Amyrah?

I stagger across the room. The hearth is cold, and the bolétis must have faded out days ago.

The emptiness of this place circles me like the specter's laughter in the dream. I can still feel its poison pulsing through my veins. A sound somewhere between a yelp and a roar escapes from deep within. I grip my head with fierce pressure and hurtle into the pouring rain.

The streets of Utsanek are drenched and deserted. I should have stayed home.

Hurrying through the abandoned market square, I pause in front of the towering fanum. The sharp steps are laden with baskets of goods of every kind, now soggy. It is rare for the valefolk to show this much devotion to the kaligorven. I resist the urge to spit, but with difficulty.

When I reach the northern boundary of the city and stumble into the center of yet another Reckoning Ceremony, my fears are confirmed.

My stomach churns. Entering the crowd, searching the faces, I hope I won't find Amyrah's among them. Kuvror Erovantus is not something she needs to see.

I press on until I am able to hear what is going on at the far end of the clearing, though it is difficult over the pouring rain. Many scowls and rude gestures launch my way. Probably because I have not bathed in a fortnight.

The Foremost presides over the ceremony, like always, his deep voice penetrating through the deluge. But I do not pay attention to his words. They are meaningless. My eyes fix, instead, to the colossal urn raised on strong poles over the bonfire.

Luminosity exudes from it, the downpour having no effect on the blood's endless combustion. Tears crowd my vision, but I do not know if it is because of the pain in my eyes or the pain in my heart. I blink, and I no longer see an earthen vessel. It is the lion-sola, noble in death. It is the stoic wren that found my daughter. It is the brilliance in my terrible dream. It is the mortal wounds in my wife.

Knees weak, I buckle forward and grab on to whatever I can to keep me from falling. Strong hands shove me off, and I sway as I struggle to stay upright.

Shaking away the vision, I focus instead on those closest to the blaze. They are not the regular band of hunters, but people. Ordinary people with hurt and vengeance written all over their faces. A tall young man with dark hair looks especially afflicted. He shifts his weight from heel to heel and clenches his fists at his sides. His face communicates more than anger; it screams self-loathing.

A feeling I understand.

The urn cracks open with a deafening snap, unleashing the deluge of the sola's lifeblood over the fire. Like every Kuvror Erovantus I have seen, the blood reacts to the ignati with an eruption of heat and light. The spectators around me cower, but I am too numb to respond.

Stillness falls. Even the storm abates somewhat. Not a soul stirs or whispers or sighs. Thousands upon thousands of people fill this clearing, and no one speaks. What are they waiting—or hoping—for?

When an unnatural wind assails the ceremonial grounds, I have my answer. Rain flies horizontally, soaking every inch of me. At the moment my courage begins to fail, everything calms. Even the rain ceases. I wipe my face and strain my eyes in the darkness, alarmed by how thick it has become. I can feel it shifting over my skin.

There are shapes in the shadows, somehow still visible in the lack of light. Several hideous forms emerge from the trees, of varied statures and shapes, but all dreadful. I dare not stare at them for long. The kaligorven advance on the gathering, and a hushed murmur infects the people. They shrink back together, carrying me with them. But no one flees.

A voice, like stone on stone, like the rumblings of the foundation of the earth, emanates from the ténesomni. I shudder.

Your offering pleases . . . The light is yours to take.

Relief exudes from the valefolk—exhales, and even quiet laughter. But they are quickly silenced.

Your faith still lacks. Our patience wears thin. When we return . . . proof of your devotion will be required.

A pall descends, dragging the hope down with it. But the mutterings of confusion and frustration become lost in the uproar of the Shrouded's retreat.

They are gone.

"Might I make a suggestion?"

The Reckoning Grounds have transformed into a frothing sea of terrified valefolk, but a silky voice slices through the hysterics. My shoulders tense as a fog of memory settles over my reason. The valefolk packed around me, the ténesomni, the kaligorven—all are beyond my notice. I latch on to that voice, feeling as though I will suffocate without proof of its owner's existence. I do not remember moving, but now only a single row of heads stands between myself and the blackened chasm that was once a roaring fire.

A lithe form appears from between the trees, and my bones turn to liquid. Sheets of darkness swirl away with each tread of the man's leather-shod feet. I blink, fighting to keep myself in the present. It is both like and unlike what I have seen occur around my daughter. The shadows part for him as they do for her, but they do not reach in as if they would devour his soul. The hair on the back of my neck stands on end.

"And who are you?" Dravek grabs a lantern from one of his men, shoving him to the side. The Foremost wears a sleeveless tunic and trousers, dispensing with the traditional robes of Kuvror Erovantus. The lantern's glow barely reaches the ink that rings his bulging bicep. He waits for the stranger to approach.

I strain to make out his face, though I do not really need to see it. I can recall it perfectly from my nightmare.

"Don't you remember me?" The man saunters to the edge of the stone pit. His sharp features twist into a mischievous grin. "After all, I am one of your own."

Ice-eyes lock on mine.

"Myrzeth," I say under my breath and immediately feel sick. My brother-in-law's name is a poisonous fume. I want him to be the first to look away, but his eyes steal the warmth of my blood. I cannot hold his gaze.

When Dravek does not respond, Myrzeth laughs in a disarming manner and paces along the edge of the pit. The last time I saw him, he hissed his lies about the solas into my listening ear. Even though the years have broadened his shoulders and lined his face, he has retained all his good looks. All his charm.

"When last I saw this place," he says, "you were in a bit of a bind with the Shrouded."

Dravek's mouth spreads to a thin line, but he remains still.

Myrzeth scans the dark Reckoning Grounds. I glance around and find every face possessed with a desperate expression. The way fingers coil around pointless lanterns and arms hold loved ones close betrays their fear.

"I hoped you would have moved on in my absence," —he clicks his tongue and shakes his head— "but it appears you haven't."

"What do you know about us, about the kaligorven?" The Foremost's hackles raise. He draws himself up taller, but the edge he had is gone. "You have yet to give us your name."

"My apologies," Myrzeth says with mock sincerity. "I thought you might still know me, although I must say I am not surprised you don't. It *has* been thirteen years." He makes a slight bow. "My name is Myrzeth. I was barely a man when I made my escape from the Vale, on the heels of my late sister."

Bitterness fills my mouth.

"While I've been gone, I've learned much about the ténesomni you fear." He holds out a hand, and the darkness dances across his fingertips —little tongues of black flame. When he faces his palms to each other, the shadows collect between them, a pulsating, black orb.

Ever the showman.

Dravek is unmoved. His eyes remain fixed on the ghost-man, following his deft movements with scrutiny. "And what made you return?"

The specter tilts his head, and his hair flops across his forehead. "The darkness called to me."

"Is that so?" Dravek sneers. His men chuckle. "Well, since you seem so much more knowledgeable than this entire city, then, please." He motions at Myrzeth with mock invitation. "What is your suggestion?"

With a flick of the wrists, Myrzeth releases the ball of darkness back into the night.

"Simply this: you need to rethink the way you approach the kaligorven."

Something resembling a growl rumbles from Dravek's throat, his levity gone. "We have done everything they have asked us to do."

Myrzeth draws his brows down and gives Dravek a quizzical look. "Have you really? Well. Pardon my interference." He shrugs and adjusts the strap of his satchel.

I look at Dravek and note, with twisted pleasure, his placid exterior has cracked. Even in the weak light, I can see the color rising in his cheeks. If anyone else provoked the Foremost in this manner, I would counsel them to stop. But it is Myrzeth. He deserves what he gets.

To my disappointment, the leader of the Vale reins in his temper. His lower jaw works as he gestures, almost imperceptibly, for my brother-in-law to continue.

Smirking, Myrzeth paces. "You've complied, yes, and that is where your allegiance has ended. But what about on a deeper level? What about your lives, the way you pattern your days? Does your behavior communicate your devotion to the Shrouded?"

"That's never been our agreement. All they require is the blood of a sola, if and when one comes into the Vale. That's it." Many throaty sounds of agreement affirm his words.

"If that were the case, I don't think I would have found Utsanek shivering in the dark, would I?" Myrzeth stops and faces the crowd, arms crossed.

His likeness to Ellehra is so strong, I can barely stand to look at him. Except this man wears his fine features like a trophy, whereas they adorned my wife like a crown. The similarities were less obvious when he was last here. With twelve years between them, Ellehra's elegance and maturity set her apart. But time and absence have lessened those distinctions in my memory. My heart throbs in a way it hasn't in a long, long time.

"But we've left them offerings at the fanum," someone calls from the crowd.

"How noble of you," he says, his raised eyebrows mocking her.

"What would you suggest?" Dravek shifts on his feet, growing impatient.

"It's simple, really. You must prove there is nothing standing between you and your worship of them. Search out those who would defy them by honoring other deities. Eradicate the ones who challenge their ténesomni. Make hunting the solas your priority. They are out there and more cunning than you realize."

"You would call that 'simple'?" The Foremost laughs mirthlessly and shakes his head. "What you're speaking of would be difficult with ten people, let alone ten thousand. And how do you suggest we 'worship' them? With incantations and rituals we must come up with on a whim?"

Dravek and his men laugh.

"What makes you think that will be acceptable to them?"

Myrzeth swings his satchel forward and unearths a tattered book from within. "Oh, I don't think there will be any 'guesswork' about it."

The volume falls open in his hands. A sinister presence seems to emanate from its pages.

"If you recall, when my sister spoke out against the kaligorven and managed to convince a few idiots to abandon the Hunt, my voice was one of reason. I warned of the consequences, but none would listen. And when her actions led to her inevitable demise, it no longer seemed prudent to waste my efforts where they would not be appreciated."

The valefolk are spellbound by his smooth words, but I am in turmoil, threatening to burst.

Dravek's silence is an invitation for Myrzeth to continue.

"Since my departure, I have made the kaligorven my study. I have wandered far and learned much about these ancient beings. To you, it may seem like they have always been here. But their arrival in the Vale is relatively recent."

"If what you say is true, maybe we should consider freeing ourselves from their dominion."

For once, I agree with the Foremost.

A shadow passes over Myrzeth's face. For a moment, his eyes gleam unnaturally. "That would be a . . . mistake." His fingers tighten around the tome, crinkling its pages. "You have not been outside of the Vale. I have. And I can assure you, there is no safer place to be. We are far better off being under their protection instead of objects of their wrath. Have you not experienced it yourselves?"

The valefolk's sorrow fills the pause like a stagnant pool.

Myrzeth's voice softens. He sounds almost compassionate. "If you do what I say, I can guarantee you more light and peace than you have ever known."

Whispers hiss through the people. He is making far too much sense.

I cannot stand to listen to it any longer.

"Myrzeth, you are nothing but a traitor to our people." I shove into the open space. My limbs shudder, my heart pounds wildly. "You abandoned the Vale—and your own family—at our moment of greatest darkness. You have conveniently avoided the thirteen blackest years any of us can remember. And you dare to step in and claim to be the salvation we have been searching for all this time?" My voice is strangled, belonging to someone else. To a madman.

"Hello, Téron." My brother-in-law regards me sadly, stoking my internal fire. "I see these years have not been kind to you."

I will not be baited. I turn to Dravek. "You cannot be considering listening to this fool. What can he know about our lives that we ourselves do not understand?"

The Foremost crosses his arms. His eyes pass from me to Myrzeth, and back again. His voice drops in warning. "Téron, stand down."

"Do not be a fool, Dravek."

"I said, stand down."

Several vice-like hands latch themselves to my arms. I struggle to pull away, but I have expended all my strength. I slump forward.

Dravek faces Myrzeth, his brow set. "Teach us the way."

"No," I wheeze.

A triumphant expression spreads across Myrzeth's pallid face. He closes the book and stares me down.

"You can start by taking care of him."

Fingers dig into my muscles with crushing force. I should be fighting. I should be repelling Myrzeth's cunning wickedness with all of my being.

But as I am hauled away, all I can think is, *Ellehra, I'm sorry.*

18
BELWYN

WHEN THE STRANGER stepped into the clearing, I took the chance to slip out of the Reckoning Grounds unnoticed. Besides, even if he could offer some hope of appeasing the kaligorven, nothing he could say would help me.

"Where have you been?"

My mother's quavering tone falls heavy on my chest when I enter the house. Her solitary form still lurks at the window, though it is well into the night. I struggle to breathe and clumsily place the lantern on its pedestal. The hearth is empty of flame, yet the room teems with something beyond shadows. Mother's shoulders angle forward, the weight of her anxieties chipping away at her strength.

Has she been standing there the whole time? It's been a lifetime since I was home.

"The Hunt, Mother, remember? I was at the Hunt. And the ceremony." My voice isn't quite right. Too high, the words clipped short. I wipe my palms on the front of my trousers, trying to hide how they shake.

"Oh," comes her muffled reply.

There isn't much more to say.

Desperate for something to do, I crouch in front of the hearth and start to build a fire, even though it's late, and the light will be wasted. I need the heat to thaw my chilled heart.

"Did you see them? The boys?"

I close my eyes to quell the guilt that stirs at any mention of my brothers. *Why is it up to me to watch them, to keep them safe? If Mother knew what I've done . . .* My stomach tightens painfully. They all deserve so much more than me.

"Mhm," I grunt, forcing myself to ignore the regret as I flake the magnesium with a knife. When I strike it again, a spark jumps into the kindling and catches. A small blaze blooms, returning a hint of warmth to my fingers. "They'll follow Father home," I say through clenched teeth.

Mother shifts at the mention of him. From behind, she resembles a child. Her hair falls in tangled clumps down her back. Once described as slender and attractive, her figure now appears angular and wan. I've been trying, but no amount of temptation can encourage her to eat. It doesn't help that the rest of us are barely skilled enough to conjure anything more than meat seared over a fire.

She's wasting away before my eyes, and it's my fault.

Whatever presence inhabits this space swarms into a fury, an audible buzzing in my ears. The flint and steel fall from my hands. I can't stay here, where unspoken words, failed intentions, and fateful decisions pummel me like hornets.

My feet deliver me out of Utsanek, this time, to the south. I don't care where I go, as long as it's as far from the forest as I can get.

I walk through several acres of farmland, my lantern hanging limp at my side. The ténesomni is less oppressive than it has been in weeks, but its presence within me has grown.

My feet kick through newly tilled earth. Black and barren, its bitter scent infuses the air. For some reason, plants do not thrive within the city limits or under the covering of the trees—unless the sola brossa shed their light upon them. Since the supply of bones has been dwindling for a dozen years, all the open land on the south side of the city has been designated for produce, where the open sky causes the plants to grow.

Shame fills me when I register that this plot of soil has already been sown. The time of sowing, Tiosh, is quickly coming to its end. When the diminutive plants decide to poke their heads through the decay, Father will declare it to be Zomré—the season of life. Usually my favorite of the six seasons. But I cannot possibly delight in the prospect of new growth on the day I took a sola's life.

Before long, I emerge onto the shores of the formidable loch that pins our city to the roots of the mountains. The cool air blowing off the black waters condenses on my face. I listen for a while to the waves assailing the stony beach. They grab at the land relentlessly, always threatening to gain purchase.

For a moment, I envision myself plunging into the opaque waters, leaving all this behind me. What lies beyond our borders where valefolk are forbidden to tread? Maybe there is a place out there where darkness can't reach.

But Loch Skythe is tempestuous at the best of times. And as my father is so faithful to point out, I'm a coward.

Despondent, I trudge along the shoreline until the beach area transforms into sharp juts of rock spiraling to the obsidian sky. I can go no further.

Pain shoots through my left temple and radiates around the back of my skull. I squeeze my eyes shut, but there is no relief.

This place is all I will ever know, just as the disappointing son of a cruel man is all I'll ever be.

I cower under the crushing weight of this thought until all the warmth vacates my hands. My head feels like it will burst with the pressure. The damp air in my face, the jagged stones under my feet, and the lifeless black encircling me all conspire to steal my identity. The lantern sputters out.

When it is too much, when I am more stone than flesh, a beautiful sound rises up over the clamor of the waves.

Curiosity replacing the malaise, I clamber over boulders and squeeze through narrow gaps. The music grows louder as I approach. *Singing.* Sharp rocks bite into my shins, but I hardly feel the pain in my haste to discover who belongs to that voice.

I see *her*, Amyrah Cantar, nestled into a cleft in the cliffside, cantering a melody I've never heard. She faces away from me, preoccupied with a task I can't see. Waves of honey-brown hair act as her cloak. I watch her in stupid silence, awed by the foreign sensation of serenity her presence has the power to kindle within me.

The odds of running into someone, especially *her*, in the middle of the night are too providential to ignore. Even so, that isn't the most remarkable thing about this scene. It's the fact that I can see it at all.

Light surrounds her—no, that's not right. It's more like she is at the heart of a strange absence of darkness. I frown, looking around her secret dell again to be sure. No, there is no other light source in the vicinity. Odd.

I approach from behind, careful not to make a sound. It's not that I wish to sneak up on her, but that what she's doing seems too sacred to disturb. Her movements are fluid as she lays something delicately against a flat stone. Flowers and leafy ferns, woven together into a beautiful mosaic. She scoops up a handful of pink blooms and tucks them, one at a time, in between the verdant foliage. Ignoring the anomaly surrounding her, I creep forward until I can see over her shoulder.

Ellehra Cantar, beloved wife and mother.

A headstone.

My foot dislodges a rock, and her gentle song, full of hope and sorrow, cuts off mid refrain. She spins around, her eyes magnified in her fair features.

"What are you doing here?" she says, fingers tightening around the bouquet of wild blossoms. Their heady perfume permeates the air. Her shoulders draw in, and I can almost feel the vibrations of her heart's elevated beat. Like a cornered rabbit, her eyes dart for her path of escape.

I hold up my hands to show I mean no threat. But from the way she shrinks back and her brows lower, I know I have made a mistake.

Unwilling to let her slip away from me a third time, I cast around for something to say. But what do I have to talk about, other than dead Light Creatures and the thing that draws me to her, the thing she tries to hide? My mouth gapes. I hate the witless fool I've been reduced to.

She moves as if to leave, and I repeat her question back at her. "What are *you* doing here?"

She stills and angles her head to the side, taking me in. I feel conscious of my mud-caked boots, my disheveled hair. And the guilt boiling inside me that I'm certain is plastered all over my face.

My heart flutters when her cool eyes meet mine. But there is no judgment in them. Her expression eases. She lifts a hand to tuck her long hair behind an ear. "It's late," she says, as if I am a child pleading with her to tell me another story before bed.

That, I realize, is exactly what I am. A child in desperate need of someone to help me forget the terrors of the night.

My reply is nothing more than silence and a cautious step closer. She bites her lip but shifts aside so I can see what she is working on.

"I come here sometimes when I need clarity." She kneels to rest the flowers reverently at the foot of the grave. "And to honor the memory of my mother."

A fresh sadness, this time not selfish in nature, pulses through me. I crouch inside her circle of light and trace my fingers across the letters, smooth and ornate. They were cut by a hand skilled with a chisel, but the marks have faded, aged by wind and weather. It has been here a while.

"Why is her grave so far from the boneyard?" I ask, although this talk of graves makes me feel like an awl is working its way through my chest.

Amyrah pinches her lips together for a while before responding. "After the Shr—" She catches herself, swallowing the word before it can escape. "After *they* took her life, my father wanted nothing to do with the forest. He needed some way to grieve, so he hid her memory as far from prying eyes as possible."

I shift uncomfortably. It is a valefolk custom that those who have provoked the kaligorven into killing do not deserve a proper burial. My brother's passing warranted nothing more than a leaf-strewn mound at the edge of Utsanek. I'm certain a headstone has already been ordered, but there won't be any other ceremony by which to remember him. That is, perhaps, one reason my mother stands at the window for days on end, growing thin. Why I feel a chaotic presence ripping at my insides whenever Rhun's name flickers across my thoughts.

But this moment isn't about me. I can't let what happened—what I've done—bleed into every single part of my life. My nostrils flare, and my chest heaves as I will myself to lock it all away.

When I turn back to Amyrah, she studies my face. Her brilliant necklace glints sharply in the soft light surrounding her.

"You need to grieve them," she says.

My mouth gapes. How does she do it? Move past all my pretense, unearth the parts of me I hate most?

"What?" My voice is small and terse. Who is she talking about, beyond Rhun? She can't know of the sola I mangled—can she?

Amyrah persists. "You need to grieve your brother and every person they have taken from us."

I sigh and disguise my relief by dragging a hand across my face, leaving it pressed against my eyes. She doesn't know the monster I am. Not yet.

"What for? It can't bring them back." It can't erase what I've done.

Air rushes into my lungs when warm fingers wrap around my wrist, gently pulling it down. She doesn't let go when it's at my side but slides her palm down until her fingers slip between mine. I hope she can't feel me shiver. She tugs on my arm until I look her in the eyes. Nothing suggestive, nothing desperate dwells in their steady gaze. Only a quiet confidence, an understanding beyond words.

"Of course, it won't do anything like that. But it can begin the healing process if you let it."

"I—" *Why does she have to be holding my hand?* I can't keep it from shaking. "I don't know how to do that."

Her fingers release mine, and I breathe again, though the absence of her touch makes me feel the cold even more. She picks up the bouquet and plucks the flowers off their stems. One by one, she sets them into the fragrant tapestry woven around her mother's name.

"You start by remembering them. All they were to you, the things they made you feel and think."

A rueful laugh shakes from my clenched jaw. "My brother was a nuisance. I hated always taking the fall for him when he wouldn't accept responsibility for his actions."

Amyrah's mouth tips in a small smile, but she doesn't look at me. "So, you loved him." She pushes in the final blossom and rests back on her heels to admire her handiwork.

I close my eyes and exhale slowly. "Yeah. Yeah, I did." Releasing those words makes my chest burn, like a thick casing has been torn off somewhere inside me.

"And if you could, you'd take the fall for him again."

The tears come, hot and acidic. "In a heartbeat."

It is silent for a while, save for my strangled sobs, until the rustling of shoes scraping stone compels me to open my eyes. Amyrah no longer faces the carved rock but settles down beside me with her knees pulled up to her chest, the shining necklace concealed as it presses to her heart. I rotate on the balls of my feet and allow myself to fall against the unforgiving granite, resting my head on the stone and staring at the sable sky. "What do I do now?"

"You let go. Let go of all the anger. Of all you think you were owed. Of all you owed him."

I shake my head, the pain shooting through my temple again. She has no idea of the debt I've incurred. "That's not so easy."

"Isn't it?" She rests her chin on her knees and stares at me, maddeningly placid.

My fingernails creep into the flesh of my palms, but as I look at her and see the midnight dew beading on her halo of lazy curls and thick lashes, they relax.

Amyrah sighs. "No, I suppose it isn't. But whether you face it or not, his part in this story is over. Except for how you choose to let him exist in your memories."

I mull on that for a beat, surprised when my brother's name passes through my mind without nausea overwhelming me. I never considered how my memory of him has been tainted by all the guilt and hatred I've been harboring.

Amyrah is right. Whatever my part is in this, I need to let him rest.

I shake my head, awestruck. A few simple words from a practical stranger, and it's like a great stopper has been dislodged in my heart. The grief has been allowed to flow at last. I lift my arm to wipe my face on my sleeve. Rhun is gone, yes, but it no longer makes me feel like I will drown. Some of the blame will always fall at my feet for his death—that knowledge has already changed me, and I can't pretend otherwise. But it can't become me.

A heavy sigh squeezes from my chest, and it echoes in the waves that crash against the rocky shore.

"How do you know so much about grief?" I ask, wincing as soon as the words leave my mouth. I'm leaning against her mother's gravestone. "I mean, you're not old enough to . . ." Everything I say sounds stupid and insensitive.

She doesn't appear to be offended but turns her face to peer between a crevice where two boulders meet. I can imagine, at a time when the ténesomni isn't so thick, one could see out across the loch from that viewpoint. She runs her hands down her shins, letting them rest around her bare ankles.

"Maybe it's because I've spent my whole life watching what the lack of it has done to my father. He would rarely even mention my mother's name, let alone share any of his memories of her. He kept it all to himself, but there were also moments when it would not be contained."

She stops, and I feel oddly eased by the sound of her sucking in a shaky breath. Her weakness makes me feel less alone.

"And now that this . . . this fantasy he contrived around her has been torn to pieces, it's like he is lost." The heels of her shoes scrape stone as her legs slide down. She crosses them and rests her hands in their crater. "I think he can't come to terms with how pointless her death was. He needed to blame someone, or something, for it. And he spent all that time hating the wrong thing."

It's Amyrah's turn to cry. I want to catch each drop as it falls, but I resist.

"He won't forgive himself for demonizing the one thing that mattered most to my mother."

A weight drops into the pit of my stomach. I clear my throat, almost afraid to ask. "What was that?"

She sniffs, tugs her sleeves so they cover her balled fists, then uses them to soak up her tears. "The solas."

Unable to keep still, my feet find their way under my shaky legs. I don't want to hear about the Light Creatures anymore I never want to hear about them again.

Amyrah continues quietly, "He blamed them for her death, you know." A little huff of disbelief emerges as she shakes her head. "Can you believe that?"

My palms start to sweat. I stuff them into the pockets of my trousers. "They can be pretty dangerous," I say, like an insufferable know-it-all.

She laughs as if I have told a joke. A soft, light-drenched sound that fills me with shame. She cocks an eyebrow. "Have you ever seen one— alive, I mean?"

That stills my steps. This is the moment when I get to decide who I'm going to be with her, this strange young woman who makes me feel like I've never truly seen the world before. As my eyes take her in, the glare from her necklace seems to me like a puncture in her flesh, spilling incandescence and growing brighter by the second. For a moment, I don't see a person sitting before me, but a shadowy form lying at my feet with my arrow lodged in its still heart. My throat is rough as the lie croaks out. "No."

Her eyes find mine, searching my face until perspiration gathers along my hairline. She senses my confliction, I'm certain. But her watery gaze is gentle. "I have. And she was the most resplendent, yet humble being I've ever seen."

I gulp, a fresh surge of guilt filling me. Here I am, standing before someone who makes me crave light like I never have before, and all I can think of is darkness.

Amyrah Cantar may have been able to help me begin to deal with my grief for my brother, but she has no idea how her earnest delight in the solas has stricken me.

That is something I never want her to find out.

19

AMYRAH

MY BROWS PINCH TOGETHER as I watch Belwyn shrink back. His broad shoulders draw up, and a sheen of sweat dampens the waves of hair at his scalp. The muscles of his jaw tense. He acts as if he is trapped, called out. Discovered.

I wish I knew what to make of him.

When I met him in the market, I assumed him to be the type of person I've actively avoided all my life. The kind that haunts the heart of every social event, surrounded by friends. The guy every girl wants to get close to, who has no idea how hard it is for most people to feel accepted, wanted. Loved.

He would never notice someone like me.

We keep being thrown together, and I can't understand why. Each time, he has surprised me with genuine concern for my welfare. And each time, I have been made keenly aware of my prejudice.

The ghost of his skin lingers on my fingertips.

I swallow down an odd shiver.

Although I hardly know him, he has changed. It isn't surprising. The kaligorven have put the Vale through countless atrocities these last three weeks. Still, the confident young man who helped me—twice—and took care of his inebriated cohort has changed, become someone different and broken. It breaks my heart.

I came to my mother's grave to search for a measure of understanding, but Belwyn's presence rattles me. The look in his eyes when he saw how the ténesomni can't touch me . . .

He is dangerous, my head warns. *You know who his father is.*

But my heart disagrees. Something is different about the way he sees me, something that makes it hard for me to stand. He may share his father's stature and some of his features, but he has a purity about him that all Dravek's cruelty has not yet managed to break.

"What are you afraid of?" It's supposed to be a simple question, but it issues out of my mouth like the steam of water hitting hot coals.

His head snaps to face me. A shadow gropes along his jaw, one wayward strand of ténesomni strong enough to push into my territory of light. I stand, and the darkness releases him.

"It's not all black and white, Amyrah," he says, oblivious to the way the murk hungers after him. His dark eyes plead with me to understand. "I can't embrace the light like you do."

I don't know why hearing this from his mouth makes me so sad. "Why not?"

Backing away, he shakes his head in the stillness. The distance pushes between us like a physical presence.

"I just can't."

He turns and steps away. The night welcomes him into its unfeeling arms.

In that moment, when the ténesomni swirls back around him and he seems so resigned to its existence, I know what my purpose should be. It's as clear as the argentilum pendant shining at my breast.

I don't know how, but I'm going to expose the darkness.

The next day, I awaken as soon as the birds begin to sing and hurry down the trail to Utsanek. The morning bell tolls as I step into the city. All thoughts of Belwyn have been chased from my mind by the unease that plucks at the strands of my thoughts.

What has happened to my father?

When I dragged myself home last night, I was too preoccupied and exhausted to notice anything. Upon awakening this morning to a cold, empty cottage, worry doused last night's burning revelations.

Disquiet coils around my chest, but Utsanek breathes easier. Something must have happened to appease the darkness—but what? I shake off the frustration of not knowing and climb onto a wobbly landing in the city's oldest district. My knuckles rap on Orlagh's front door.

After a lengthy wait, it cracks open. Her face appears through the gap. I wait for her to invite me in, but she doesn't. Fear taints her eyes as they strain to see around me.

"Have you seen my Pada?"

The old woman pulls back slightly. "No, child, I'm afraid I haven't."

I swallow the urge to cry, rubbing my fingers over my mouth as I take a deep breath. When my eyes wander past her, she inches the door in so it is barely open. The subtle motion inflicts a sting of rejection. She's never denied me entry before.

There will be a good reason, I tell myself, but I'm sure something must be wrong. Her house is quiet and dark. The oven must not be lit—something that only occurs when she's ill. My brows descend. "Are you feeling alright?"

She tries to diffuse my concern with a breathy laugh. "Of course, I am. Why would yeh ask such a thing?" Knobby hands tug the shawl closer around her shoulders.

Her evasive behavior elicits an exasperated sigh from me, and a dull ache grips my forehead. "Can I at least come in for a bit? I could use a place to think."

She shakes her head. "I'm sorry, dear, but I can't righ' now. It wouldn't be safe for yeh jus' yet."

My palm flattens against the door as she goes to shut it. I flex my fingers so my nails claw the rough wood.

"What aren't you telling me?" I am unable to withhold a note of desperation from my voice.

Orlagh's brows arch. Her lips purse, but she shakes her head. "If I could say, I would. But yeh need to trust me righ' now. It's not the time for this."

All it takes is one glance into her solemn brown eyes for me to relent. This is a woman who loves me, who knows me better than anyone in the Vale. Reluctantly, I nod, and she cups my cheek in one of her weathered palms.

"Watch out for yerself today, dear girl," she says, and latches the door in my face.

Resting my back against it, I let my eyes lose focus in the gloom. Defeat builds within me, exacerbated by my lack of sleep.

What good is this ability to repel darkness if I can't do anything useful with it?

With a nagging feeling I should avoid the marketplace, I thread through the alleys, careful not to get too close to anyone I see. Not many people have begun stirring yet, but I'm beginning to doubt my lantern's ability to disguise the way the darkness disagrees with me. I'd rather avoid curious eyes.

A dry laugh crumples out. *Imagine being afraid of the light.*

I come out at Utsanek's west side and try to get my bearings. The road is wider, caked with mud, and crisscrossed with ruts. I stand to the side as a mule-drawn wagon bounces by, weighed down with timbers. Glancing up, I find the buildings aren't stacked on top of each other like mismatched stumps, as they are in the inner city. This is the trade district where my father works. It makes me exhale in relief. I know this place.

The smells of burning coal and fresh-cut wood circle around me. I pass a lamplighter as he ascends a wobbly ladder to replace the candle in a lantern clinging to the side of the carpentry guild. I'm sure he's grateful his efforts have a bigger impact.

The stonemasonry that employs my father lies at the end of the strip. I slow my approach. If by some miracle Father is here, what will he say to the way I left him a day ago? I can't bear for him to repeat my spite-filled words. And if he's not here, I risk agitating the foreman.

But when I peek inside the window and scan the handful of forms completely engrossed in their labors, I do not find him among them.

Anger and dread battle for dominance in my heaving chest. He never let me out of his sight for seventeen years. And now this?

As I step away from the building, a voice booms. "Amyrah."

I close my eyes and summon an unaffected smile.

A short man with a bald pate and arms thicker than his thighs emerges from the workshop, wiping his hands on a rag tucked into the waist of his trousers. Even though he's easily twice my weight, his eyes are level with mine.

"Good morning, Harvel," I say. It takes all my resolve not to wither under his critical stare.

"What do you think you're doing here? Did you come expecting a welcome?" His fleshy forehead is a mass of thick ridges squeezed between wild brows. He plants his palms on his hips.

I swing the lantern by my side to disguise how it shakes. "I came to see my father. It's been ages since I visited him at the shop."

Harvel scoffs, a puff of sour breath hitting me in the face. "And it's been a long time since he visited the shop."

I feign ignorance. "What are you talking about?"

He laughs as he shakes his head and looks down at his huge leather boots. "Don't you go denying you knew anything about it. I'm sure you noticed him holed up in that rat's nest he calls a home for the past three weeks."

I wither a little. Harvel is a tough man, but he has been my father's employer for ten years. It wasn't easy for Pada to find work after my mother died, and Harvel was the only person willing to give him a chance. I've always respected him for his pragmatic approach to life. To hear him belittle my father like this is especially hurtful. "He hasn't been well for a while." A sickening heaviness expands in my gut.

Harvel assesses me with narrowed eyes. His tone drops. "So I've heard." The abrasive sounds of metal striking stone ring in my ears. He takes a step closer, and I fight the urge to move back. "I've also heard talk he's been making things difficult for the Vale—again."

I swallow and pinch my lips together.

"Now, I've never bothered much with what you folks believe or do in your own home, so long as Téron's work has been up to my standards. He's had his bouts of illness over the years, which I've overlooked." He comes so close I can see flecks of green in his granite eyes. "But this is one step too far. Opposing the Foremost, risking the Shrouded's anger like he did yesterday . . ." He paces and rubs a hand over his bristly hair, the calluses scraping against it audibly. "You realize I've had to find a replacement for him, Amyrah. I won't have him coming back here. Especially if he can't keep his mouth shut."

"What happened yesterday?" I ask, because to me, it's even more significant than my father no longer having an occupation.

Harvel's hand falls to his side. The folds in his forehead smooth slightly. He leans in again. "All I know is things are changing, and it will not go well for anyone who stands in the way."

I open my mouth to respond, but Harvel says, "If people don't start considering what their actions cost the Vale," —he pauses, his shoulders rising as he sucks in a deep breath— "they don't deserve a place here."

His expression is so layered, so intense, that I am forced to turn away from it. I watch the masons as they work, chipping away at giant slabs of rock.

When I make my eyes focus on their projects, my stomach cramps painfully. They are making headstones.

I turn back, and surprise has overcome Harvel's swarthy face. His eyes widen at the glowing pendant, then rove up and around me. My heart responds by flinging itself against my ribs. I bring my lantern under my chin and push against his chest. He steps back, his jaw working in a silent question as a blind panic seizes my limbs. I stagger backward.

"Th-thanks for your help," I mutter breathlessly, "but I should probably get—"

Confused, he stares after me as I spin away and hurry out of the trade district as fast as I can.

"Watch it, girl."

I barrel around a corner, right into a wealthy merchant stepping off his front steps. Gasping for air, I mutter my apologies without looking back.

Once he is out of sight, I fall against a wall and wait for the deafening rush of my pulse to quiet.

Harvel's words gnaw at my thoughts until my mind screams, *What have my actions cost the Vale?*

I shake my head to knock the question loose.

I am not responsible for the evils of others.

But the seed has gained purchase in my mind, and I can feel its weed-like roots taking hold.

I force myself to keep moving, but my resolve evaporates like a physician's liquor. I don't resist as Utsanek reels me back into the heart of its oblivion.

Mixed with the clouds of doubt, my father's words join the tangle of thoughts. *Your love of light will get you killed.*

When I thought it was only my own safety on the line, I didn't even question the danger. I believed the beauty of illumination was worth it. But I can no longer deny how my heedless actions—my light—brought the retaliation of the kaligorven.

The intersections around me begin to blend with sinister sameness. I try to take deep breaths, but the feeling of dread won't leave me alone.

If this light is so good, why does it bring so much devastation?

My pulse and pace quicken, and every turn I take leads to more long passageways and too many people. I need to get out, but I can't find a way. The longer I remain, the worse the ténesomni pursues me. I have never felt it like this before. It spirals angrily at the boundary between darkness and light, pushing in closer and closer to my skin. A muffled scream tears from my chest. I look behind me and see no evidence of a physical pursuer, but the fear remains.

Throat dry and lungs burning, I dart down alleys and squeeze between fences, desperate for relief. When I slip between two dilapidated structures and find an open gate at the end of a narrow passage, I land in a scene that banishes my panic and makes my breath catch.

An entire city block is lit up—not with sola bones or gloomy lanterns, but with a myriad of bolétis. They line both sides of the wide street and greet me from delicate woven cages hanging overhead. A rainbow of colors to feast my heart on and ease my mind.

It is another world.

Pressing a hand to the wild pulse in my throat, I stare around in wonder. The countless mushrooms form an effective barrier between the looming shadows and the street below. A girl shakes out a carpet on a balcony and sends a burst of wind that makes the rustic pendants sway and dance. Their rays of light sprinkle in every direction.

A linear garden runs in spurts down the street's center, fragrant with forest herbs and a few early blooming flowers. Rusted signs dangle from the buildings, boasting of a tea house, an apothecary, a weaver, a mercantile. And a library.

Children run past, squeezing themselves behind doors and crouching below the garden planters. Two women converse in low tones and chuckle quietly beside a cart overflowing with preserves, keeping an eye on the impish play.

"Ex-excuse me," I say, holding the lantern close to my heart so I can feel its tremulous warmth.

The taller of the two leans forward and tilts her head. A flash of unease runs through me when she exchanges a wary look with the other. "Anything in particular I can help you find?"

"No." I shake my head. "No, I was just—what is this place?"

"Ah." She nods, her eyes not leaving mine. "Came here by mistake, have you?"

When I don't answer, a knowing smile thins her lips. "Well," she says, catching a toddler who comes careening through a doorway. She hoists her onto a hip. "This is Utsanek's best kept secret."

The other woman rolls her eyes and swats her friend's shoulder with the back of a hand. "Tress, it won't be for much longer if you go telling every stray cat that crawls in."

Tress laughs at the rebuke and sets down the fussing child after kissing her curls. She scampers away to ruin the big kids' hiding spots. "Loren thinks we should have a warning system so we can hide all this" —she waves her hand in the air— "and pretend we are just as depressed as the rest of this city."

Loren purses her lips as she rearranges the jars on the counter.

"But I keep telling her that would be impractical. Besides." She smiles. "I trust Elyōn to send us exactly the people who need us."

My lantern lowers a little. "You aren't—" I bite my lip. "You aren't afraid the kaligorven will punish you?"

Tress laughs airily, banishing the thought. "What can they do to us beyond bodily harm?"

I frown. Bodily harm seems bad enough.

Tress tucks a stray strand of mousy hair behind an ear and tilts her head in an invitation to follow. I glance at Loren, but she resolutely avoids my eyes.

Not knowing what else to do, I join Tress. She weaves through the planters and pranksters who dart every way. They avoid her respectfully but are not so careful with me. After a few jostles, warmth returns to my fingertips, and I find myself smiling. When did I last see children playing in Utsanek?

Tress leads me to a quieter courtyard tucked beside the library. Several benches surround a twisting tree covered in a riot of colorful mushrooms. She motions to a bench, and I sit.

"Now. What's your name?"

I peer between the lights at the tree's branches. They are bursting into buds, promising Tiosh will soon give way to Zomré. The hopefulness of this sight encourages the muscles in my back to relax.

"I'm Amyrah," I say, her question finally registering in my mind. "Where did you find all these bolétis?" I marvel at the little mushrooms' quantity and vibrancy. My small collection was the product of many weeks' and miles' worth of searching.

She points behind us to a wooden gate camouflaged in a tangle of leafless vines. "This neighborhood lies on the southwest corner of Utsanek, right up against the forest. Over many years, our community has worked to hem a portion of it in for our own private use." She smiles, the light from the bolétis sprinkled within her faint green irises. "Our own little Ellithïm."

Paradise. I chew on the word. It feels like an intruder in my troubled heart.

"We have cultivated it into a rich garden for many things," she continues, "but mostly as a place to grow bolétis."

"I did not think anyone else cared for them," I whisper, an emotion I can't explain making my throat ache.

"Few can see their value, it's true. Alone, they seem of little worth. But in great numbers, they can prove something the ténesomni finds difficult to overcome."

It's as if a cord wraps right around my neck, preventing me from swallowing.

There's been community here all this time—a beautiful, thriving community. Collecting mushrooms for light, living in the middle of this darkness . . . together. And my father and I have spent ten years alone.

I can name what I am feeling. *Longing.*

The colorful tree blurs in my vision.

"Tress, there you are."

A man wrapped in thin layers of wool steps into the courtyard and strides over to us. He bends to embrace the woman and kisses her cheek. A chain slips out of his shirt, weighed down by an ebony soapstone ring. Tress slips her hand into his black hair, a matching band on her fourth finger. I look away as they share a moment, hastily wiping my tears on my sleeve.

"Tell me what happened." Tress's face creases with concern.

He straightens and glances at me with misgiving. Dark circles rim his eyes.

For a reason I don't understand, Tress places her hand on mine and says, "She's safe, Bryn." Her glance flicks down to my necklace, and she gives me an assuring squeeze.

Bryn regards his wife thoughtfully, then proceeds as if not in the presence of a stranger. "It's bad, my love." He runs a hand down his face and over his beard. "This newcomer is intent on causing trouble for anyone who will not fully subject themselves to the dark beasts."

"What does that mean?" Tress sits up taller, her eyes tracing her husband's motions. A tremor runs through her fingers.

The man sighs wearily. "He has convinced the Foremost to go after all those devoted to Elyōn, to begin with."

Tress gasps and pulls her hand away from mine. "What?"

Bryn nods slowly. "Yes, I'm afraid Dravek has been sending his men to search out caeruméni meeting houses. He's offered a considerable reward to anyone who will turn over the fidrélas."

"Fidrélas?" I say before I can stop myself.

Bryn cocks his head at the interruption. The frown still dominates his brow, but kindness fills his deep-set eyes. He hesitates as he searches my face, but his wife's endorsement appears to have been enough to convince him. "Those faithful to the ancient teachings of Elyōn. In the long absence of Sola Vinari and Kuvror Erovantus, our numbers have been increasing. But in secret. As confidence in the provision of the kaligorven has dwindled, the interest in the beliefs of old has grown."

Tress's soft features form a contemplative expression. "Yes, it has been a relief to see the Shrouded's hold on the souls of the valefolk weaken over time. Although, it has been difficult to encourage the people when they've seen the bones that light our city grow dim."

My fingers travel to the little pendant at my throat. No matter how the Foremost insists hunting down the light will bring us peace with the kaligorven, he can never banish the truth that light will always symbolize hope.

Tress raises her eyes to the tree. "Elyōn will always shine light in our hearts, but people tend to lose their faith when darkness is all they see."

"Hmm, yes." Bryn sits heavily on the bench beside his wife. "And their devotion is easily bought by the bones of the innocent."

"The bones of . . ." I shift forward on the bench so I can see Bryn's face better. "Have the kaligorven lifted the command of darkness?"

He nods. "Yes, and with a fresh beast to harvest." He grimaces. "I'm sure Utsanek will be in a state of celebration for days to come."

I inhale sharply. Another sola? The air seems to press down upon me. I stare at the buttons of my dress and dig the toes of my shoes into the soft earth beneath the bench.

"Bryn." Tress's gentle voice breaks through my fog. "You said they were looking for the faithful." I can hear the concern in her voice, but I can't bear to look at her face. Her next words come out in a whisper. "Did they find any?"

My fingers tighten around handfuls of my dress as my heart cries in a groan too deep for words. An eternity passes before Bryn responds.

"No, thank the Highest. They did not."

Tress closes her eyes and exhales, and I find I can breathe again.

Getting to his feet, Bryn squeezes Tress's shoulder. "But we need to be prepared for what is coming."

She nods. Something unspoken passes between husband and wife, and while I'm still trying to figure out what it was, he leaves.

"So. Amyrah." Tress turns her soft green eyes upon me once more. I meet her gaze. "Tell me about that necklace."

20

WEHNA

WHERE DOES ALL THE LIGHT COME FROM?" Arvo's voice bounces between the stone walls of the alleyway.

"Don't go too far," I call after him, but it's useless. My little brother has already disappeared around a building. I shiver as I run to catch up, shadows close at my heels.

A distinct hum of excitement emanates from ahead, but it only adds to my anxieties. I pick up my pace, barely able to keep Arvo's tiny frame in sight. When I turn a corner and see what all the commotion is about, I stop short.

Blinding orbs light up the market square—only a few bones from a freshly hunted sola. I lower my lantern.

Arvo plants himself under one of them, gazing at it with a slack jaw.

"What is it, Wehna?" he asks as I approach.

I glance up. The brightness makes my eyes smart. "It's a bone, Arvo. A bone of a Light Creature."

He tilts his head and absentmindedly takes my hand when I hold it out to him. Together, we walk into the busy marketplace.

"But they're so much brighter than normal," he ponders, finishing with "That's not nice," in the same breath. He scowls at the garish display.

"No." I sigh. "It's not." I usher him past two men bartering loudly over an enormous hog. The market froths with more people than there have been in weeks. I stare blankly at a group of women exchanging pleasantries as if it is the most beautiful afternoon there ever was. Their gaiety seems almost comical. Are the valefolk really so fickle?

Oblivious to my mental anguish, Arvo continues to mull over the bones. "But without them, I guess we wouldn't be able to see much. Light is a good thing." His little mind works double-time.

I know what my parents would say to him. *As long as we take a life, we will remain in darkness, no matter how much light continues to shine.* But I can't make myself form the words, because all I feel is relief that there is a place where I will no longer be haunted by the ténesomni.

A delicious aroma wafts by, causing my stomach to cramp. Arvo's eyes go wide as he sucks in the smell and licks his lip.

"Oh, Wehna, can we get some meat pies? Please?"

His innocent request sends a dagger through my heart. I let him pull me over to a stand overflowing with golden brown pastries. He reaches out to grab one, and I yank him back before the vendor notices. Swinging my purse around, I dig inside and cringe. Only a few coins of arlum are left from a love offering my parents' friends insisted on taking for us at the last caeruméni. They gave out of charity, and I should save the money for something more practical, like one more sack of lanuum. That's what Mother would do. I bite my lip.

Arvo yanks his hand out of mine. I look at him in surprise. His cheeks flush with sudden anger.

"Mada would let me have one," he practically shouts at me in a burst of temper completely out of character. Stunned, I pull back.

I fight to rein in my own anger. "Well, I'm not Mada," I say through clenched teeth.

Here I've been, trying to hide all my worry from my brother, telling myself we're managing fine, that I can provide for everything he needs in my parents' absence.

What a liar I am.

"I wish she was here and you weren't."

I take a calming breath, but as I crouch down to his level, he shoves me so I lose my balance. I catch myself and look back in time to see him grabbing a pie from the counter and darting into the milling crowd.

"*Arvo*," I yell, but he is gone.

Dread washes over me as I scramble to my feet. I shout his name again, my vision bouncing around the square wildly. He doesn't respond, and I can't find him anywhere.

Just as I am ready to rush off and chase him down, a stern voice calls me back.

"Not so fast."

I whirl around, tears stinging my eyes. "What?"

A woman, as wide as she is tall, puckers her face, fixing me with what I'm sure she thinks is a withering gaze.

"That boy yours?" She makes a motion with her chin, causing her entire jowly face to shake.

"Spare me the lecture," I spit out, burying a hand in my purse and pulling out the coins. I thrust them underneath her nose and hope she'll take them before I feel compelled to apologize for my brash words.

She glares at me for what feels like forever, until I almost shriek with frustration.

"*Just take it.*"

With grumbled words I have no desire to interpret, she holds out a hand and accepts the payment. I don't wait for them to clink in her meaty palm before I dart away and begin the frantic search for my brother.

The air has grown oppressively hot and humid by the time my panic fizzles out into despair.

Arvo isn't anywhere.

Though I implore them, the valefolk are in too much of a mood for merriment to concern themselves with finding one wayward child. I enter every shop and knock on every dwelling that faces the square, but there's no sign of him. I would search the side streets, but even as desperate as I am, I am too afraid to push back into the shadows. Near hysterical, I pass by the vendor's stalls again and again, seeing Arvo's face everywhere in my mind's eye and nowhere in reality.

Where could he have gone?

He knows so little of this city. And he's only five.

Keep him safe, I plead with the Highest.

Exhausted, I crumple onto the steps of the shrine to the Shrouded. I set down the lantern and bury my face in my hands. First my parents, and now my brother. Am I destined to lose everything in this cursed valley? Sobs tear my chest apart.

Elyōn, why did we ever come here? I ask in silent whispers. *Why would you lead my family to a place that has caused us so much pain?*

We've been in Utsanek for three years, and as far as I can see, nothing good has come from it.

Are you listening? my heart groans. *Do you even care?*

All I hear is an unfeeling rumble of ambient chatter.

Why won't you show yourself to me? I don't know if you are even here.

The pernicious thought slips in between my prayers, taking advantage of the frailty my failings have exposed. I raise my head and wipe the wetness away from my face. Seething shadows obscure the sky. Oh, what I would give to see it again.

As if summoned by my melancholy, the expanse opens and a curtain of rain descends. Patrons shriek and laugh, running to find shelter in buildings and beneath awnings. I turn my face up to it and wonder if this is a punishment from Elyōn, or if it means nothing at all.

Maybe I should look for help elsewhere.

Behind me, the door of the fanum creaks open. Curiosity piqued, I enter.

I wait for my eyes to adjust to the darkness, blinking and hugging my damp frock close to my skin with one hand, clutching the lantern in the other. A dusty smell mingled with a heady musk assaults my senses. My footsteps sound abnormally loud on the stone floor.

"Hello?" I say, almost unable to make the word come out at all. My voice bounces around the space.

Moment by moment, the room reveals itself to me. A huge sola skull hangs from above, faintly illuminating the space. It must be very, very old if it emits such little light. A high roof arches overtop of it, supported by thick pillars. Images of cryptic creatures and ancient Atsunic script I cannot read are carved into their sides. My fingers trace the grooves as I move around the room.

Far more impressive than the pillars, a massive monument dominates the far wall. I approach it slowly, forgetting to breathe as I take in its intricacy.

Whoever created this statue was tremendously skilled. The artist has managed to convey the impression of a terrifying beast with razor claws and eyes that seem alive, while purposely leaving out the finer details. What looks like swirls of vapor curl around it and obscure most of its form. If I didn't know it was made of stone, I'd expect to reach out and feel nothing but the brush of wind against my fingertips. An ephemeral creature locked forever in time.

I gasp when something moves—a ribbon of smoke folding in on itself as it travels upward. Looking down, I find a lit rod of incense resting in a polished metal bowl.

A frown claims my brow. What am I supposed to do? Take it and wave it around? I don't know what I'm doing here. Do the kaligorven always listen, or is there some ritual I'm supposed to perform?

"It's splendid, isn't it?"

The voice makes me start. I hold up my light and peer around.

A man sits in the far-left corner of the fanum with his back against the wall, his legs splayed carelessly out to the side. He looks up at me between strands of white-blond hair, pressing a finger into an old book to keep his place. My heart pushes into my throat and heat spreads into my face. I turn to leave.

"No, no." He holds out a hand, arresting my retreat. Dust mushrooms from the volume as he snaps it shut and gets to his feet. "Stay."

"I-I'm sorry. I shouldn't be here." I brush a spiral of black hair away from my eyes.

"And why shouldn't you?" he asks as he stretches out his stiff limbs. Respecting my reluctance to banter with him, he flips open a leather bag on the floor and slips the book inside. Returning his attention to me, he strides over.

He has such a peculiar look about him. Not overly muscular, but tall and well-proportioned. Undeniably attractive. My blush deepens. He is definitely not a boy, but someone coming into the peak years of manhood. The lack of pigmentation in his hair and skin makes them so similar, they almost blend together. I squirm inwardly under the scrutiny of his shadowed eyes and look determinedly at the statue. He follows my lead and regards the image.

"I would have every person in Utsanek visit this place and see it for themselves."

Something about his voice makes me shiver. There is nothing particularly sinister about it, but I can't help but identify a distinct tone of reverence. A silent warning blares in my soul.

I can feel him looking at me again. My mouth goes dry. Why have I come here? I don't remember. "H-have you seen one up close?" I ask stupidly. "A real one, I mean."

His eyes do not leave mine. The corner of his mouth and one of his eyebrows hitch up as if attached to the same invisible string. "Yes, actually." His smile broadens when I flinch. "Does that frighten you?"

A shudder runs down my spine as I remember my brother, somewhere out there in this city of darkness. I peel my eyes away and glance back at the door. But my feet stay planted.

He holds me in his sights for a few breaths longer, then releases me and paces around the room. I feel my insides uncoil.

"This fear you hold is a good thing, although I think, like the rest of the Vale, you don't fully understand what you are missing. When your only goal is to satiate the kaligorven, you completely lose sight of the power they offer."

He steps toward the statue and raises his hands, muttering under his breath. As if at his call, the shadows skirting the room rush to circle around him. I stare, awestruck at how vividly the pillars that guard the shrine are painted, at how much the darkness concealed.

The man turns around, still holding his arms aloft. "Think of how prosperous this city could be if it simply tapped into this might."

You need to be strong, Wehna. Isn't that what my mother always wanted of me? Well, here is proof of strength. My eyes eat in the spectacle, my mind filling with images of banishing the ténesomni so I can find my brother, so I never have to be afraid again.

But this is not the strength she had in mind.

With an enormous effort, I tear my eyes away.

Highest, give me courage.

At the same moment, something springs to life inside of me—something new and bold.

"What true strength can there be in a power that blinds, that demands death?" I whisper.

The irises of his eyes swarm with wisps of shadow, making me shiver. "Spoken like someone who has yet to give herself to the night."

A phrase of my mother's rises to the surface of my mind, finds its way onto my tongue. "The darkness may assail the light, but it will never overcome it."

The stranger's expression goes from open to forbidding. He throws his arms down, and with a flick of his hands, the shadows return to fill the room, thicker than before.

"If you choose to remain in that attitude, I promise you will soon find yourself paying the price."

The spike of his words startles me, but I'm thankful for it. It has woken me up.

"I'm sorry I bothered you," I say, backing toward the doorway. "But that's a risk I'm willing to take." I am surprised to hear that my voice is confident.

Strong.

I turn my back on him and leave the fanum, chills running down my arms.

Elyōn, forgive me for ever setting foot in there.

The sheets of rain weave into a blurry tapestry. I pick up the search again, plunging into the water with a calm I can't account for, even though I am shivering with cold. My lips move in inaudible prayer as I go, ignoring the darkness, resolved to take Utsanek one block at a time.

Highest, keep him safe. I know you will keep him safe. I trust you to take care of him, wherever he is. You know where he is. Lead me in the right direction. Keep him safe. Make him brave. Keep him safe . . .

Slowly, the shower relents. The warmth of Tiosh resumes in its absence, but the chill in my heart remains. There is no sign of Arvo on any of our familiar routes, and dread threatens to extinguish the unfamiliar daring. Still, I press on.

Until my lantern goes out.

It's as if all my fears converge on me at once, making up for the reprieve I didn't know I was experiencing.

My chest pumps rapidly, and my limbs shake. A shrill whistling cuts out all other noise, but I know no one else can hear it but me. The shadows move in. Can they sense my weakness? Have they been waiting for me to drop my guard?

Elyōn, help!

My lips form the words, but no sound emerges. I struggle to keep upright, scream at myself to keep moving, to keep searching for Arvo. But the curtain of defeat descends.

Then, a still, small voice.

You are not alone.

It is almost as if I can hear the words spoken audibly. I feel around, but no one is here. Only this wicked veil of shadows.

Even in your darkest moment, you are not alone.

My father's words, long since folded away in my childhood memories.

I suck in wretched breaths and push them out again in slow exhales. The smallest measure of calm returns as the knowledge of the Highest's nearness holds the ténesomni back. I look around, waiting for my eyes to see what's around me.

How could I have been so absorbed in my prayers that I didn't even realize where I was? I have ended up right on Orlagh's doorstep.

He hears me.

Relief covers me like a warm blanket. I scramble up the steps and pound on her door.

No answer. I bang again and again and again.

Still, nothing.

An exasperated sound drags itself out of my throat, and I crumple.

"Wehna?"

Like a sharp-edged sword, the word dismembers my fears from reality. I stare into the gloom, tremulous hope flaring.

The glow of a lantern illuminates Orlagh's hunched form, holding tightly to the hand of a tiny person.

"Arvo," I gasp, tripping off the landing.

The diminutive shape frees himself from the woman's grip and hurtles toward me. I gather him into my arms, my tears flowing freely into the softness of his neck.

His words muffle against my shoulder. "I'm sorry, Wehna," he sobs.

"It's alright. You're alright."

I hold his face in my hands and look at him when Orlagh catches up, holding her light out so we can see.

"Where did you go, little fledgling?" I can hardly speak, my heart pumps so hard.

"I just wanted to hide from you and eat my pie. But when I ate it, I didn't know where I was."

Tears gather in his huge eyes. His bottom lip quivers. I pass a hand over his damp brow as fresh tears of my own crawl down my cheeks.

"I was scared, but I remembered Pada's promise that—that—the Highest is always with me, even when I don't think he can see me."

My arms wrap around him again, and I breathe in the sweet scent of his curls.

"You're absolutely right, Vo."

He pushes back. "I wasn't afraid anymore. And I asked him to help me find the light."

I draw in a long breath, amazed I am getting lessons in faith from a five-year-old. My soul sings to Elyōn. *You really do care about the smallest sparrow.*

"Then this girl found me. When she came close, the darkness backed away."

He sniffs loudly and wipes his nose with the back of a hand. "I went with her."

I cock my head, trying to make sense of what he's telling me. "Did . . . did this girl have a name?"

His head shakes fast. "She never told me." Worry shines in his green eyes. "Did I do something bad, Wehna? I made sure I didn't tell her anything about me, like you told me. She was so nice. She made me feel not afraid."

My fingers find his and give them a comforting squeeze. "It's alright." I smile weakly, and the dimples return to his cheeks.

But the enigma of the girl troubles my thoughts.

"Wehna?"

I return my attention to Arvo.

"She gave me this."

He holds out a hand wrapped up in leather cords, and a many-rayed pendant dangles beneath it.

21

BELWYN

MY SHOULDERS ACHE under a heavy sack of books. I struggle to keep up with Shemai and Korvin. I really should be making them carry their own work to the house of the maevotér, the withered old man in charge of their education. But I don't have the heart to wish another trial on them as long as they live—even if it's as small as being made to carry their own schoolbooks. I heft the bag up higher and quicken my pace.

The boys snicker with each other as they work out various insults in the Atsunic tongue. Even as a subtle ache throbs my heart, a smile tips the corner of my mouth. I remember Rhun and myself at their ages— nine and twelve—doing everything in our power to thwart the lessons of our unflagging private tutor. Rhun had dubbed him "Old Man Splutters" for the way he was either always working up his incurable phlegm or spluttering over our terrible pranks, for which I always got in trouble. I still chafe when I think of it.

Unbidden, Amyrah's words pop to the surface of my turbulent thoughts. *If you could, you'd take the fall for him again.*

I grab my chest, fruitlessly attempting to rub away a pain that only exists in my mind. Something in me is always surprised Rhun is no longer here. It's like the root suckers that spring up long after the tree is taken out. They appear at such random intervals, ages after the giant has been cut down. You can make yourself forget it happened for a while by snipping them off, but they will keep coming—an untimely reminder that something big is missing in your life. And the pain will start afresh.

I'm thankful every time my feet take me away from the place I last saw my brother.

Our house lies in the wealthiest sector of Utsanek—the Oputae, as it is known by the valefolk—at the northeast corner of the city. The yards there are vast and opulent, the streets wide and well-maintained. Over the last couple days, workmen have been busy lining the main roads to the heart of the city with bone fragments from the last sola—the one I killed —every couple hundred feet. I feel sick when I draw near to them, trying not to look up when I pass. But it's obvious the presence of more light than the Vale has seen in thirteen years does not affect the valefolk in the same way.

I'm somewhere between glad for them and disgusted at this whole corrupt system.

As we approach the tutor's house on the edge of the Oputae, an illogical feeling of having done something wrong creeps into my gut. It wasn't long ago that he caught me breeding wood frogs in his water cistern—Rhun's idea. A breathy laugh bubbles from my lungs.

I draw even with my brothers and drop the bag down at their feet.

"Well, aren't you going to go in?" I ask.

Korvin's hand falls from the doorknob, and he turns to me with a puzzled look. "It's locked."

Shemai's eyes widen, and his jaw drops. "No way! We don't have school today?"

I pound on the door and peer through the windows. No light emanates from behind the dusty curtains, and no one comes to answer. "I guess not."

My youngest brother gives a little hoot and dances on the spot, but Korvin's countenance falls. "So . . . what are we supposed to do all day?"

Good question. I glance at him, and he chews on his bottom lip. There is a dark smudge across his cheek, and his light hair is greasy and matted in places. Shemai tugs at his shirt. His nails are black, and he hasn't bothered to clean up a bloody scrape on his elbow. A twinge of guilt plagues me. My brothers bear serious indications of neglect.

"What do you both want to do?" I cross my arms and lean against the house to appear more flexible than I feel.

"Go swimming," Shemai says without a moment's hesitation.

I roll my eyes. Only a nine-year-old would think taking a dip in a loch that lost its ice only a few weeks ago is a good idea.

Korvin takes longer to ponder it. "I don't want to go home," he says, and his troubled eyes flick up to my face.

Something cracks inside me, because I know what he's thinking. I feel it every time I step inside our house. It's been difficult enough for me to process, but I wonder how these two are dealing with our mother's paralyzing depressions, our father's withering disdain. I want to do something for these boys, something that will take their minds off this nightmare they've been living.

But what?

My eyes drift over to Old Man Splutters' house and land on the stone cistern along its side. A wicked grin appears on my face.

I step forward and grab the boys each by a shoulder, bending to their level. "I've got a plan."

"This one is covered in *slime*," Shemai squeals, lurching after a wood frog as it leaps from his hands.

I smirk and hold open a small leather sack for Korvin to drop in his catch. He beams at me and wipes his dirt-stained hands on his trousers.

"You and Rhun really did this to the maevotér?" he asks, his face flushed.

"Well, technically, I caught the frogs, and *he* dumped them into the cistern." I laugh. "But yes."

Shemai runs up the bank of the slough, peering into a gap in his cupped hands. "This frog is huge. It looks pregnant."

"Frogs don't get pregnant, morvus."

I smile inwardly but knock Korvin on the shoulder. "Hey, be nice to your brother. And some actually sort of do."

Korvin rolls his eyes and slips down the bank to find another specimen.

I carry the sack to a tree and slide down against it.

For a moment, I close my eyes and think back to those years when all we had to worry about when we left the house was carrying a lantern with us. No solas. No ceremonies. Just two brothers and a mysterious kingdom of our own.

This was always the place Rhun and I would escape together when Father was overbearing. Rhun could always tell when his expectations weighed too heavily on my shoulders. He'd catch my eye and give a subtle jolt of the chin that meant to meet him behind the house.

I liked to believe we were the only ones who knew about this hidden slice of calm in the middle of the forest. Sometimes, we'd amuse ourselves by building rafts, other times by hand fishing for huge bottom feeders. We even had our own treetop fortress at one point. I raise my lantern and look up. The platforms are still visible above. I resist the urge to point them out to the boys, because they are probably not safe anymore.

The ache in my chest deepens, but it feels less caustic now that I've allowed the grief to flow. This is how I want to remember Rhun. As the brother who knew how to lighten the load of the world and occasionally got me into trouble with our tutor.

I realize now that we made our own light.

As I wipe fresh tears off my face, I wonder why I have never taken Korvin and Shemai here before.

An eerie wailing reverberates through the trunks of the trees and makes the hair on my neck stand on end.

Not again, I say, except the words don't actually come out.

"What's that about?" Shemai puffs as he runs over to me, much too excited.

I snatch up the lantern and get to my feet. "Don't know," I say, then call for Korvin. He stares down at his cupped hands, shrugs, and releases the fortunate amphibian.

"We should hurry."

Korvin catches up to us, and I hand him the squirming bag. We head back toward Utsanek, following the direction of the hunting call.

Can there already be another sola? I swallow hard to try to convince my stomach not to eject its contents. Shemai runs ahead, eager to find what all the commotion is about, but Korvin hangs back with me. He wears a familiar expression of concern.

"What are they like?" he asks quietly.

I look at him as we walk. "What are what like?"

He twists the mouth of the sack in his hands. "The solas."

I don't want to talk about this, I think. But I'm done with avoiding the hard stuff.

"I've only seen one, but it was . . . beautiful." I shrug. There isn't another word for it.

"Are they dangerous?"

My brow furrows as I ponder. The one I shot had seemed so gentle. So . . . intelligent. I try to shake the image of its eyes boring into mine.

"No, I don't think so."

Korvin sighs. "I don't understand why we are supposed to . . ."

The scraping of our shoes seems oppressively loud.

"Kill them?" I finish.

He nods.

"That's not the agreement we have with the kaligorven." Even saying their name has the power to frighten me.

Korvin is not satisfied. "Wouldn't it be better to let them live among us? What if we could . . . I don't know . . . find a way to make the Vale a place where they wanted to dwell. Couldn't we have light and let them live?"

This honest line of questioning makes me uncomfortable. "It may be better for them, but there is so much more to this than simply having light to live by." There's much about them and the Shrouded that he doesn't understand. That I don't understand.

As we approach the northeast entrance to the city, we both grow quiet. Shemai slouches against the gate, his face communicating his impatience.

At least he waited for us, I think, which is more than Rhun would've done at his age.

Even though an atmosphere of uncertainty hangs over the three of us, I can't resist making a detour at the maevotér's house. As I get down on one knee and lace my fingers together to hoist Korvin up, a smile chases away his troubles. He climbs up, and Shemai tosses him the bag with a fit of wild giggles. Korvin dumps the frogs in and hops down. We stumble away, barely able to contain ourselves.

"Remember," I wheeze when we are at a safe distance, "if you get in trouble, tell him Belwyn did it in memory of Rhun."

By the time we reach the city center, all our lightheartedness has vanished.

The square festers with people. I have quite a time keeping my brothers in sight. It is a new sensation, being so concerned for their well-being, and I'm finding it difficult to let go. Maybe it's because I should have been there for them long before this.

On the steps of the fanum, my father and the newcomer stand side by side. I frown. Can I ever remember him inviting someone to be on the same level as him?

Father holds up his hands to silence the crowd, although it isn't necessary. The prospect of Sola Vinari has left most speechless.

"You've done well to come at the call of the Hunt." He congratulates the masses. "And I am certain your devotion to the kaligorven will be rewarded." His arms lower. "You can leave this in the capable hands of me and my men. We will all celebrate upon our return." A smile hills his cheeks, but it does not reach his eyes.

The audience remains in uneasy silence for a beat, and a voice speaks up. "We don't want you to decide who gets to hunt for us."

A ripple of anger passes over my father's face, but he masks it quickly. Beside him, Myrzeth is unreadable.

"What would you have me do? Surely, you do not wish for us to jeopardize this Hunt."

"You should not get all the credit every time a sola wanders into our lands," another person yells. Cheers of agreement ring out.

The Foremost holds up his hands again. His veins stand out along his biceps. "Silence."

Something keeps drawing my eyes back to Myrzeth, a pillar in front of the frothing audience. He makes my skin shiver.

My father's mouth draws taut, and he projects his next words through gritted teeth. "If it would satisfy you, we will arrange for a lottery to decide who gets to join in the Hunt."

Cheers of approval ripple through the square. Dravek motions to two of his men to make the necessary preparations. In quick order, a line snakes through the city center. Valefolk scribble their names on little strips of paper and cast them into an urn.

I quietly shift out of sight.

Thankfully, Shemai has found a group of his friends and pays no attention to me. But Korvin turns and watches me draw back.

I cannot give any explanation except a slow shake of the head, but it seems enough for him.

"Don't worry. I won't tell Father," he whispers.

Relief floods me as I am freed to watch the proceedings from the shadows.

In no time ten names have been read out, and a ragtag group of hunters stands before the crowd. One may doubt their capabilities based on stature, but a single look at their determined faces is enough to assure that a sola will be killed this day.

Father disguises his feelings at how everything has unfolded, but to my trained eye, his anger is as obvious as the lantern in his white-knuckled hand.

A knot of dread slips into my intestines. I know he will save his rage for behind closed doors.

Through all of this, Myrzeth remains unmoved. I frown. What's his game?

Turning to the valefolk, the Foremost says, "When we return to you, we will once again have an opportunity to prove our devotion to the kaligorven."

A halfhearted cheer answers him, and I make out his conflicted face as he turns to lead the hunting party out of Utsanek.

Once they are gone, Myrzeth steps forward. He does not need to motion for silence. Every eye is on him.

I creep from my hiding place.

"Good people, aren't you tired of this pathetic system that requires you to wait for a sola to find you?"

Mumblings ripple through the captive audience.

"You have been taking a passive role with the kaligorven for far too many years. It isn't your fault. I blame it entirely on poor leadership."

My stomach twists.

"But we've had peace for years," a woman cries.

Myrzeth raises a brow. "Have you really? Or has it been a steady descent into darkness?" He paces across the fanum steps. "What would you say if I told you we could not only have peace with the Shrouded, but light as well? And not just that—we can have power."

The whispers of the crowd grow into louder conversations. He is playing off their fears and desperation, enticing them with something that has been an altogether foreign concept in the Vale.

A reedy man emerges from the people and approaches Myrzeth. "Show us the way."

Who does this man think he is? I wonder. No way the rest of the valefolk will be so eager to change our method of doing things.

But I am wrong.

A cheer—much more enthusiastic than the one my father received—erupts.

"You have already begun the process by reporting those who hold to an alternate system of beliefs. They will be prosecuted and made to pay. And I assure you, your efforts will be rewarded."

A disheveled man a few feet from me grins hideously, revealing a maw filled with gaping holes and blackened stubs of teeth. He makes me feel filthy.

"I counsel you to take it one step further. Don't merely report those worshippers of Elyōn. Actively persecute them. Make them feel the consequences of their misguided beliefs so they may be convinced to recant their ways."

My jaw drops. Is he condoning violence against our neighbors?

"The more we can assure the kaligorven their presence and ways will not be challenged in the Vale, the more willing you will find them to share their strength with us."

The men give throaty grunts of appreciation, but I notice the women are more hesitant to voice their approval. Myrzeth is appealing to a more masculine obsession with power.

"And consider whether you are making your own home a welcoming place to the mighty dark beasts. Do not merely lay offerings on these ancient steps, so far removed from your daily lives. Set aside shrines to the kaligorven within your houses, showing them they are welcome in our midst."

The women look at each other nervously. This entreaty to the womenfolk is not quite as well-received.

Sensing their unease, Myrzeth smiles. "I can assure you that, when properly acknowledged and honored, they pose no threat to you or your children. A decade's worth of neglect has made them so hostile to the valefolk."

Myrzeth's words are so calm, so smoothly delivered, I am not surprised to see the women's faces relaxing. But I have lived under the roof of a man skilled in manipulation for too many years for them to sway me.

"If you listen to me, I promise we will transform the Vale into a place even the Grovesha come to respect and fear."

I cock my head at the word, which means "the Outlands" in Atsunic. Hardly anyone ever mentions or thinks of that mysterious land beyond the Vale. It's forbidden. A chill settles on my skin. Whatever Myrzeth's motives, it's clear they are far more complex than I realized. He was cunning to wait until my father had left Utsanek to reveal them.

"And above all else," he continues, the blackness agitating and gathering around him until he holds everyone's attention, "if you discover someone who poses a threat to the darkness, who may have a strange ability to repel it" —the ténesomni seems to emanate from his eyes— "bring them to me."

Nothing in me wishes to stay and hear more.

As I beckon my brothers to me and escort them out of the square, a new burden weighs upon my shoulders, but I can't slip this one off like I can a sack of books.

I know exactly the kind of person Myrzeth would be eager to eradicate.

22
TÉRON

THE SOUND OF WOOD-SCRAPING STONE echoes in the dank room. I try to sit, but my head screams in pain, and the world pitches around me. My body falls against the cold floor, and I groan.

I have given up trying to figure out how many days I have been kept here. In fact, I do not care.

My mind is stuck in a nauseating cycle, one word swirling around again and again until it makes me sick.

Myrzeth.

It lingers in my mind like a filthy stain.

A thousand questions consume me, but one burns more deeply than the others.

Where has he been all these years?

I have tried for so long to bury the memory of the last night I saw Ellehra. How could I have worked so hard to forget the things that pained me most—adding layer and layer overtop, piling on new memories and passions and joys and sorrows, burying it all down deep— yet something could come along and disturb the topsoil, revealing heartache waiting right under the surface?

I thought I had moved past the hurt of Ellehra's death a thousand times. I thought time would make me stronger. I thought I could be better for Amyrah.

But then the solas returned to the Vale, and I saw one die up close for the first time. Then my daughter grew in her passion for the light, and I could see my wife shining out through her eyes. Then this wicked relation returned, and every last bit of control I thought I had achieved washed away in a moment.

Now I know the man I became was a lie. He has been cracked, broken, torn open.

Tears run down my face. They rush stronger than a river, flowing from the depths of my soul, stinging as they touch the parts of me that have lost every protective layer.

Yielding, I let the deluge take me, dredging up all these old recollections with it.

"You can't expect me to sit by while this happens again."

Frustration marred Ellehra's beautiful face. She paced around the kitchen, her bare feet making hardly any sound.

"We are talking about a life, Téron. Not some instinctive animal, but an intelligent creation." Her white-blond hair flicked around her waist when she turned her watery eyes on mine.

They usually had the power to untangle all my apprehensions, but not that day.

My head shook slowly from side to side. "It is the way it must be." I gripped my spear tightly for a moment, then sighed and set it against the wall. Crossing the large room, I caught her by her hips and pulled her close, breaching that strange place where ténesomni could not reach. She kept her arms tucked between us and looked away from me, the fingers of her right hand curled into a fist against her lips.

"I wish you could understand." Her teeth bit into her knuckles for a few breaths. "They are not the ones we should be afraid of."

My hands released their hold and buried themselves in the roots of her hair. "What kind of husband would I be if I did not do everything in my power to keep you safe?" Her eyes flitted up to mine as my hand moved to her cheek. "What kind of father would I be?"

The tenseness between her brows eased a little as she covered my hand with hers. "But don't you see? By giving in to the kaligorven's demands, you allow this system of fear to become her future."

My hand dropped, and so did my tone. "I will do what I am required to do, Ellehra, even if it means killing one of your beloved solas. Your brother says they are more dangerous than—"

A mirthless laugh interrupted me. She pulled back and wrapped her arms around herself protectively. "You would listen to an arrogant nineteen-year-old instead of your own wife?" Thinly veiled anger tinged her voice.

I bit my bottom lip and exhaled through my nose. "He may be young, yes, but if you would just listen to him" —she clicked her tongue and rolled her eyes— "you would find he has some very interesting thoughts about the kaligorven that are worth considering."

Her lips parted as if to speak, but the sound stuck in her throat. Her eyes widened with mock levity. "I don't believe this. He's fooled you, too, like he fooled my mother."

My wife was no longer the only one struggling to contain her emotion. A growl rumbled somewhere inside my chest, and I turned my back to her.

Why can't she trust me to provide for her? I thought, but her voice, typically a sweet sound in my ears, assaulted them like the tip of a spear.

"They mean us harm, Téron. They want to break us over and over again until we are emptied of ourselves."

I wheeled around. "And what makes you think the solas will be any better? What makes you think that once they have grown in number, they will not do the exact same thing to us that the kaligorven have done?"

Her shoulders dropped lower, and she untangled her arms from around her body. They fell limp at her sides, her hands hidden by folds of golden linen. "*Faith*, Téron," she replied.

It hit me like a blow to the stomach. She walked across the room and picked up a book from the mantlepiece. My eyes trailed her, distracted by her loveliness even though my heart quaked within me. She flipped through the pages reverently, and her voice fell like an early rain. "I wish you could believe me when I tell you there are good intentions toward us in the midst of this darkness." She sighed, and I cringed. I knew what would come next. "I wish you could know the Highest as I do."

I erased the separation between us and grabbed the book from her hands, tossing it onto the table behind me. She looked up, alarm written across her face.

"It is time you set aside these old superstitions, Ellehra. It is time you start paying attention to the real world" —I motioned to the cozy room in which we stood— "and let Elyōn exist exactly where he has always been: far removed from us."

Her white face grew whiter still, and a tremble shivered across her lips. "You think I've chosen him over my family?"

"That is not what I said." I sighed, rubbing a palm roughly over my forehead. "I cannot believe you could actually think you are the only one in Utsanek to hold the answer to this riddle of darkness." When my hand dropped, she stared at me with hurt mounting behind her eyes.

"Do you think I'd actually risk it all—your reputation, our daughter's safety—because of a silly delusion, a child's fable?"

A horn blared outside, only a few blocks away from our home, and Ellehra started at the unnatural sound.

"Don't go," she whispered, her fingers finding my skin.

For a moment, I considered giving in to her plea. I considered loving my wife as I would myself. I considered laying down my pride for her sake. But the weight of the expectations of the Vale came crashing down on me when the horn sounded again. A primal need to purchase protection for her in the only way I knew how consumed me. I tore my arm from her grip and made a motion to grab my spear.

Ellehra groaned in exasperation, the sound setting my teeth on edge.

"Mada?" The trembling voice came from around the corner, halting me in my tracks. A bedraggled bundle of blankets and wispy hair stood in the passage to the front room, staring at me with eyes almost too wide for that little face.

When I risked a glance at Ellehra, her expression communicated both frustration and sadness. *Look what we've done.*

Ellehra sighed heavily and met our daughter on her level. "I'm sorry, little flower. Did we wake you?"

Amyrah's curls bounced as she shook her head. "I didn't yike da youd sound." She followed obediently as her mada took her hand and led her to a kitchen chair.

I watched as Ellehra poured her a glass of water and set a spiced tea biscuit in front of her on a clay plate. She bent over and whispered something in Amyrah's ear, and soft giggles followed.

Seeing my two girls like this made me want to stay. How could I possibly worry about the ténesomni while surrounded by so much light?

Slowly, as if afraid to frighten away the tender moment, I approached the two of them. Amyrah beamed up at me, a crumbly bit of biscuit stuck to her apple cheeks.

"Pada, wanna have a bite?" She held it as high as she could, and for a moment, all my shadowy fears vacated my mind. A smile claimed my lips, and I proceeded to nibble on her chunk of biscuit—and the fingers surrounding it—until she shrieked with delight.

In the middle of that purest moment of happiness, I hardly felt Ellehra's gentle hand between my shoulder blades. I hardly heard her whispered words.

"If you will not put a stop to this evil, I will."

When I straightened and turned around to question her, our back door swayed ominously in the obsidian night.

Amyrah weighed no more than a bundle of farrow in my arms as I set her down on the wooden landing.

"*Mercy*, Téron. What is this abou'?" An aged woman with silver-streaked hair opened the old door and stepped out of the dwelling.

I stamped my feet and strained my neck toward the forest edge of the city. "Ellehra—she—"

The horn sounded again, further away this time, and a filthy Atsunic word shot past my tongue. A warm hand gripped my wrist, and I turned to face the woman. Her eyes filled with concern as she placed her other hand on my daughter's head.

"*Shades and whispers.*" Orlagh let me go. "Is she all righ'?"

"I don't know. I don't . . . ." Another curse, another agitated shuffle of the feet.

Her mouth pressed into a thin line. "Go, then. Go to yer wife." She turned her attention to Amyrah, waiting calmly at her feet. "I'll take care of this sweet bairn." She gave a tender smile.

With little more than a dip of the chin, I took off down the street.

"Téron."

Myrzeth seemed to glow in the gloom. I raced up to him and slid to a stop.

"Have you seen her? Ellehra?" I panted, staring wildly into the trees.

"You need to calm down." The young man planted himself between me and the forest. I lurched to go around him, but he stepped deftly into my path. "The Hunt has already started. There's nothing you or I can do about that now."

Furious, I glared at him with all the intensity of a furnace. "I am calm," I said, eliciting an eyebrow raise from Myrzeth. "But she is out there, throwing herself right in their path. I can bring her back."

His cold hands clamped around my forearms. "Think about it, brother. The kaligorven are only interested in the solas. They will pay no attention to her. And I am sure the hunting party is too far ahead for her to interfere."

Beads of sweat dripped down my temples as I looked from the blackness to Myrzeth and back again. His firm hands rose and fell with the heaving breaths that shuddered my entire frame. I shook my head. "No . . . no, I have to go out there."

He jolted me until my eyes were his again. "What will it accomplish? Let the Hunt take place. Don't make a fool of yourself."

For a beat, I wondered if he was right. Ellehra was foolhardy. Maybe this would be the moment she learned to back down. But reason broke through.

"Who are you to counsel me?" I ripped my arms from his grip and took a step back. "You are just a boy—not yet a man."

Tentacles of ténesomni seemed to wrap around Myrzeth, and a darkness filled his irises. But he said nothing.

"I have let you fill my head with nonsense about the Shrouded, but I really should have been paying attention to my family."

As I stepped away from him and under the roof of the treetops, holding my lantern out ahead of me, I caught his subdued reply. "One day, you will know how wrong you were."

I would have turned around right there and given him a physical answer to his poison-tipped words, but that was when the screaming started.

I do not remember that wild plunge into the woods. I do not remember dropping the lantern or earning the gash that spilled blood all over the side of my face.

What I do recall is the surging of my heart inside my chest, so hard and fast that pain rushed through my body at each pump.

Somehow, I never questioned where to go. An irresistible force propelled me to the exact place where light died, where the tether between me and my beloved snapped.

What did I expect to find? A horde of dark beasts feasting on her flesh?

There was nothing there except her, incandescence seeping from the hundreds of punctures in her once-perfect skin.

Mangled body, twisted limbs. Yellow dress, torn to shreds. Her face oddly peaceful. I tried to press my hands to the gashes, my hands soaked in the blinding light that flowed from those mortal wounds.

The solas did this, I screamed inwardly, but only strange wails issued from my lips. *They rewarded her pure faith with a violent end.*

That wicked lie took root that day, sending me down a terrible path that would haunt me for years to come.

"It's been a long time since we've been able to have a chat."

Myrzeth's voice draws me back to the present. What should fill me with rage is a welcome interruption to my brutal recollections. I crack open my eyes and wince. The light from the lantern in his hands is painfully bright.

"I want nothing to do with you," I slur, once again attempting a sitting position. I inhale sharply as vertigo threatens to throw me down.

When my spine is safely propped up against the stones of the cell, I let out my breath and raise my eyes to the ghost-man.

A charming chuckle escapes him, a stark contrast to everything about the current circumstances. "I thought you might say that." Myrzeth crouches and balances on the balls of his feet. "But as my brother-in-law, it seemed only right to give you a second chance."

A jagged burst of wind that is supposed to be a laugh lurches from my lungs. "Why would I want that? You cost me the one thing I cared about."

Myrzeth tilts his head a little, and I shiver at how the shadows play with him—as if fond of him. "Really? Is that what you've told yourself all these years?"

I grit my teeth in a maniacal snarl. Spittle flies as the retort propels itself out of me. "Because of you, I trusted the Shrouded would not hurt her. Because you stopped me, I let her run into the forest. If it had not been for you, I may have been able to get to her before . . . before . . ." The words shrivel up in my throat, and my vehemence loses its power.

Lowering the lantern until it clangs resonantly on the ground, Myrzeth rests his palms on the floor and makes a patronizing click with his tongue and teeth. "Oh, Téron. I think you're wrong."

That makes me straighten. "What?"

His eyes narrow slightly, peering at me from between strands of colorless hair.

"Ellehra was not the only thing you cared for."

"What are you talking about?"

He stands, leaving the lantern on the ground as he brushes the grit off his hands. "I'm disappointed in you." He paces a few steps, then becomes still. "As your daughter would be, I think."

Shame washes over me. My head sags so my chin hits my chest. How could I forget Amyrah?

"Would you really endanger her, I wonder? You know the truth of the Shrouded now. They are jealous and eager to remove any who may pose a threat against them."

"She is no concern of yours," I growl.

"Oh, on the contrary. If she is at all like my deceased sister, she is of great concern."

Panic fills me. What does Myrzeth know of Amyrah, of her gift? I raise my eyes and follow his movements around the room.

"Amyrah could not be more unlike Ellehra," I lie, relieved when my voice does not warble.

Myrzeth spins on his heel and stares me down.

"I hope you are telling the truth."

"She respects the kaligorven's strength. After Ellehra's death, I made sure to raise her with that knowledge." The words burn.

It is silent for a while as Myrzeth inspects my features. His jaw shifts, and his brow knits, then smooths.

"Well." He stoops to pick up the lantern. "The one factor between her and safety," he says as he hands the light to me, strides to the door, and unlatches it, "is you."

He melts into the shadows, leaving the cell wide open behind him.

23

AMYRAH

I PAGE THROUGH AN OLD BOOK, its musty scent rising to greet me. The thing has sat on the mantel in my house for three days, and it has taken me this long to find the courage to crack it open. Tress put it into my hands the morning I discovered her secret community, making me promise to bring it back someday soon—and find her for a visit when I do. I didn't want to accept it, but she insisted.

At first, I could only look at it with apprehension. What would I find in there about my gift—and what if it has the power to change everything?

Now, it is a timely diversion from the fears that have grown within my heart since my father went missing.

I have heard nothing of him, and none of my inquiries have proved fruitful. Orlagh has resumed her market baking, and she assured me that if his absence had anything to do with Dravek or his men, they would be boasting of it. The gossip would have made it to her ears by now.

This knowledge does nothing to ease my troubles. If nothing has happened to him, where is he? Have my fitful words caused him to shut me out forever?

He wouldn't abandon me like this, would he?

Swallowing down my fears before they consume me, I make my eyes focus on the book. The cover is made from a rich, burgundy leather. A single Atsunic phrase is scrawled across the front. *Avis ténesomni luvem.* After darkness, light.

The book feels heavier than it should in my hands, and I press my fingers into the soft cowskin.

It is an ancient collection of verses I don't understand. They speak of beauties and sights that thrill my soul but conjure confusing images in my mind—things I have only seen in my dreams. Within these fragile pages unfamiliar lights blaze, and there are references to a time when darkness did not have dominion at all.

I am not sure how to even fathom such a thing.

The sound of the waves tucks me into the rocky alcove around my mother's grave. My breaths are freed to move through me, slowly and evenly. No one can see or hear me here. The lantern glows at my feet, and I curl myself around the precious book.

My hands go still when familiar words stare at me from the page. My heartbeat flutters in my chest.

"Shaluth Cantu," I whisper. Salvation Song. My eyes travel over the lines as the inborn tune plucks at my heart.

> *My eyes have seen a glim'ring beam*
> *Piercing through doomed bracken's core,*

And although it has made my heart to hope,
I fear I shall see it no more.

Thus grows the ever dark'ning gloom
From the glen to the ne'er ending moor.
And although Light has filled me with wealth unknown,
I fear it has left thee poor.

I pause.

How could light ever make someone poor? Perhaps for those who have fought for darkness, light is a terrifying thing.

The next section sweeps through my mind.

Long past, on that ill-fated night,
When the hearts of men grew weak,
There came by the woods a Shrouded beast,
Of which we now do not speak.

And on that day no spear was raised;
The strong did not shelter the meek.
Then all the brilliant goodness fled,
And of that light we now do not speak.

Could it really be true that these beasts are not a natural part of the Vale at all?

I graze the words. If more valefolk knew this song, maybe we could find a way to fight the kaligorven. Maybe it would give them the courage to stand.

Lo, there will be a coming day
When bird, beast, man shall see,
For all the darkness will fade away
And all of the Vale will be free.

Thus grows the ever bright'ning day,
From the fields to the ne'er ending sea,
And the Light of Life will shine on all,
For rich and whole we shall be.

I can hardly breathe as I come to the end of the song. It speaks of—no, *promises*—a day of freedom. Could such a thing ever come to pass? Can I find the faith to believe it?

But my soul screams for a more pressing question to be answered. Why do I know these words?

My eyes travel to the gravestone.

Father made it himself, even though his skills lie more in building with stone rather than carving it. I remember him going to great pains to find a secluded spot, clearing away debris and rocky boulders. The memorial was completed years after her passing.

At first, it bothered me that he chose to commemorate her here, so far from the other graves in Utsanek. But now that I no longer depend on him to chaperone me around the Vale, I'm thankful for the secrecy and the solitude of this place. It is mine.

I've never asked him why he doesn't visit it anymore.

The thread of my thoughts leads me right back to my mother. Did she teach me this song? Did she take care to sing it with me until I knew every word, every note by the age of four? I do not know. If it was her, why can I sing every verse of this song but not remember her voice?

The longing for her is a gnawing pang of hunger that can never be satisfied. Oh, how I wish she was with me now. Would she be able to help me understand this gift? Or maybe we would discover its meaning together.

The knot of pain tightens within my core. I set the book on the stony ground and rub my arms. Pressure builds behind my eyes. When I blink, tears spill down my face.

I don't understand any of this. Why this gift, why now? How can it be of any use? Maybe in the hands of someone more powerful, or someone who has the whole of Utsanek on his side, it would be. But who am I? A motherless girl with a broken father.

A strangled sob reverberates around the dell. I bury my head in my hands, and my shoulders shake.

I have never felt so alone.

Elyōn, my inner being moans, *where are you?*

Like a soft caress, the wind passes over my brow. The voice of Orlagh flits through my mind.

I am more and more convinced tha' he's more'n just a story mothers whisper to their bairns as they fall asleep. He's keepin' all things together, an' he's workin' it all according to his purpose.

How can she be so sure? What evidence can there be in the middle of this unending night? It feels like my world is falling apart, like the true day will never come.

There is no one I trust more in this world than Orlagh, but I don't know if I can take her words and make them my own.

The pages flap in the cool breeze. An abrasive sound escapes me as I suck back the fluids issuing from my sinuses. I lean forward and still the papers with my fingertips. My lips part as my eyes fall on a familiar image. I pull in a sudden breath.

An eight-pointed shape, the rays alternating in length, with long ones at the top and bottom—identical to the pendant of the necklace.

I run my fingers greedily across the verse on the opposite page.

> *At the dawn of the world's birth,*
> *the fire lights were ignited;*
> *An unquenchable flock without number,*
> *piercing the black cloak of the sky.*
>
> *They shone through the ages,*
> *a lasting gift from the Highest.*
> *The crystalline constellations rested*
> *when the Burning Star drew nigh.*

I roll the word 'dawn' across my tongue like an unfamiliar fruit, uncertain whether I should sink my teeth in. But it tastes sweet there, like new beginnings and life. 'Fire lights' piercing the sky, however, leaves me perplexed. My lungs deflate. Is this supposed to make sense? I read the rest of the poem again and again, and each time, I am more confused. I glance upward, and there is only inky blackness.

My eyes land on the illustration's Atsunic description and translation —*Istilatum Ideralis: Burning Star*—and what must be the earliest memory I possess ignites in my mind's eye.

I felt scared for some reason, alone in my bed and awoken by a loud noise. The blankets I wrapped around myself were heavy, and I tripped on them as I walked down the hallway. My parents were talking loudly. Their voices made me want to cry.

Mada found me and made all the yucky feelings leave. She gave me a big cup, and I squeezed it tight so I wouldn't drop it.

When she bent over, her soft hair tickled my cheek. She whispered in my ear, and it made me giggle.

"I'm so glad the Highest gave me my little star girl."

Star girl.

My hand travels to where my collar bones line up, only to find the necklace not there. I close my eyes and let out a sigh.

Right. It is now in the possession of a scared boy with curious green eyes.

I could never shake the image of that other poor, hungry scavenger my father and I met in the overturned market the day Sola Vinari began again. Crossing paths with a second needy child was like a chance to reach out and make something right, even though I had nothing to offer but the jewel from my neck.

Although I am frustrated that I no longer have it to compare to the image, I can't make myself regret the act of generosity.

Besides, there's something more important staring me right in the face.

Istilatum ideralis is the term the girl at the market booth used to identify the pendant's shape. This book has translated the Atsunic word as "star"—not that it means anything more to me. But it cannot be a coincidence that, in one of the few memories I have of my mother, I recall her coining me "star girl" as clearly as if she was whispering it into my ear at this very moment.

A gust of wind shakes the treetops, causing a commotion of wings and melodic chirping to fill the skies.

I don't grasp how all this links together, but the longer I think about it, the more my tumultuous heart pants for the peace that understanding brings.

Didn't the merchant girl mention something about things that lay outside the Vale? It struck me as an odd phrase that day, thrown into even bolder relief when she seemed mortified that such a thing had escaped her tongue.

Perhaps it wasn't chance that made the pendant fall, that led my hand to pick it up. A chill spreads down my arms and legs. Perhaps Elyōn really is working things together for a purpose I could never even imagine.

A peace overwhelms my heart, however brief. But enough to assure me none of this is a coincidence.

Pushing myself up and brushing away dust from my dress and tears from my face, I grab the book and lantern and slip out of that place of security.

I need to find the girl from the marketplace.

"How dare yeh!"

In the middle of a crowded market, painfully bright with the presence of new sola brossa, that single voice is all I hear. My fingers go numb when I recognize who it belongs to.

Jeering laughter rings out, and I force my way between a multitude of shoulders. I pull up short and raise a hand to my mouth.

Orlagh kneels on the unforgiving cobbles, surrounded by her beautiful loaves and rolls. The time-worn market stall lies on its side behind her, damaged beyond repair. I catch sight of her face twisted with pain. But no tears stain it.

For a moment, I stare, uncomprehending. I see the expressions of the young men surrounding her. They are animated with wicked glee as they watch her scramble, as they grab buns and whip them at her. I recognize one of the brutes, although I can't place him.

Goaded by his friends, he whoops and lunges forward, stomping on a loaf and crushing the poor woman's fingers beneath his boot. She yelps in pain, eliciting a fresh wave of wicked cackles from the onlookers.

As if in slow motion, I see the same idiot pick up a wooden cutting board and raise it above his head. It takes a moment for comprehension to click into place, and white-hot rage fills me.

"*Stop*," I scream, throwing myself between my friend and her attacker. As I face him with fire in my eyes, he lets the board fall.

Somewhere within me, there must be a lioness. I feel her tearing through my core, giving fierce power to my words.

"You pathetic cowards. What gives you the right to attack an elderly woman in the street?"

The sick smile on the young man's face falters as I stare him down. He's tall and weaselly, and I have encountered him before. This time, he is not inebriated.

"What's the matter, Flip?" One of his friends snickers behind him. "Are you scared of a little girl?"

My cheeks grow warm, but I will not be intimidated. Balling my shaking fists at my sides, I do not break eye contact with Flip.

Flip glances at his companions, and when he turns back to me, all his mirth has melted away. "Get out of my way, little dog."

"Not until you promise you'll leave this poor woman alone." My teeth grind against each other as I try to contain my fury.

Flip's eyes narrow, and he takes a menacing step forward. I do not shrink back.

"Do you know who she is?" Flip jabs one finger toward Orlagh.

The kindest woman in the Vale, I think.

He sniffs derisively. "She's one of the fidrélas. She's a myth-worshipper, a filthy smear on the backside of Utsanek."

Cackles ripple outward at his words—from more than just his simpering troop. A satisfied smirk slants his lips.

Unease grows within me, but I refuse to acknowledge it.

"I'm surprised anything could be filthier than that mouth of yours," I say, keeping my lips tight so they do not tremble.

The laughter dies, and his friends exchange affronted looks. One of them gives Flip a nudge from behind, and he moves in closer still.

"You'd better watch it. You kind of sound like that old hag. Maybe you're one of them too." Eyes the hue of rotting squash stare down at me, daring me to retaliate.

I hold my lantern below my chin. I'm sure it is much too bright in the square to notice the anomaly surrounding me, but I can't help feeling self-conscious.

"Amyrah . . ." Orlagh's soft voice breaks the tension of the moment. I gasp like I have forgotten how to breathe and crouch beside her. "Amyrah, yeh don't need to be here. I can manage by mysel'."

Tears prick at the corners of my eyes as I pull her off her knees and lean her into my side. She trembles all over, clutching her bruised hand in the other. My heart breaks.

"Whatever you think of her, there is no reason for this despicable treatment." I turn my eyes on the brood again, hoping my words will make some impact.

Instead, Flip looks about to burst out in laughter. He crosses his arms and raises his chin. Under the glaring light of the bones, his face appears skeletal. "Myrzeth would disagree with you," he says with a shrug.

Myrzeth? There is something familiar about the name, but I can't place it.

I focus instead on helping Orlagh up. She's trying to act like there has been no harm done, but the way she grimaces and gasps when she tries to stand tells a different story. Once she's found her feet, she clings to me the way I clung to her as a small child.

"What are you talking about?" The continual burn of my indignation is starting to take its toll. But I need to be strong for Orlagh, so I force myself to stand a little straighter.

"Haven't you heard? Myrzeth is making some changes around here." He struts around us, and I wonder if he's ever had so much attention in his whole life. "He's given permission to make trouble for everyone who resists the Shrouded."

"Is that so?" I ask, unable to keep the sarcasm from my voice. I should be more careful, but he is a ridiculous peacock.

He doesn't seem to notice and turns away from me for a few steps. "Yup. So, I guess you could say me and the boys are doing our neighborly duty." He spins around, and a maniacal expression claims his features. "What do you say we make this a two-for-one, boys?"

They shout and move in like jackals.

I turn to Orlagh and cringe, not entirely because I'm afraid, but because I can't believe these fools are so seduced by this corrupt sense of power. They aren't even questioning the morality of their actions.

"I think you've made your point," says a low voice, slicing through the noise.

I look up. Belwyn shields the two of us from the onslaught. Relief, and something *different,* wash over me.

Flip's voice sounds muted from the other side of him. "Come on, Bel. We're just having a bit of fun. Let us take a few shots."

Flip yelps as Belwyn grabs his wrist and forces him to his knees.

"Alright, *alright.*"

Belwyn releases him. "Get out of here," he growls.

I shift so I can see around Belwyn's broad-shouldered frame.

"You used to know how to have a good time." Flip cradles his wrist and scowls. "What happened to you?"

Almost inaudibly, Belwyn replies, "More than you can possibly understand."

With that, it's over. No one offers one more word in protest. The assailants slither back into the crowd, and the marketplace resumes business as usual.

Orlagh pats my arm, and I release her.

"Thank yeh, child," she wheezes into my ear and squeezes me painfully tight. "Yer ma would be proud of yeh." Without a glance at her devastated merchant's stall, she limps toward the crowd where many hands and several aged friends receive her.

As I stand in the middle of the carnage, an overwhelming feeling of loneliness overtakes me. My eyes travel from the ruined loaves and find Belwyn's warm irises fixed on me.

Without questioning what I'm doing, I walk into his empty arms.

This . . . this is absurd. A moment to which I never gave a single thought. But here it is. And now I know every fiber of my being has been craving it since the moment I met him.

Slowly, cautiously, his arms wrap around me, pulling me into his embrace. I start to think about my hands. What do I do with them? Should I hug him in return? The idea makes my insides twist. I held his hand before, but that was different. I didn't have to think about it. It felt right in the moment. But I don't know what's expected of me, or what I expect of myself. Relenting, I let them rest, limp and awkward at my sides.

I press my cheek to his chest and suck in a shaky breath. One of his hands slides to rest between my shoulder blades, and the other presses into the middle of my back.

A shiver spreads through me from the epicenter of his touch, and I feel him shaking too. Is it cold? Was I cold? I don't remember. I don't know anything anymore, except the feeling of safety, the smell of leather, and the sound of his heart beating much faster than it should be.

Too soon, the moment passes. His hands slide down my arms, find my hands. They slip between my fingers and pull me in a daze through boisterous people I don't hear and sights I can't see.

When the light and commotion has been fully exchanged for the darkness and stillness of the side streets, I find the courage to look at him.

I notice things now that I would not have dared before. How his hair is longer and wavier at the front. How the gold ring in his nose mimics the faint ring of gold around his pupils. How when his eyes find mine, it's hard to breathe.

"Amyrah." Belwyn faces me and takes hold of my arms. His fingers leave tingling impressions. "You should be careful."

His severity is a gust of icy wind. I blink several times and try to make my mind focus on anything other than the space between us.

"Wha—"

His hands tighten, and he stoops a bit lower to make sure he has my attention. "I believe that because of your—your *ability*—you may be in danger."

I know this, but hearing it from his mouth makes it sink in. My eyes probe his olive skin, fixate on the crease between his brows.

Why does this matter to me now when it didn't before?

He grips me tighter still, and my eyes widen. "I'm afraid that soon you won't be able to hide this." He glances up at the border between ténesomni and my inner light.

A weight lurches in my heart, like an anchor has been tossed over its edge, pulling it down into the depths of my being.

He cares for me, I think. And it wakes me up, snaps me to the thing that needs answering more than the mystery of my gift.

My hands find his for a change, and I clutch them between us. "Belwyn, I need you to help me."

His eyebrows, which hitched upward when I touched him, fall back and shadow his eyes. "Of course," he says.

I swallow, wishing this moment could last, wishing we were anywhere but here, any time but now.

"I need you to help me find my father."

Confusion flits over his features, but after considering me for a moment, he nods almost imperceptibly. I bite my lip, then continue.

"Because I think he might be in even more danger than me."

24

BELWYN

HOW DO I SEARCH for a man I've never met?

Amyrah came to me. She sought *me*. I don't know what prompted her to do it. Maybe she didn't mean to—maybe it was a primal reflex for comfort. But my heart tells me otherwise. When she caught my eyes, I thought I saw something deeper than that. It was more like . . . yearning.

And when she came to me, when she filled more than the void between my arms, I was supposed to be the strong one. For her. Yet, it felt like I had been the one on the cusp of danger.

The girl I haven't been able to stop thinking about for weeks came to me. And though my thoughts about my own father are complicated, I see how earnestly she loves hers. Her only family. And she trusts me.

I can't let her down.

There's one obvious solution, but knowing I will have to face my father again to attain it makes my skin crawl.

I can hear the shouting blocks before I've made it home.

"Who does he think he is?"

A large crash adds speed to my steps.

"Where did he come from? What gives him the right to challenge me like this?"

When I'm about to turn the knob of the front door, my intestines twist. I will be sick. I almost turn back right there but imagining my mother or brothers on the other side of that door prevents me.

Upon entering, I find my father tearing up the room in a fit of fury. A small table lies in splinters against the far wall.

My eyes dart from side to side, and I exhale. My brothers are nowhere to be seen, and Mother sits calmly in a chair pulled close to the fire, a blanket hemming her in. A mug issues swirls of steam as she cups it between her thin fingers. It is the best she's looked in a long time.

Who got those things for her?

The latch snaps shut, and Father spins to face me, his tirade cut short. I avoid his eyes, looking instead at his hands. They have traces of dirt in the crevices.

When I meet his gaze, a wild look dominates his eyes. My heart lurches hard in my chest, and I swallow to keep it from escaping through my throat.

"Where have you been?" he asks, cracking his knuckles out of habit. It makes me cringe.

I regret the reaction when he notices and strides toward me. His hissed words increase in volume. "I asked you where you've been."

Fighting to appear unruffled, I slip off my jacket and hang it behind the door. "Just at the market."

Father's face twists. "So, you've become one of Myrzeth's pupils too."

I don't like where he has me, with my back to a wall. I like the tone of his words even less.

With an approximation of calm, I shoulder past him, sit on the edge of a footstool, and make a show of rewrapping the cords around my leather boots. His breath creeps down my neck, but I resist the urge to shrug away from him.

"No," I answer, taking my time fiddling with my footwear. "I don't care for him."

He snorts and moves off. I pinch my eyes closed for a beat and steady myself.

"I spent an entire day and night chasing down a sola with a bunch of idiots who wouldn't know how to take out a baby rabbit." A curse slips between his lips. He peels the bearskin vest off his tunic and throws it on the couch. "We thought we caught a glimpse of it multiple times, but every time we got close, it vanished."

That explains his sour mood and unkempt appearance.

My mother flinches when he flops onto the couch. I watch her closely, waiting for the glazed look to return, for her to become an empty shell. Instead, her hands curl around the mug, and she raises it to her lips. Her eyelids close as she breathes in the aroma and warmth. She seems to be doing better than she has in a while.

"And when we got back to Utsanek empty handed, that meddler had the gall to confront me in front of my own men." The fingers of his left hand drum the couch armrest with ferocity.

I peel my eyes from the anomaly of my mother and focus on my father's words. "What?"

His face distorts even more than before, like something putrid hovers right under his nostrils.

"*Myrzeth*." He curses again, causing Mother to turn her face quickly to the fire. "That idiotic reptile. He invoked the rite of Privotus Vimorteth against me."

I mentally flip through all the Atsunic lessons I endured over the years, trying to place the phrase. I wait for him to explain. Instead, he bends forward and snatches a new sola bone from the table.

More and more bone fragments have been making their way into our house now that they have been distributed around Utsanek. Perks of being the Foremost family.

He stares at it in his palm for a while, though I don't see how he can stand it. The shard is blinding, more than bright enough to illuminate this entire room. With calm purpose, he wraps both hands around it and snaps it in half with a forceful jerk.

"He would steal the rule of the Vale right out from under my nose."

And then it makes sense. Myrzeth has challenged my father to the ritualistic competition for Foremost.

Inactivity rarely suits my father, but it's even more egregious to him when he feels his control slipping. After holding the whole room hostage in his brooding silence, he stands and moves to leave. I don't think about trying to prevent him, even though I haven't been able to question him about Amyrah's father yet—the thing I came home to do. But it's best to get out of his way when he is like this.

The front door slams behind him, and there is air in the atmosphere again.

I approach my mother and lay a hand on her shoulder. She surprises me by resting hers on top of it. No words pass between us, and she doesn't look up. But we communicate, nonetheless.

A clatter from the back of the house draws my attention.

I stop short in the doorway to the kitchen, trying to understand what I see.

Korvin and Shemai bend over a large pot, jostling each other as they drop in diced onions and carrots.

"What are you doing?"

Korvin raises his eyes from his task, and his cheeks blush a shade of pink. "I-I thought Mother might like some—some soup," he says, jolting when Shemai tosses two whole carrots in with a splash.

"*Shem*," he scolds. My youngest brother giggles like a lunatic and grabs a long spoon to retrieve them from the pot. Korvin wipes his brow with the back of a hand and looks back at me.

"Do you want help?" I browse the ingredients lined up carefully on the table. The onions, carrots, and garlic are from our root cellar, but the boys have also managed to procure a bundle of delicate herbs and a whole plucked chicken, cleaned and ready for cooking.

I pinch a tiny leaf between my fingers and raise my hand to breathe in the fragrance. My eyebrows raise when the spiced scent matches perfectly with the meal they have planned. "This looks amazing. You did this all on your own?"

Shemai hops off his stool and pulls a stained paper from under a pile of carrot peelings. "We found this old recipe in one of Mother's cupboards. Korvin spent all morning gathering the stuff."

I take the recipe from his hand, and he scampers back to Korvin's side. *Grandmada's Everything's Alright Soup* is penned in fading letters across the top of the page. Memories of the caring and zany matriarch flip through my mind. A wistful smile creeps across my lips, and the warm kitchen air swells around me like an embrace.

My focus flicks toward my brothers. Korvin hands Shemai a mortar and pestle, and the latter gets to work grinding dried peppercorns into a gritty powder.

"I think we've got this under control," Korvin says, wiping his hands on a kitchen towel.

I watch him for some time, wondering when the shift out of boyhood began. Only a day ago, he was catching frogs—but that was my idea, not his.

The tea in Mother's hand must have been his initiative. For a moment, it irks me that all my efforts to draw her out have not been received, but the feeling passes quickly. Korvin is deeply thoughtful and quietly observant. Nothing, it would seem, slips past his notice. His gentle, unassuming manner and intuitive gift for caring is probably exactly what Mother needs.

It is good there's someone in this house who can lessen her sorrow.

"Korvin," I say, drawing closer and resting my elbows on the counter. "Have you heard Father talking about a man named Téron? You've been home more than I have lately."

He looks up from the herbs in his hands, patiently pulling leaves off one by one. "Father talks about a lot of people."

I nod. He is a calculated man, and when acting the role of Foremost, he chooses his words very carefully. But within these walls, where he knows none of his sons would dare cross him, he lets his grievances fly.

"You may have heard him mention a person who risked the Hunt," I prompt.

A shadow of misgiving shivers over his features, but he masks it quickly and sends Shemai to fill a bucket with water from the pump in our back garden. Once the grumbling has faded from earshot, Korvin turns back to me.

"He was shouting about something before you got here. Something about the new guy . . ."

"Myrzeth?" I nod. "Father told me he's challenged him for his position."

Korvin shakes his head. "No, it was more than that. He wasn't pleased that he had released someone from the Cellar while the Hunt took place."

Utsanek doesn't have a dedicated prison, but one place has grown to a legendary status among young miscreants—the place mothers threaten to send their children when they misbehave. No one knows where it is, but with the high quantity of old stone buildings in this city, it could be anywhere. To the sons of the Foremost, the Cellar isn't just a myth.

My brows lower as I ponder this. "Well, couldn't that have been anyone?"

The sound of water splashing percussively drifts in through the open kitchen window. Korvin lowers the raw chicken into the pot.

"Make sure you wash your hands," I remind him. He crosses over to the water basin and begins scrubbing his palms with a cake of soap, and again I am struck with what a special soul he is. Not many boys of twelve would endure an older brother giving them directions.

He shakes off the excess water. "No, I don't think so. I heard Father say he wanted to make an example of him, because of what he did, and what his wife had done in the Vale before."

His wife.

I am almost entirely sure Korvin is right. He spoke of Amyrah's pada. It's something. At the very least, I can tell her he isn't being held anywhere.

A sigh issues from my chest, a welcome release of pressure. "Thanks, brother."

I swing open the back door and pause as Shemai sidles into the room, huffing under the weight of the sloshing bucket. I turn back to watch Korvin help him heft it up and dump its contents into the pot.

Yes, they squabble from time to time, but they are both a marvel. Products of darkness, brought up in adversity, children of a tyrant behind closed doors. And yet, somehow untainted by it all. My family.

Korvin catches me watching him, and I avert my eyes. As I duck out the door, his gentle voice slows me.

"I like it when you call me that," he says. I look over my shoulder, and he seems embarrassed.

"Call you what?"

A subtle smile pulls at his lips. "Brother."

25

WEHNA

THE CART BOUNCES ACROSS the uneven cobbles behind me. I spin around and throw out my hands to steady it, but I am not fast enough. It escapes my reach and overturns, spilling all the drawers of necklaces, bracelets, and earrings everywhere. The wares I failed to sell in the market today—our last means of survival—are all over the street. But I am too numb to react.

Forcing myself to action, I grit my teeth and scramble to retrieve them before they get trampled by valefolk.

"Let me help, Wehna."

"Wait—"

Arvo dashes after a ring that bounced across the street before I can stop him, right into the path of two large oxen being driven mercilessly by a sneer-faced man.

The scene slows strangely as I envision his tiny body being trampled by the huge animals. Even if I could unglue myself from the ground, I wouldn't have enough time to get to him. A scream tears through me, cuts my vocal cords to shreds.

At the last moment, a strong hand grabs him by the scruff of his shirt and hauls him to the side. Arvo yelps as he is plucked out of harm's way. The livestock and the wagon rumble by, and I lay a hand to my heart and breathe a prayer of thanks to Elyōn.

Arvo's rescuer crouches down in front of him, hands firmly clamped around his forearms. My heart, which is already racing, picks up pace. But when the man looks my way, I want to cry with relief. It's my father's friend, Bryn.

With a pat to his back, Arvo scurries across the street. I stand in time for him to throw himself into my side.

"Hey, you're alright," I say when I feel him shaking.

He says nothing, choosing to bury his face in the folds of my dress instead.

Bryn crosses over to our side and inspects our fallen cart. "Nothing appears to be broken," he says as he rights it.

I shake my head, brushing my hair away from my face. "Thank you." I don't mean to whisper the words.

When he merely pauses to throw me a smile before setting to work gathering the jewelry, I wake up.

"Here." I lead Arvo to a wobbly stool outside a bustling tavern—not my first choice, but I need to keep him close and stationary. "You sit here while I clean this up. Then we'll go home and have a drop of honey with the cakes I made for dinner. Deal?" I gently press a finger to his button nose.

He sniffs and runs his hand under it. "Deal."

I straighten and return to the task. Bryn has already begun placing the items in the narrow drawers that line the merchant side of the booth. Pada's clever craftsmanship.

"Thank you," I murmur, stooping to snag a long necklace with a glowing soapstone pendant in the shape of a rosebud—one of Mada's more delicate carvings.

"These are really remarkable." Bryn hands me a pair of identical earrings, watching me as I deposit them in the appropriate drawer. "How did your parents manage to make them shine like that?"

My eyes dart to him for a few seconds, and his kindness makes me feel filthy. Every time, this lie gets more difficult to tell. The words tumble past my lips.

"They use bolétis. Many more varieties can be found in the forest if you know where to look ."

A curious expression crosses his face—a half-smile and a raised eyebrow. I can't interpret it. "Is that so?"

It almost sounds like he finds something amusing.

I nod and grab another bracelet—this one with simple spherical beads. Their light is barely visible anymore. It was already a weak thing, but now that Utsanek is lit with shards of sola brossa in every major place, they seem almost worthless. Probably why no one wants to buy them anymore.

He goes back to gathering the jewelry, and I am glad I'm no longer his object of interest.

I look over my shoulder and find Arvo still on his stool, pressing his nose up to the window of the tavern.

"You've had no word from your parents, I take it."

Bryn's deep voice draws me back. A heaviness tugs at my heart, and I bite my cheek to remain in control.

"No."

They left in a hurry that night, promising Arvo they'd be back as soon as they could. He believed them—they had done it before countless times. But he didn't know about the kaligorven, about how they were on the prowl again. He had no reason to doubt their ability to keep themselves safe.

Just once, I wished they would have bothered to make such promises to me. They always thought I didn't need them. For one moment more, I wished they would have treated me as the needy child and not the competent seventeen-year-old. Did they know how hard it was to see them go, again and again, whether for a good cause or not? Did they realize how quickly the responsibility drained me, or how much more difficult I found it to battle my incessant fears when they weren't there? I wished they could've seen how I needed them as much as the countless hurting souls they ministered to without fail.

Bryn is silent for a while as I organize the items into drawers, trapped in a labyrinth of thought. People mill all around us, moving from one point of business to another, conversing and getting worked up about things that don't matter. They are heedless of the two statues in the middle of the commotion, or of how pointless all their strivings really are.

"Wehna—"

I raise my head and fix the most paradoxical smile I can manage. "They always said not to hold too tightly to this world." My voice quavers strangely through the last two words. I swallow. "I guess they are putting their faith into practice."

He shuts his mouth, a frown throwing his deep-set eyes into even further shadow. "I'm sure they wouldn't have left you if they thought there was any chance they would not be coming back."

Closing the final drawer, I look back at him reluctantly, not even able to pretend to smile anymore. "I guess we can't know, can we?" My breaths grow shallow, and the panic I've worked hard to mask over the last few weeks rises to the surface. If Bryn were to offer words of comfort right at this moment, I'm certain I would lose every last ounce of self-control.

"Whot ye got there, love?" A hunched, beggarly woman walks up to my cart and invades my personal space, mercifully sparing me from a complete emotional breakdown.

The odor surrounding her assaults my senses, and it is almost impossible to keep from reacting. "Ye peddlin' some more baubles?" she asks in her abrasive tone, one wide eye fixed determinedly on me.

Remembering that I would like to earn a bit of arlum if I can, I pull open some of the drawers. "Yes. Please, look."

Without hesitating, she snatches a bracelet and holds it high, fingering the carved beads. They are in the shape of leaves. Bryn lifts a hand and opens his mouth like he is concerned she's going to make off with it, but I give him a subtle shake of the head.

"Do you like that one?" I ask instead, taking a small step back so I don't make her feel like I'm hovering. And to hopefully put myself in the path of a breath of fresh air.

"Oh, it's love-a-ly. Just a *love-a-ly*," she croons. "Gots me a matching piece, I do." She digs into the front of her stained frock and pulls out a long necklace.

My jaw drops. The green beads are identical to the one on the bracelet.

"Where did you get that?" I ask, now doubting my first inclination to trust the woman.

She smiles, revealing a mouth full of rotting teeth. "Well, it was ye who gave it to me, wasn't it?"

I reach for the bracelet, and she pulls it back beside her ear and scowls.

"Now, now, dearie, don' ye say ye be forgettin'."

Heat climbs up the back of my neck. "I don't remember because I didn't do it." In my peripheries, I see Bryn step closer.

"Perhaps you are mistaken, ma'am," he says.

She tightens her fist around the bracelet and brings it under her chin. "I ain't crazy, if that what ye be thinkin'."

"No one said that." Bryn holds a palm out to ease her.

"I remember ye and that husband of yers." She fixes her eyes on me again. "Ye were always kind to me. Whot happened to him, I wonder?"

I think I understand.

"Could you possibly be thinking of my mother?" I ignore the way my throat wrings at the mention of her.

Her eyes narrow, and she comes far too close to search my face. I hold my breath.

"Whot, it weren't ye tha' brought me food when I was nigh to death?" Confusion clouds her already clouded eyes. "It weren't ye tha' pressed this jewel in me hand?"

I shake my head slowly, chewing on my bottom lip.

She gives an abrasive sniff, then puffs out a stale breath. "Nah, it weren't ye."

I smile weakly, relieved her memory is returning.

"It weren't ye I seen lyin' side by side on the road with a man. It weren't ye I seen with the life drained right out of ye."

I go cold from the roots of my hair to the tips of my toes and slump to the side. Firm arms hold me upright.

"Wha . . . what did you say?" I whisper.

But she shakes her head over and over again, thrusting the bracelet into my face. I take it from her.

"It weren't ye. It weren't ye . . ." She backs away, muttering, her eyes boring into my soul until the bustle of the street obscures her.

It's as if heavy chains have wrapped around my chest, dragging me into the earth, squeezing the air out of my lungs. Bryn fights to keep me upright.

"Steady, Wehna. She doesn't know what she's talking about."

But she does, my mind responds. *She knows exactly what she's talking about.*

Because in my heart, I know it too.

My parents are dead.

"Arvo," I croak, my throat as dry as mortar. I swallow and try again, eyes still fixed on the place where the woman disappeared. "Arvo, let's go."

I feel myself push against Bryn's firm chest, feel his hands release their grip on my arms. His voice sounds distant, counseling me to pay no attention to her. I think. He relents when I lurch away from him.

"*Arvo.*"

Forcing my eyes to register my surroundings, I spin toward the tavern, with its warm light leaking through greasy windowpanes. And its empty stool out front.

I gasp, something that barely clung to life expiring within my heart.

The street pitches toward me.

I've lost him again.

26
TÉRON

BROWN ALE SLOSHES over the side of the mug and dribbles down my fingers. I take a swallow. The bitter liquid churns my stomach. Food would be a better choice right now, but I have not been one for good decisions lately.

Useless. Everything about me screams the word. I raise the flagon to my lips, but the sour smell makes me feel like vomiting. With a loud crack, I bring it to the counter. A dry laugh wheezes from my lungs. I cannot even drown my sorrows properly. What a pathetic fool I am.

"If you break that, it'll go on yer tab," the taverner warns before moving to another customer. I stare at my thumbs as they try to dig themselves into the earthenware.

All those years of mourning for Ellehra were miserable. I thought a man could not get lower, but I was wrong. Because in all my pain, I still had a purpose. I had a little girl who needed me. My hands found relief in their work, and something inside still drove me to existence—not the life I had wanted, but one I could at least find a reason to keep living. And whether hatred or the brightness of my daughter motivated me, I do not know. But I did keep going.

I fail to see the reason for it all now. My job has been given to someone who will show up each day, I don't doubt. The plan I made for vengeance shriveled up the moment I found out it had always been focused on the wrong target.

And now my daughter has seen all my inadequacies—every last hateful quality of who I am—on full display. She has grown past her need for me.

Worst of all, I am a danger to her.

She is better off without me.

I squeeze my eyes shut and tighten my hands around the mug so much it could snap. I want it to crumble.

"Can I sit with you?"

The little voice is so out of place in this den of inebriates that I think I must have imagined it. I let go of the mug and look around.

A boy heaves himself up onto the stool next to me. He does not look to be more than four or five. I am so thrown off at the sight of him that I just stare.

"Is there anything to eat?" he asks. I forget for a moment who or where I am.

"Hello there," I say, mildly bemused. I beckon the taverner over. He looks as confused by my tiny companion. "Could we have some bread?"

He recovers and disappears through a doorway at the back of the room for a moment before returning with a small loaf.

"I'm 'fraid it isn't fresh," he says as he hands it over.

I thank him before other patrons call him away.

"Here you go." I split the loaf in two and hand the boy the larger portion.

He takes it without hesitation and munches on it thoughtfully for a while. Not sure what else to do, I take a bite as well. It is so dry, it almost chokes me. I have to drink a mouthful of ale to get it down, but the boy does not seem to mind how stale it is. He continues to chew, his feet swinging from the tall stool as if this is a perfectly reasonable place for a five-year-old to be.

"Do you mind me asking what you are doing here?"

He looks at me with bright-green eyes, odd against his dark skin tone and hair. "I'm eating some bread," he mumbles through a mouthful, and I spot a mischievous lift to his dimpled cheek.

Despite myself, I smile. "And are you alone?"

He swallows with effort and shakes his head. "Wehna's outside."

I don't know who Wehna is, but I am glad, at least, to hear he has someone with him. Although I am not sure I trust her if she lets him wander into a place like this.

The boy continues to eat until he has consumed every crumb. I offer him mine, but he crinkles his eyebrows at me. "Aren't you hungry?"

He is not wrong. My insides growl. Under his watchful gaze, I manage to eat all the dry bread. It settles my stomach.

With that out of the way, I turn my attention to him again.

"What are you doing here?" I gesture at the room. "This is no place for a man like you."

He wrinkles his nose and giggles. I almost want to laugh too. Almost.

"I was bored, and you looked sad."

Again, I am struck by how intuitive this little boy is. "I was, a bit." There is no use trying to hide it from him.

"Whatcha sad about?"

I frown, wondering how I can put this into words, or if I even should. But he keeps looking at me with those innocent eyes. To tell him anything but the truth would be a crime.

"I lost someone, a long time ago. And I am remembering it all a little more these days. But I am also sad because I have a daughter, and my sorrow has made me do and say things I regret."

Look at you, baring your soul to a child, a voice in my mind chides. *You really are pathetic.*

The boy has no consideration for my brooding thoughts. He raises a hand and scratches an itch at his temple. A bracelet made of tiny flying birds adorns his small wrist. "I did a bad thing to Wehna when I was mad. I stole a pie and ran away, but then I got lost." A look of complete contrition plays across his boyish features.

I clear my throat. "Well, I am glad she found you."

He nods and kicks his feet against the counter. "My mada and pada are lost." A sigh much too big for his small frame whooshes out of him. "Sometimes it makes my sister sad like you."

Compassion strikes at my core. "But not you?"

He thinks for a moment, puckering his mouth up and staring hard at the ceiling. "Not really. Elyōn will keep them safe."

Elyōn. The mere mention of the ancient deity washes me in a flood of guilt. Ellehra always spoke of him, and I always brushed her off.

"I bet she misses you," he says.

"What?"

"Your daughter. I bet she misses you when you aren't with her." His face falls. "I miss my parents," he whispers.

My heart breaks. I want to comfort him, but I don't know how. And anyway, I am a man and a stranger. In a tavern. Nothing I could do would be appropriate.

"I'm sorry," is all I end up saying.

He looks at me and lifts his chin. Again, something about his eyes unnerves me. I am about to get up, to insist he go outside and find this girl—what was her name? Wehna? He should not stray from her like this.

But he speaks again. "Did you say that to her?"

My mouth drops open to respond, but I close it as my mind wanders down the maze of this last week. It halts at the last time I saw my daughter. Refusing to move on, it settles in and forces me to relive it all. I hear Amyrah shout those terrible, true things all over again.

I know enough to keep things running while my useless father wallows in the past.

Her words carried the force of a sledgehammer. But they were honest. Painful and honest, like the edge of a blade. I cringe when I recall the way I responded, channeling my hurt into a weapon against her.

You think this makes you special, but it means nothing.

Lies. More and more lies.

And that final, stinging blow, the one intended to cut her, that ended up lodging itself even deeper in my own conscience. *If you are intent on ruining yourself, I want no part of it.*

I have never spoken anything more untrue in my life.

"What would you do if you found out your parents were not lost, but had left you?" Even as I ask the question, I hate myself for it. Is it fair to make a child think of such things? But something about him suggests he is no ordinary little boy.

He looks at the floor and thinks for a while. "If they did that, I know they'd be sorry."

"What makes you think that?"

He shrugs and shuffles a little on the stool. "I know them. I'll always forgive them."

At that moment, there seems to be a lull in the conversations surrounding us. My eyes travel down the bar. Two men are on the brink of coming to blows. I register their mouths moving, but no sound escapes. The taverner bangs the counter and cuts their scuffle short. I feel the vibrations, but everything is a silent blur around me.

Is it really possible that after all I have said and done, my daughter could forgive me—has forgiven me all along—even in the midst of the hurt and the loneliness I have put her through? Could such astounding grace really exist?

A hand drops on my shoulder, and the world comes back into focus, fills my ears with the sounds of life once more.

"Excuse me, sir."

I turn to regard a man bent over me. He has an imposing frame—broad from his shoulders right down to his feet. His dark eyes, overshadowed by a prominent brow, glint in a heavily bearded face. I would have found him intimidating, perhaps, if I were alone. But the boy does not shrink from his presence. Not all children are excellent judges of character, but I suspect this one is.

"Yes?" I respond.

"Arvo says you looked after him." He motions to the boy on the stool. "I want to thank you."

I glance at my new friend. "It is actually more like he was looking after me."

Arvo grins.

The man's mouth moves slightly with an unasked question. He holds his hand out to me and introduces himself. "Bryn Peren."

I take his hand. His strong fingers grip mine and give them a firm shake. "Téron Cantar."

Bryn smiles warmly and turns to the boy. His expression becomes stern.

"Arvo, you gave your sister a fright. I'm glad you're safe, but you shouldn't run off on her like that."

Arvo lowers his head sheepishly, and his lip begins to quiver. The man's features soften. "But all is well now." He puts an arm around him and points to the entrance of the tavern. "Do you see that woman outside? She's my wife, Tress. She's waiting with your sister until we can get her some help. Go to her now."

The boy slips off the stool and takes a step toward the door, then turns back to me. He digs into his pocket for a while, sticking his tongue out the side of his mouth, until he finds what he is looking for.

"Here," he says, holding out a fist and waiting for me to open my hand underneath it. "A girl gave this to me when I was sad. You can have it now."

Intrigued, I hold out my palm. He drops something into it—a many-rayed silver pendant on a leather cord. I frown. I recognize it, but when I go to question him, he has already scampered out of the tavern. I stare at the place where he disappeared.

"He's quite the little man, isn't he?" Bryn asks, taking the empty stool.

A slight nod is all I can manage. I finger the necklace, picturing it around Amyrah's neck. But something does not fit the memory. Didn't it emanate light? At least, it did when she wore it. It looks like ordinary metal in my hand.

"Forgive me if this is an intrusion, but you seem to be a conflicted man."

I do not meet his eyes.

"I recognize the look in your eyes." He rests his elbows on the counter and leans into his clasped hands. "I know what it is to have your actions condemn you."

I merely grunt. What could he possibly know about my situation?

"It's probably not what you want to hear, but I can guarantee you will not find any victory by continuing to trust in your own ability to fix the wrong in your life."

"You're right," I say, setting down the necklace and taking a gulp of ale. I plunk the mug down again. "I don't want to hear that."

He smiles good-naturedly. "Are you a man of faith?"

Even though Bryn doesn't come out and say it, I know he refers to faith in Elyōn, not the kaligorven. My shoulders rise and fall with a heavy sigh. "Not really," I reply, and before I can hold it back, I add, "I left that to my wife." The words leave a bitter taste in my mouth.

This is the day for admitting things to strangers, apparently. At least I will not be looked at with speculation for talking to this one.

Bryn sits in thoughtful silence for some time before he speaks again. "I was as you are, several years ago. My wife found it so easy to trust in the goodness of the Highest, but it was always a battle for me. I felt shamed by her easy belief."

It is so familiar, my chin bobs.

He lowers his hands to the rough counter. He has an easy manner about him—the furthest thing from intimidating, I realize now. "But I've since learned I was merely trusting in my own ability to believe." He laughs. "And I was not very skilled at it."

"Nor am I."

"That's the thing. It isn't about our skill at all. Faith is a gift from

Elyōn, not something we can cultivate on our own." He looks at me. "The absolution you seek from your guilt—it can't be earned, either."

I sigh and cover my face with my hands. This is not the kind of conversation I need right now.

But Bryn plows on. "Friend, no one is beyond hope. If the Highest can implant even the tiniest grain of faith in a heart like mine and cause it to grow, he can do the same for you. If he can remove my guilt from me, he can do so for you as well."

A dry laugh shudders out of me. I am beyond redemption.

"I don't pretend to know your situation, or what brought you to this place this evening," he continues, unfazed, "but I recognize your expression. You believe you are not worth saving."

"Are any of us truly worth it?" I bring myself to look at him. "You just told me not to trust in my own efforts."

Sadness flickers briefly in his eyes. "No," he answers softly. "We are a fallen people, and completely undeserving." Bryn pauses, and his eyes travel to the flickering candlelight. "And yet, he loves us still."

I want to retaliate, to tell this naïve man he is wasting his breath. How can he believe in a deity so gracious when we are trapped in the clutches of this never-ending shadowland?

But something stops my tongue when I think of Arvo. In his childlike innocence, he would forgive his parents for leaving him, for lying to him. He would love them still. And I know my daughter would do the same for me, if I asked. Perhaps Bryn is right, and they are both faint reflections of Elyōn. Perhaps I can be forgiven for what I have done.

But the guilt still burns in my soul. "I have made a mess of everything in my life. It is too much."

He shakes his head. "You can't fix everything all at once, and you don't need to. Confess your need to Elyōn, and I promise he will move you forward, one step at a time."

My hand covers the necklace.

Bryn gets up and pushes the stool in. "Walk in the light, friend," he says as he hands me a small scrap of paper. "Darkness need not dwell in you any longer."

I unfold the paper to find directions to a specific area in Utsanek scrawled across it. I do not recognize the location.

"When you're ready to discuss this again, you can find me here."

When I look up, Bryn Peren is gone.

I sit in the tavern, lost in thought, until even the regulars have stumbled into the night in search of rest. The taverner shelves the last flagon and points at the door.

Once I am in the street, I feel like something has shifted within me, something I cannot put into words. So often, Ellehra would speak of similar things, but I was too proud to listen. What need did I have for Elyōn when my life functioned fine without him? But this stranger has now reminded me of the things she said, the things I have long forgotten. And I am broken enough to hear them.

So much has happened in thirteen years. I am not the same man I once was.

Elyōn, forgive me.

Before I understand what I am doing, silent words pour out in a torrent of prayer. Oh, how long my spirit has been bound by bitterness. But a ray of mercy has pierced the hidden dungeon of my soul. My griefs drain away, and hope fills the void. Words of confession become whispers of praise. As my feet move through the streets of Utsanek, I exchange guilt for forgiveness, resentment for thanksgiving, turmoil for peace.

My chains fall off. My heart is *free*.

Without a lantern to guide my way, the ténesomni is nothing more than a passing shadow. I make it back to our cottage without difficulty. It is no longer a place of oppression; rather, it is a promise of a new start. Even in its sadly neglected state, it welcomes me in.

What an amazing, astounding, incomprehensible love.

As I take up the old routines of caring for the goats and chickens, fetching water, and lighting a fire in the hearth, one troubling question remains. How can I possibly keep silent as Myrzeth distorts the Vale to his purposes? And if I do oppose him, like my heart compels me to do, what will it mean for my daughter?

27

WEHNA

WHEN I OPEN MY EYES, a mosaic of impossible colors hangs above my head. For one disoriented moment, I think I'm seeing the stars again—until I blink, and they come into focus.

Much too close to be stars. The timid flicker of hope puffs out.

"You are alright, dear. Just relax."

Something soft cushions my head, but the rest of my body aches from the unyielding surface on which I am lying. My brows scrunch together when a throb of pain floods my forehead. I press a palm into the pain.

"Where am I?"

A strange sound makes me pull my hand away. I blink into the gentle lights again. A woman with compassionate eyes stands off to the side, under a canopy of branches covered in multicolored bolétis. She smiles and holds out a hand. I hesitate before taking it. Carefully, she pulls me upright. My legs swing down, and my feet are steadied by a hard surface.

"You're somewhere we should have brought you weeks ago." She sits down beside me on the bench, and a dirty blond braid slips off her shoulder and swings gently. "But we didn't want to risk your parents returning to an empty house."

There's that sound again. High-pitched shrieking, mingled with sounds of . . . *joy*. Children playing.

"Arvo." I gasp, my whole body springing up.

The woman puts a hand on my shoulder to still me, and her touch brings the threat of tears to my eyes.

"It's alright," she says, her fingers tightening when I try to get up again. "He's here." Her green eyes are a peaceful shade, less vibrant than Arvo's. I fix onto them like a lifeline. "My husband searched for him after you took a turn, and he didn't need to look for long." Something feels like it's trying to pry out of my lungs, but I lack the courage to give it utterance.

"He's safe," she says, eyebrows going up with the word that calms my fears.

Melodic laughter fills the courtyard as a troop of seven or so kids tumbles in under the reach of the tree. My eyes dart around until they fall on a small shape, with curly hair that bounces and a smile that fills the whole world with unquenchable light.

The tears come, hot and fast and without mercy. I do not protest when the woman pulls me into her embrace, and she does not protest when I drench her shoulder.

We don't have to be alone.

PART THREE

come

*You have heard the call,
"Come out of the darkness,
Child of the Day."
Can you now remain
where darkness dwells?
You are no longer of the night,
for it has run its course
and the day is at hand.
Darkness, with all its fury
and malice,
could not overcome it.
It is already passing away
and the True Light
is shining.*

28

AMYRAH

A LITTLE BROOK RUNS PAST OUR COTTAGE and through Utsanek. It flows right by the tiny house we used to live in. I've always thought it an uncommon seam of beauty in that hostile city—a physical reminder that there is still kindness even for all the broken things in this world.

I can still recall how I would stop to listen for its tinkling requiem on the days when the streets were loud and my pada was not nearby. If I kept quiet for long enough, its song never failed to find me. It led me home. At the age of six, my father moved us out of the city so we wouldn't bear the valefolk's scorn any longer. The thought of living away from the lights frightened me, but the consolation was that we would still live near the brook. Like before, I could follow its path with careful footsteps. The knowledge that it didn't change, that it would always take me to the places I needed to be, soothed my fears. And if I ever got lost in the ténesomni, I could calm myself, listen, and find evidence of its existence.

I follow it now, willing it to whisper those words of comfort I have long since forgotten. Even though I no longer fear the dark, and it can no longer reach me, I feel as though I am six again, placing all my faith in the water to lead me home. My lungs contract and expand with a steady rhythm, and my footfalls are nothing more than soft thuds along the bank. The noise of Utsanek fades completely.

It is only me and the brook.

The snapping of a branch across the babbling water sends a rush of blood pounding through my eardrums. I peer as far as my circle of illumination will allow, but I am able to see nothing on the other side of the stream.

"It's just a doe."

His voice makes my heart lurch.

I turn around and find Belwyn standing a few yards behind me. There is a bow and quiver on his back, but the lantern in his hand proves he has no intention of hunting. It looks as though he only grabbed the weapon as an excuse to leave Utsanek. I don't trust myself to speak, so I stand and clutch the old book to my chest.

He regards me until I feel heat creeping up my face. Raising the lantern to eye-level, he pries open its hinged door and blows the candle out. There is hardly any difference in the ambient light. Even still, a small sound escapes my lips when he extinguishes the ignati.

"Why would you do that?" I breathe, hugging my arms around me even tighter as he approaches. I shiver, though I'm not cold.

Even without firelight, his irises appear golden brown. "It doesn't seem necessary," he says with a smile slanting into his cheek.

"But how are you going to get back?"

I laugh when his forehead furrows, and he points a single finger into the air.

"Ah. Right."

I let the warm feeling of mirth flow through me for a beat. But then I remember. My hand finds his arm, and he gawks at me in surprise.

"Did you learn anything about my father?"

His face becomes grim, maybe even a little disappointed. "Yes and no. I'm pretty sure the Foremost kept him in a holding cell." My fingernails press into his skin. "But someone released him."

"Oh." I sigh, despair flaring in my heart.

Why hasn't he come to find me? Is he hurt somewhere? I let go of Belwyn's arm and pull my cloak closed with one hand. Pinching my eyes shut, I swallow down the panic and force myself to focus on what is right here in front of me. Who is in front of me.

"What brings you out of the city so late?"

"Is it late?" A look of honest perplexity claims his face as he stares around at the trees. "It's been hard to keep track lately." His eyes fall back on me, and he takes a step even closer still. "I came to find you."

The way his voice lowers makes my insides twist.

"It's lucky you happened to set off in the right direction, isn't it?"

He smiles for a moment, and the twisty feeling deepens.

"Well, it only took one look at you to know you do not belong in the city, and you said you didn't come to Utsanek much." He lifts his head and arches an eyebrow. "It turns out there aren't many people who would willingly live outside of Utsanek. None, actually, other than you and your father. So, you weren't hard to track down."

My shaking hand casts around for the wayward locks of my hair. When they find one, I weave my fingers into it. "What's wrong with how I look?"

The smile fades from his lips but stays in his voice. "Absolutely nothing at all."

Something snaps across the brook again, stealing our attention. I suck in a breath, but I can't tell what caused the fright which made it necessary —the sound or Belwyn's eyes?

Not willing to dwell on it, I set down the book and step carefully down the bank, ignoring how he holds out a hand to stop me.

The waters are no longer swollen with the effects of the thaw, and I walk across the stones lining the creek bed without getting my boots wet. My sphere of sight extends far enough to touch the reeds on the other bank.

With a noisy thud—how did he manage to sneak up on me?—Belwyn joins me.

I raise a palm to still him.

We each hold our breath, watching the unmoving foliage for so long, it begins to feel foolish.

A tawny form parts the grass. It steps through on long, lean legs and raises its elegant head toward us. Two large ears fan out to the side, twitching ever so slightly in our direction. Dark eyes latch on to mine. My heart slows its pace.

"See? I told you it was a doe."

I risk looking behind me at Belwyn, mostly to make sure he isn't nocking an arrow. As I suspected, he has no interest in hunting today. My attention turns back to the animal.

The deer should have responded to our movement, to Belwyn's voice, but she hasn't moved. I stretch out a hand toward her, foolishly hoping she will come closer. Belwyn's clipped breaths sound softly behind me. He is as enraptured as I am.

For some reason, the doe steps forward. She isn't afraid. She descends the bank and crosses the water. Without a moment's hesitation, she reaches forward and sniffs my hand with her soft nose.

"Hello," I whisper.

Her ears lower, relaxed.

When Belwyn steps from behind me, she lifts her head to full height but doesn't bolt. She is easily as tall as me—maybe taller.

I glance at him. "Have you ever seen a deer so big?"

A visible shudder runs through him. He licks his lips and stares.

Unsure of what to make of his response, I turn back. I should probably be wary of a wild animal that shows no fear of humans, but I'm only feeling a strange sense of familiarity.

I desperately want to touch her fur. Careful not to startle her, I hold out a shaking hand. She keeps an eye on it but does not back away.

The noise of the bubbling water fades to the background as the space between me and this magnificent creature diminishes. I feel the warm air rushing out between my lips in measured breaths. I see her hide ripple to shake off an insect. My fingers stretch out and—

The instant my skin touches her fur, an explosion of luminescence leaps from the doe, filling the entire vicinity with brilliant light. I bring my hand back to shield my eyes, but the blinding display does not diminish. Confused, I stagger back a few steps.

And I laugh. "Belwyn, she's a sola."

I can't tear my eyes away. Her entire body has been transformed by the all-consuming blaze. Intricate designs blossom across her cheeks, down her neck. Ribbons of gold unfurl like a carpet, filling the creek bed with a river of flame.

My joy escapes in a torrent of tears. I approach her again, laying a hand on her beautiful muzzle. She does not pull away but remains as if awaiting instruction. Gently, I bend her head down and draw near, closing my eyes and pressing my forehead to hers. Incredible warmth causes every bit of cold to run to the extremities of my body in great waves. Something swells in my chest, something I've never felt at this potency.

Hope.

I breathe in the intoxicating air between us one more time, turn around, and dry my eyes.

"Belwyn, can you believe—"

The words evaporate on my tongue.

He is on his knees, his tall frame curled in on itself, face buried in his forearms, fingers lost in his thick hair. Heaving motions shake his shoulders as he drags in breaths like he has been held underwater.

I rush to help him, kneeling and ignoring how the frigid water begins to seep into my dress.

"What's wrong?" I lay a hand on his back.

His body jerks away from my touch, and as his arms lower, his eyes fix on me with an undeniable expression of anguish.

"I . . . I can't . . ." He shakes his head too fast and pinches his eyes shut. "It was . . . I can't . . ."

My hands find his—icy cold. I kneel right in front of him, shielding him from the sola's intensity, clutching his hands firmly between us. "It's alright. You're alright."

He shakes his head faster and tries to curl up again. I let go of his hands and use mine to hold him up by his shoulder and to keep his face from turning away from me. "Tell me."

The tremors threaten to break him loose, but I will not let him go.

"You wouldn't look at me again," he says between breaths.

A prick of doubt punctures my optimism, but I stay firm.

"Belwyn," I whisper, and his eyes finally see mine. "I'm not going anywhere."

No change takes place in his tormented expression, but slowly, he raises a tremulous hand and grabs my fingers that rest against his cheekbone. An encouraging smile begins to form on my lips when his eyes darken, and he drags my hand down.

"Not even if I told you I killed a sola?"

I can't help it. I pull away from him, my hands falling limp into my lap. "What?"

He rests his palms on his thighs and leans into his arms. "I killed one. Just like that" —he motions with his chin to the doe behind my back— "except it was a buck."

Tears pool in his eyes as he watches me draw further and further back. I don't mean to.

"I didn't want to do it. I told myself I would stop it from happening. And it was just . . . there. On top of me. And I . . ." His hands ball up against his trousers. "I killed it."

Before I know what I'm doing, I've risen and walked back to the sola, still waiting for me with the intelligence of the ancients brimming in her eyes. I lean forward and whisper in her ear, gently nudging her toward the forest stretching to the Askonnet Mountains. She steps away slowly at first, but soon bounds up the bank and disappears into the trees. After a short while, her light fades from sight.

When I turn around, Belwyn is no longer in the bed of the stream. Panic flares in my heart. I scramble up the slope and locate him before he passes out of my range of vision.

"Belwyn?" I cry, desperation pinching my voice.

He turns around, pain etched across his features. "Yes?"

I try to say something several times, but the words won't come. The hurt in his face deepens. I grind my teeth in frustration.

Tell him to come back, my head screams. *Tell him it's ok, what he's done doesn't matter. It's not his fault.*

But my lips won't obey. Not yet.

Give me time, my heart cries. Except there is no time.

The moment before he is about to disappear from my light, I make my voice submit. "Follow the water. It will lead you home."

What just happened?

Can all solas withhold their light, or did I witness something spectacular?

My hands still tingle with warmth from contact with the creature. I try to preserve their heat by wrapping them tightly around the book as I journey home.

Walking in the exact opposite direction of Belwyn, my chest tightens. I hate that I am reacting this way to his confession. But what choice do I have? It isn't me who can absolve him of guilt. How else did he think I could respond—especially at that moment?

To me, the solas represent all that is good and true and life-giving in this world. They represent my mother. Something about them has awoken a fire within me that has lain dormant my whole life.

I don't understand how anyone—especially him—could have been so heartless.

But it broke him. I can't deny it. It cost him everything to confess it to me. How is it fair to hold this against him?

Let me be mad at him for a little while longer.

Oh, but it hurts my heart.

I stare at my feet and stumble through the forest, oblivious to the night that surrounds me.

When the spongy floor hardens and the trees no longer surround me, I lift my eyes to a surprising sight.

The cottage glows with warm firelight, with the scent of woodsmoke in the air.

"Father?" I murmur, barely daring to hope.

I throw out caution and sprint toward my home. I need him to be there.

My hand finds the crude planks, slides down to pull the latch. The door swings open, and . . .

He waits for me with open arms.

I abandon all attempts at maintaining composure and throw myself into his embrace. He holds me tightly, so tightly it hurts, but nothing could ever make me tell him to let go.

My face buried in his shoulder, I shake and cry and heave in breath after shaky breath. He slips a hand under my mass of hair and presses my head closer, closer still, kissing my temple and whispering words I don't catch. They calm my soul, nonetheless.

"Pada," I say, pulling away after an eternity and looking into his steady blue eyes. "I was so scared." My voice trembles, my head shakes. "So, so scared."

His lips press together, an effort to keep calm, and he brushes away strands of hair that my tears have slicked to my cheeks. "I am sorry, my girl. I should never have shut you out like that."

My hand covers his.

"I treated your mother's loss as my pain, and mine alone. I did not allow myself to believe it was yours too. And I was not strong enough to bear the thought of losing you to those—" He grits his teeth and pinches his eyes closed. "Those monsters."

"I'm fine, Pada. I'm alright. The darkness can't touch me."

He slips his hand out from under mine and grabs it, pulling it down and trapping the other with it between his. "But it can. I saw it with your mother."

Leading me to a chair at our humble table, he sits in the one on the other side, all the while not letting go of my hands. "She thought she was invincible too. But this ténesomni is more sinister than you know."

I lean in closer, my heart beating fast. "Can you tell me more about her? Please? You hardly ever speak of her." I want to know about her gift most of all, but I don't say it. I just wait.

A sad expression wobbles across his face, but it doesn't drag him down like it used to. "You are so much like her that it hurts sometimes to look at you." He smiles softly. "I am sure the only thing you inherited from me is my crazy hair."

My hand shoots up to my wayward waves, and I smirk.

His humor fades and he sighs. "I didn't know what drew me to your mother in the first place—except that she was breathtaking, of course. But there was something else I couldn't figure out."

The fire illuminates half of his sallow face. His eyes see somewhere far, far away. "She showed up in the market one day. I had never seen her in Utsanek before, yet I felt as if I had known her my whole life. She chose me, someone endlessly plagued by darkness. *Me*." A shimmering reflection appears in his eyes, and he blinks it away. "I still cannot understand it."

He clears his throat. "When we were together, there was never any darkness at all. She had a way of setting my fears aside, and I found it hard to be apart from her for even a moment. When she showed me what she could do, how she could keep the ténesomni at bay with a mere flick of her wrist, she awoke in me a consuming instinct to guard her." His hands release mine, and he drags a fingernail across the wood grain.

"Maybe it was because the light within her could not be held back," he continues, "but she became so restless living in the city. I never knew much about her background, and she turned strangely evasive when I would mention it. I started to wonder if she even came from the Vale at all. All I knew was the day she showed up, it became a better place."

Oh, Mada . . . I squeeze my eyes closed, trying to picture her. *What secrets did you withhold?*

"But with each sola the valefolk hunted, she grew more and more distressed. And the power within her that held the shadows back became even more potent. I was afraid for her safety and sought counsel from her brother."

My mouth falls open. "She had a brother?"

He nods. "Yes, and he was equally as gifted as Ellehra. Only he took a different view of it. He insisted that if she could change her attitude and seek how the darkness could be appeased, there could be harmony and prosperity as a result." His fists clench on the table. "To my everlasting shame, I listened to him, not her. I chose to back the Shrouded instead of the solas."

A heaviness presses down on my soul as I watch my father rake his hands into his hair and stare at the tabletop. His shoulders rise and fall as he tries to gain control of his breaths. I would reach out to him, to offer him comfort, but I feel just as wrecked as he does.

"After they took her from us," he says, raising his eyes to find mine, "I pretended not to see the same gift in you. It was small at first, easily ignored. Or hidden with a good lantern. If I could not see it, and nobody else could, I didn't need to think about what it could mean for your future. But I always knew you gave light back to me, as Ellehra did." His eyebrows go up, pleading. "Can you ever forgive me for pushing it—you —away?"

"Yes," I say. "Of course, I can."

We sit there in silence for a while. My mind winds through the events of the last few weeks. How I noticed my gift spark to life the moment the solas came back to the Vale. How I witnessed even the smallest light dispelling the darkness. How Elyōn has led my steps to those who are hurting and awoken a yearning to see the shadows broken.

"What should I do with it?"

He sniffs loudly and looks at me. "With what?"

"My gift. My *light*."

Folding his hands and leaning his chin into them, he thinks for a beat and sighs.

"I do not want to tell you to hide it, the way I did for seventeen years. It is yours. A part of you, as it was your mother. As you are a part of her." Shaking hands move to encase mine. "I know it means you will be endangered, but maybe . . ." He gulps and steels himself. "Maybe Elyōn meant for you to shine at such a time as this."

I suck sharply through my nostrils, struggling to absorb all he's told me. Who is this broken man who sits across from me? Broken not as he was, torn to shreds by guilt and fear, but broken away from the influence of that fear over his mind and heart.

Without waiting for me to respond, he reaches into his pocket and pulls something out. He holds it up, and it dangles between us.

The necklace.

My eyes go wide, and so do his, for as he holds it, the dull metal begins to glow, bright and piercing. He stands up, the chair scraping the floor, and comes to me. I grab my hair in two fistfuls and hold it up and out of the way as he ties it around my neck.

"Amyrah," he says, coming to kneel before me, "my 'quiet song.' You were made for so much more than this shadowland."

Pressing the beautiful pendant to my throat, I slip off the chair and hold my father tight.

29
WEHNA

"ELYŌN ÉRIT AGÉRTU."

The phrase spirals around the secluded sanctuary of the forest, acting as the cue for the congregation to disperse. Bryn smiles at his wife as he closes his book and joins the stream of people. I stand in the middle of it all, unable to make myself move, watching women find each other with outstretched arms, men slap each other heartily on the back, and parents struggle to keep track of their rambunctious children.

It's been a week since Arvo and I arrived in this secluded community, and in that time the number of people in it has increased significantly. In a way, it's nice our faces aren't the only new ones here.

The acts of violence against the fidrélas are on the rise in Utsanek, and Bryn and Tress have responded by shepherding the most vulnerable to this place of safety. I worry for my friends, constantly putting themselves in danger like that. After all, I know what the consequences can be.

My heart shakes in my chest, trying to rid itself of the black thoughts sticking to it like tar.

Focus on the good.

I do not have to worry about Arvo's safety. We have food to eat. Someone is always willing to lend a listening ear. We have a community. Our needs have been supplied—abundantly.

So why does my heart feel unsatisfied?

"Wehna?" Arvo tugs on my dress.

I force a smile to chase away every hint of inner turmoil before fixing my eyes on my brother. "Yes?"

"Orlagh wants me to help her try out her new oven Can I go?"

The elderly woman walks to us with slow steps, the kindness in her lined face a soothing balm.

My grin is real now. I exchange a questioning look with her. "Are you sure you know what you're taking on?"

The squeeze on my arm is an answer itself. "Don't yeh worry abou' a thing. Time past, I had three bairns of my own, and I know wha' kind of shenanigans they're capable of." She looks at Arvo and pinches his cheek, but I recognize a hint of sadness in her gaze.

How could such a wonderful lady have no grown children to look after her? I feel guilty for how absorbed with my own problems I have been.

Arvo grabs both of my hands and tugs down on them. "She said I can help her make spiced buns."

I gasp playfully and reflect his expression of wonder. "Well, then. How could I say no?"

After hugging me so hard I almost fall over, he grabs Orlagh's hand and chats her ear off as they exit the wooded area. I am left alone.

I take a slow breath and exhale heavily.

This is the most beautiful place I've ever been in the Vale. The close-growing trees have been trimmed of all lower branches, and the ground cover has been cleared. It has the feeling of a cathedral stretching to the heavens, a hidden grotto in the middle of a depressing wilderness.

Everywhere I look, bolétis grow in huge clusters in all the colors I could ever imagine. No wonder Bryn saw right through my lie about the glowing jewelry if he already knew about the forest's unending variety of bioluminescent mushrooms. I'm certain if anyone could impart their luminescent qualities to other objects, this community would have figured it out by now.

Bryn has, at least, left off questioning me about it. I'm thankful, because it is impossible for me to dwell on life before the Vale without the air in my lungs thickening like sap.

I walk along the border of the enclosure, trailing my hand through the brambly hedge that keeps this space private. A myriad of five-petaled white flowers dot it like constellations. The sweet fragrance of new life rises to greet me. Surely it is Zomré by now, although the Foremost has not officially declared it.

It was Zomré when my family came to Utsanek . . .

I sigh. How much different would our lives have been if we had come to live in this peaceful place instead of the forever-darkened streets outside of it?

The beauty and peace around me become too much for my overburdened soul. Rather than drawing my heart to praise, it reminds me of all I have lost. With the frightful beast of grief assailing my stomach, I leave.

The haunted cathedral grasps at my heels.

30

AMYRAH

I RAISE AN EYEBROW as my father purchases a cake of a sickeningly sweet confectionery he has always been partial to. It's made of a compacted paste of dried fruits, tree nuts, and spices. He offers me a bite as we walk away from the stall, and I wrinkle my nose.

"I don't know how you can eat that."

He makes a show of being offended. "What? It's *good*." He sinks his teeth in and groans with exaggerated pleasure.

I roll my eyes and link my arm with his as we walk down the alleyways. Utsanek seems like a lighter place, but it isn't because of the new sola bones, or the lantern held out in front of me. I squeeze my father's arm tighter, and we continue in comfortable silence. The bag slung across my body gently bumps my hip as we go, weighed down by Tress's book.

"Isn't it odd how empty the streets are today, Pada?" I ask as he smacks his lips, taking his enjoyment of the treat to a humorous level.

Father swallows and shrugs. "It's likely some other ceremony we have no need to witness."

I know he wants to dispel my concerns, but his eyes give him away. Even mentioning the dark deeds of Utsanek bothers him. Squeezing closer to his side, I let the silence carry us for a while.

"So, where are you taking me?" Father looks around at the unfamiliar buildings and passageways that converge upon us.

"Somewhere you will like, I promise," I answer, but a frown follows.

Which way is it? I try to dredge up the memory, but it's all a haze. Father watches me, a bemused smile barely peeking through his beard.

I let out a sigh, frustrated with myself for forgetting where to go.

Without berating me, my father takes the lantern gently from my hand and rotates in a slow circle to get a look at the intersection. He makes a strange face and digs into a pocket in his trousers, pulling out a scrap of paper, unfolding it, and holding it up to the lantern light to get a better look. Wonderingly, he turns his eyes on me and holds it out for me to read.

"Is this the place?"

Curious, I take it from him and read, and my eyes widen.

Directions to a place called Ellithïm.

A laugh of amazement bubbles out of my lungs. "Yes, Pada. That's exactly where we're going."

Enter when the way is empty flows along the bottom of the paper. Tucking it into my bag, I check the area, but Father and I are the only ones here. Blowing out the lantern, we duck down the alley and stop at the shadowed gate. Father gives me a little nod, and I raise a shaking hand to push it open.

The scene behind is like a gigantic exhale. It's even more stunning than I remembered. As we enter the hidden neighborhood, I steal a glance at my father. His slack jaw and amazed expression are every bit as gratifying as I hoped they would be.

"Well, what do you think?" I nudge him forward and close the gate behind us.

He replies with an arm around my shoulders and a squeeze.

We walk down the street, him gawking at the bolétis canopy, me admiring the new blossoms that have opened in the planters since I was here last.

"Téron."

My brow furrows as a tall man with a mass of dark hair brushes past me and makes straight for my father, gripping his hand in a firm shake.

"You found your way to us."

A shy smirk blooms across my father's face. "Yes, but it was my daughter's doing." He motions toward me with his chin.

The man turns around. It's Bryn. I don't know what to do when he envelops me in a hug. He smells like tree sap and dust.

"Amyrah," he says, straightening and looking back and forth between my father and me. "I don't believe it. You're his daughter?" He laughs, low and warm, and it loosens something around my father's eyes. But it has the opposite effect on me.

"You two know each other?" I can't explain why I feel a weight sink into my stomach as I watch my father act familiar with this . . . stranger.

"Not as well as I'd like, but enough that I am truly grateful for the opportunity to know him better," says Bryn.

My father nods. "Yes, me too."

I turn to my him. "How did you meet?"

His mouth shifts to the side. "I could ask the same about you."

Heat paints my cheeks. I shrug. "A lucky chance."

"That pretty much sums it up for me too." Fondness slips over his features. "A peculiar little boy introduced us, actually."

Bryn chuckles. "That he did. And what I may have written off as a fluke meeting before, I can no longer ignore. That you happen to be Amyrah's father . . ." Wonder overcomes his face. He shakes his head to clear it, then extends his arm out to us. "I should have known. The resemblance is strong." He smiles. "Please, I insist you both join me at my house."

Father nods, but I step back, swinging the bag in front of me. "I actually want to return the book Tress gave me, if you don't mind." The excuse is a convenient way to hide my shock at my father making a friend for the first time in thirteen years.

Disappointment dampens Bryn's expression, but he concedes and gestures toward the library with an incline of his head. Clapping an arm around my pada's shoulders, he leads him down the street. I am left with the cloying scent of flowers forcing itself into my lungs.

31
WEHNA

LOSING MYSELF IN A BOOK is the only escape I can think of to free myself from my paralyzing thoughts. I step through the door of the library, a little bell making a middle-aged man look up from his counter. He smiles briefly before returning to repairing a tome with a crumbling spine.

Though the library in this neighborhood is diminutive, it's moderately varied and beautifully maintained. I run my hand along the meticulously polished shelves. There are children's fables, school primers, manuals on husbandry and various trades. Only a few history books dot the shelves, which strikes me as strange, considering how vehemently the Vale clings to its traditions.

This small collection is more than I have found anywhere in Utsanek. The valefolk do not place a high importance on literacy, largely because of the hand-to-mouth existence most people have been forced to live. It wouldn't surprise me if lack of education contributes to the fear-based system enslaving the Vale. It makes me sad.

My mother brought her own collection of books when we came here, determined my education wouldn't be wasted, and her son wouldn't be held back. I bite my lip, remembering how I left them at our little apartment. I wonder how long it will take me to work up the courage to retrieve them, or if they will even still be there when I do.

You need to be strong, Wehna.

I grit my teeth and force my brain to focus on the lines of books in front of me. I came here to distract myself from my troubles, didn't I?

For the next while, I travel around the room to every shelf, looking at the titles, slipping some out, and thumbing through the pages. Once I've visited all the sections, a frown creeps across my brow. Each book I've looked at has something in common, and it troubles me. I approach the counter where the librarian works in silence.

"Excuse me, do you have any books written about or by someone outside of the Vale?"

His hands go still, and he looks up from his task, his smile growing brittle. He glances around the room and out the window, like he is checking to make sure no strangers are around.

Is no place in Utsanek free from fear and suspicion?

His eyes return to mine. "That's a dangerous question to ask, young lady."

My eyes narrow. "Why is that?"

He sets down the pot of glue and paintbrush he's working with and rests his hands on the countertop. Although his red hair is relatively untarnished by age, he has a maze of wrinkles around his eyes and mouth. He's older than he looks.

"I'm surprised your parents wouldn't have told you about such an important event in Utsanek's history."

I shift uncomfortably as his dark eyes bore into me, casting around for an excuse. "They had better lessons to teach."

He scratches his temple with a long index finger, no doubt perplexed by my answer.

"Please," I say, slipping my fingers under the bracelet Arvo made me. "I really do want to know."

Weariness claims his features after a long silence. He rubs the space between his feathery eyebrows. "To me, it feels like only yesterday, but I suppose it has been over thirty years."

"What happened?"

The librarian drops his hand and pinches his lips together for a long while, as if waiting for me to give up and walk out. But I don't. Eventually, he gives in. He leans forward and lowers his voice.

"It happened during the season of Elberu when the harvest was at its peak. The attacks from the kaligorven had been growing more numerous, and no matter how many solas the people hunted down, the dark beasts would not relent. Bloodied bodies were found in the forest daily."

The image of my parents lying dead in the streets pops to the forefront of my mind, threatening to undo me. I swallow against the surge of sorrow and try to make the librarian's face come back into focus.

"People grew fearful and desperate, and a sect soon formed that wanted to leave the Vale. The idea caught on, and Jakkor, Foremost of the Vale—Dravek's predecessor—could do nothing about it except issue idle threats."

"Why would he oppose them if people were only trying to protect their families?"

The man scratches an eyebrow "Control. The entire structure of the Vale depends on it. If people knew they could leave and were successful in doing so, what would keep anyone here?"

I know that if I could have, I would have left this dreadful place the moment we stepped foot in it. But it was never my decision to make.

"They organized a grand exodus for the day after the harvest's completion," he continues, oblivious to my thoughts. "Several hundred valefolk strapped all their belongings to their backs and headed toward the Askonnet Mountain range. Even though we were armed with weapons to defend against the Shrouded, we did not stand a chance against the shadow beasts."

He grimaces and closes his eyes, taking a moment to collect himself.

Oh, I think. *Of course. He speaks from experience.*

After a long inhale, the librarian finishes the account, but his words are fitful and hard to hear. "It was a massacre. Out of the hundreds who attempted to flee, only a handful were spared. My wife and I were fortunate, but loss either touched or claimed most households." A tear slips down his cheek. "The damage it did to people's minds was . . . significant." He shakes his head. "No one ever thought the Shrouded were such a mighty force."

I reach over and cover his hand with my own. He regards me with surprise, but a grateful smile follows.

"What happened next?" I ask, not impatiently, but in a whisper.

"In an act of desperation, Jakkor had every single record of the Outlands purged from Utsanek history. He burned all literature originating from outside our borders, and the people gave it all over willingly, so great was our fear. He also forbade the people from speaking of what could lie beyond."

He wipes his face with a hand and clears his throat. His features are so grim, so pale. I regret making him relive it all.

"Those were the darkest days I can ever remember. It did a number on the valefolk. We've been scrambling to appease the kaligorven ever since." He gives his head a sad shake. "So many Light Creatures were killed, and so many rituals were observed.

"When that poor woman opposed the Hunt a couple decades later, it made a lot of folks nervous. But it also spurred some of us to remember the horrors of our history. Her bravery kindled hope in many. But when she got herself killed, it smothered all confidence. What we did not expect, though, was the mysterious silence of the Shrouded. I think the people were so grateful for the reprieve from both the kaligorven and the solas, they didn't mind watching the sola brossa fade over time. They had never known such peace in their lifetime—until the Light Creatures came back."

A thousand new questions crowd my mind. Who was this woman who so bravely challenged the system? And why did the solas stop coming when she died?

But I don't have a moment to put them into words when his eyes find mine again. "So, miss, no, you won't be finding any books or records from the Outlands within Utsanek. Believe me, I've tried. And it is best to leave it that way."

He acts as if this is the end of the conversation. My mouth opens to protest, only to be stopped by the dinging of the doorbell.

I turn around and find myself facing a girl with a familiar pendant shining at her neck.

32

AMYRAH

THE TINKLING BELL WAKES ME from my stupor. As I step through the doorway, I dig into my bag to retrieve the book. When I look up, warm hazel irises stare back at me. Recognition flickers as I take in the girl's face, her clothes, the dozens of bracelets wrapped around her wrists.

"I-I remember you," she says, eyes growing even wider than they already were.

I frown at the awkward greeting, but I can't deny I'm as surprised to see her. "Yes, from the market, right?" The book feels heavy in my hands as I set it on the counter. I glance at the man behind the desk as he reaches for it with a puzzled expression on his face.

The girl swallows and nods, her eyes falling to my necklace.

Oh, right. Shame rushes through me like an icy wind.

"I'm so sorry," I say, rushing to untie the pendant and hold it out to her. "You made this, right?"

She cocks her chin, confusion only deepening the surprise. "How did you get that?" she whispers.

My stomach weaves itself into knots. I bite my lower lip. "I found it in the market square after the first Hunt."

She shakes her head quickly. "No, I mean, I'm positive my brother had it."

It's my turn to be confused. "I . . . did . . . give it to a scared little boy." My mind reels. The lost child was her brother?

The girl's mouth presses into a line as her eyes follow the sway of the blinding star. Strange shadows slip across her smooth features.

"But it made its way back to me. I'm not sure I understand how." I drop the necklace into her open hand. "I'm glad it can be returned to you."

We both gasp. The moment it touches her skin, its light goes dim, looking just as it did when my father held it.

"Do you know why it does that?" I ask. She holds it up again, and the closer it gets to me, the brighter it shines.

"It doesn't make sense." Her mouth works for a while, and she shakes her head. Dark curls bounce around her shoulders. "I mean, yes, it's made from a metal that's supposed to not only reflect incredibly well, but also absorb the surrounding light—or so they say. But it usually doesn't do anything more than glimmer." She touches the pendant in her palm and smiles sheepishly. "When I was younger, I'd even try to get it to glow by holding it up to different things." The smile fades, and her eyes jump to mine. "But I never saw anything make it shine until you held it at the market."

Pursing her lips, she thrusts it back at me. "I think it belongs with you."

I take it from her hands—it immediately shines bright again—and tie it back around my throat. It feels heavy there, like a kindness I will never be able to repay.

"Excuse me, miss, but why have you handed me this book?" The librarian pushes the leatherbound tome across the polished wood counter. "It isn't one of mine."

"What do you mean?"

He slips it into my hands, weighing them down like a brick.

"What I said," the man answers. "I know every book on my shelves. I've never seen that one before in my life." He leans forward, looking both ways, and the market girl and I can't help but lean in too. "But I'd be keeping it a secret, if I were you."

Confused but not wanting to appear obtuse, I nod at him and drop the book into my bag, trying to ignore the way the girl watches me. The librarian stares at me for a while, not convinced I understand the gravity of the matter, then clicks his tongue and resumes painting glue onto a coverless spine.

The girl faces me. "I was . . ." She grabs a coil of hair, stretching it down while avoiding my eyes. "I was pretty much done here. Would you like to take a walk with me?" Without giving me time to respond, she exits the library and waits for me to follow. Her bold actions stand in stark contrast with how shy and unsure of herself she seems.

"I suppose we should learn each other's names, if we're going to be friends," I say once outside, feeling my heart flutter with nervousness. I don't have much experience making friends. Is that something a friend would even say? I cringe inwardly as my palms begin to sweat.

"That seems like a good first step." The corner of her mouth tilts up. "I'm Wehna Qaith." She adds her family name like an afterthought. I wonder why she felt the need to tell it to me at all.

"Amyrah Cantar," I reply in kind. We shift awkwardly, as if we both wanted to shake hands, then reconsidered. It makes us giggle softly.

We walk into the charming courtyard, the tree now almost fully leafed out. An elderly couple sits on one of the benches, smiling widely at us. I give a small wave, which they return with enthusiasm.

"I actually wanted to speak with you about something," I say, shooting a look at our small audience. They watch us with rapt attention. "Is there anywhere we can talk that's more private?"

Her eyes dart to the courtyard's gate, and she sighs in resignation. "Yes, we can go to the cathedral."

I have never heard the word 'cathedral' before, but when I step into the walled-in forest, I can infer its meaning. Everything in this place draws my heart to praise. The trees coax my eyes up, up, up to where they are lost in the expanse, and the symphony of colors fills all the spaces between their lacing roots. A large clearing that a hundred people could fit in comfortably lies in the center. At the far end, where the ground curves upward and meets a rocky outcrop, a tinkling brook splashes over smooth stones and into a deep pool.

Wehna leads me beside it, and we sit on spongy moss. She pulls her legs up and wraps her arms around them, resting her cheek on her knees. I can't decide whether she seems tired or sad. Her eyes caress my void of darkness, less visible with the thousands of bolétis crowding in around us.

Having it revealed like this should make me feel exposed, but in the presence of this girl I hardly know, I am *seen*.

"You don't make sense to me," she says, curiosity pinching her lips.

I don't make sense to myself. My hand wiggles into my sack to pull out the book. I rest it on my lap and press a palm to its tattered cover. "There's a lot I'm struggling to understand these days."

She raises her head and blinks at the book. "Where did you get that?"

"Tress made me take it when I found this place, said it would give me answers. But all I have is more questions after reading it."

I flip through it, the verses rushing past in a blur. When the illustration of the star appears, I smooth out the pages and turn the book toward Wehna. "You used this phrase to describe the pendant of this necklace the other day—istilatum ideralis. I didn't know what it meant at the time, but I found this."

Her eyes pass over the picture and the words. She exhales slowly, troubled.

"What does it mean by 'firelights in the sky' and 'burning star'? How could they 'shine through the ages' or 'pierce the sky?'" I hold my breath.

Tugging at a bracelet, she stares at the pages for a long time, until I give up the hope of an answer.

"I'm not sure what I can or should say," she says. "There is a lot I know, and a lot I've been forbidden from speaking about."

"By whom?"

Her chest rises sharply. "My parents." A breath leaves her in broken bursts. Her eyes seem to sparkle for an instant. She sniffs and looks away, shaking her head. "I know what they would say if I told you anything."

I reach out and trap her twisting fingers beneath mine. Her head snaps back to me. "Please."

She chews on the inside of her cheek. I force myself to release her, to ease up. To wait.

Weakly, she nods. "Have you ever been outside of the Vale?"

"No," I say, wrinkling my brow.

"Well, I have." She gulps. "That's where my family is from. We came here three years ago, because my parents felt compassion for this place." There is a note of bitterness in her voice—not strong, but like a fragrant candle mixed with the subtle scent of a burnt wick. "They plunged me and my brother into shadow for the sake of those living in darkness."

"Wait—are you saying there's a place beyond the borders of the Vale where the ténesomni doesn't have dominion?"

The bolétis reflect in her eyes. She doesn't nod or shake her head but leans forward and whispers, "I can't say anything else. Don't you know how dangerous it is to speak of such things?"

"Fine." I can't hide my disappointment. "Just tell me about the stars."

Instead of answering, she grabs the book and whispers the verse.

> *At the dawn of the world's birth,*
> *the fire lights were ignited;*
> *An unquenchable flock without number,*
> *piercing the black cloak of the sky.*
>
> *They shone through the ages,*
> *a lasting gift from the Highest.*
> *The crystalline constellations rested*
> *when the Burning Star drew nigh.*

She hands it back. "I can't tell you much more than what's written here. It is true, there are lights in the sky. What fuels them, I don't know.

But they never burn out, always giving heat during the day and lighting the path at night." A wistful look claims her fair features. "I think the night sky is what I miss most from before."

A hunger growls within me as she weaves her riddles, a hollowness reaching ever deeper into the core of who I am. I've felt it before, when the solas left me. When I discovered the Ellithïm I could have been living in all my life. When my father connected with Bryn on a level I've never witnessed.

When I watched Belwyn walk away.

A weight spreads over my chest, turning my lungs to lead. I fight against the pressure, sucking in breaths in quick succession. My ears ring as my pulse picks up, drumming in my fingertips, my throat, my head, until the rhythm is audible.

Wehna stands up, staring into the onyx canopy with alarm plain in her posture.

She can hear it too.

I scramble to my feet, grabbing the book and dropping it in my bag. "What is it?"

Her head shakes. "I don't know."

Dread clings to my skin like an icy mist as the drumbeats roll in on the wind.

"It's the beginning of the Challenge Ceremony," a voice says behind us. We turn around, finding Tress approaching. She hugs her arms around herself, her face as white as the flowers blanketing the hedges. "I haven't heard it since I was a little girl."

Wehna and I exchange glances.

"The what?" she asks.

Tress blinks a few times, as if surprised to find us standing here. "Someone has challenged the Foremost for his position in the Vale."

"Can people do that?" I ask.

She nods. "Anyone who thinks they have a chance at defeating the Foremost can." A shiver runs through her body. "It's usually a bloody affair, and it almost certainly will end in death. I first saw one when I was seven years old, and I'll never forget the way the Foremost's family clung to each other."

The Foremost's . . . *family*.

"Belwyn," I whisper, fear gripping my bones in its claws.

Without explaining, I dash from the cathedral, through Ellithïm's idyllic street, and into the veins of dystopian Utsanek. I don't stop running until I hear Wehna's call.

"Amyrah, wait."

I slow and hold out my arms to cushion me as I come to a stop against a crumbling column of brick. My breaths come in stabbing gasps.

"Where are you going?"

I shake my head. What am I doing? Running to the aid of a boy? No, it must be more than that. "I should be there, to see . . . to know what happens." My hands shake. I grasp for my long hair.

Instead of questioning me further, Wehna traps one of my hands in hers.

"We're on the wrong side of the city. We'll never get there in time."

Still, the drums continue. Pounding, pounding, incessantly pounding.

"I need to be there for him," I say in a whisper, lip trembling. *I need to fix what I did to him.*

Wehna's soulful eyes search mine, and I hate how feeble, how unstable I must seem. But her hand tightens.

"We'll exit Utsanek and circle around it until we come to one of the main roads. Then we can cut right through the middle and end up at the ceremonial grounds. If we hurry, we might make it in time."

Gratitude swells as she leads me through the streets. They are darker than they should be, the ténesomni pushing in more than it has since the solas returned to the Vale.

I breathe a sigh of relief when the crooked buildings no longer loom overhead. I recognize where we are, but I still let Wehna direct us. We pass fields of tender shoots reaching toward the sky. Do they reach for the light hidden behind the shadows, the stars we cannot see?

Once we step onto the shores of the loch, I stop. Wehna turns around, a question in her eyes.

"Do you hear that?" I ask.

She tilts her head and frowns, confused. "Hear what?"

"The drums. They're quiet." I stare toward the city, defeated. We're too late.

Wehna comes close to me, and we stand together for so long, my feet start to ache. The wind passes through the treetops, the waves drag at the shore.

"Do you ever feel trapped in this place?" I say, daring to interrupt the Vale's unfeeling melody.

"Every single day," she says.

Tears trace shining lines down her bronze cheeks. I feel her sadness stir my own. Her jaw clenches, and sorrow slips seamlessly into anger. "Once you're in it, there is only this darkness." She looks at me, her irises rings of ignati.

"We must find the light together," I say.

In that moment, when our spirits become kindred and we share a kindling of hope, I look up.

My vision fills with the impossible.

33

BELWYN

THE DRUMS ECHO THROUGH THE DARKNESS, then leave the air ringing with their silence. Ignoring the gnawing sensation in my chest, I pull on the awful ceremonial garb.

Strange to think this could be the last time I will wear it.

Again, the deep thumps sound, rhythmic, penetrating the cavity of my chest.

I pull on a leather boot, muttering in frustration when I can't find the other. Casting my eyes around the room, they fall on the pair laying in a heap against the far wall. Exactly where Rhun threw them.

The gnawing feeling intensifies.

As the drums continue to rattle my brain, I locate my other boot and complete the ensemble, holding my breath to keep all the wounds and regrets at bay.

Without giving another moment to this ghostly place, I bound down the stairs and out the door, leaving that trap of memory behind me.

No one my age or younger has any experience with the custom of Privotus Vimorteth. I remember the lessons I endured on it now. It states that any person may challenge the current Foremost to ritualistic combat for dominance and wrest control of the Vale at any time. The ceremony has not taken place since my father claimed the title nineteen years ago. That no one has bothered to invoke the rite since says much about his strength and character. The only reason I know anything about it is because my ancient tutor grilled me on every facet of the histories of the Foremost and every ceremony related to the position.

The rules maintain that if the challenger comes out the victor, all embodiments of status will be conferred from the Foremost family to them, including their home. But if the challenger is not successful, the Foremost can decide to issue the command of banishment, or death.

It explains why no one is eager to overthrow the Foremost—especially a man as formidable as Dravek.

The Reckoning Grounds have been transformed for the occasion. I may not have personal experience with Privotus Vimorteth, but there are plenty who do. Banners the color of dried blood hang at intervals around the clearing on long wooden poles, a sola bone suspended between every few of them. Valefolk in their best garb stand shoulder to shoulder around a smaller area forming a half circle, delineated by normal animal bones pushed into the hard earth. Six enormous drums are placed along the north line, with six identically clad women swinging long mallets in perfect unison.

Do they get together for weekly practices? The thought bubbles up a laugh in my throat, and I have to work to keep it in. Ridiculous to find humor at a moment that could bring death and ruin to my family.

Or freedom.

Another thought I fight to push aside, but it won't budge. If no one had challenged my father, he would have been allowed to pass on the responsibilities of the Foremost to his firstborn before he became too brittle to fight back.

A role I have no desire to play.

Maybe this is a good thing, I think. *Maybe Myrzeth will win.* Noxious guilt seeps through my skin the moment the words flick through my mind. Even though he's a tyrant, I can't wish ill on my father.

My brothers stand at my side, like they did at the first ceremony when the solas returned. Unlike last time, my mother is with us. Gone are the featherweight fabrics, the golden designs on her face, the elaborate hairdo. Robed in a modest frock with her simple blond plait draped across her shoulder, she clutches my brothers to her sides, her unadorned arms locking them in fiercely, protectively.

She's never looked more beautiful.

Drumbeats fill the clearing incessantly, bending every breath, every pump of every heart to their pulse. The moment I think my body might fail under this unnatural rhythm, the drummers withheld their mallets. I swear I can hear all Utsanek take a collective breath.

The time has come.

My father steps into view between the centermost drummers, once again draped in his fur robe the hue of midnight. He walks into the core of the clearing, followed closely by his most trusted man, Krandel. When my father undoes the clasp of the cloak from his throat and lets it fall, Krandel lurches forward to catch it. As he wraps it up in his arms and bows out of sight, a look of barely contained revulsion swims across his features.

Spinning around to assess the gathering, my father raises his arms and reveals the intimidating broadsword sheathed at his side. There's no question what tactic he will take in the fight. Deadly force.

"And where is my would-be challenger? Has he crawled back into the slimy pit from which he emerged?"

When my father makes a joke—albeit a macabre one—he is used to at least some form of reciprocation. But the attitude toward him has shifted. Not one person laughs or grunts in return.

He hides his alarm well, but there is a subtle tilt to his head, a tightening of his fingers. Neither are good signs.

The people on the other side of the clearing part, and Myrzeth steps into view. My nails bite into the flesh of my palms as I watch a young woman trailing him. The jaunt to her step and the position of her chin communicate her infatuation with Myrzeth. And the spotlight.

Ketra, what have you gotten yourself into?

Father's opponent does not wear any frivolous garb, and there isn't a weapon anywhere on him. Instead, he holds his time-worn book up in front of him, a slight smile tugging at the corner of his mouth.

I can feel my father's patience wearing thin, even from fifty feet away.

"How good of you to show up" —Father bows in mock respect— "to your own challenge."

Only then does Myrzeth look up from his page. He holds a finger in his place, obviously enjoying the reaction he can provoke in the Foremost. He snaps the tome shut and places it tenderly in Ketra's hands. I feel sick as I watch her plant a passionate kiss on his lips before sauntering to the sidelines.

The newcomer faces my father again. "Well, then. Shall we get this over with?"

Dravek's jaw clenches, and he reaches for his sword, drawing it and holding it outward in a practiced motion. "With pleasure."

They circle each other for a while, my father looking like a beast about to spring, and Myrzeth appearing amused by the whole thing.

"To be clear," he drawls, bringing his hands together in front of his chest and massaging his knuckles. "If I win, you will immediately lose all your rights as Foremost in the Vale."

"I won't lose," Father says.

Myrzeth raises an eyebrow. "Oh? Then don't let it concern you."

A snicker ripples around the clearing, causing a cold chill to race down my spine.

"But if you do?" The ghost-man paces in his nonchalant manner.

Father's response is more a snarl than actual words. "The Vale will be yours."

"Excellent." Myrzeth drops his hands to his side and gives them a quick shake.

A roar erupts from the Foremost as he lunges at his adversary, bearing down on him with a powerful swing of his sword. The slight man, narrowly avoiding the edge of the blade, lets my father's momentum propel him past. The valefolk's derisive laughter adds insult to his fumble.

It isn't exertion that makes my father's skin redden. He glares at Myrzeth and tries a different approach, lunging forward and stabbing to the full reach of his arm. Again, Myrzeth seems to anticipate Father's actions. His feet are quick, and where he pales in comparison to my father's strength, he outstrips him in speed. As the Foremost's temper flares and each swing loses him energy, a wicked laugh emanates from the challenger's pale face.

Instead of demoralizing him, it seems to renew Dravek's vigor. In a succession of quick blows, my father manages to take Myrzeth off guard, clipping him across the fleshy part of his forearm. Black blood drips from Myrzeth fingertips, and all the levity drains from the challenger's face. My father grimaces—his version of a smile.

"So, you are flesh and blood after all," he taunts.

A mistake. With a summoning motion of his wrists, Myrzeth calls the ténesomni to his aid. The shadows rush in, congealing together so I almost feel them whipping past my skin. They collect above him, and I look around the clearing in alarm. It is . . . bright. I can see the treetops, leafy and lush, and shockingly green. And above that, a vast sea of deep blue.

But my eyes are drawn back to the writhing black entity suspended above Myrzeth's uplifted hands. A hideous smile slices across his face. Time stops as my eyes find those of my father's, huge with confusion and fear.

The challenger makes his final move. He flings his hands toward the Foremost, and the darkness obeys. My heart jumps to my throat as I watch every black thing in the entirety of the Vale collide like a gigantic fist in the center of my father's chest.

The impact throws him backward, knocking the sword out of his hands. And that's when Myrzeth springs into action. Releasing the shadows so they enshroud the world once more, he dashes to the blade and holds it over my father's throat.

Unblinking, I stare at the still shape of my father, broken on the ground.

Don't be . . .

A spluttering cough, a shuddering of the chest, and he comes to life.

Something akin to relief flutters in my chest, though I don't understand it.

Myrzeth bends forward and says loud enough for all to hear. "Do you concede?"

Eyes wide, he gazes up at the newcomer. My father nods. The tension in his body evaporates in the humiliation of his defeat.

With that, I am freed from the burden of taking up his mantle.

And our family has been made destitute.

34

AMYRAH

I COULD SEE THE SKY, PADA. Only for a moment."

He peers at me with skepticism, as if I'm eight years old. "Can't we always see it?"

I shake my head. "No, this was different. There was *more*."

He grimaces, his hands moving in a steady rhythm as he milks a goat. His voice comes out low, distant. "There is nothing else up there, Amyrah."

"But you're wrong. I saw it as clearly as I see you now. It wasn't black at all, but the purest blue imaginable. It felt as though it went on forever." He refuses to look at me, flaring my frustration. "You may not have witnessed it, but I'm sure others did if they were at the ceremony."

He rests an elbow on a knee, staring at the straw beneath his feet. "Amyrah . . ." He rubs his face. The nanny goat bleats impatiently.

I rush forward, kneeling before him and clutching his arm. "Don't you see what this means? This darkness is just a passing thing."

His hand falls as he considers me in my sphere of light. "Fine. Let's say you are right, and it is not something that continues forever. What can you possibly do about it?"

I draw back, his bluntness smarting. His shoulders rise and fall with his steadying breaths, and he closes his eyes. I swallow back my anger. This can't end like our last argument.

"You think I'm only going to get myself hurt," I whisper, "but inside I'm gasping for light. Real light. Every time I see it, my soul craves more. I can't sit back and watch people stumble around in darkness, or what they think is light."

He sits up straight and rests his palms on his knees, sighing deeply. His gentle eyes find mine. "I know."

My stomach unknots itself.

The milking completed, I pick up the pail and step into the warm Zomré morning. Father follows close behind.

"I am going to Utsanek again today," he says, heading toward the lean-to along the sheds. He bends and lifts the handles of the small wooden cart. "We need fresh feed for the goats. A few of them will be kidding soon." The cart bounces out of its ruts and onto the packed dirt path. Father smiles at me. "Should we go together?"

"I'd love that. Let me get some things together."

I screw the lid on the milk pail and climb down to the stream. Lowering the jug down, I slip it into a gap Father created with rocks, and the icy water flows around it.

Back in our yard, Father follows me to the cottage. He leans against the doorframe and watches as I dump the few remaining nuts into a bowl and add the empty basket to the stack I'll take to the market. He motions for me to give him the handled one full of eggs I collected this morning. Looking around the cottage, I try to think of anything I'm forgetting.

It looks cheerful today, with a crackling fire in the smooth-stoned hearth, a vase of tiny pink flowers on the mantelpiece, and the scrubbed table in front of it, adorned with a centerpiece of bolétis. I take in the neatly arranged storage shelves with their textured baskets, the two narrow beds draped with simple but sumptuous wools. My eyes fall on the purse on the foot of my bed.

When I grab it, something thuds to the floor. The book. Father bends to retrieve it, and his face goes white.

"Where did you get this?" He rasps, shaking fingers touching the cover gingerly.

I move closer to him, watching the lines deepen on his face. "Bryn's wife gave it to me the first time I met her."

Pada's jaw quavers. He swallows forcefully. "I got rid of it long ago."

I frown. "You've seen it before?"

He cautiously lifts the front cover, still acting like he's in the presence of a specter.

"Why would you want to throw it away?"

He looks at me, sparkling tears losing themselves in his thick beard. One long finger taps at the page, and I peer down. A faint E.C. is traced inside the cover. I hadn't noticed it.

"Because it belonged to your mother."

I grab the book before it falls from his hands. He backs up until his legs rest against his bed, and he sinks down.

He takes some time before he speaks. "She read from it every day. Every single day. I acted like I didn't care, but only because I envied her faith." He laughs dryly. "Or feared what it could do if I let it in."

I join him on the bed, regarding the book with renewed wonder.

"After she died, I raged against Elyōn. I wanted even less to do with him than I had before. I went into the forest and threw this thing away as far as I could. I hoped the decay would take it, that I'd never have to hear anything about Elyōn again."

"Someone must have picked it up," I say, wonder filling me.

He shakes his head. "I can't believe it."

We sit in stupefied silence until Father sniffs and looks at me. "You know what this says to me?"

I tilt my head, waiting.

"It says nothing is truly impossible."

He reaches for my hand and gives it a reassuring squeeze.

Gathering up our things, we leave the cottage behind and find the cart waiting where we left it. Father fixes a couple lanterns on two hooks meant for the purpose and hitches up the cart by its handles. We set off down the trail, carried on with the music woven by stream and songbirds and souls knit together.

For a moment, I pretend everything is right in the world.

The illusion breaks upon entering Utsanek. On every street corner, the gossip hisses.

"Did you see how awful Ketur looked?"

"Yes, so drab and dispirited."

"Well, you can't blame her with that excuse of a man she calls her husband."

"And her youngest boys. Did you see? Cowering in her arms like babies."

"The older one must be nearly twelve by now. Shameful he is so dependent on her at that age."

"And what of her oldest? He showed so much promise before, but he looks as wrecked as his mother."

"Pity."

"Yes, well. It was bound to happen. We always knew they wouldn't lord their status over us forever."

I try not to stare at the women as we pass. Who are they talking about? Disquiet threatens to smother me. My steps slow, the cart trundling on behind my father.

"But what about the newcomer?"

"Have you ever seen such power?"

"Nowhere but with the Shrouded."

"And he's easy on the eyes."

"That young lady sure thinks so."

"He says he's going to usher in a new age for the Vale. Do you believe that?"

"A new age? Well, I'm all for that. It could hardly be any worse than the one we just lived through."

"It's about time we had a new Foremost."

So, the challenge was successful.

The urge to run off and find Belwyn is strong, but I realize, with a sinking heart, I have no idea where to find him. Every single one of our meetings has been by chance. Why did I never find out more about him?

Elyōn . . . my mind whispers. But I don't know what else to say.

Thankful the abundance of sola brossa means I no longer need to be worried about people seeing my light, I hurry to catch up to my father as he approaches the market square.

I am uneasy entering it, remembering how hostile it turned the last time I was here, but the mood feels different today. Everyone buzzes with excitement. Stall keepers and shop owners alike have decorated with banners of dyed fabric and fresh gathered foliage from the forest's edge. There are more fine wares on display than normal.

Father weaves the small cart through the throng with extraordinary patience. I trail after him, trying to make sense of the shift in mood.

The sola bones lighting the scene nauseate me. I keep my eyes downward, scanning the faces, the stalls, everywhere I can possibly see, for one particular person.

Belwyn is nowhere in sight.

My eyes fall on the fanum at the north end. More offerings crowd the steps than I have ever witnessed before, and the doors are open. People move in and out of it, their faces full of pious sobriety.

What has happened to my city? I'd like to think it has changed for the better, but I know it hasn't.

"Amyrah, give me a hand with this, would you?"

My father's voice summons me from my fretting. I rush over, catch the other end of the giant sack, and help him heave it to the cart. We load three more, and I dust off my hands on my dress as Father gets the heavy load rolling.

"What other business did you want to attend to?" he asks between puffs.

I look down at the basket of eggs, recalling how I don't have anyone to trade with now that Orlagh stays in Ellithïm.

"Nothing," I say, feeling foolish.

We push on as the valefolk shift around us. Their mood is so vibrant that I feel more keenly than ever how I do not belong.

The cart stops. My father stands stock still, face to face with a man I've never seen before, yet who stirs up ghostly memories. A girl close to my own age, with a wine-colored dress and blond hair that must have taken ages to arrange, hangs off his arm. She tilts her chin in challenge at everyone who dares to stare.

"Téron." The man nods.

My father's shoulders inch upward. "Myrzeth," he growls.

"It's actually Foremost now." He smirks at the girl. I'm certain she must be half his age.

"Forgive me if I don't congratulate you."

The girl's gaze travels lazily away from my father, toward me. She looks me up and down, raising an eyebrow.

"That's exactly the kind of petty answer I expected from you, although I must say I had hoped you would've grown out of it." He leans his head as the girl whispers in his ear, then shoots his icy eyes to mine.

"And who do you have with you today?" Moving past my father, Myrzeth plants himself in front of me. Something like a fist clamps around my heart. "Could this be . . . of course. Little Amyrah."

The girl snickers. An unbecoming sound for such a pretty face.

"Don't say your father has not told you who I am."

I almost believe his look of surprise.

My father's livid features prove the man treads on dangerous ground.

"He has not," I answer, holding my head higher.

Myrzeth tilts his chin, and a smile tugs on his mouth. "I see you inherited my sister's spirit."

All the air is knocked from my lungs. My mouth falls open, and I struggle to form words. "You're my . . . my—"

"Uncle." A playful smile tugs at his lips. "You don't remember me at all?"

I frown, struggling to make a memory surface. His fair looks are cloying, churning my stomach as only something foul can. "Not a bit."

He makes a crestfallen face. "How sad. You and I had a particularly special bond."

"That's a lie, Myrzeth." Father takes one step closer. "She saw right through you, even at a young age."

The girl clings to my uncle's arm protectively, staring at me.

"Well," he says, holding out his arms in a gesture of defeat, "you can't blame me for trying." He strides forward. "You might not look much like your mother, but I'm curious to know what other attributes she may have passed down to you."

Instantly, my guard is up. My father's fists clench at his sides as he watches Myrzeth like a bird of prey.

My uncle leans forward and whispers in my ear, "Because if you are at all like her, we could either have something that could become unstoppable, or something that could tear this whole valley apart."

The repulsive sensation of his moist breath on my cheek sends shivers down my spine.

He straightens and smiles wickedly.

"I can't wait to find out which it is."

35

BELWYN

I CLIMB AN OLD LADDER to the roof of our family's new dwelling and investigate the shingles. As I expected, half of them are rotten or mysteriously absent. As if the dozens of pots strewn all over the inside after last night's rain weren't proof enough.

"Shem," I call down. "Go help Korvin with the handcart."

He scrunches up his face. "But you told me to hold the ladder."

"Never mind that. I'll be fine. We need to get the new shingles on before the rain picks up again. Just go help him."

I hoist myself onto the ledge of the roof and look out at Utsanek in the damp darkness. From the glowing lanterns in the streets below and the few sola bone shards that have made it to this poorer district, I can make out the dim picture.

This neighborhood is a slapped together collection of sloped rooftops and snaking chimneys. Ours isn't the only roof with problems. The one across the alley from us has a gaping hole, two feet across at least. But no one cares enough to fix it.

Inactivity invites my darker thoughts to seep in, like rainwater through the gaps in these weathered shingles.

Come on, boys. Hurry up. I rub my hands across my trousers to keep them warm.

Father has not been home in days. 'Home' sounds wrong. He hasn't been *present*.

Why doesn't that bother me?

Probably because he hasn't been present for most of my life. Being present means more than showing up to berate your sons for their failings, or only partaking in your wife's company when she will make you look good.

I've done my best to respect him, to live up to his insatiable standards, but I lost a bit of that childlike trust at the Challenge Ceremony. I watched the faces of the valefolk when they celebrated his fall, when they were released from his rule of fear. In his pride, he could not see what has been plain for years. He's a joke to the people. They didn't want to disrupt the eerie quiet of the kaligorven's absence—the only reason no one opposed him until now.

The whispers wherever I go are the worst—not because I don't agree with what they say about him, but because of how my brothers and my mother are being dragged into this with him.

My fingers press into my thighs. If he had been with us more, would Rhun have been so uninformed about the dangers of the kaligorven? If he had been a real father to him, would I be the one constantly having to brace for wave after wave of guilt for not protecting him as I should have?

I let the anger build in me, filling every empty space. My muscles contract painfully under its influence, straining against the tendons and moving my bones against my will. It pushes on my lungs, yet I am incapable of making their air escape. I tighten my fingers around the ledge of the roof and feel like, if I squeezed, I could reduce it to splinters.

This rage—it's intoxicating.

The clatter of wheels punctures it, lets out the pressure. Korvin and Shemai roll the cart to the foot of the ladder, arguing about the best way to position it.

A cold fear radiates across my skin. If I'm not careful, I could be every bit as frightening as my father. Or worse.

I must be better for my mother and my brothers.

Swallowing forcefully, I call down to them. "Leave it like that. It's perfect."

Over the course of the morning, the three of us work together to solve the problem of the leaky roof. Shemai grips the base of the ladder while Korvin shuttles shingles up and down with caution. I hammer the planks on one at a time, sealing up the gaps. It is satisfying to do physical labor like this, to see the value of an action manifested. To be able to assess worth, look at a job and know it is well done.

"Here, Mother told me to bring this to you."

I glance at Korvin curiously as he grips the ladder tightly and holds out a spiced bun. A perfect spiral glazed with a shiny, sweet syrup.

"Did she make these?" I ask, tucking my hammer into my belt and slipping the treat from his hand.

He nods. "They're really good."

I look at him and frown.

"I know. I'm just as surprised as you."

Korvin descends the ladder. My eyes follow him down and land on my mother, waiting at the bottom. She wears a flour-stained apron and a soft smile. Both become her.

I sink my teeth into the pastry and close my eyes. I've never tasted anything so delicious.

"Belwyn?"

I open my eyes. My mother is no longer alone, but in the company of two young women and a child. I get a sinking feeling. Korvin goes down first, and I follow him, my twisting stomach making it hard to keep my footing.

"This young lady says she knows you."

I wipe my hands on my tunic and turn around. Amyrah and another girl watch my every move, both carrying several books. I evade Amyrah's eyes, looking instead at my stained garb. Warmth rises under my collar. Clearing my throat, I approach them.

"Yes, Mother," I say, keeping my eyes fixed determinedly away from them. "This is Amyrah. We've met, uh, a few different times."

My mother raises an eyebrow at me, and the grin I force on my lips feels more like a grimace. She turns to the young women. Amyrah's necklace glints from her throat, brighter than ever.

"And your friends?"

The other girl tugs the child closer. "I'm Wehna, and this is my brother, Arvo."

I nod at them. The little boy stares around me at my brothers, a shy smile dimpling his cheeks.

"Hello, Belwyn," Amyrah says softly, and I can no longer avoid her.

Her cool eyes, which I expected to heap condemnation on me, act more like a balm, stilling my accusatory thoughts.

"We should talk," she says.

I can do nothing other than nod dumbly.

Picking up the hint, Wehna motions at the books in Amyrah's hands. "Here, between Arvo and me, we can take those."

With a grateful smile, Amyrah hands the volumes over.

"Thanks for helping me get them," Wehna says, letting Arvo take ownership of the lantern. "I wouldn't have worked up the courage to do it without you."

Amyrah hugs her friend's neck, then watches as brother and sister move down the street.

"Would you care for a spiced bun, Amyrah?" Mother moves toward the entryway, looking back in question.

"No, thank you." She smiles. "But would you mind if I took your son for a walk?"

I can feel my cheeks heating up as well.

Mother smiles. "Well, since he's been a good boy and finished his jobs for today, I don't see why not."

I mumble something that sounds like 'thanks' as she hands me a lantern. I catch up with Amyrah, hoping she won't be able to see my burning face.

We stroll quietly for a while, weaving through the streets without a destination in mind. When we step into the open air outside, she breaks the silence.

"Belwyn, the way we parted—"

I put out a hand, finding her forearm. "Please, don't. I deserved that response."

When my fingers travel beyond the edge of her sleeve and brush her skin, she draws her arm away. A soft shade of pink spreads across her cheeks.

"No, you didn't." She looks down, her eyelashes fluttering. I find the subtle freckles dotting her nose and the bunches of her cheeks. "I can't blame you for this broken system we're trapped in."

"Even so," I say, my chest considerably lighter, "you don't know how bitterly I regret it."

Her eyes flick up to mine, studying them so closely that my heart picks up pace. Judging by how she reaches for a lock of her hair and turns away, hers does too.

"You have a lovely family," she says, changing the subject. We resume walking.

I exhale. "Yeah, they're alright."

"I didn't know you had more brothers." She pauses, our footsteps padding almost noiselessly on the soft earth. "How are they doing with everything?"

I scratch the back of my head as I try to work out how much I should tell her.

Everything, I decide.

"We all seem to be dealing with grief in different ways. My youngest brother doesn't really grasp what's happened. As long as there is an activity to keep him focused, he's been fine. Korvin, the next oldest—" I suck in a sharp breath and close my eyes. That title used to belong to Rhun. "He's a lot quieter, more attentive to the needs of those around him. I think that's his way of processing things. Projecting outwards."

I hold the lantern tighter. "It's my mother I've been most worried about. Her grief immobilized her for weeks. I wonder if she's been going through it a lot harder than the rest of us because her confidence in the life Father had built for us shattered. When she lost her dearest boy, she also lost the man she thought would protect us."

Amyrah stops and stares at me, her mouth falling open.

I cringe and raise a hand to my brow. "Sorry," I mumble. "I said too much."

"No," she whispers, moving closer and reaching for my hand, pulling it down. Chills run up my arm. She's done this to me before. "It's fine. I understand."

Clearing my throat, I cast around for words in my foggy brain. "She—she's been a lot better lately, though. In a lot of little ways." The heat dies down in my face somewhat. "And it's kind of like I'm only seeing her for who she is now." I watch her eyelashes flutter. Are other people's so thick?

She continues to hold my hand, staring up at me. "And what about you?"

I frown. I don't want to talk about myself.

"Have you been able to move forward?"

A rough laugh fills the space between us. *So little space between us.*

"I've . . ." my mouth goes dry. I lick my lips and try again. "I've been noticing the little things that help lessen the darkness. And Rhun's name doesn't dredge up the same pain it used to. It's different now. Duller."

Her hand squeezes mine. She says nothing—and everything.

My eyes dip to her necklace, then back to her face, framed by her wild curls. I raise a hand to touch them, brushing one gently away from her cheek with the back of my fingers. My hand feels heavy; I lower it slowly, so it rests on her shoulder against the curve of her neck. Her throat shivers as she swallows.

"How do you do it?" I whisper, my eyes tracing her features.

"Do what?"

"How do you keep fighting the shadows? How do you make your own light?"

A frown skitters across her eyebrows, and she looks away. "Part of it I can't explain. It awoke in me the moment the solas returned. It's not only the light around me. It's like there's a calling on my heart I can't ignore. Something planted inside that drives me to fight it."

My stomach squeezes as she talks. Her passion, her heart, *everything* about her makes me hunger for more. And it has stirred a fear for her safety that increases every moment I'm in her presence.

"Please be cautious, Amyrah."

"What? You don't think I'm capable of looking after myself?" She raises a brow and tilts her chin at me, mildly offended.

I shake my head. "It's not that. Everything is growing more . . . tense. Don't you sense it? There are more consequences for opposing the kaligorven than there have ever been before."

"I'm not afraid of them."

"Well, you should be. Were you at the Challenge Ceremony?"

She shakes her head and releases me.

I draw my other hand away from her face and pace back and forth, unable to hold in my nervous energy. "You didn't see what I did. Myrzeth . . . he has unusual powers. The darkness listens to him. And he wields it like a weapon. I've never witnessed anything like it."

Amyrah's jaw sets defiantly. "I have a weapon of my own."

I grab her by her shoulders. "Not like this. Please. I'm begging you, Amyrah. Think about your actions."

She pries my hands off her and steps back. "I do, Eelwyn. But I think about the cost of silence more."

Dread slips into my gut. "What do you mean?"

"The solas. You have dealt with your own guilt for killing one. But the answer isn't simply to stay your own hand when the time comes to strike. It's in defending those who cannot do so for themselves." She clutches the necklace at her throat, her fingernails biting into the tender skin, turning it white. "You keep telling me to think about myself, but what about them? Who will stand up and fight for them, if not me?"

I shake my head, desperate for her to understand. My words are strained, pleading. "It's a fight you can't win."

Doubt pulls at her lips, like she fears the truth of my words. But with each breath the white fire in her eyes screams against it.

"Maybe you're right," she whispers, backing even further away from me. "But I can still be their voice."

"Amyrah—"

"No, Belwyn. I won't hide anymore."

A curse rides my sharp exhale. I step toward her, ready to make her understand by any means possible, but I'm interrupted by the sound I dread most in the world: the haunting timbre of the hunting horn.

I have a brief glimpse of Amyrah's wide eyes before she spins around and threads through the trees, without a lantern or a single method of defense other than her stubborn belief that her light will protect her. And even though I know I should go with her, I should do everything in my power to bring her back, I cannot.

Terror has sent out long, immobilizing feelers that root me to the ground.

36

AMYRAH

I RUN, PROPELLED BY THE SOUND that can only mean one
thing: death to a sola.

I must stop this from happening.

The thought rages through the cells in my body, fills it so I experience
every leaf and branch touching my skin as a crackle of energy. The
whisper of wind in the treetops drives me. Faster, *faster*.

If I hurry, I can get to the sola before any of the hunters from Utsanek
even have a chance to get organized. I can urge it to leave. And if that
fails, I can stand and convince them to leave it alone.

My legs do not tire as I pass through bush and briar, as I skirt streams
and scramble over boulders. The horn sounds again, spurring me on.

For such a time as this.

Perhaps this is what Father meant.

Perhaps this is the moment I was made for.

I taste blood, my lungs scream in pain, but I don't care. I won't let that stop me.

After more miles than I can guess, I see it ahead: the brilliance only a sola can give. I come to a racing stop, clinging to the rough bark of a tree to catch my breath.

Elyōn, give me strength.

As I approach the light gasping for air, nervousness possesses me so my limbs begin to shake.

You've faced the kaligorven before. Remember the hope that came to you then. You are not alone. You've been made for this moment.

Bolstered, I approach the blinding display.

But something is wrong. I squint at the light. It does not flow and ripple in rays and ribbons. It does not sparkle or shift. Not a breath of warmth exudes from it. The light, which should be clear and life-giving, has a green tint. It feels like death.

Then disappears entirely.

"So nice of you to come, Amyrah."

The voice slides over my skin like oil. I grab a nearby sapling for support as my uncle steps out of the shadows. A curving horn hangs at his side, and he holds something in his hands—a small bundle wrapped in leather.

My legs wobble beneath me as I gasp for air. He watches me carefully. "Oh, did you like my little ruse?" A quick movement of the hand, and the leather shroud flips off, revealing a whole handful of fresh sola brossa. "No sola, but they do the trick in a pinch. Especially when one's mind is predisposed to look for a certain *luminescent* phenomenon."

"Why would . . ." I swallow and determine to stand on my own two feet. "Why would you do such a thing?"

He wraps up the bones carefully again and stoops to set them at the base of a tree. "How else could I get you on your own? I knew after I threatened your father, it would be difficult to get you away from his overreaching protection."

His sharp eyes cut deeper than any blade. My heart jumps into my throat.

"But won't others be coming?" I ask, the words barely audible.

"Oh, no. My men have been given orders to keep the valefolk busy in the city square. Some trouble-making youth stole the horn for a joke, you see." His eyes twinkle maliciously.

The adrenaline that sped me here dries up, and I feel tired. So, so tired. My shoulders slump forward, and I struggle to stand.

"I assume you've already been made aware of what my particular skill set includes." An ugly smirk pulls at his features. He raises his hands and makes the shadows dance in twirling pillars above each. With another gesture, the ténesomni rearranges itself into a swirling dome that rushes around me, obscuring him from view.

At once, my stupor leaves. I stand straighter, settling into a sturdy stance. Feet shoulder width apart, hands balled firmly by my sides. *No*, I think, opening my hands and staring daggers into the blackness. A pulse of energy rushes through me, blasting the shadows far, far away. I blink in surprise.

"Impressive. Very impressive," Myrzeth says, releasing the shadows and approaching me with slow steps.

I stare down at my hands, shaking with exhilaration.

"If I were to hazard a guess, I'd say you didn't know you could do that."

My lips push together in a tight line. I will not satisfy him with an answer.

He laughs and shakes his head, circling around me. "You are more like your mother than I thought. She would never degrade herself to banter with me, either."

I resist the urge to spin around and keep him within my range of vision.

"And I bet you couldn't have been more different from her," I say.

"Ah, well, there you are both right and wrong." He comes around to my other side, stopping when he looks me in the eyes once again.

"It is true that in the end we could not have been more opposed. She was always so annoyingly good. Of course, to a person like that, the only one answer is to blindly accept the light. It's your only option, really, if you refuse to budge on your convictions."

"Some would say honor can only be found within conviction."

He nods his chin. "True, niece. And those of a more antiquated mindset will cling to that ideal even as the last remnants of life drain out of them."

I close my eyes and suck in a sharp breath. How can he so callously make reference to how my mother—his own sister—died?

"But those with the willingness to imagine other possibilities soon find that narrow, moralistic view . . . limiting." His hand clamps around my wrist with an iron-like grip. I open my eyes with a gasp. His fingers are so cold.

"Your mother, Amyrah, was one of those narrow-minded fools. While she was off being enamored by a deity she could not see, I explored a more tangible source of power."

Bile builds in the back of my throat. I yank my arm out of his grasp, and he lets out a peal of amused laughter.

"We could have been allies, your mother and me. Right from the beginning, we were special. We could call and banish the darkness at will, as all the Luvesti are able."

I blink several times as I try to digest what he's saying. "The Lu . . . Luvesti?"

He smiles, broad and obnoxiously white. "Ah. Didn't you know?" His mouth curves into a pitying expression. "Of course, I should have realized your father wouldn't tell you."

Unease climbs up my spine, vertebra by vertebra.

"You do not belong here. Even with half your blood tainted with Utsanek dirt, you are Luvesti by race."

I shake my head, unwilling to let him into my head. A different race? The Vale is my home. Every word that comes out of his mouth is a lie.

Isn't it?

He snorts in disgust. "Ellehra and I have our wonderful parents to thank for messing us up like this. For sending us here in the first place." The pungent mulch silences his steps as he paces, never breaking eye contact with me for a moment. "But really, I should thank them. It turns out there really is no better place to become intimately acquainted with the darkness. They had no idea what a gift they gave me."

My mouth opens and closes. I grasp around for some lifeline of sense. My mother. My grandparents. The Luvesti. My thoughts swirl more than the ténesomni, looking for somewhere, anywhere, to find purchase. But there is nothing but this sinister man and the incriminating knowledge burning at my core.

I do not belong here.

Myrzeth leans in, his pale face filling my vision. "So, what will it be, Amyrah? Will you broaden your mind with me? Share in the knowledge, share in the power?" He straightens and backs away. "Or must I arrange for the kaligorven to take care of you, as they did my sister?"

My eyes flit around my orb of light—it seems smaller—wondering if the Shrouded wait just beyond, where I can't see. "C-can you control them too?"

The corner of his mouth twitches, ever so slightly, but he masks it with a self-assured grin. "They respect what I have. As long as I perform for them, I find them more than willing to perform for me."

The shivering starts in my chest and spills to my extremities. I open and close my mouth multiple times, trying to form the words. But it's like I am underwater.

"Yes?" Myrzeth says, coming closer, closer still.

I shake my head and try again. His amused expression begins to fade after a while, his patience with this game wearing thin. When his hands move out from his sides and he spreads his palms, when his lips begin to move with whatever unnatural language he's speaking, I find my voice. It leaves my lungs in the form of a song.

> *Lo, there will be a coming day*
> *When bird, beast, man shall see,*
> *For all the darkness will fade away*
> *And all of the Vale will be free.*

The last verse of the ancient tune spills from my lips like warm cider. Just as the trembling overtook my body from the inside out, the music replaces every grain of weakness with a fire-like strength.

I am no longer afraid.

> *Thus grows the ever bright'ning day,*
> *From the fields to the ne'er ending sea,*
> *And the Light of Life will shine on all,*

For rich and whole we shall be.

A dark fury erupts from my uncle's livid face as he summons the ténesomni to throw itself against me. And it is his one mistake. In the second the darkness is lifted, and I can see beyond my limited range of vision, there isn't a dark beast in sight.

The shadows slam against me but break apart like mists in Elberu's heat. When they rush back to their original posts, my uncle's pale face is aghast with confusion and fear. His eyes look beyond me, to something that makes the back of my neck tingle with warmth. I risk a glance behind.

High in the branches, a dazzling light sends down spiraling tendrils that curl around me, embracing me. A pure, sweet trilling fills the air.

The wren's song.

I can't help it. I laugh, and the tiny sola chirps with me.

When I turn around, my uncle is nowhere.

37
WEHNA

ARVO'S WHOLE BODY TIPS FORWARD, ever so slowly, until his forehead rests on the book open before him. He hangs there, suspended between table and chair, with his arms dangling straight down between. The bracelet of flying birds shines softly around one of his little wrists.

"I don't wanna learn how to read," comes his voice, muffled against the pages. He sways his arms apathetically. "You can't make me."

With difficulty, I hide my smile behind pinched lips. "Not even if I . . . tickle you?" I lunge forward and attack his exposed armpits. He shrieks and pulls his elbows in to his sides, his malaise giving way to a level of glee fitting for a five-year-old. I flick my hair out of my face and kneel on the wood floor. His grin fades as he pulls his right arm onto the tabletop and rests his cheek on it, looking at me with those green eyes.

"Mada and Pada aren't coming back, are they?" he whispers. His soft voice pierces me like a blade.

I reach for his hand, pin it between mine, and open my mouth to say something—anything—other than the truth. But I stop. He deserves to know. He probably already does, and it would only hurt him more to keep lying to him like this.

"No," I say, watching him carefully. He sucks in his bottom lip and gives a tiny, shattering nod. My brave, brave baby brother. Two solitary tears creep out of the corners of his eyes, leaving shiny trails across the bridge of his nose and his squished cheek. I stop them with a finger, taking the crystal droplets and pressing them to the fabric right above my heart.

"You're keeping them?"

"Always."

"In your heart?"

I nod, my own tears falling freely.

"Good." He sighs, and a smile bunches his other cheek. "Mada and Pada will want them."

A swirl of girls in dresses and braids and flower crowns enters the kitchen and consumes the quiet moment Arvo and I were sharing. My brother sits up and wipes his eyes.

"Do you wanna help us make a garland for the door?" one of the little girls whispers loudly in Arvo's ear as her sisters drop armful after armful of blooms on top of his schoolwork. He frowns, but then brightens and looks up at me hopefully.

"Can I be done learning for today?"

"Of course," I say as I pat his head and back out of the room. The happy chatter, which felt like a noose around my heart, fades behind me.

Bryn and Tress have been so accommodating. Even though they have five children of their own—all daughters ranging from the ages of two to thirteen—they've welcomed Arvo and me into their house without a single word of complaint.

I feel like a terrible human being as I grab a lantern and escape their company, leaving Arvo to the girls' dotage.

Sucking in a long breath of the cooler evening air, I hold it in my lungs for a while before letting it escape. Sometimes, the noise and busyness get to me. I'm just a pebble in a sea of activity, refusing to be carried by the waves of life, sinking lower and lower no matter how I'm tugged about. And although my soul knows it needs this—this sense of belonging and carefree levity—I feel like I'm one girlish giggle away from a complete meltdown.

What's worse is I know I should be setting some sort of example for these young ladies. They probably look up to me for some unaccountable reason. But I can't make myself stay with them a moment longer.

"Wehna." A breathy laugh animates my name, and I spin around to find its source. Amyrah jogs down the street, her face rosy, her eyes aglow, her necklace bouncing against her throat. The weight on my mind eases a little.

"What happened to you?" I ask, reaching out to stop her. She laughs again, her fawn waves floating in a crazy halo around her. *I have to give her some curly hair tips,* I remind myself.

"You wouldn't—" a gasp for air interrupts her. "You wouldn't believe it."

I loop my arm through hers before she falls over and lead her down the central street of Ellithïm. "I'm heading to the market. Walk with me and tell me after you catch your breath."

She nods and leans against me.

"I don't even know where to start," she says once the color has normalized in her cheeks. We duck out of the gate together and pull close to fit down the dark alley side by side.

She and Belwyn must have had quite the talk, I muse, irritated with myself for the twinge of jealousy that rises at the thought. I don't even know the guy, but I saw the way he looked at her. No one has ever looked at me like that.

"Start with that boy," I press, making her stop short.

"Oh—no. No, this isn't about him." Her cheeks flush scarlet. "Um, yes, I guess it started there. That was, uh, confusing. And . . . wonderful. Well, mostly." She laughs at the knowing smile creeping over my lips. "It's not what you think. And we may have ended in an argument, to be honest."

I roll my eyes and tug her to keep walking. "Well, since I haven't had a chance to get to know him, I must say I approve of how slow you're taking it."

She nods and goes quiet for a moment. Embarrassment washes over me. *Did I say the wrong thing?* Maybe I'm being too familiar with her.

"So." I clear my throat. "What was it?"

She gives her head a little shake. "Right. Yes. Did you hear the hunting horn?"

I nod. "Ellithïm has gotten good at ignoring them. Everyone continued as if nothing happened."

"That's actually good. It was all a ruse."

"What?" I slow and stare at her.

She turns toward me and nods. "It was a ploy to get me to come out in the open."

My fingers squeeze her wrist. "That sounds bad, Amyrah."

"I think, well, I think it could have been. Myrzeth—he's my uncle, by the way—*ow*!"

"Sorry." I pry my fingernails from her arm. "But he's your uncle?"

A grave nod is the only answer I get.

"That's . . . whoa. That's significant."

"Yes, and he tried to see if I had the same kind of powers as he has."

"You mean the creepy ones that tease the shadows into submission?" A shiver runs down my spine.

"Something like that."

I back away, peering at her through narrowed eyes. "Do you?"

Her body pitches forward in a mirthless laugh. "No. But I do have something that could challenge them." She turns to me, and her eyes twinkle. "Wehna, he threw all the powers of darkness at me, and they broke against me like water on rocks."

I tilt my chin, trying to make sense of what she's saying.

"And a sola showed up. Do you want to know the strangest thing about it? He was afraid of it. I saw it in his eyes." She grabs me by my shoulders. "Don't you see what this could mean?"

I continue to regard her in dumb silence.

"This darkness doesn't have to endure. I think . . . I think I'm the one who can bring it to an end."

A skeptical chuckle escapes my throat. "Do you actually believe that with the fidrélas growing in number by the day, with the undeniable signs that Elyōn exists and orchestrates our lives, he has honestly been waiting for you to come along and end this night?"

Hurt flickers in her eyes. Her hands drop from my shoulders, and I regret my words.

She looks down. "Maybe. I don't know."

I sigh and grab her hand. "Here's what I do know. Elyōn has definitely given you a gift. Who am I to say how it's meant to be used?"

Her pale blue eyes find mine and search them, pleading. "I'm not saying all that has been done to fight the shadows until now has been wasted. That place back there" —she motions toward Ellithïm— "is a testimony to how powerful small acts of faith can truly be. But maybe he has chosen me for a role in this. And I think he's shown me he will supply the power to complete it when the time comes."

I chew on my lip and start walking away—not because I'm angry at her, but because for some reason Elyōn keeps dropping people in my life with far greater faith than me. And it's starting to become more than I can bear. I've been put in my place by my five-year-old brother, humbled by the whole hidden community, and gently rebuffed by this new friend —not to mention how I could never live up to the self-sacrifice of my parents. Why does it seem so easy for everyone else to believe, yet for me it is a daily battle to put aside my doubts and fears?

How can someone born in the light be so easily swayed by the darkness?

"Wehna?" Amyrah's soft touch lands on the back of my shoulder. "Did I say something wrong?"

I reach back and clasp her hand, pulling it down and uniting it with my own.

"No. You didn't. I just . . . I think Elyōn is teaching me something through you." I manage a half-smile and a glance into her eyes.

She squeezes my arm with her other hand, and we continue through the streets of Utsanek in companionable silence.

As we approach the marketplace, however, things begin to change.

There is a frenzy of activity. People cart produce and merchandise all over the place, laughing as they bump into each other and hurry through the crowd. We enter cautiously, pressing even closer to each other.

"What's happening?" Amyrah whispers into my ear. "It's like there's some sort of festival going on."

I frown and glance around. She's right. There is an unusual number of vendors, food stands, merchants, and even a few troubadours in the mix. It reminds me of—

"It's exactly like the day the solas returned," Amyrah says.

"Yes." But what could be as important as the first renewal of Sola Vinari?

We push into the heart of the square, and Amyrah yanks me back.

"What?"

She shakes her head darkly. "Believe me. We're better off if we avoid those guys."

I look back. A circle of teenage boys, possibly under the influence of alcohol, are getting rowdy with each other. One of them looks our way, and his idiotic smile dies on his lips. I let Amyrah lead us in the opposite direction.

We weave through the mass of people, but the unnerving sensation that we are being followed pricks at the back of my neck. I turn around multiple times, but there is only the incessant rumble of strangers preoccupied with their own pursuits. A frown plants itself on my brow. I pull Amyrah's arm.

She spins around. "It's getting crazy in here," she almost shouts. "What do you say we forget about the market today?"

I bob my head and follow her as she cuts toward a side street. Maybe this worry will stop plaguing my mind if we can get out of here.

The quiet, dark alley is a welcome reprieve from the chaotic square. I glance over my shoulder at it, amazed so many people could be crammed into one place, and walk right into Amyrah.

"*Oops.* Sorry, I—"

The teenager from the market stands in front of us, wearing the most twisted grin I've ever seen.

"Thought you'd get away with insulting me the other day, didn't you?"

Amyrah stays perfectly silent. My skin tingles with dread.

He snorts. "Turns out I'm not the only one that's eager to see you get what's coming to you."

I grab a fistful of her dress and whisper into the back of her hair, "Amyrah, we need to move."

But she remains still.

Two more shapes appear out of the darkness, but they aren't wiry boys. They are tall and muscle-packed men, each like an apex predator.

The boy's hideous cackle tears through the air. "I'm gonna be so stupidly rich when the Foremost hears what I brought him."

The men approach fast, but Amyrah won't budge, no matter how much weight I sink into her limp arm. The man on the left makes a move toward her, and the other lunges at me, knocking the lantern from my hand. It puffs out. I swing at him with all my might, but my blows glance off. His deep laugh churns the pit of my stomach.

In my struggle against him, I lose track of Amyrah. I look around frantically to find her, only to see arms bulging with muscles dragging her into the darkness.

"*No!*" I scream. An explosion of pain bursts across my skull, and all goes black.

38
TERON

SOMETHING IS WRONG. Its gnawing presence grows within me like a thorn in my flesh.

I force myself to complete my tasks at the homestead instead of letting my anxieties overtake me. It takes all my resolve.

When the call of Sola Vinari sounds, yet again, I want to shake it from my mind like a mule frees its skin of pests.

Don't let it in. This battle is not for you. Keep your head down, and no harm will come to Amyrah. It is not up to you to fix all the wrong in the Vale. Don't let it in.

I repeat the same words over again, but with each blast of the horn, they become more difficult to say.

What if there is a sola out there, and I can stop this? What if I can make right what I failed to do thirteen years ago?

With great difficulty, I ignore its timbre until silence claims the valley once more.

But the ominous feeling increases. Can I trust that Amyrah did not run off into the woods as her mother did? Can I trust Myrzeth to leave her alone?

The answer to both questions is *no*.

Dread takes complete possession of my body, urging me on with an insistence that almost hurts.

Rushing through Utsanek's streets, I meet a familiar, tall figure in the alley leading into Ellithïm.

"Bryn, have you seen my daughter?"

He pulls me out of the shadows and into the wider street, where I can identify the concern that paints his features.

"No. In fact, I'm on my way to make a search of my own—for Wehna, Arvo's sister. She left him with my daughters a while ago, and we have not heard from her in a very long time." He pauses to think. "She went with Amyrah earlier today to retrieve her books from her apartment. I wonder if they've met up again."

I sigh and run my hands roughly through my hair. "Things are bad in the Vale, Bryn. Can you feel it? A current below the surface, flowing through the shadows? The tension is growing. It has always been there, but we have become used to it. This younger generation, though, does not have the benefit of years behind them. I worry everything seems so new and thrilling right now. But this evil—it is ancient. Perhaps Wehna and Amyrah know more about it than most, but I am certain not even my daughter understands the full extent of my brother-in-law's wickedness."

Nervous energy makes me pace the ground. Bryn's steady gaze follows my movements.

"There is none more cunning than him. He can twist his words like he twists the darkness. Even when you think you have resisted him, it is like he always anticipates your response and uses your strength against you."

Bryn lays a hand on my arm. "Peace, friend. We will find her."

I close my eyes and exhale, nodding slowly.

We have not yet arrived at Utsanek's central square when the drumming starts. Ahead, a living sea of people passes the narrow gap between buildings, heading to the northern gate. I growl in frustration and turn to leave. I want no part in whatever this is.

"No, wait." Bryn's grip arrests me. "We should go with them, Téron." He turns. "The sound makes my stomach flip just same as yours, but we cannot risk being uninformed of any developments in the Vale."

I shake my head and move to slip past, but he positions himself in front of me. "We need to be wise as serpents, for the sake of our families."

My chest deflates. Perhaps he is right. Now is not the time for ignorance.

Bryn's gaze drifts past my shoulders and down a branching side street. He stares in confusion for a moment, and his eyes widen.

"*Wehna.*"

He shoves me to the side, but I do not blame him when I see a heap of fabrics thrown to the gutter. Except it isn't just a heap. It's a person.

Bryn kneels beside the still form. A girl. An ugly gash snakes across her brow, trailing sticky blood across her face. Even in this awful state, I see the resemblance to Arvo.

I crouch down and feel for a pulse. It is weak, but steady.

"Let me go for help," I say, rising to my feet.

"No, Téron. I can manage on my own." He grabs a cloth from his pocket and tries to wipe the blood from her features, but it has already started to dry and will not come away.

"Please. Let me find someone."

"I assure you, I'll manage." Bryn looks at me and points in the direction of the Reckoning Grounds. "You need to be there. Someone needs to know what other dangers we should expect to encounter."

He says the last words darkly as he stares down at Wehna. I imagine he cannot look at her without seeing his own daughters.

A rush of nausea threatens to upend me.

I wish I didn't know exactly how he feels.

39

BELWYN

"THESE BUNS ARE STALE." My father squeezes one without trying it and makes a face.

Hardly, I think. *They were baked fresh this morning.* But I keep my mouth shut.

He throws it on the table and paces the length of the kitchen. It only takes four of his long treads.

"Is there nothing in this rat's hole to eat?"

Mother stands over a basin of dishes, her shoulders drawing upward. I open my mouth to answer for her but stop when she turns around. Her smile only looks slightly forced.

"What would you like? We still have a bit of pork shoulder left from last night's dinner, if you think that would appease you. But I'm afraid there isn't much of it, since it also served as our dinner for three days."

Father scowls at her and grabs the bun he tossed, sinking his teeth into it. He grunts and sits heavily at the table, placated for the moment. I glance at my mother. Her brow arches along with her subtle smirk of triumph. She turns back to the washing.

I approach her and rest my hand between her shoulder blades. "Why don't you let me take care of that?"

She nudges a clump of blond hair away from her face with the back of a sudsy hand. Her eyes communicate her question.

"I mean it. Shem and Korvin are upstairs trying to work out the kinks in a new game they've concocted. It involves dice and some sort of . . ." I chuckle. "Actually, I have no idea. I'm sure they'd love to explain it to you."

When I drop my hand and roll up my sleeves, taking the brush from her, she squeezes my wrist and bumps me with her shoulder.

If she had told me she loved me, I couldn't have heard it louder.

"That woman has made you soft," my father says after she's dried her hands and ascended the creaky stairs.

I scrub the dish in my hands with extra force and bite my tongue.

"Did you hear me, son?"

The chair shrieks against the floor, and the wet brush is yanked from my hand. I grip the edges of the basin and prepare myself.

"Look at me," he says, inches away from my ear. His voice carries with it a warning if I should ignore it.

Clenching my jaw tight, I face him, dishwater dripping on the rough planks of the floor.

Slowly, I raise my eyes.

His are not as dark as mine, but volatile. Fire and ice pressed up together, barely contained in a glassy case. They are set deep into his skull, and I can see the ridges of his eye sockets clearly pronounced around them.

"You've always been a disappointment, you know that?"

My fingers curl.

"I am aware," I whisper.

He tilts his chin. "What was that?" His tone causes a rush of weakness to course through my legs. I lean against the counter and suck in a breath.

"I said, I'm aware of how I've fallen short of your expectations. You've made it abundantly clear I am not the son you think you deserve."

Father's nostrils flare, and I should back down right now. But I can't.

"And maybe you're right. Maybe you don't deserve me."

I glance at the bandage wrapped around his forearm. He must have had his tattoos modified after his position was stripped from him. No doubt he wishes to transfer the burden of his failures to me. My throat tightens, but I shove my next words through, ignoring how the corners of my eyes prick with the threat of tears.

"Has there ever been a moment where I did not do exactly what you asked?"

He answers with a snort of disgust.

"Even my best has never been good enough for you. Because obedience isn't really what you desire. It's fear."

"Watch your words, boy," he growls. "I've only ever wanted to make you into someone strong."

"Really? Well, you've succeeded in that. But not, I think, in the way you intended."

He leans back and hitches up his brows. "Enlighten me."

"Strength—" I stop and lick my lips, but my tongue is dry. I try again. "Strength has nothing to do with beating someone into submission." I flinch as his fingers twitch but force myself to get this out before I lose my nerve. "I'm not talking about fists. You do it with something much more cunning. Words and actions." I stand straighter, anger beginning to take precedence over fear. "All this time, you thought you were the one dominating, but you've really taught us how to persevere under adversity."

His lips press so tightly together, they all but disappear. A flicker of doubt causes that hard line to wobble, but he makes no other motion.

He doesn't seem so intimidating anymore.

I almost laugh, but it sours in my mouth before it can escape. Is this how he feels when he uses words to cut us down?

You are just like him.

I push the thought aside. *Not now.* "I guess I have you to thank. What you've labeled as weakness—looking out for another person, seeing their needs, and standing by them in the face of opposition—has made me stronger than you can ever know."

My speech hangs in the musty air, growing heavier with each beat of my heart. I run the words over in my mind again. No, I don't regret a thing. It needed to be said, and it is better for him to take out his fury on me instead of my mother or brothers.

Silence is a tempestuous thing with my father. The tension between us builds to a caustic level, burning in my veins like acid, threatening to suck the stamina right out of me.

Wouldn't it be easier to fold, to let him win? He's my father, after all. Isn't it wrong to oppose him like this?

But in my heart, I know the most difficult and necessary place to stand up against evil is in the home.

Beads of sweat form on my brow, and I utter the first prayer of my life. *Elyōn, give me strength.*

This time, when the drums ring out, they are my saving grace.

"Get out," he says, and it's not venomous; it's more like something slowly deflating. "I never want to see your face again."

40

AMYRAH

A GROAN PARTS MY LIPS as a hand slips beneath one of my armpits and yanks me upright. I struggle to get my feet underneath me, yelping as the strong fingers dig into my tender flesh. My wrists ache, bound behind me with coarse rope. A meaty palm reeking of rendered animal fat clamps over my mouth. I struggle against my captor, but the grip tightens, bringing tears to my eyes. I blink them away and try to make my surroundings make sense.

Where am I?

"I wouldn't fight it if I were you." A slick voice tickles my ear, causing a shudder of pure revulsion to flow through me. "It won't do you any good."

My breath escapes in forceful bursts through my nostrils. The smell of his hand makes me want to retch.

I nod my head as much as his grip will allow.

"Good." He starts to peel back his fingers, but I rip my jaw out of his clutches and suck in a mouthful of air not marred with his stench.

"Relax, lass. Don't embarrass yourself."

His hold on me slips down so it no longer digs into my armpit. I stand under my own strength.

A quick glance above and behind reveals we're on the edge of the forest. The trees are lit with a sickly light. A raised platform lies ahead, with sola bones at its corners. Beyond that . . . darkness.

The rippling of many voices being shushed to silence washes through the clearing like a wave. My brows knock together as I try to understand.

I decide a whispered question is worth the risk. "What is this?"

The person behind me sputters out a grating laugh. "Your debut."

My debut? I try to spin around to see him, but he jerks me to keep me where I am. "What are you talking about?"

Another man's leering face comes into view on my right. He motions to the platform with his giant, stubbly chin. "Wait and see, sweetheart."

Straining my eyes to pick out anything past the blinding bones, I see a person on top of the platform. He is robed in so many inky linens, I mistook him for the darkness itself. But the glow of his anemic hair is unmistakable.

My uncle.

He holds up his arms, his white hands reflecting sola light like mirrors.

A collective gasp emanates from the audience—presumably the whole of the Vale—as if he conducted them to do so. I look up to see what has provoked their speechless awe.

A vortex of ténesomni spirals overhead, visible even in this dense night. It is so thick, it's a marvel there are any shadows left anywhere in the whole world.

I wonder at the purpose of it. The display unnerves me, I'll admit, but I can't shake the feeling Myrzeth is showing off. And that takes the edge off my fear.

How could this narcissistic man ever be related to my mother?

With a wave of his hands, he releases the shadows, to the delight of the crowd. Ténesomni rushes back to its natural place—everywhere except around me.

He nods subtly. I jump when the booming of drums eviscerates the silence. They rattle in my chest, as if it is a hollow cavern. Three drums to my left, three to my right.

"Welcome, valefolk."

His voice projects unnaturally. Does the darkness carry it for him?

"You've been called here to witness the beginning of a new era in the Vale."

Whispers slither through the air from the valefolk, and I don't blame them. Even my curiosity is piqued.

The tilt of my uncle's head shows he finds the reaction to his liking. He raises his hands and waits for the people to still once more.

"But before I get ahead of myself, I need to welcome our guests of honor."

At first I think he means me, but I am only one person. And I know he would never honor me. When he bows his head and mutters, I understand. He is summoning something.

Strange words escape his lips—a language that feels even older than Atsunic. After a beat, I hear something else. Something I've experienced before in the dead loneliness of the forest. Heavy footfalls.

This time, it's not only from one huge creature. This sound issues from dozens.

41

TÉRON

MORE OFTEN THAN I CAN RECALL, I have stood within these ceremonial grounds and witnessed things that still cling to the back of my mind. Every time I watched the sola blood pouring out, every time I whispered that it was all for our good, the black edged its way deeper into the crevices of my soul. It was a relief to avoid it for so many years.

Because this place . . . it is the haunt of death.

I come to the clearing with that knowledge already bearing down upon me, but the eerie silence achieved by thousands of valefolk makes it ever more apparent.

Holding up my lantern, I slip into the crowd. Everyone stands strangely still. And there is something else odd about the scene I cannot quite identify.

A woman looks over at me and curses. "Put it out, you fool."

That is it. No one has brought any light.

Not wanting to draw attention to myself, I open the door of the lantern and blow out the flame. Have the people become so accustomed to the illumination of the sola brossa that they no longer carry lanterns with them wherever they go, or is something else at work here?

I follow the gazes of the crowd to the far edge, along the tree line. A makeshift platform has been erected, with sola bones raised on stands on its four corners. The new Foremost stands in the middle of it, looking out at his people. Even near the back of the gathering, I can feel the frost emanating from his eyes.

The drums sound again. Myrzeth uses their frenzy to his advantage, grinning as the valefolk shift and grab each other, the tension in the clearing like a pulsing, living thing.

"Welcome, valefolk. You've been called here to witness the beginning of a new era in the Vale." His words, timed perfectly for when the drumming ceases, are like a burst of oxygen. People inhale them hungrily. But not me. He tilts his chin, a deceptive smile dimpling his cheek.

"But before I get ahead of myself, I need to welcome our guests of honor."

Leave, leave now, my thundering heart warns when the footsteps sound. The bone-rattling wind follows, bending the trees wildly. But my body is stuck in place, my eyes trained to the platform, my breath catching abrasively in the desert of my throat.

Muffled cries ring out as the sounds draw nearer. A chill crawls down my neck. There is no doubt the kaligorven are approaching, but this time from every direction, all around the perimeter of the gathering.

Why have they come? I can see no bonfire, no urn of sola blood.

"They promised they would return, did they not?" Myrzeth booms, as if in answer to my question.

I remember. The last Kuvror Erovantus, when they lifted the order of darkness. What is it they said? Something about our offering being acceptable but our faith still lacking. And . . .

Oh no.

I move through the people, drawn like a moth to flame. With each step forward, each shoulder I brush past, the unease within me multiplies. As my eyes strain to see who stands behind the platform, I pray to Elyōn that I will not find her among them.

The winds cease.

"And now, we welcome them back with open arms."

A commotion arises amid the valefolk as the Shrouded make their presence known. The crowd presses in as the beasts materialize from the ténesomni, penning us in like a pack of wolves. But I don't even notice, I don't even care. The fear they inspire is nothing like the crippling terror that possesses me when I get close enough to see the person held between the two towering men standing at attention behind the Foremost. She is serene and determined, and so much like her mother.

My legs give out. I remember what else the kaligorven said at their last visit.

That proof of our devotion would be required.

42

AMYRAH

THEY ARE ALL AROUND US. I hear their great shuddering breaths, and every footfall sends shockwaves racing up my legs.

Myrzeth, head lowered as he utters diseased words, now stands straight and holds out his hands, palms up. Night comes to his call and he sends it to fill the clearing, making even the sola bones appear dim. He eases the path of the Shrouded, coaxing them closer, closer, closer. They bulge on the cusp of shadows like black waters.

I keep my eyes fixed to my left, where a chill like the depths of Vestri emanates. The beast remains concealed behind the vibrating curtain of ténesomni, safe from the reach of the sola brossa. I can only imagine how frightening it must be for those closer to the back of the gathering, further than the bones' glow could ever stretch.

My uncle nods to four people standing by, and they approach the posts on which the bones are balanced. As they reach up, I feel pressure building behind my ribs.

No, do not take the lights.

It's one thing being resigned to facing darkness day by day. It's quite another to do it when you know there are monsters nearby.

The men take down the bones and slip them into satchels. When they close the flaps, everything except the space around my uncle and me is left in total blindness. I swear I hear a moan of relief from the creature to my left. I wish I could reach up and cover my necklace, now conspicuously bright.

"Praecéro" the Foremost says, and the shadows split to the edges of the clearing and stay there without him holding them back. We stand in a gentler, dusky darkness in which black forms can be made out.

"Kaligorven," —he gestures to either side— "we invite you to walk among us. Make your presence known, and we will honor you."

A form emerges to my left, and I yank against the man who holds my arm. His grip does not slack. My pulse pounds in my ears; the heaviness of terror binds itself around my chest. I squeeze my eyes shut and try to make the words to the song run through my mind. But it's like my head is packed with moss.

Sharp cries force me to open them again, but I wish I hadn't. On both sides of the platform, more beasts have gathered. From behind, very little detail can be seen other than their misty shadow cloaks and twisted horns barbing to the sky. But they are still terrifying.

Uncontrollable shivering overtakes me. I throw a panicked glance behind me, but there are no more monsters there.

Words, if you can call them that, form out of the beasts—but not just from one. All. The sound circles around, a guttural grinding, bouncing off the trees behind me and the walls of the city on the far end of the ceremonial grounds.

You have summoned us, and we have come . . . But our patience will not last . . . Present to us your offerings or bear our displeasure.

Restrained murmurs sound from the valefolk. I watch my uncle carefully, curious to see if this speech hits him with even a fraction of the force with which it has struck them. It might be my imagination, but I think I see a slight tremor in his hands before he laces them behind his back.

The smallest spark of courage flares in my mind, burning away the cobwebs. He takes several steps across the platform and spins on his heel.

If he is afraid, he conceals it well.

Trepidation tugs on my insides as he shoots a meaningful glance in my direction and waves me forward. I feel the cords around my wrists tighten and jolt briefly. My arms swing free. I rub them, then lurch as the man shoves me forward, snickering under his breath when I stumble.

"Let me first introduce someone to the Vale," my uncle says as he steps to the side.

The kaligorva closest to me rumbles menacingly.

Myrzeth lets out a contrasting laugh in response. "I promise, you will be well-satisfied with what I've brought you."

Crying out in wordless groans to Elyōn for courage, I ascend the platform with shaky steps.

43

BELWYN

THIS IS AN ABSURD MOMENT to feel so light of heart. *Did I really stand up to my father?*

A trembling laugh pushes past my lips as I pass my fingers through my hair. *Yes, yes, I did.*

But the pounding of the drums siphons away the rush of adrenaline. They are the footsteps of doom. Absolutely nothing in me wants to investigate, but I must.

I pass through the still-unfamiliar sector of Utsanek, avoiding mysterious puddles and heaps of rubbish. Small parcels are left on almost every doorstep. I bend to look at one of the piles closer. A country loaf, lanuum cakes, fresh sprouts, and even a cask of some fermented beverage —lavish gifts for such a destitute neighborhood. Other porches are even beautified with dried foliage. Offerings to appease the kaligorven.

Do they walk the streets of the city? I wonder. The image of a horrifying beast bending to sniff a bundle of flowers almost makes me laugh again. Either people have no common sense, or they are so desperate to please the Shrouded that they will try absolutely anything.

The drumming picks up again, this time sending a shiver down my spine and awakening a sense of urgency.

I run through the alleys, cursing when I lose my sense of direction. The streets in this poorer sector do not all go through, and some of them subtly twist until you are going the exact opposite direction than you intended.

Mercifully, I step out into one of the major thoroughfares and recognize where I am. This passage is lit with sola bones, and if I follow it, it will lead me to the northwest side of the Reckoning Grounds.

My feet pound the cobbled streets like drumbeats.

When I emerge through the northwest gate and into the clearing, I skid to a stop. This is where the drums sound, but I can see nothing. An ominous chill hangs in the air.

As I listen, the hushed sounds of thousands of valefolk reaches me. Then there is another voice, talking above it all. With trembling hands, I raise my lantern and blow out the light.

Stepping lightly, I approach the gathering, straining my eyes to make sense of what lies before me. But it's all shadows as thick as mud.

It's like I've stepped through a waterfall. To my darkness-trained eyes, I've walked into the middle of the day. Looking behind me, a wall of ténesomni shudders. This must be one of Myrzeth's darkness-bending tricks.

When I turn around again, a brighter spot at the north side of the clearing draws my focus. And dread assails my core.

The need to get closer overwhelms me. I almost don't see what I'm walking into until it's too late.

A massive, Shrouded form prowls directly in front of me, gripping the earth with four deadly paws. The darkness clinging to it shifts and undulates, sending out cold feelers in my direction.

I've seen one of these before.

I clamp my mouth shut just in time to keep in the sound of fright.

It must have heard me anyway. It raises itself up to its hind legs and turns to probe the ténesomni with hellfire in its eyes.

I close mine, and terror sinks its cold claws into my mind. It can only form one, desperate thought.

Elyōn . . .

The kaligorva sniffs the air tentatively, even those small breaths sounding like huge rushes of wind.

It sees. It can smell me. It knows I am here.

By some absurd stroke of luck, it lets out a heavy breath and turns to continue pacing the edge of the crowd.

My muscles convulse madly. I back away as quickly as I dare and lurch along the edge of the ceremonial grounds, losing track of how many kaligorven I shift past.

Are they protecting the valefolk or making sure none can escape?

When my heartbeat decelerates, I can concentrate on what is happening beyond them.

I don't like what I see.

Myrzeth prowls a large platform, much like the kaligorven that circle the clearing. I can't make sense of why he has called everyone here.

Until I see Amyrah standing next to him, clasped hands resting calmly against her simple dress. Myrzeth's own aura of darkness manipulation conceals her light, for the time being.

"Amyrah," I whisper, a feral sound that does not originate from my lungs. It tears from my soul.

What have you done?

I would run to her, except I am on the other side of the beasts that have subjugated the Vale for longer than anyone can recall. My father is right about me. I am a coward.

Myrzeth's voice rattles around my skull. "These last few weeks have been . . . *difficult* for the Vale. Many of you have suffered the loss of loved ones. And we have endured an unprecedented level of darkness."

Careful, Foremost, I think as the kaligorva ten yards from me rumbles threateningly.

I continue looking for a way to penetrate the circle but find nothing. Slipping into the trees behind the platform, I keep my eyes fixed to Amyrah's back.

"What if I told you all the Vale's recent troubles could be traced to one specific source?"

Whispers hiss from the gathering. I feel as though I will be sick.

He walks in a loop around Amyrah, stopping behind her. When he rests his hands on her shoulders and leans in to whisper something in her ear, a jolt of rage runs through my marrow.

Myrzeth lets his hands fall and steps away. My jaw unclenches.

"Why don't you show them what you can do, niece? Show them what you've been hiding. Show them what made the kaligorven steal their children."

With that, he steps off the platform and beckons in the ténesomni with a twitch of his fingers. It fills the clearing as it normally does, then swirls angrily around Amyrah. The hairs of my arms stand on end when I think of how Myrzeth used the darkness as a weapon against my father. But I know Amyrah is stronger than him. She has to be.

Oh, Elyōn, let her be . . .

Her tremulous voice cuts through the gloom. "*Stop.*"

With one word, the shadows are flung away. They hang in the air everywhere but around her. The absence of darkness surrounding her is on display for all to see.

No, I will name it for what it truly is. *Light.*

And even though this terrifies me, even though I know this means danger for her, I can't help but feeling a sense of relief that the Vale gets to see her as I do.

44
TÉRON

IDRAG MYSELF THROUGH THE CROWD on hands and knees, strength ebbing as my despair grows.

Here I am again, powerless to save the most important person in my life.

You will fail your daughter just as you failed your wife, a voice slithers through my mind. *My* voice. The serrated words tear as they pass.

I rest my forehead on the backs of my hands and let the sobs thunder through me. The last wicked dream of Ellehra plays out before my eyes.

The knife in my hand . . . the knife in her heart.

This is all my doing.

"Morvus, what are you doing down there?" a stranger says. The sharp toe of a boot finds the space between my ribs. Air whistles through my teeth.

"Get up."

I push myself so I rest back on my heels. The gray gloom deepens to black. A sheet of darkness whips by, heading to the podium. But I can make out nothing beyond the endless skirts and trousers of the valefolk.

As I try and fail to gain my feet, the shadows rush back, filling the air like a heavy mist once more. Gasps and mutters erupt. A plume of light ahead calls my spirit to action.

I need to be there.

Begging Elyōn to remove the false image of Ellehra from my mind, I find the strength to stand.

I grab shoulders and part the people like water, fighting through the current of bodies until I come out at the front.

The platform is flanked on either side by two monstrous kaligorven teeming with the shadows they create and shed continually. I cannot look at them for long without the blood in my veins freezing.

Instead, I fix my eyes on the lone figure, the only thing that matters to me right now. Soft waves of hair crown her head. The nondescript cloak adorns her like a robe. And the pendant at her throat is more dazzling than the fairest jewel.

My daughter.

Myrzeth hops onto the platform and orders the darkness to move to the side. The putrid taste that generally accompanies his presence fills my mouth.

"Do you see?" Myrzeth spits out an incredulous laugh. "Because of this girl's insolence, the kaligorven have retaliated. When they gave the order of darkness, she opposed them with everything she is. Of course, she spared no thought for the cost of her actions. Her comfort was worth your sacrifice."

I am jostled as the people I have lived with my whole life agitate into a roiling sea.

"She must pay," someone shrieks. It is echoed out of hundreds of mouths.

A smirk stretches Myrzeth's lips as his words hit their mark, but I choose to watch Amyrah's face instead. Pale, but determined. *Stay strong, my girl.*

Her long hair bounces around her shoulders as she shakes her head. "You speak only lies."

The Foremost turns to regard her. "Oh?"

"My only desire is to see this ténesomni broken. I could not care less about my own comfort." She turns from him to the valefolk. "Don't you see? Where there is true light, darkness fears to dwell." Her clear eyes probe the faces of her people, desperate for them to understand, to believe. But they are too enslaved by fear to do anything so radical.

A collective roar splits the air. The kaligorven advance a few paces on the valefolk. Cries of alarm ring out as they approach, but when Myrzeth holds up his hand, they halt. I frown. How has he managed to control them—the very beings that have held us in bondage for centuries? It is absurd.

"Careful, dear niece. They do not appreciate your sentiments."

She pushes her shoulders back and projects out into the night. "We should not be afraid of them. Don't you see? One little word, one little *light,* is enough to ruin them."

I close my eyes to hold back the tears. Is this how Elehra looked as she made her final stand?

It was. I know it was.

Screams erupt from the far end of the gathering. The kaligorven are attacking.

My eyes dart to Myrzeth, no hint of surprise visible on his placid face.

"Do you see the price of your careless words yet, Amyrah?"

Her lip trembles.

"Peace, friends," Myrzeth addresses the beasts, and the onslaught stills. Anxious energy pulses through the throng. "I feel your rage as if it were my own. This girl cannot be allowed to keep offending you in this manner. If it would appease you, I would offer her in exchange for your favor."

No...

My soul is being burned right out of me, leeched from my body with excruciating pain. I will myself to move forward, but the gravelly voices of the kaligorven rise as a wall of ice to halt me.

We accept.

A mad rush of wind assails the clearing, prompting more screams from the valefolk. The Shrouded push themselves through the heart of the mob with alarming speed and spread themselves out in an oblong circle around the edge of the platform.

Through a small gap, I see Amyrah's white face shaking with fiery determination.

Myrzeth hops off the stage and backs out of the ring slowly. "Do you have any final words?"

Her mouth opens and closes, but there is no sound. She tries again, but all she manages is a broken whisper. "I am not afraid."

But they are not just darkness. They are living creatures, flesh and blood and tooth and claw. Her gift may protect her from shadows, like Ellehra's did, but it will do nothing to hinder a physical force.

No one can survive this.

I gape at her, paralyzing denial making all this seem like a terrible, terrible dream. When her hands shudder up to her hair and her fingers run down the long strands, smoothing both the lock of hair and her mind with it, I wake up.

Elyōn, give me strength.

As my brother-in-law raises his hand and turns his wrist to release the dozens of blood-thirsty kaligorven, my legs find their power. I throw myself into the circle right as the brutes' claws dig into the earth to propel them toward her.

With more force than I could have anticipated, I lunge at my daughter and shove. I feel her body pressed briefly into my palms and wish to Elyōn that I could keep her that close forever. But she lurches away from me, tumbling off the platform and out of the Shrouded's reach. Her scent lingers in the gap she left—earth and rain and sweet blossoms all dancing together. When I look up, I see an infinitesimal flash of her horror-stricken eyes before I am swallowed by the ténesomni.

45

BELWYN

THE MOMENT BEFORE THE KALIGORVEN DESCEND, Amyrah's light flickers. Terror tries to drag me down to the earth.

I am going to lose her.

But the man, who looks so like Amyrah, changes everything. Chaos erupts throughout the clearing as he thwarts the Foremost's plans, and the horrible beasts become a single, writhing mass on the platform.

I throw myself forward and cushion Amyrah's fall. Her screams tear through her slight frame as I drag her away, away from the horror. Away to the safety of the woods.

I press a hand to her mouth, desperate to get her a safe distance from what was meant to be her execution. I hope the confusion of the moment works to my advantage, that no one notices us. She struggles in my arms, but my determination outmatches hers.

When we are out of earshot of the commotion, she manages to tear my fingers from her face. "Let me go!" she shrieks and pushes hard against me, catching herself before she hits the ground. Shoulders heaving, she scrambles to a sea of ferns and vomits. I run to her and lay a hand on her shoulder, but she twists away from my touch.

"Why did you do that?" she sobs, turning her frozen fire eyes on me.

Her fury hits me like a blow to the gut, and I recoil.

"W-why would you . . . would *he* . . ."

A moan distorts her words as she wraps her arms around her knees and rocks back and forth.

I close my eyes and exhale slowly. *She isn't angry at me.* A wave of relief tainted by a drop of guilt hits me.

Now I understand. It was her father who took her place.

Crouching, I pull her away from the pile of sick. Her entire body tremors, but she obeys. I lean against a tree, and she curls up against my chest.

I have wanted to hold her from the moment I met her, but not like this.

Brushing hair wet with sweat and tears away from her face, I gently tuck her head beneath my chin and give her grief a place to land.

The shudders racking her body gradually begin to calm until it is just her warm breaths condensing on my neck and the rising and falling of both our chests together. My arms hold her secure. Her gift might protect her from the dark, but only I can shield her from the cold.

We sit like that for as long as I dare. But it can't last forever. Even though I am afraid to break the spell, I know I must.

"Amyrah, we should keep moving. It isn't safe for you here."

She shakes her head violently.

I grit my teeth and grab her shoulders, peeling her away from my body and looking into her eyes. The necklace glints between us.

"I know nothing matters to you anymore—how could it?—but you have to listen to me. If you stay here and let Myrzeth or those beasts find you, what was your father's sacrifice for?"

She blinks, freeing more tears to join the damp of her hair. Lip trembling, she nods.

I stand slowly, reaching to help her up, but she rises without my assistance. I pull my hand back, fighting down the hurt.

This moment is not about you, morvus.

When we've advanced only a few paces, however, her hand slips into mine.

We cut through the trees as fast as we can until the tinkling sound of water rises out of the shadows. The stream that leads past her cottage. A knot tightens in my gut. Maybe we should head in a different direction.

Amyrah surprises me, like she always does, and descends the banks to cross to their side of the brook.

Crouching low, she cups water and splashes it onto her face. I follow her down and stand guard.

A noise disrupts the sameness of the babbling water. I wheel around, staring uselessly into the shadows.

The reeds along the bank's edge shiver, and I hold my breath. Whatever this is, it is too small to be a kaligorva.

Amyrah stands and follows the direction of my gaze. A soft gasp parts her lips.

A foxlike creature bounds to the water's edge. It is small, only knee-height, but its two huge ears are like sails raised to the sky. Unlike any animal I've ever beheld, the white-tipped tail sways behind it and flattens into a broad fan rather than a tapered point.

The creature creeps by me cautiously, leaving plenty of space, but approaches Amyrah with boldness.

I watch, dumbstruck, as she crouches low and holds out a hand. The fox sniffs tentatively, and Amyrah's mouth falls open. She reaches out with both hands, and it doesn't flinch when her fingers graze its silky fur.

In an instant, the stream bed fills with light and heat. The animal completely transforms at Amyrah's touch.

Of course, it is a sola. I should have known.

As I should have realized that she has the power to awaken them.

Wonderment claims Amyrah's face, but only for a moment. She gathers her wits and leans toward the golden thing, her mouth issuing words I cannot hear.

With an impressive bound, the fox clears the stream bank and dashes out of sight.

"What—" I stop and lick my lips, trying to make sense of what I saw. "What did you say?"

She turns her lamp-like eyes on me. Her chin trembles.

"I sent her" —a breath shudders from her chest— "to be with him."

I don't need to ask who she's talking about.

The cottage would be a lovely place if it wasn't crawling with darkness and memory.

I hang back and let Amyrah approach it at her own pace. I am well acquainted with the unpredictable beast grief can be.

But she is not like me. Her footsteps never falter, and she only pauses briefly to rest her hand against the lintel before unlatching the door and ducking inside.

Exhaling slowly, I follow.

Her light fills the small room. My eyes take in the humble furnishings and the beauty infused into every corner.

I take it back. This cottage absolutely overflows with loveliness, and I am an intruder within. It is too raw, too sacred. But Amyrah turns around, and though she doesn't exactly smile, her face communicates a welcome that sets my mind at ease.

Instinctively, I set to making a fire. It might be a risk to settle into the cottage like this, but I'm hopeful this is the last place anyone would look for her. It's too illogical. Besides that, I am fairly certain no one will want to be wandering through the woods after the display they just witnessed.

Amyrah stands over me. She makes a quick motion, but when I glance at her, she's simply running her fingers across the smooth stones of the fireplace. The flames catch, and heat blooms. She sighs softly.

Straightening and dusting off my hands, I lead Amyrah to sit on one of the narrow beds.

She may not be falling apart at the seams, but the far-off look in her eyes proves she is nowhere close to fine.

I crouch and gather her hands together between mine. My thumb runs across her knuckles, and my eyes search her face until she sees me.

"You can't stay here," I say.

A breath whistles sharply into her lungs. "I know." She slips a hand out of mine and flicks a rogue tear off her cheek.

"Any idea where we can go?"

She blinks at the word 'we' as if it alarms her.

Yes, I think. *You heard me right.* Because there is no other option for me now. A strange providence has been twining us together for long enough. I can't ignore it any longer.

"Uh, well," she says, recovering herself, "there's always the Grovesha."

"The Outlands?" I lean back slightly and rest my hands on my knees.

She nods. "I know it sounds crazy, but there is more out there than we know. This book" —she motions to a leatherbound volume on the mantel— "isn't from here. And I have a friend I'm convinced knows more about it than she's saying." Her hands tighten around fistfuls of her linen dress.

I marvel at her for a little while, letting my eyes linger on the freckles dotting her nose and the barely perceivable flecks of gold pricking her cool irises. Her thick hair has been teased into tangled tresses. Her beauty is wild and untamed. Free.

The longer I look at her, the more difficult it is to resist the longing she ignites in me. It isn't what I've felt in the company of Ketra, where everything about her person was always meant to draw out a very specific response. It's much deeper than that.

I think it could break me.

Before my heart bursts through my chest cavity, I tear myself away and pace the room. My mind races with all the things we would need to get in place to go on such an open-ended journey. I look around the dwelling, my eyes landing hopefully on the shelves in the back corner.

"Amyrah, if I go into Utsanek to gather some things and get more information from this friend of yours, can you handle packing what you can find here? Anything that would be useful for traveling."

She cocks her head toward me. Dark circles cushion her eyes. I fight the urge to abandon everything and hold her in my arms again. Not that she needs me to. Even in her exhaustion and pain, I know she is strong.

Her chin bobs definitively. "Yes, I can do that." She stands and trails me to the door, digging a slip of paper noisily out of a pocket concealed in her dress. "If you follow these directions, you'll come to a hidden community. My friend's name is Wehna. Give her my name and explain what's happened, and I know she'll help us."

When I go to leave, Amyrah's hand catches mine and pulls me back gently. With slow steps, she swallows the space between us and reaches to touch my jaw. Her fingers, at first tremulous and light, tense and draw me in. I follow their lead.

She kisses me only once, slow and gentle, and I forget to breathe as her fragrance fills my senses. Fresh earth and forest blossoms.

It is over almost as soon as it starts, but I lived a lifetime in that kiss.

"Thank you," she says, breathless, "for doing this for me."

I trap her fingers beneath mine before they can slip away. "Always."

A pall of gloom hangs over Utsanek. In the market square, the few people out at this hour of the evening studiously avoid making eye contact with anyone. It sets me on edge, seeing people's guilt written so plainly in their body language.

I pick up my pace as I approach the fanum. It has always unsettled me, but it's even worse now. Who in their right mind would want to worship such hideous, murderous creatures? In the wake of the ceremony, the gifts strewn all over the steps look less like offerings of devotion than heaps of rubbish.

As I pass its steps, a hair-raising roar issues from within, spearing the silence. Knowing that I should back away, that I don't have time for this, I climb the steps and pull the heavy door open a crack.

Myrzeth rampages around the cavernous building, tossing pans of incense and screaming at the towering statue.

"I have done everything you asked of me." He kicks a pan again, sending it skittering across the flagstones. "You gave me this power, and I have used it as you taught me."

Who is he talking to?

He paces in front of the idol, thrusting his long fingers into his platinum hair. "Because she lives, your name is mocked. And I look like a fool." He throws his hands down and addresses the statue directly. "How do you expect me to wield this power if the valefolk think one act of sacrifice can thwart you?"

My blood runs cold. I back away and let the door fall closed, but too late. The Foremost spins around and shoots me with an insane, frozen gaze.

I scramble down the steps and lose myself in the oblivion of the side streets.

"You're going *where*?"

My mother pulls her shawl tightly around her shoulders, watching my frantic preparations.

"I'm not sure, but I need to get her somewhere far away from here."

I lunge up the stairs and burst into the bedroom. Korvin bolts upright, reaching impulsively for a heavy mug on the table next to his bed. When recognition lights his features, he relaxes.

Shemai continues to snore deeply.

"What's happening?" Korvin says quietly, throwing back the covers and tiptoeing across the creaky floor.

I thrust my arms into my leather jacket, then toss an additional cloak overtop.

"I'm going to be gone for a while."

He opens his mouth, but I shake my head as I fasten the strap of my quiver across my torso and grab my bow.

"I can't explain right now."

My eyes pass around the room for anything else that could be useful. I grab an old satchel of Korvin's. "Do you think I can borrow this?"

He bobs his chin quickly. When I face him, he bites his lip. I bend and lay my hands on his shoulders.

"Listen, Korvin. You need to keep stepping up like you've been doing. Mother is going to need you. She already depends on you so much."

His head nods again. "I will."

Something about his determination eases the anxieties that wrapped around me when I walked in on Myrzeth's tantrum. I drag in a deep breath and allow my heart to slow down a beat.

"I'll do everything I can to come back, I promise. But I don't know when that will be because there's someone else who needs me."

"I understand." He puffs out his chest a little. When did he get so tall? "You won't have to worry about anything here."

I study him, surprised to find myself holding back tears for the first time this evening. I pull him to my side with my free arm.

"Elyōn watch over you, brother."

Without giving him a chance to respond, I dash out of the room and down the stairs. Mother stands by the door, holding out a parcel wrapped in waxed cloth. "We don't have much at the moment, but this should get you through a day or two."

Taking it from her carefully, I slip it into the satchel. A pang of guilt stabs my chest. I know how much this will cost my family.

When I look up, she is right in front of me, throwing her arms around my neck and embracing me the way she did when I was small.

"Elyōn keep you safe," she whispers into my ear. I pull back in surprise. She's never spoken the ancient deity's name before. "Now, go." She motions toward the door with her chin.

Dangerously close to losing my resolve, I duck out the door before I can change my mind.

I've only gone a few steps when I hear a voice that infuses weakness into every bone of my body.

"Belwyn."

My father steps out of the shadows, right into my path. I cringe when I see his muscular hands tightened around his broadsword. Do I really have to fight him? Now?

But one look at his sour face and I know that's not what this is about.

"What you said earlier today—"

"I'm not apologizing for that," I say.

His mouth tenses dangerously but soon eases. "No, I don't want you to." He moves closer to me, a tortured mind shining out through his hazel eyes. "I wanted to tell you that—that you were right."

I throw out a hand against a railing to steady myself. "What?"

"You're strong. And I . . . I don't deserve you."

My mouth sags. I clear my throat and clamp it shut. I can't do this right now.

He seems to understand and doesn't push it. His eyes travel over me, taking in the jacket, cloak, provisions, quiver, and bow. They rest on my face. "If you're going out there . . ." His fingers twitch around the sword hilt. "Well, what kind of man would you be if you didn't have one of these?"

Haltingly, he thrusts the sword out, as if it takes every bit of his resolve to do so. When I don't take it immediately, he grunts and pushes it against my chest. I barely manage to clutch it before he lets it drop. While my mind is still trying to comprehend what happened, he brushes past me, toward the house.

I stand there, stupefied, until his hand lands heavily on my shoulder.

"I know I wasn't the best Foremost, and an even worse father, but I want you to know I would have never stooped to such animalistic tactics."

With that, he's gone.

Taking a moment to remind myself what I'm supposed to be doing and swallow back emotions I don't have names for, I pull out the scrap of paper Amyrah gave me. Just one more thing to do, then we can get out of here. I flatten it against my chest with one hand and hold it up to read the directions.

But before I can, a roar—this time not from human lungs—shakes the stillness of the night.

Panic possesses me. It's coming from the direction of Amyrah's cottage.

In what feels like only a few breaths, I tear through Utsanek and down the wooded path, not bothering to bang on the door before I burst inside.

It is empty.

46

AMYRAH

I SLIP MY HAND INTO MY POCKET and rub the thick paper between my fingers. I only read it once, but I know it by heart.

My daughter,

There is so much I should have told you, but I do not have time to write it all now. The Vale grows restless, and you should know two things before it is too late.

First, your mother is not from here. She came from the city of Ketsé, which lies on the north side of the Askonnet Mountains. If you follow the stream that runs past our house, it will lead you to a safe passage through them.

And the second is this: I love you.

I drag in a breath of cool air and swallow down the lump that squeezes my throat.

Belwyn didn't see me grab the letter from the mantle while he built a fire. I don't know why I hid it from him, but once I had read it after he left, I was glad.

Pinching my lips together, I steer my thoughts away from how his breaths sent shivers racing down my spine. Or the way that once his arms were around me, I never wanted them to let me go. A dull ache spreads somewhere in the region of my heart.

The familiarity our souls shared in that moment . . . the final three words I will ever have from my father . . . Both are compelling reasons for me to be out here on my own, running into the night with nothing more than a cloak on my back and an old book weighing down my bag.

I can't afford to lose anyone else.

As I stop to catch my breath and adjust the bag's strap, a terrifying sound wakes the birds and sends them squawking to the skies.

My fingers go numb as the memory of the kaligorven converging on my father is triggered. A strangled yelp lurches from me as the last image of his face swims before my eyes. His tawny hair falling over his forehead. His brows pressed together, that single crease between them standing out in bold relief as his palms made contact with my ribs.

Falling to my knees, I gasp and rub the place where I can still feel the impact of his hands.

Get up.

The sound rings out again. A roar.

Shaking uncontrollably, I claw through the damp grass along the water's edge, unable to bring my limbs under control.

Get up.

But I can't. There is no strength left in my frame. It disappeared the moment my father shoved me off the platform. I used every scrap I had left pretending I was fine for Belwyn's sake.

Get. Up.

As another roar echoes through the night, I drag myself to the skeleton of a fallen tree and rest my head against it, exhausted. The smell of rotting wood washes over me.

Who was I to think I could be the one to break the ténesomni? Elyōn may have given me a gift, but it is no match for the festering evil that lingers where darkness dwells.

At least, if this is where I meet my end, no one else will see it.

The kaligorva must be getting close by now. I close my eyes. A strange sense of calm fills me like spiced tea. I breathe deeply, drawing the aroma of decaying things into my lungs.

Wouldn't it be better to let nature take its course? The cold is already creeping over me, its fingers finding a way inside my skin. Maybe it's right to let this giant's grave become mine as well.

But as the clamor of the beast draws nearer, I pick out something else from the aroma. Something so green and fresh I can almost taste it on my tongue.

In the midst of death there is also life.

A flutter of warmth touches the top of my head, brushes the side of my face. It grows in intensity until every trace of chill has fled and I can see blood red from beneath my eyelids. I open my eyes.

You are not alone.

'Star' is the only word that comes to mind when I see the brilliantly burning creature standing guard to my left. I turn toward it and slip my knees under me, adopting an unintentional posture of humility. It towers over me to the height of a man. The glossy fur sways with each pulse of light. A holy fear consumes me as I raise my eyes to behold the sola's face.

It is wolf-like and long, with pointed fangs peeking out of its solemn muzzle and thick fur around its neck and chest. It bends its awesome head down and sniffs my forehead before anointing me with the penetrating warmth of its smooth tongue, making me doubt I will ever be cold again. A peculiar scent of rain and fire and freshly tilled earth swirls around me.

I could bask in this creature's presence forever.

A rumbling growl shakes the ground beneath me. The sola's head turns to face what's coming. Reluctantly, I tear my eyes away from it and stare into the ténesomni.

Something is odd about this beast of darkness. It does not hesitate when it comes to the barrier between my light and the shadows, but steps through boldly. A scream lodges in my chest as I get a full picture of one of the kaligorven for the first time.

Its face is wild and twisted, with a myriad of sharp teeth and shocks of matted fur sprouting from all directions. The broad snout is marked in places with shiny black skin that looks like scars. The eyes are terrifying, filling my soul with the sensation of being on fire. Two gnarled horns protrude from its skull, making it seem a foot taller than it is. Its body is harder to identify, as it stands upright like a man, but bears no resemblance in any other respect. Shadows shift all over its gargantuan frame, enshrouding it protectively. There is something distinctly rotten and festering about its presence that forces me to breathe through waves of nausea.

It is a thing not quite living, a massive predator raked through a furnace or dragged from an open grave. While the aura from the sola emanates, the presence from this monster oozes.

The wolf-sola steps toward it, and a deep growl makes the hairs on the back of my neck stand on end. The chasms of the kaligorva's eyes lock on to the burning beast, and the air between them crackles.

When they propel themselves at each other, the world stops.

Teeth shear sheets of shadows into threads; claws rip ribbons of radiance into tassels. The air around me begins to rush as cold and hot clash violently. Deafening snarls swirl through my senses.

The two giants are evenly matched, even though the sola's frame is smaller. I gasp as the kaligorva throws it off its back and crouches to pounce, but the wolf recovers and darts deftly out of the way.

Enraged, the Shrouded lets out a throaty scream and tears wildly at its opponent's chest. The sola's luminescence pulses powerfully through its locks of fur, protecting it from what could have been a fatal blow.

The battle rages on for an eternity, until the work of keeping up with it becomes a burden I can no longer bear. I crawl shakily along the trunk of the tree, putting as much distance between myself and this otherworldly tempest as I can.

When my strength is spent, I turn around in time to see the sola make a desperate attack at the kaligorva's exposed underside. It succeeds in knocking the monster back, and the wolf goes to work, tearing the enemy to pieces. For a moment, it looks as if the fight could be over.

But the Shrouded rallies and bends all four limbs underneath the sola, kicking it off with alarming force. The wolf's huge body sails to the side and over the stream, hitting a boulder with a sickening thud. The dazzling illumination disappears in an instant.

"*No,*" I shriek.

A mistake. The kaligorva staggers to full height and turns to face me. A hideous sneer pulls its grizzly muzzle. It moves toward me with heavy, unsteady footsteps.

There ... is ... no ... escape ...

The voice rattles through my brain like a sickness. The beast does not physically form the words, yet I hear it.

My hands feel around for something, anything with which to protect myself. But there is nothing.

The light around me flickers as my eyes close.

I am not afraid.

As a rush of air swings a wispy lock of hair across my face, a scream that sounds neither like sola nor kaligorva shakes me from my stupor. My eyes spring open, and I can't make sense of what lies before them.

A shadowed figure crouches between me and the Shrouded, pulling back a long blade that reflects my light and the sparkle of my necklace. With another deafening yell, the form thrusts the blade upward, right into the core of the attacker as it descends upon us.

I scream as we are knocked back together under its crushing weight.

Stillness follows. I struggle to breathe.

With a groan and a cry of exertion, the kaligorva is rolled away.

I scuttle back, eyes wide as the figure stands and turns to face me, broad shoulders heaving.

Belwyn.

"What—what are you doing here?" I cry, finding I do, indeed, have the strength to stand.

He stares at the beast, at his hands, then at me with wide eyes. "I came for you," he huffs between breaths. His mouth opens to say something else, but I run into his arms before he has a chance. He stumbles, and we both sink to the ground before we fall down the slippery bank of the stream.

I bury my face in the warm leather of his jacket and sob, then laugh, then sob again. His breaths puff hot against my head, and he shakes with the aftereffects of adrenaline.

"You shouldn't have followed me," I say after a while, and his arms tighten around my back.

"And you shouldn't have left without me." His stern voice makes my stomach spiral. Warm fingertips find my jaw and turn my face toward him. His eyes search mine. "Why would you do that?"

I lay my palms against his chest and push him back. "You don't understand. I have felt alone my whole life. And my father . . ." I gulp against the tears burning the inside of my skull. My head shakes too fast. "I can't bear the thought of anyone else hurting because of me."

The fire in his gaze dulls to a warm glow. "And I've spent my whole life afraid of standing up for what I know is right. But you were the one who gave me the courage to do that." His voice drops to a whisper that stirs a tingling sensation deep inside my core. "I feel it, Amyrah. Can you?"

My fingers tense against him. "Feel what?"

His lips pull into a soft smile. The ring in his nose glints. "Whatever happens after this moment, we're meant to face it together."

47

BELWYN

I BELIEVED NOTHING COULD RUIN ME like the thought of losing Amyrah.

But as we curve together beside the clear, flowing stream and it whispers to us, I know I am wrong. I am ruined by the way her head nestles into my shoulder and the night wraps around us like a blanket. I am ruined by the subtle rise and fall of her chest, like waters lapping on the shores of Loch Skythe. As my hand moves over her hair of its own accord and my fingers lose themselves in their lengths, I am ruined.

She sighs heavily, ending the ephemeral moment. I resist the urge to tighten my arms around her, to keep her always next to my heart.

"The sola," she says as she sits up. "I need to see it."

I nod and get to my feet, reaching a hand to her, but I draw it back slightly when I remember how she rejected it last time.

As she flicks her hair out of her face and looks up at me, a curious expression twists her lips. "Wasn't this how we met?"

The corner of my mouth twitches with a roguish smile, and her laugh flits through the night on bird's wings.

She slips her hand into mine.

The crumpled body of the sola lies on the other side of the stream. I splash across the water and crouch next to Amyrah.

I can find only a couple large wounds emitting glittering light as the blood drips from them. It's impossible to know how many more internal injuries the wolf sustained.

Fresh tears slip down Amyrah's cheeks as she reaches a trembling hand to the creature. A moment before she can touch it, its chest lurches, sending both of us sprawling back.

"It's alright." She laughs breathily.

I close my eyes for a beat and plead with my heart to quit trying to kill me.

Amyrah approaches it again, slowly slipping her fingers into the dense fur.

The wolf's breaths, ragged at first, fall into a steady rhythm. Amyrah pushes her palm even deeper into the fur, leaning forward and whispering into its ear. I can barely make out what she's saying, but it sounds like a story.

> *At the dawn of the world's birth,*
> *the fire lights were ignited;*

An unquenchable flock without number,
piercing the black cloak of the sky.

They shone through the ages,
a lasting gift from the Highest.
The crystalline constellations rested
when the Burning Star drew nigh.

As if her words hold some sort of magic, luminescence crawls out in a steady wave from her fingers until the whole magnificent creature glows once again, as a sola should.

"How do you do that?" My jaw falls slack as I avert my eyes from the blinding heat.

She holds up her hand and turns it over, scrutinizing it. "I don't know. But I don't think it comes from me."

The sola stirs, and I grab Amyrah's hand and tug her to me as it shudders and draws its legs underneath it.

Still weak and haggard, it manages to find its feet once more. It turns its great head to regard us. Intelligence shines behind its jeweled eyes.

I swallow down a swell of emotion. The stag had looked at me much the same. Will I ever be free from the guilt of having taken a sola's life?

Like she can read my thoughts, Amyrah leans in and wraps her palms around my arm. "You saved this one, you know." She squeezes until I angle my chin toward her. "And me."

With a groan more human than animal, the wolf claws up the sloping sides of the stream and moves away from us with padded footfalls.

"Look," says Amyrah, her eyes reflecting the dazzling display. "It's heading north."

She's right. The wolf does not veer away into the woods but sticks to the path carved through the forest by the flowing water.

As it fades into the distance, reality sets in.

"Do you still want to stick with the plan?" I ask as we climb up the bank. Stooping to grab my sword, I wipe it as best as possible with a fistful of moss.

Amyrah crosses her arms and stares down at me. "What plan are you talking about?"

Rising, I slip the blade into the sheath buckled to my side. "Finding these nebulous Outlands."

"Oh." Amyrah touches a hand to her mouth. Her eyebrows angle upward in the middle. "I probably should mention something." She grabs a handful of her hair and twirls it nervously around her fingers. "There's at least one city I know of on the other side of the mountains. Ketsé. My father said it's where my mother came from."

I snap up from bending to grab my bow and quiver, which I had thrown off to defend Amyrah. My lips part, and after a moment, I chuckle. "Is there ever going to be a day where you stop surprising me?"

Amyrah's cheeks flush a soft shade of pink. "That's not all. Myrzeth told me I'm . . . I'm . . ." She bites her lip and blinks at me, nervous.

"Go on. Today's the day for unexpected revelations."

"I'm of a different race than the valefolk. The Luvesti, I think he called it."

Luvesti. A strange word I've never heard. But that doesn't mean it isn't real.

I grab the bow and quiver and swing them over my back. "How are we supposed to find them?"

Amyrah joins me at my side and turns her attention to the north. "Father said a safe passage lies where the water flows through the mountains." She turns her clear eyes on me. "So, if we follow the stream . . ."

I exhale. "It will take you home."

48

AMYRAH

WE BEGIN OUR TRAVELS TOGETHER as the birds wake up and drizzle their masterpiece over us. Our pace is easy but steady. Sometimes I forget who walks by my side, and when his fingers trail down my palm and insert themselves between mine, a pulsing warmth fills me, and it becomes difficult to breathe.

The terrain around us changes subtly as we press on. The trees thin as the ground starts to dip and rise like frozen waves. Warmth flows down from the mountain ahead, teasing us with the promise of life and causing us to peel back layers. The shadows thin, although they still drift in wispy swirls wherever I look. But we are nearing the end of their dominion. Even if we didn't have my light, we wouldn't need a lantern.

As the day floats by and draws down the exhale of evening, Belwyn sits down against a pine and calls me over. I settle in beside him. He takes out a parcel of smoked meats, hard cheeses, and dried fruits from his satchel for us to share.

"My mother's final gift to me." He shrugs as I throw him a questioning look. He tries to appear nonchalant, but I can see the way his mouth pulls down at the corner.

We both partake without reservation. I can't remember the last time I ate, and even stale bread would taste phenomenal at this point, but I know I will never enjoy a more delicious meal in my life.

By the time we finish, the songs of night have begun to warm up. Belwyn yawns and stands, stretching his limbs.

"What do you want to do? Find somewhere to shelter for the night —" His breath catches, and I think I see him blush for the first time. "Or push on?"

I frown and listen to the waters splashing. The stream has grown considerably in size as we've journeyed. To me, it's the sound of someone beckoning, calling me on. I can't ignore it now.

Standing and brushing pine needles off my dress, I shake feeling back into my legs. "Night hardly means anything to us valefolk, does it?" I smile at the way he cocks his chin. "Yes, Luvesti or not, I'll always just be Amyrah from the Vale."

He nods and gathers all our supplies.

When he returns to me, his expression is somber. He hands me my bag and looks at me intensely. "Don't use that word, alright?"

My brow furrows. I can't think what he means. Perhaps he doesn't like me talking about the Vale. Is he so eager to forget what we've come from?

But one look at his face eases my mind.

"*Just.* It's much too small for someone like you."

Heat blooms into my cheeks.

Belwyn presses a palm to my back, and we continue chasing the stream.

Over the next few hours, the path turns into a punishing trek over ledges and up increasingly steep slopes. Without being able to see what lies ahead, all we can do is press on, one climb at a time. I wish the sola had stayed in sight. I wonder where it slipped off to.

The night settles in, bringing with it a chill and bone-racking exhaustion. We stop frequently to catch our breath and scoop what we can from what is now more of a waterfall than a stream. The noise of it grows as we press further and further into the Askonnet Mountains.

"How are you doing? Should we stop here?" Belwyn asks after saving me from a clumsy step on loose shale.

I shake my head and dab the sweat away from my forehead with the back of a hand.

No. We're getting close. I can feel it.

He doesn't argue, but lets me go ahead of him, holding out his hands to catch me whenever he thinks I'm about to slip.

When the night is almost pitch black and my legs shudder beneath me, I must admit it would not be safe to continue. I close my eyes and suck in air through my nose.

It's fine. There's always tomorrow, I console myself. But in my depleted state, I am one small disappointment away from a complete breakdown.

"We don't need to go on, you know." Belwyn pulls me close to him— not to embrace me, but to be my strength.

I can't form words. How can I make him understand? This isn't about my safety, or even my need to discover what secrets my mother hid.

It's about *him*. My father. The one who lay down his life so I might be free.

My shoulders heave forward as a silent groan rips from my soul. *Elyōn, you've led us this far. Don't let me despair now.*

A familiar melody sweeps overhead, carried on golden wings that flutter impossible hope into my heart.

Belwyn's hands grip me almost painfully. I glance at his awe-stricken face.

A warm sound that shouldn't come from me emerges. Laughter.

"That's my sola, Belwyn. That's my wren!"

He glances down at me, confused, but a disbelieving smile soon claims his features.

Stamina renewed, shadows forgotten, we follow the sola up and over one last embankment. The shining songbird sits perched on a lonely pine at the top, waiting for us.

Belwyn makes it up first and reaches back to give me a hand. He pulls me up easily, and we stand together, chests heaving, on the welcome reprieve of a long, level surface stretching beside the stream—now more of a river. It bends to the east, flowing from higher up in the mountains.

"The darkness," I gasp, a chill washing over me. "Do you feel it?"

The ténesomni is thicker up here, and it reaches toward me as if desperate to stake its claim.

He nods, holding out his hand and letting the shadows slide across his arm. I shiver.

But the bird sings again, calling us higher up, further into the safety of the mountains.

On legs threatening to give out, I walk forward, Belwyn at my side.

The shadows crowd in around us. They whisper words of doubt into my soul. My hand finds Belwyn's, and we cling to each other as the ever-night—the darkness I've known my whole life—tries to keep us within its clutches.

As I consider all we've lost and those we've left behind to come to this point, my courage threatens to flicker out. But Belwyn's fingers tighten around mine, sending a dose of kindness to my aching heart.

Like one being submerged in a hot spring, we step out of the ténesomni and into incomprehensible light.

I draw in a shaky breath and fall to my knees.

Brilliant oranges, pinks, and purples fill the sky, anointing the heads of leafy trees far down below with breathtaking halos. At once, I understand what the word 'dawn' means. I can see farther than I've ever been able to before.

For a while, we bask in the delicious light pouring in from the east, painting our faces with warmth and hope. I raise a hand as I try to behold it, but it is brighter than any sola there has ever been.

"Burning Star," I say in hushed syllables.

Belwyn walks ahead, mouth agape, as he takes it all in. "I didn't know this much color existed anywhere in the world."

Looking over my shoulder, I shudder at the raging wall of black shadows. But it only reaches about fifty feet into the sky. It does not go on forever.

The sola, a burning star itself, hops in the treetop overhead and flutters its wings.

A laugh tumbles out of me, surprising me again as it pushes through the veil of grief that enshrouds my soul.

I always knew I was never meant to dwell in the night.

EPILOGUE

WHO'S THERE?"

The voice makes both Belwyn and me start. He comes to my side and helps me up, wrapping an arm around me protectively as we turn toward the west. My heart jumps to my throat when I see a small hut nestled in between a copse of conifers. But I am more surprised by the two people standing outside it.

They wear tattered clothes, mended in multiple places, and careworn expressions that tug on my heartstrings.

Belwyn's grip around my shoulders tightens as they approach.

"Tell me who you are," the man repeats. The woman behind him touches her hand lightly to his shoulder as she brushes past him.

"Rael, *no*," he says through gritted teeth. When she ignores him, he growls and follows.

Rael's eyes fall to my necklace, and she throws out her hand against the man, stumbling backward and fighting for breath. He catches her, then looks at me with suspicion. But his face blanches when he sees what undid his wife.

Stepping toward me slowly, tears begin to course down his pale cheeks. His green eyes grapple on mine.

"Have you seen our daughter—and our son?"

The woman, strangely familiar, recovers and walks up to me with lurching steps. She reaches out shaking fingers, sucking in a sharp breath as she rests them on the pendant.

"Have you seen Wehna?"

APPENDICES

THE BOOK
of
ELLEHRA CANTAR

Flee as a bird to your mountain
Thou who art weary of sin
Go to the clear, flowing fountain
Where you may wash and be clean
Fly, then th'avenger is near thee
Call, and the Savior will hear thee
He on His bosom will bear thee
Thou who art weary of sin
O thou who art weary of sin

(From "Flee As a Bird" by Mary Dana Shindler, 1840)

GLOSSARY

NAME PRONUNCIATIONS

Amyrah *(uh-MEYE-ruh)*

Arvo *(AR-voh)*

Askonnet *(ASS-kon-neht)*

Atsun *(AT-soon)*

Belwyn *(BELL-win)*

Dravek *(DRAY-vehk)*

Ellehra *(el-LAY-ruh)*

Ketra *(KEH-truh)*

Ketsé *(KEHT-say)*

Ketur *(keh-TUR)*

Korvin *(KOHR-vihn)*

Myrzeth *(MEER-zehth)*

Orlagh *(OHR-luh)*

Rhun *(ROON)*

Shemai *(SHEM-eye)*

Teron *(TAIR-uhn)*

Utsanek *(OOT-san-ehk)*

Wehna *(WEH-nuh)*

ATSUNIC TRANSLATIONS

argentilum *(ar-JENT-ih-loom)* : a type of precious metal that
 absorbs and releases light and heat

arlum *(AR-loom)* : a form of currency used in the Vale

bolétis *(boh-LAY-tees)* : bioluminescent mushrooms

caelaveth *(chay-LAH-veth)* : become as one

caeruméni *(CHAY-roo-MAY-nee)* : a worship service

Ellithïm *(el-ih-THEEM)* : paradise

Elyōn *(EL-ee-ohn)* : the Highest; deity of Atsun

fanum *(FAHN-oom)* : shrine

Grovesha *(groh-VEH-shuh)* : the Outerlands; beyond the Vale

ignati *(eeg-NAH-tee)* : fi re

istilatum ideralis *(EES-till-a-toom EE-dair-all-iss)* : burning star

kaligörva *(kal-ih-GOHR-vuh)* : a lone Shrouded beast of darkness

kaligorven *(kal-ih-GOHR-vehn)* : the Shrouded beasts of darkness

kuvresh *(KOOV-resh)* : bloodshed

Kuvror Erovantus *(KOOV-rohr air-oh-VAHN-toos)* : the Blood
 Reckoning Ceremony

lanuum *(LAH-noom)* : an edible tuber, similar to a petato

luvem *(LOO-vehm)* : light

ATSUNIC TRANSLATIONS
(continued)

maevotér *(MAY-voh-tayr)* : private tutor

morvus *(MOHR-vuhs)* : idiot; fool; moron

praecéro *(pray-CHAIR-oh)* : split; break apart

Privotus Vimorteth *(pree-VOH-toos vih-MOHR-teth)* : the right to challenge the Foremost to ritualistic combat for his or her position

Shaluth Cantu *(shuh-LOOTH can-TOO)* : salvation song

sola *(SOH-lah)* - a Light Creature

Sola Vinari *(soh-LAHT vih-AR-ee)* : the ancient custom of hunting the Light Creatures

sola brossa *(soh-LAHT BROH-suh)* : the light-imbued bones of a Light Creature

sola kuvror *(soh-LAHT KOOV-rohr)* : the incandescent blood of a Light Creature

ténesomni *(TAY-neh-SOM-nee)* : living darkness

ATSUNIC PHRASES

avis ténesomni luvem *(uh-VEES TAY-neh-SOM-nee LOO-vem)* : "After darkness, light"

habith ténesomni eth noér lurum *(huh-BEETH TAY-neh-SOM-nee ehth noh-AIR LOO-ruhm)* : "Dwelling in darkness is our good"

Elyón érit agértu *(EL-ee-ohn ay-REET uh-JAIR-too)* : "the Highest will act"

DAYS OF THE WEEK

Sunday	Satus *(SAH-toos)*
Monday	Soporiat *(so-POH-ree-aht)*
Tuesday	Vindéré *(vihn-DAY-ray)*
Wednesday	Tavilun *(TAH-vih-loon)*
Thursday	Jotesta *(joh-TESS-tuh)*
Friday	Bézeqor *(BAY-zeh-kohr)*
Saturday	Xitus *(ZEE-toos)*

SEASONS OF THE YEAR

Ice	Vestri *(VESS-tree)*
Thaw	Niatev *(NEYE-uh-tehv)*
Sowing	Tiosh *(TEE-bhsh)*
Life	Zomrĕ *(ZOM-ray)*
Harvest	Elberu *(ELL-ber-oo)*
Decay	Morpa *(MOHR-puh)*

ORLAGH'S SPICED BUNS

INGREDIENTS

FOR THE DOUGH
5-6 cups flour
1/2 cup white sugar
1 Tbsp salt
1 Tbsp instant yeast
2/3 cup butter, melted
2 eggs, room temperature
2 cups warm water

FOR THE FILLING
1/3 cup butter, softened
1/2 cup brown sugar
1 Tbsp cinnamon
1 Tsp pumpkin pie spice

FOR THE GLAZE
1 cup butter
1 1/2 cups brown sugar
1 tsp vanilla extract

DIRECTIONS

1. Combine 1 cup flour, white sugar, salt, & yeast in a large bowl.
2. Thoroughly mix in 2/3 cup melted butter, eggs, & warm water.
3. Stir in 4-5 cups flour, a cup at a time. When it is tough to stir and the moisture is incorporated, dump out on floured work surface and knead it together. Add more flour if the dough is too sticky. Dough will be soft. Knead for 10 minutes.
4. Let rise, covered, in a warm environment for at least 30 min.
5. Meanwhile, prepare glaze: Melt together butter, brown sugar, & vanilla in sauce pan over medium heat and whisk until combined. Pour glaze equally into two 9x13 baking pans.
6. Punch down dough and roll out into a thin rectangle. Smear the dough with remaining 1/3 cup butter and sprinkle with brown sugar and spices. Roll into a long log. Cut into 18-24 rounds. Place on top of glaze in baking pans.
7. Let rise, covered, at least 30 min.
8. Preheat oven to 400°F.
9. Bake until tops are all golden brown, minimum 18-25 min.
10. Flip pans upside down onto cookie sheets, letting the buns fall out. Scrape any remaining glaze onto buns.

SHALUTH CANTU

My eyes have seen a glim - 'ring beam Pierc - ing
Long past, on that ill fat - ed night, When the
Lo, there will be a com - ing day When

through doomed brack - en's core, And al - though it has made my
hearts of men grew weak, There came by the woods a
bird, beast, man shall see, For all the dark - ness will

heart to hope, I fear I shall see it no more. Thus
shrou - ded beast, Of which we now do not speak. And
fade a - way And all of the Vale will be free. Thus

grows the e - ver dark - 'ning gloom from the glen to the ne'er end - ing
on that day no spear was raised The strong did not shel - ter the
grows the e - ver bright - 'ning day, From the fields to the ne'er en - ding

moor; And al - though Light has filled me with
meek. Then all the bril - liant
sea, And the Light of Life will

wealth un - known, I fear it has left thee poor.
good - ness fled, And of that light we now do not speak.
shine on all, For rich and whole we shall be.

ACKNOWLEDGMENTS

I must begin by honoring my Savior, Jesus Christ. You have redeemed my soul and lavished Your mercy on me. You have led me out of darkness and into Your marvelous light. The glory is Yours.

The journey to writing this book was one that began alone. I wrote to engage my mind and process many difficult things about this world. But I was too afraid to let anyone else witness those tender places of my heart. As the words and passion for this story began to grow, so did the circle of people I let in to the process. It started with my family. My children, who heard the earliest chapters and ideas forming. This tale of hope will one day be for you. My husband, who graciously gave me time and space to write and let me geek out about "weaving in my threads of story." My mom, my number one fan and best friend. My dad, who has always been the best sounding board for all things theology and writing. All of you gave me the courage to believe this novel could ever be something worth reading.

And then came my Flash Fiction Magic family. You inspire me with your creativity, your kindness, and your charming weirdness. It was because of your fellowship that I first truly identified as a "writer". I don't ever want to stop making memes and stickers in your honor.

I cannot forget my faithful three Sola Sisters. Rachel Lawrence, who read this story as it was being written, whose tears are imbedded into nearly every page. This story holds as much of your heart as it does mine. I can't wait to read your beautiful books. Amber Kirkpatrick, my person to nerd out with over fonts and slay the great beast that is the Instagram algorithm. Your stories are epic, and you sharpen me. Emily Barnett, who always asks the right questions and gives sacrificially. I am inspired by every word you pen. And the chapter graphic is *perfect*. If this story goes nowhere, I have already gained everything in you three.

To my beta readers: your insight and kind words were more helpful and life-giving than you know. Thanks for taking a chance on me and giving so willingly of your time.

My editor, Elle Fort, whose attention to detail and commitment to my writer's voice was exactly what I was looking for. Thank you for sharing your wisdom with me in such a kind and helpful manner and making this book truly shine. My proofreader, Meghan Kleinschmidt, who polished the text up to perfection.

As for my ARC readers and street team, your enthusiasm made the terrifying task of marketing this book much more fun than I thought possible. I'm so glad I met you, and I'm grateful for every one of you.

A debut novel is a precious, fledgling thing. It may not be a sweeping tale that sets people on fire, but it has a strength all its own. I have no delusions of grandeur when it comes to where it will go. But if it touches even one heart, if it causes even one soul to look to Christ, then its purpose will be complete.

After darkness, LIGHT.

ABOUT THE AUTHOR

Andrea Renae grew up wandering the Canadian prairies. She thrilled in stories of all kinds. As an only child she was usually accompanied by her cat while lost to daydreams or finding new things to create with her hands. As an adult writing became a way to process life's countless beauties and hardships while solidifying her hope in the Author of it all.

When her fingers aren't typing away, she can often be found teaching her children, playing piano, experimenting with watercolors, knitting sweaters, or practicing for her inevitable fame on the G3BO. Her favorite activity, however, will always be spending time with her family, her friends, and her goofy goldendoodle, Charlie.

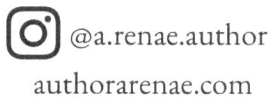 @a.renae.author

authorarenae.com